Praise for the Romances
of Amanda McCabe

"Flawlessly crafted historical romance." —*Chicago Tribune*

"An enthralling spell of tender romance with a hint of danger,
set against the glittering backdrop of Regency London."
—Diane Farr

"[A] terrific book that kept me engrossed the entire time! A
real winner." —Huntress Book Reviews

"Amanda McCabe has been delighting readers since her de-
but, and this sweetly engaging tale doesn't disappoint. She has
a talent for bringing ordinary characters into soft focus and
making us want the best for them." —*Romantic Times*

"An extremely talented new voice."
—Romantic Reviews Today

"McCabe is a welcome addition to the ranks of Regency
authors. She creates well-developed characters, both pri-
mary and secondary. She re-creates the world of Regency
society with a sure hand. She provides a sweet and moving
romance." —*The Romance Reader*

Spirited Brides

One Touch of Magic
and
A Loving Spirit

Amanda McCabe

A SIGNET ECLIPSE BOOK

SIGNET ECLIPSE
Published by New American Library, a division of
Penguin Group (USA) Inc., 375 Hudson Street,
New York, New York 10014, USA

Penguin Group (Canada), 90 Eglinton Avenue East, Suite 700, Toronto,
Ontario M4P 2Y3, Canada (a division of Pearson Penguin Canada Inc.)
Penguin Books Ltd., 80 Strand, London WC2R 0RL, England
Penguin Ireland, 25 St. Stephen's Green, Dublin 2,
Ireland (a division of Penguin Books Ltd.)
Penguin Group (Australia), 250 Camberwell Road, Camberwell, Victoria 3124,
Australia (a division of Pearson Australia Group Pty. Ltd.)
Penguin Books India Pvt. Ltd., 11 Community Centre, Panchsheel Park,
New Delhi - 110 017, India
Penguin Group (NZ), 67 Apollo Drive, Rosedale, North Shore 0632,
New Zealand (a division of Pearson New Zealand Ltd.)
Penguin Books (South Africa) (Pty.) Ltd., 24 Sturdee Avenue,
Rosebank, Johannesburg 2196, South Africa

Penguin Books Ltd., Registered Offices:
80 Strand, London WC2R 0RL, England

Published by Signet Eclipse, an imprint of New American Library, a division of
Penguin Group (USA) Inc. *One Touch of Magic* and *A Loving Spirit* were previously
published in Signet editions.

First Signet Eclipse Printing, September 2009
10 9 8 7 6 5 4 3 2 1

One Touch
of Magic

With love to my family,
Mom, Dad, and Sean
(and Gilbert, Diana, and Victoria, too!)

Prologue

The Legend of Thora's Treasure

And now, if you will gather around me, I will tell the story of Thora's Treasure. There is Viking silver and jewels of great worth. There is true love, love that transcends all time; there is deepest, most bitter loss.

You can see the treasure. But if any person whose heart is not pure removes this treasure, or any part of it, he will be struck from the earth and his name forgotten for all eternity.

The treasure can only belong to Thora's true heir—to the one it waits for.

"And now we commit the body of the Lord's servant Sir John Iverson to the earth, and we commend his soul to Thee. Amen."

Sarah, Lady Iverson, barely heard the vicar's voice. It seemed to come to her from a very long way away, as if in a dream—or a nightmare.

She stared through the black tulle of her veil at her husband's coffin placed across the drawing room. She felt oddly numb. Surely she should feel something? John had been her husband, her dearest friend, her mentor. He had taught her all about history, about how to dig in the earth to find ancient secrets. She should feel such deep grief. Not just this distance, this chill unreality. This . . .

numbness. It was so very much like those odd dreams she had been having ever since they started working on the Viking village. She saw the village come to life around her, but she was apart from it all. Just an observer.

But perhaps the grief would come later, when she was alone. Perhaps this numbness was God's way of keeping her from breaking down in sobs in front of everyone.

The vicar ceased speaking, and Sarah automatically murmured "Amen" along with everyone else. She watched as the men stepped forward to prepare to carry John's coffin from the house to the waiting grave in the churchyard. Still, she could not feel that he was gone. Surely he would wake her up from this dream at any moment, and tell her to quit lazing abed, as they had excavating to do.

She closed her eyes tightly. *Wake up,* she thought. *Wake up.*

A hand touched her arm, and she opened her eyes. It was not John, of course; it was her best friend, Mrs. Phoebe Seward.

It was so odd to see Phoebe in black, Sarah thought distractedly. Ordinarily, she was dressed in the brightest colors of the rainbow.

Phoebe's pretty, usually merry face was somber as she leaned forward and whispered, "Do you want to say good-bye, Sally?"

"Oh, yes. Of course." Sarah stepped up to the coffin, and laid her hand on the smooth wood.

The chill of it, even through her black glove, at last broke into her numbness, and she knew this was no dream. It was reality. John was gone, and she was alone.

A sob broke from her, and she pressed her hand to her mouth. Phoebe's grip tightened on Sarah's arm, and she led her away from the coffin back to the settee, as the men carried John out. Sarah's mother, Lady Bellweather, her two younger sisters, Mary Ann and Kitty, and John's friend, Mr. Neville Hamilton, waited for Sarah to be settled, then sat down around her.

Sarah was glad of their familiar company, glad to not be alone.

Until her mother started talking.

Lady Bellweather smoothed her heavily jet-beaded cloak over her capacious bosom, and said, "Well, Sarah. You know how I hate to say I told you so, but I knew when you married Sir John it would end badly. He was so much older than you, and always mucking about in the dirt digging up old things. He was rich, to be sure, but not suitable for a pretty, young girl. Now here you are, a widow at twenty-two." Lady Bellweather sighed deeply, setting the black feathers in her bonnet to trembling.

Sarah stared at her mother in shock. She had certainly heard her make some tactless remarks before—Lady Bellweather was *not* known in her circles for finesse and tact. But this—this was beyond endurance. Sarah pressed her handkerchief hard against her mouth, so hard that she tasted blood, so she would not say something very rude indeed. Words no lady ever spoke to her mother. She owed John the respect of not making a family scene on today of all days.

Sarah's sister Mary Ann looked at their mother with wide, shocked dark eyes. "Mama! Sarah is grief-stricken. She loved Sir John. How can you say such things?"

Lady Bellweather had the grace to look at least a bit ashamed. She smoothed her cloak again, and said in a quieter voice, "I am sorry, Sarah. But you know that I must speak as I find. Sir John was a good man, but not the most suitable of husbands for a young girl."

Sarah looked away, out over the drawing room. The very chairs and tables were well known to her, since she had lived in this house with her husband for over four years, but she did not see them. Her anger at her mother's words ebbed away, leaving her just tired and sad.

It was true that there had been no passion in her marriage with John. He had been thirty years her senior, a famous scholar and antiquarian, and still devoted to the memory of his late first wife. But there had been fondness, and a shared love for his last project—the excavation of a Viking village on an estate near York.

Sarah smiled as she remembered their work. That village was John's legacy to her, and she would finish the work as her final gift to him.

She looked over at where Neville Hamilton sat, his sunburned face, nearly as red as his hair, pensive and sad. She knew that Neville, her husband's friend and colleague, who had been assisting them with the village, expected her to give the work over to him now. He— and everyone else—expected her to go off to Bath or Brighton, and live as a rich young widow until she remarried.

Well, they could *expect* all they wanted. That sort of life was not for her. It never had been, and never would be. She was going to finish excavating the village, and write a monograph on their findings there.

And then—she would find a new project and start all over again.

"Please, sir. A coin for a wounded soldier."

Major Miles Rutledge stopped abruptly in his hurrying tracks to stare down at the man who sat on the pavement, carefully balanced on a low stool. The thin, dirty hand that held out a battered tin cup shook slightly; a crudely carved cane lay on the ground beside him.

Pinned to his tattered coat was a brightly shining Waterloo medal.

Miles had seen dozens of such men in just the three days since he had arrived in London to spend what was left of the Season with his mother. There was no work for them at all; the economy was in such poor straits that there could not possibly be incomes for so many returning soldiers. They had served so bravely, had risked their very lives for their country, only to come home and watch their families starve, while they stood by helpless. Beggary was rampant.

Miles felt anger, white hot and futile, well up inside him, as it had so very often in these last few days. He had become accustomed to taking care of the men in his regiment while on the Peninsula. Here, he felt a helpless rage. He gave them coins and food, listened to their stories, gave them advice whenever he could. That was not nearly enough. It did not make their lives better. He sat awake at night, feeling guilty for all the advantages he enjoyed, for his family's more-than-comfortable situation, when good men were hungry.

There *had* to be more he could do.

As he stepped closer to put a coin in the cup, the man looked up. He was quite startlingly young, and thin faced. His bloodshot eyes widened as he saw Miles's uniform.

"So you're an officer in the Forty-first Foot," he said.

"Not for much longer," Miles answered. He dropped the coin with a clatter—it had obviously not been a good day, for the cup was nearly empty. Then he knelt down beside the man, uncaring of his greatcoat that swept into the dust and rubbish of the pavement. "I am resigning my commission. It's time for a civilian life."

The man laughed bitterly. "Aye, well, the civilian life isn't all they said it would be. I'm Lieutenant Patrick O'Riley, as was, of the Twenty-first. Your regiment did some brave fighting at Talavera."

"As did yours." For one moment, Miles allowed himself to remember that day, the smoke and mud and blood, the stink of death. It had been hell on earth, and this man had also faced it.

Miles shook his head to try to clear it of the horrible images, and stared out at the busy London street. People bustled about, going on their business, not even seeing the men sitting there. Sometimes, a well-dressed gentleman or lady would eye his officer's uniform with puzzlement, or frown as if they knew him from somewhere, but they, too, were quick to pass.

"What did you do before you went into the Army, Lieutenant O'Riley?" he asked.

"I lived and worked on my uncle's farm in Ireland, and was very good at it, if I say so myself. I would have gone back there after the war, but there was a quarrel with my cousins, who own the land now." Lieutenant O'Riley eyed Miles speculatively. "You wouldn't happen to have a farm, would you, sir?"

Miles laughed. "I fear not! My father was a younger brother, before his death last year, and had only a very small estate. It's mostly given over to raising horses."

Then he thought of something. His uncle, Lord Ransome, had a vast estate, with much farmland lying fallow. There had to be many jobs there, and he, Miles, was his bachelor uncle's heir. . . .

A great wave of self-disgust broke over him. It was all his mother chatted about, him inheriting Ransome Hall, but he could not wish for anyone's death to bring him good fortune. Even though he and his uncle were not close—Lord Ransome was a dedicated scholar and antiquarian, something that military Miles could not fully appreciate—he liked the old man. And what he did with his land was his own business.

Miles just had to find some other way of helping these poor, gallant men.

Chapter One

"Death! Destruction! Betrayal!" Phoebe Seward gasped melodramatically, twirled about in a flare of bright yellow silk skirts, and fell back onto a settee, one hand pressed to her brow. "The curse is upon me!"

Sarah laughed helplessly, and pushed aside the piles of books and papers on her desk. Who could concentrate on studies when Phoebe was about? "Oh, Phoebe, do stop," she gasped.

Phoebe peeked at her from beneath her hand. "Aren't you just the tiniest bit worried about the curse, Sally?"

"Not a bit! Except that it has scared some of my more superstitious workers away. Thora's Treasure, and its accompanying curse, is just a legend. All places like this have them. That site in Ireland John and I worked on supposedly had leprechauns guarding it! I never saw hide nor hair of the little men, though."

Phoebe lounged back on the settee, stretching her legs out on the brocade cushions. "What about the cave-in at the cellar of the old leather-worker's shop?"

Sarah shook her head. "That was merely some of the aforementioned superstitious workers trying to frighten me away. Some of them believe that if I leave, and the village is covered up again, Thora will not be tempted to smite anyone. But I will not be frightened away by such nonsense. This work is far too important, and we have learned so much from it already." Sarah picked up one of her sketches from the village, a plan of the great-room of a house. "There is much still to be found, I am sure."

"Such as treasure?"

"Such as burials, and goldsmiths' shops, and bakers!"

Phoebe sighed. "I have always said you have no romance in your soul, Sally Bellweather."

Sarah laughed. "Perhaps not. You have enough romance for both of us! You and my sister Mary Ann. And I have better things to worry about than curses."

Phoebe leaned forward, her golden hair falling back over her shoulder. "Has something happened that you have not told me about? Something to cause you worry?"

"The new marquis is coming to Ransome Hall. I had a letter last week from his attorney."

"Oh, no! Does he want you to leave?"

Sarah shook her head. "Not at present. But he will want to meet with me to . . ." She dug about in her papers until she found the letter, and read a bit of it aloud. "To discuss my future tenancy of the property."

The paper trembled in her hand. The Viking village was located on a corner of the estate owned by the Marquis of Ransome. The old marquis had been a friend of Sir John's, and had gladly let them do what they liked on it, had even rented them this house, an old hunting box. He had continued the arrangement with Sarah after John's death, but now the marquis himself had died, nearly a month before.

Sarah knew nothing of the new Lord Ransome, except that he was the old marquis's nephew, and a military man only lately returned to England after valiant service on the Peninsula and at Waterloo.

She feared a military gentleman might have no patience with her work, with the scholarly nature of it, and the fact that it was a female who led the project. She had tried not to think of it these past few days, tried to just enjoy Phoebe's visit, but it was always at the back of her mind. She had hoped Lord Ransome would stay away for a good long while.

Phoebe came and took the letter from Sarah's hand to read it herself. "Surely, though, this new lordship will see the importance of what you are doing! He has to let you keep on, as his uncle did."

"I pray you are right, Phoebe."

"I know I am. Your work is valued by scholars all over the kingdom."

Sarah looked up at her dearest friend. They had been friends for so very long that Phoebe was one of the few people Sarah felt she could share her true doubts with. To the rest of the world, she always kept up a careful facade of self-assurance and coolness. It was the only way she could maintain respect in the scholarly world she and John had occupied.

"Will the opinions of scholars matter to a major in His Majesty's Army?" she asked. "Or will he see it as a waste of good property?"

Phoebe put the letter back down on the desk. "I should stay with you until Lord Ransome comes. I will write to Caro, and tell her not to expect me next week."

Sarah shook off her moment of vulnerability, her instant of doubt. She was always strong—she had to stay strong now. "Nonsense, Phoebe dear! Your sister needs you, and I know you are eager to see your new baby nephew. And did you not say Harry will join you there?"

Phoebe blushed, and turned away with a carefully careless little laugh. "My husband will not miss me for a few more days! And baby William will still be there next month."

"But he will be so much bigger. No, I cannot be selfish and keep you here. It is not as if I will be all alone. My sister Mary Ann is coming to stay, and Neville Hamilton will return soon from his wedding trip. He has been of invaluable help at the village, and perhaps he could speak to Lord Ransome, if the marquis has no wish to have dealings with a woman. So, you see, Phoebe, you *must* go to Caroline, or there will be no room here!"

Phoebe still looked doubtful, but she smiled and went along with the talk of Sarah's family. "How is dear Mary Ann? Did she not have an infatuation with poor Mr. Hamilton last year?"

"A schoolgirl infatuation only! I hope she will be over it, now that he is married. She is to make her bow next year, and Mother has great hopes for her."

Phoebe sat back down on the settee, watching Sarah closely. Sarah knew what that speculative look meant— her friend was up to some scheme.

"So Mary Ann is to go to London!" Phoebe said cheerfully. "And what of you, Sally? Have you not considered going to Town? You would be a much better chaperone for Mary Ann than your mother. And you could stay with Caro and me! What fun we would have! And think of all the eligible gentlemen you could meet."

Sarah laughed. So it was another plea to go to Town! She should have known. Phoebe had been trying to persuade her of it for months, dropping hints here and there about the delights of the Season. Phoebe, a voracious novel reader and happily married herself, was convinced no woman could truly be happy without romance in her life.

"I cannot go next Season," she said. "I have my work here." And her one Season, where she had met Sir John, had been a crashing bore, so vacuous and such a waste of time. She had no desire to repeat it.

"This work cannot last forever," Phoebe said gently. "Surely it will be done before the spring, which is months away!"

"After the excavation is finished, I will have to write about it. I have no time for London fribbles."

"It would not be all balls and routs," Phoebe argued. "You love the theater, and there are the libraries, the British Museum, antiquarian societies you could join! I know you did not enjoy your Season very much, Sally, but things are different now. You are a widow, and can do as you like. We could have such fun."

It *did* sound tempting, when Phoebe put it like that. She was a member of several antiquarian societies already, but kept up with them only by correspondence. A chance to attend their meetings in person would be most welcome, as would the chance to visit museums and libraries. The society of the nearby village of Upper Hawton was most congenial, but had nothing like that to offer.

She looked over her cluttered desk, at the drawings and notes that represented her work. The work she *owed* John. He had been a good husband to her, had given her a good life. The work on the village was far from over; she could not abandon it for the frivolities of Town.

But she could not bear to disappoint Phoebe, either, not when her friend was only trying to help, and looked at her so hopefully. "Perhaps," she said. "We will see how things are going here later, after—after Lord Ransome arrives."

Phoebe smiled. "I will be content with that—for now. But we must find some merry things to do this week, some assemblies or card parties before I must leave, and you must face the new marquis."

Sarah laughed. "Indeed! But perhaps, if I am fortunate, I will never have to meet Lord Ransome after all."

"How so, Sally?"

"Perhaps the curse of Thora's Treasure will smite him down before then!"

The breeze was soft and warm against her cheek, the sun hot where it beat down on her head. Sarah leaned back on her elbows in the sweet-scented grass, closing her eyes to let the summer day wash over her.

She knew it was just a dream; it had the blurry edges of unreality, the perfection a real day would lack. She also wore something that looked suspiciously like a nightdress, loose and white and soft, with tight sleeves, bound at the waist with a thin silver chain. Her hair spilled over her shoulders onto the ground.

Never in real life would she have gone about so disheveled! She intended to enjoy this dream while it lasted, though. It would vanish, as so many others before.

She lay flat on the grass, and opened her eyes to stare

*up at the spreading branches of the ancient tree above
her. Sunlight filtered through the leaves, casting shifting
shadows around her.*

*Suddenly, a face appeared between her and the sky, a
figure leaned over her. A man, a beautiful, godlike man,
with golden hair that fell to his shoulders, and eyes a color
to rival the sky. And he was smiling at her, her, a smile
full of secrets and a hot sweetness.*

He smiled as if he knew her—intimately.

*"So here you are," he said, his voice rough and rich.
It sent a shiver along her skin to hear it. "I have been
looking for you. You are always running from me."*

*"I am not running now," Sarah murmured. As if com-
pelled by some overwhelming force beyond her control,
she slid her hand behind his neck, drawing him down to
her, closer and closer. His hair was satin soft to her touch,
his skin hot.*

*Sarah's eyes drifted shut. Never had she felt like this
before, never! A terrible longing seized her in her very
heart. She wanted his lips on hers, needed them. . . .*

A sudden chill touched Sarah's flesh, driving away the
heat of a summer's day's passion. She tried desperately
to hold on to the dream, reached out for it with a cry,
but it slipped away. As all dreams do.

She sat up to find herself in her own chamber in the
hunting box. She had kicked aside the bedclothes, and
the breeze from the half-open window was cold on her
legs.

She rubbed at her face, her head aching with unful-
filled longing and the remnants of sleep. "It was just a
dream," she whispered. "Just a foolish dream. Like all
those others I have had."

Just a dream. But *who* was that dream man?

Chapter Two

Miles Rutledge, the new Marquis of Ransome, sat on top of a tree-shaded hill, surveying his uncle's land, spread out before him in a patchwork of green meadows and speckled farmland.

Or rather, it was *his* land. He could not get used to that idea. He did not feel in the least like a landowner, or a marquis. He was just plain Major Rutledge, and all the bows and uncertain expressions on the faces of the tenants as he passed were most unsettling. It left him with the strange sense of being in some unreal dream-world, one he would awaken from to find he was back in the dust of Spain, sleeping on the sun-baked ground.

But the dirt beneath his horse's hooves now felt very solid, as Zeus pawed at the ground, eager to be off on a gallop. The Ransome estate, spreading as far as the eye could see, was real. What he had seen of it today was prosperous and tidy, yet strangely underused. Fields that could be under cultivation, providing jobs and food, lay fallow. His uncle had been a scholar, wrapped up in his studies of ancient Britain, and obviously not much interested in the mundanities of the modern world.

Miles thought of all the men who had returned from brave service in the war to find no jobs, no way to take care of their families. It made him feel so helpless—and angry.

Mr. Benson, the bailiff of the estate, rode up to Miles's side, breaking into his thoughts. "So, we've seen most of the estate today, my lord—the most important sections, anyway," he said.

"You've obviously been a fine caretaker since my uncle died, Mr. Benson," Miles answered. "And perhaps even before that?"

Mr. Benson laughed ruefully. "Aye. His old lordship wasn't much concerned with the farm, that's true. But he was a good man, and took care of his tenants and workers."

"What workers he had," Miles murmured. Louder, he said, "The buildings are all in excellent repair, and it looks to be a good harvest this year. I fear I do not know much more about farming than my uncle did—I have been in the Army since I was eighteen, and that was seventeen years ago. Perhaps you could assist me, Mr. Benson?"

"I would be happy to help you in any way I can, my lord."

"Excellent. Then tomorrow morning, we can ride over the rest of the estate, and in the afternoon take a look at the accounts."

"There's not much more of the estate left to see," Mr. Benson said. "Just the northwest section, but Lady Iverson is there."

Miles frowned as he pictured in his mind the map of the estate. "The northwest section? Is that not where the river cuts into the estate?"

"Aye, but it's more a stream than a river. That's where it is deepest."

Miles might not be much of a farmer yet, but he *did* know that river—or stream—valleys often yielded the richest land, ripe for cultivation. That was a large tract of land there, enough for two farms of a middling size at least. "Lady Iverson? She does not sound like a tenant."

Mr. Benson laughed. "Oh, no, indeed, my lord! Lady Iverson and her husband, Sir John, have been digging up an old Viking village there. Sir John passed away last year, but she still works on it. They were friends of your uncle, and he let them stay there. I believe the attorney spoke of talking to you about the situation soon."

It sounded like a whopping waste of good land to Miles, some spoiled Society lady digging about in the dirt where crops could be growing. "A Viking village?"

"Oh, yes, my lord. My brother sometimes works there, hauling away rubbish and the like."

"I see," Miles said slowly. "Do many people work there?"

"A few, though not as many as used to." Mr. Benson glanced around a bit nervously. "They say there's a curse on the place."

Miles almost laughed aloud. He had the sense that the tale of Lady Iverson and her Viking village was going to prove quite amusing. Perhaps that was why his uncle had let her stay on the land—for the sheer diversion of it. "A curse?"

"There's said to be treasure there, but if anyone touches it they will die horribly. They say the treasure was cursed by a Viking witch named Thora, and she doesn't want anyone messing about with it. Things have happened there—a cave-in, some objects smashed. People don't much want to work there, for fear they'll accidentally disturb the treasure."

"What about you, Mr. Benson? Do you go to the village?"

Mr. Benson shrugged. "My job is to look after the estate. The village is Lady Iverson's business."

"I see." Miles decided he would just have to have a thorough look through his uncle's papers, and see if this lady and her husband had some sort of contract on that land. "And what does she intend to do with the village once it is dug up?"

"My brother says she is writing a book."

"Is that so? I should like to meet Lady Iverson soon."

"You may get to meet her sooner than you would think, my lord. That's her now."

Mr. Benson pointed with his riding crop down to the road below them. It was not much of a road, more of a pathway really, that wound around the edge of the estate until it joined the main road into the village of Upper Hawton. In the distance, stirring up a small dust cloud, was a bright yellow phaeton drawn by a pair of matched grays.

As it came closer, Miles saw that it was indeed a lady driving it, going at a rather improvident speed that sent the elegant equipage jolting over the ruts in the road. She wore a purple carriage dress, and a tall-crowned black hat trimmed with jaunty purple plumes. Glossy dark brown curls peeked from under that hat, and Miles had a glimpse of a pale oval of a face as she drove past. She raised one black-gloved hand to wave at Mr. Benson as she went by, then she was gone, her carriage jolting on its way down the road. A snatch of some song she was singing floated back to them on the breeze.

She was far more dashing than Miles would have expected a lady scholar to be. He found himself very curious to meet her.

But he could hardly just gallop up to a lady, and stop her carriage without an introduction. She might think he was some sort of highwayman! She appeared to be heading into Upper Hawton, though. Surely there was some errand he needed to accomplish in the village? Some purchase to be made?

And surely there was someone there who could properly introduce him to Lady Iverson.

Chapter Three

Sarah sang a merry little tune as she drove along, basking in the sunshine. It was truly a lovely day, with a cloudless blue sky and the hint of autumn in the air. She felt better than she had since Phoebe left last week. The work on the village was progressing most satisfactorily; she even had two new workers, a brother and sister from one of the tenant's families, who seemed to have no fear of any curses. And she was on her way to meet her sister Mary Ann. Not even her odd dreams could disturb her this day.

Best of all, she had not heard from the new Lord Ransome, or his attorney. She knew he was in residence at Ransome Hall, had heard of him from all her friends and workers. They said he was very handsome, if a bit weather-beaten from his years on the Peninsula, and quite charming. She confessed herself curious to catch a glimpse of him—but not curious enough to face his questions about her residency on his land. Not yet, anyway, not when the work was going so well.

She knew she would have to face him sooner or later, and persuade him to let her stay. She just hoped it was later, perhaps even so late that the work was complete and she could leave.

As she turned a bend in the road, she saw that Mr. Benson, the bailiff, sat atop a hill with another man. Ordinarily, she would have stopped the phaeton and had a little chat with Mr. Benson, for he was a most pleasant

man, and she wanted to ask how his wife was doing after
the birth of their new baby. But she had a suspicion that
the other man was Lord Ransome, so she just drove past.

She turned her head, trying to get a glimpse of him as
she drove. All she had was an impression of thick blond
hair, uncovered and ruffled by the breeze, of a military
posture in the saddle. His head also turned to watch her
progress, and she had to resist the urge to stop and try
to get a better look at him.

But stopping would mean speaking, and she was already late meeting her sister in Upper Hawton. Her
mother's friend, Lady Hammond, who was dropping
Mary Ann off on her journey to London, would not wait
in the village for very long, and it would never do to
leave Mary Ann alone there. She drove down the road,
until the men were left far behind her.

Unfortunately, fate seemed to be against her. Attempting to cross a shallow stream, something she had
done dozens of times before, she felt a great jolt, and
her phaeton tilted and would go no farther. Her horses
tossed their pretty heads, as if indignant that their jolly
run had been so rudely interrupted, and tried to move
forward. The carriage was quite thoroughly stuck.

Sarah twisted about to look down at the offending
wheel. It was obviously caught in some muddy rut of the
streambed, and she would have to walk to the nearest
farm for help. She glanced down at the water, frowning.

She had dressed so carefully today to meet her sister,
leaving behind the stout boots she used for digging in
favor of dainty new kid half-boots. She certainly did not
want to ruin them! Perhaps she could climb over the
front of the phaeton onto one of the horses' backs? But
then how would she release the horse from the carriage
without getting muddy?

She sat there for a moment, absorbed in this conun-
drum, until she heard the rustle of hooves on the road
behind her. She turned, full of relief, to call out for rescue—only to find that it was the man who was perhaps
Lord Ransome approaching.

A half-smile curved his lips as he reined in his horse next to her carriage. He *was* handsome, Sarah thought, just as everyone said, and not the least weather-beaten. He was rather sun browned, to be sure, the darkness of his skin in contrast with his guinea-gold hair. His eyes were a brilliant blue, surrounded by only the faintest of lines that deepened when he smiled at her fully.

They sparkled in the sunlight, blue as the sky, making him seem very friendly and easy. Not at all the stiff-backed prig she imagined an Army man would be. And he seemed very—familiar.

She smiled back, caught by his handomeness, his smile. She didn't think she could speak even if she tried, she was so breathless. And he hadn't even said anything to her yet! He had just smiled at her, and she was staring like a silly schoolgirl.

Stop it right now, she told herself sternly. *You are not some young miss; you are a respectable widow, and he is the one who holds your work in his hand.*

If he thought she was a simpering lackwit, he would never let her stay at the village.

She twined the reins around her fist, and sat up straight on the carriage seat. "Good day, sir," she said, deeply grateful that her voice emerged in a normal fashion, and not as a high-pitched squeak.

"Good day, ma'am," he answered, his own voice deep, and rich with humor. "It appears you are in quite a situation."

She smiled at him. "Indeed. The wheel is stuck," she pointed out unnecessarily. "I am meant to be in Upper Hawthorn to meet my sister."

"Well, I would offer my assistance, but perhaps I should introduce myself first. I am Miles Rutledge."

"The new Lord Ransome. Yes, I thought so. I've heard much about you. I am Lady Iverson."

"I have heard of you, as well."

Sarah looked up at him quizzically. "Have you indeed?"

"Of course. The famous Lady Iverson, the lady antiquarian. I am eager to hear more of your activities. But, in the meantime, perhaps we should turn our attention to this emergency, and get you into the village to meet your sister."

He leaned down to look closer at the wheel, one hand on the edge of her phaeton. She stared down at it, fascinated. It was a strong hand, dark, long fingered, capable, with a small white scar on its back. In the deepest, most secret part of her mind, she saw that hand resting on her bare arm, sliding along her skin. . . .

She shook her head to clear it of this new silliness, and managed to paste a bland expression on her face just as he straightened up.

His eyes narrowed, as if he suspected her improper thoughts. Or maybe he was just preoccupied with his problem, for he said, "If you will permit me, Lady Iverson, my house is not far, and I would be happy to lend you my carriage to fetch your sister. Then I could return here with some of my men, and free your phaeton."

Sarah was tempted. Mary Ann would be waiting. And the chance to be with Lord Ransome a bit longer was also a most prospect. More extensive conversation with him would reveal that he was just a man, like any other, no doubt wrapped up in hunting and drinking and other such dull pursuits, with no appreciation for the beauties of history and culture. His good looks would have no charm for her, then.

Then, too, she truly needed more time to examine her predicament, vis-à-vis Lord Ransome. Her fate, as it were.

"The horses . . ." she began, glancing toward the pair. They stood there calmly, while the cool water lapped about their knees. Occasionally, they bent their elegant heads to take a drink, apparently enjoying the holiday.

"It is not far to the house," he assured her again. "They won't be here very long."

"Very well," Sarah agreed. "Thank you, Lord Ransome. You are most kind."

"Not at all, Lady Iverson. My reputation in the neighborhood would suffer grievously were I to leave a lady stranded out here!" He laughed, that warm, whiskey-dark sound that made Sarah want to laugh along with him, despite her plight.

Her life had been devoid of laughter, *true* laughter, for so long.

"Now, try to stand up, and I'll pull you onto the horse," he said, holding his hands out to her.

Sarah balanced herself carefully on the carriage floor, and reached up for him. In one quick, smooth motion, he drew her up before him on his horse, so swiftly that she hardly realized what had happened until his arms came around her to adjust the reins. She straightened her legs along the side of the horse, and smoothed the cloth of her skirt down as far as it would go.

She felt suddenly breathless, and uncomfortably warm. She sat forward, but Lord Ransome was still close at her back, his heat flowing through the very cloth of his coat and her gown to her skin. He smelled of sunshine and soap, and his chest when he brushed, ever so briefly, against her back was hard. She didn't know if she could make it through even the short ride to Ransome Hall without breaking down into giggles, or something equally unseemly. She doubted her mind could focus on anything at the moment, not even on simple polite conversation.

No man except her husband had ever been this close to her before, and John, as dear as he was, had never caused such confusion in her usually ordered mind.

And that had to be the explanation, she told herself. This was simply a new experience for her, and the sensations would fade as soon as the novelty of it wore off.

Somewhat reassured, Sarah smiled and leaned back, until she remembered that solid, warm chest behind her, and sat bolt upright again.

"Mr. Benson tells me you are working on, er, digging up a Viking village," he said, his voice rumbling pleasantly against her back.

Sarah glanced back over her shoulder at him, surprised at the sound. Thus far, he had seemed content to ride along in silence, for which she was most grateful. It gave her time to get her thoughts together, so she could string words together in coherent sentences again.

Fortunately, he had asked her about something she was *always* willing to talk about, even if he had described it in those odious words "digging up."

"Yes, indeed," she answered. "My late husband was a well-known antiquarian, with a particular interest in the Vikings. When your uncle found some tools and coins on his property, he wrote to Sir John and we came here to explore further. It has proved to be a unique discovery; there is nothing else like it in all of England. Nothing yet found, that is. It is a complete village, probably dating from around the nine hundreds, with streets, houses, shops, things like that."

"I see," Lord Ransome said slowly. "How long have you been working there, may I ask, Lady Iverson?"

Sarah, who had just gotten worked up for a good lecture on her favorite subject, closed her mouth. She had forgotten for a moment, in her enthusiasm, that this was the man who now owned the land "her" village sat on. The man who could toss her out without a fare-thee-well.

He probably didn't want to hear her yammering on about shops and firepits and rubbish heaps. He probably didn't care two straws about such things—most people did not—and wanted the old hunting box she was living in to use for hunting again.

Hunting! When she was collecting vital artifacts about England's very heritage.

She took a deep breath, telling herself not to leap to conclusions, and answered, "About a year and a half."

"So long? I did not realize it took so much time to dig such things up."

There were those words again—"dig things up." As if all she was doing was mucking about in the dirt looking for trinkets. She could see that Lord Ransome was in great need for an education.

But not right at that moment. She had learned the value of subtlety and diplomacy, of not charging right in after what she wanted, from her husband. This was the time to begin to persuade Lord Ransome of the true importance of her work—not hit him over the head with a history lesson. Much as she would like to do that.

"This is a very extensive site," she answered. "My husband's methods, which I am following, are to excavate very carefully in order to preserve the historical evidence as much as possible. Most people simply want the artifacts and objects, but Sir John saw the deeper significance of such finds. Also, the work was delayed for many weeks when—when he died." She decided not to mention how short staffed she had been, due to fear of the "curse."

"I see," Lord Ransome said. "It all sounds most interesting, Lady Iverson. I would be fascinated to take a look at it."

That was even better. If she could show him the actual village, it would be easier to point out all the things they had learned so far. And she relished any chance to show it off for new people.

She smiled up at him over her shoulder. "Please, do come at any time, Lord Ransome. I would be most happy to show you the village."

He smiled back, and only then did she realize that, in her enthusiasm over her project and her fear that he might take it all away, she had forgotten how very attractive Lord Ransome was.

She remembered now.

She also remembered why he seemed so strangely familiar. She had seen him before—in her dream.

Lady Iverson was not at all what Miles had been expecting.

His uncle had been seventy if he was a day, and Sir John Iverson had been his crony. Miles had pictured an elderly couple scrambling over the fields, digging about for Vikings coins, leaning on their canes. But Lady Iverson looked as if she could not be more than twenty—and she was dashed pretty.

The eyes that looked up at him, flashing with enthusiasm as she spoke of her work, were the golden brown color of fine Spanish sherry, slightly tilted up at the corners and framed with a sweep of long lashes. Her skin was touched with pink by the sun, with a small smattering of pale freckles over her nose and cheeks. Dark curls bounced from beneath her stylish hat, occasionally brushing his throat when she turned her head.

She seemed impossibly young and enthusiastic, vital, warm, and so *alive*. Completely unlike the powdered, mannered, flirtatious ladies he had met in London after his return from the war. They had flocked about him, flattered him, when they learned he was to be the new Marquis of Ransome, but their manners had been so artificial, so shallow, after his experiences in Spain that they made him impatient.

He was glad to escape them to the country. He was even more glad now that he had met this lady. She seemed real, full of real emotions and enthusiasms in a world of artificiality.

He looked forward to seeing her work, to hearing her speak of it more. He still believed that that particular section of his land could be better served by crops and jobs, and he would have to tell her that very soon. He doubted that seeing her work would change his mind. But he did not have to say that just yet. Right now, he wanted to enjoy her company.

All too soon, they arrived at Ransome Hall, and he was forced to take his arms from around her small, slim figure and help her down from the horse onto the graveled drive. Almost immediately, the front doors opened, and his uncle's butler—*his* butler—Makepeace appeared.

"Lady Iverson," Makepeace said, too well trained to show any surprise he might be feeling at seeing her there. "What a nice surprise to see you today."

"Hello, Makepeace," Lady Iverson said. "It has been far too long! I fear I had a bit of an accident, and Lord Ransome very gallantly rescued me."

"An accident, my lady?" Makepeace asked, his tone alarmed.

"Her phaeton is stuck in the stream not far from here," Miles explained. He had stayed on his horse, intending to ride back immediately to fetch her team. "I thought I would take some of the stable lads back to help free it. In the meantime, could you order the carriage to be brought about for Lady Iverson's use? She is to meet her sister in Upper Hawton."

"Of course, my lord. Right away," Makepeace answered. "Perhaps you would care to come inside for a cup of tea, my lady, while the carriage is summoned?"

"Thank you, Makepeace. That would be most welcome." Lady Iverson climbed up the stone front steps behind the butler, then turned back to Miles and said, "And thank *you* again, Lord Ransome. I do not know what I should have done without you!"

"Not at all. I was glad to be of assistance, Lady Iverson. I trust we shall meet again soon?"

She smiled at him. "Of course. Please do come to the site, whenever it is convenient. We are working on it most days."

"I look forward to it."

He looked forward to it very much indeed.

Chapter Four

"Sarah! Here you are at last. I've already finished my luncheon, and quite despaired of your appearing before teatime. I was so worried—what happened?"

Mary Ann leaped up from her seat before the fire in the private parlor of the King's Arms Inn. The remains of a meal were indeed scattered about the table, and a book lay abandoned on Mary Ann's chair.

Sarah put her arms about her sister, and kissed her cheek. "I am so sorry, dear, but I was unavoidably delayed. There was a tiny accident with the phaeton. You know how Mother is always saying I'm a fool to drive that dangerous carriage about!"

"An accident!" Mary Ann pulled back to examine her carefully. "Are you injured?"

"Not a bit. But where is Lady Hammond?"

"Oh, she left almost as soon as we arrived. She said she had to get to York before dark," Mary Ann said carelessly. She took Sarah's arm and drew her over to sit by the fire. It was a warm day outside, but the thick old walls made the room chilly. "It is quite all right, though. Rose is here, you see, and everything is very proper." She gestured toward a young maid who sat in the corner, quietly sewing. "Let me get you some tea, Sarah. You must be so tired after your ordeal!"

Sarah gratefully accepted the cup of tea Mary Ann poured for her; its smoky warmth was soothing after the long, arduous morning just past. But her mind still kept going back over her meeting with Lord Ransome, kept thinking about him, wondering about him and if he would keep his word to come look at the Viking village. It took a great deal of effort to pull herself back into the present moment, and her new duties as a chaperone.

"Lady Hammond never should have left you alone here," she murmured.

Mary Anne laughed, and sat down in her abandoned chair opposite Sarah. "Do you expect anything else of a friend of Mother's? All most of them are concerned about is their own convenience. I was surprised she agreed to convey me this far!"

Sarah had to smile, for it was all too true. All their lives, ever since the death of their father when Sarah was ten years old and Mary Ann and Kitty just babies, they had been dealing with the vagaries of their mother and her empty-headed circle of friends.

"All the same, it was most irresponsible of her," she said, setting her empty teacup down on the nearest table.

"I felt perfectly safe here," Mary Ann said. "The innkeeper gave me this lovely parlor to sit in, and the serving maid has been telling me all the local *on dits*. Besides, I am glad Lady Hammond is gone! You are much merrier company than she is."

Sarah smiled at her. "I am glad to see you, too, Mary Ann! You are looking very well."

And she was. Mary Ann had always been the prettiest of the Bellweather girls, with darker eyes, smoother, light brown hair, and a creamy skin untouched with freckles. Her dainty prettiness was set off by her stylish dress of white muslin printed with tiny blue flowers and a pale blue spencer. It was easy to see why their mother had such hopes for Mary Ann on the Marriage Mart.

It was just too bad that she, like Sarah before her, displayed absolutely no interest in Society and a proper Season.

"I have been reading a great deal about the Vikings," Mary Ann said, holding up her book. It was a study of the Viking voyages of the ninth and tenth centuries, a work Sarah was very familiar with. "I cannot wait to see your village! It sounds a bit like this site in Scotland."

"I'm very glad you're so enthusiastic, Mary Ann dear! You will be a great help to us, I am sure. Your sketches are wonderful. But what does Mother say about your studies?"

Mary Ann shrugged blithely. "She does not know! As long as I go to teas and musicales and shops with her, she never notices how many books I take out of the lending library."

Sarah had a suspicion about why Mary Ann displayed this sudden interest in the Vikings, but she hoped she was wrong. Just in case she was not, though, she said gently, "Mr. Hamilton will be coming back from his wedding trip soon. He will be glad of your assistance, too."

The animation faded from Mary Ann's face, and she looked down to her lap. "Yes, that is what the maid said, that the—the Hamiltons are returning soon from Scotland. I must say I was surprised when we got your letter telling us of his marriage. Was it not rather sudden?"

"Perhaps. He did not know Miss Harris very long, to be sure. But sometimes love will not be denied." Sarah rather suspected that the marriage had more to do with the former Miss Emmeline Harris of Bath's ten thousand pounds than passionate love. She could hardly say that to Mary Ann, though, remembering her sister's infatuation.

"No, of course not," Mary Ann said. She looked up, a fixed smile pinned on her lips. "I am sure you are remembering my silly infatuation of last year, but you needn't worry. I am quite past that! Mother says I will meet far more dashing men in Town."

Sarah smiled and nodded, even though she did not believe it. In her own experience, most of the men in Town were silly fools and peacocks, but she didn't want to dash any of Mary Ann's new excitement. "You will have your choice of beaux, I'm sure."

"I am more interested in what's happening here. The maid told me there is a new marquis at Ransome Hall. Have you seen him yet?"

"Once," Sarah answered shortly. She didn't really want to talk about Lord Ransome yet—she was still puzzled and confounded by him, and wanted to think about him some more. "Only briefly. I am sure we will see him while you're here, though."

Mary Ann gave her a laughing glance. "The maid said he is handsome, and a dashingly brave Army officer."

Sarah laughed. "He *is* handsome, I admit, but I could not say if he was 'dashingly brave,' having never seen him in battle. Are you thinking of trying your hand at some matchmaking, Mary Ann?"

"Of course not! I am not our mother."

"Good. Because I am not thinking of marrying again at all. Now, are you quite finished here? We should be getting back to the hunting box before tea. Mrs. Taylor made you her special almond cakes." Mrs. Taylor was Sarah's faithful cook, who had been with her since her marriage to Sir John.

"Oh, wonderful! And I can't wait for a glimpse of your village, too."

The drive back to the hunting box proved to be a quiet one. After Mary Ann imparted all the news of their family, and Sarah told her about Phoebe's visit, Mary Ann took out her book again and instantly became absorbed—or seemed to be.

This left Sarah time to reflect at length on her odd morning—and reflect she did, on Lord Ransome particularly. It was hard not to think about the man, when she was riding in his very own carriage.

She leaned back against the buttery-soft leather of the squabs, and ran her hand over the tufted seat. It was a most comfortable and luxurious equipage, and she could swear she caught a whiff of his sandalwood soap and sunshine scent.

Sarah pressed one hand against her mouth to hold in a laugh at her own silliness. One glimpse of a handsome man, and she was like one of the ridiculous heroines in the Minerva Press novels Phoebe and Mary Ann loved so much! Sarah had never had time for such things. Even as a young girl she had been too wrapped up in dusty old books and history to care about gentlemen and flirting and, besides, her and John's circle of friends would have found those frivolous. Why, then, did her mind keep turning back to Lord Ransome? Why did she wonder when she would see him again?

Perhaps it was because he was not what she had feared—not thus far, anyway. He had not been one of those obnoxiously bluff and stiff military men, lecturing her about women's proper spheres and ordering her off his land. It was true that he was quite ignorant of the true purpose of her work, but he seemed willing to listen to her. He wanted to look at the village.

He was kind, as well as handsome. He had rescued her neatly from her dilemma, thus saving her nice shoes, and lent her this fine carriage. It was that kindness, and the good humor shining from his sky blue eyes, that so disarmed her.

But she would just have to be sensible now. She had digging and studying to accomplish, and Mary Ann to look after. Despite her sister's protestations, Sarah strongly suspected she was not over her infatuation with Mr. Hamilton. Mary Ann could not even look directly at her when she spoke his name.

So there was really no time for any infatuations of her own, Sarah thought with a little sigh. Surely Lord Ransome would not be around very often, and she seldom had reason to go to Ransome Hall. If he was out of sight, she would not think about him. It was only the novelty of his presence that made him so interesting. In fact, he would be out of her thoughts by supper.

Surely he would.

Thus satisfied, Sarah straightened her gloves, and turned her attention to the scenery passing outside the window.

There, just visible in the distance, she could see the graceful, pale gray stone of Ransome Hall. She wondered if Lord Ransome had returned there yet. . . .

* * *

Mary Ann was not truly absorbed in her book; she just held it before her eyes, so Sarah would think she was. She dearly loved her sister, and was delighted to see her again, but she didn't think she could indulge in polite conversation any longer without crying.

She knew that her family considered her feelings for Mr. Hamilton to be mere infatuation, and they smiled about it behind her back.

It was true that she had been just fifteen when they met last year, but her feelings had *not* been a schoolgirl crush. She often borrowed novels from Phoebe Seward, and her emotions were just like the ones of those heroines. Even now, thinking of Mr. Hamilton's handsome auburn hair, her heart pattered in her breast, making her breathless.

He had spoken to her so seriously and earnestly about Viking history, as if she was quite grown up and intellectual. Not like she was a child, as almost everyone else did!

Why, now that she was of an age to marry, did he have to go off and wed someone else?

The thought made her eyes itch with tears again, but really she was rather tired of crying. She tried to behave as the tragically romantic Minerva Press heroines did, delicate and brave, though sometimes it was dashed hard.

She peered at Sarah over the top of her book, and saw that her sister appeared quite absorbed in her own thoughts, as well. In fact, if Mary Ann did not know her sensible sister so well, she would almost have said Sarah had a secret infatuation of her own.

Yet who could it be? The only men Mary Ann ever saw Sarah with were dusty old scholars like Sir John. And surely Sarah was far too old to be infatuated with anyone! Why, she was a widow.

What, then, accounted for the unaccustomed soft expression in Sarah's eyes? Glad of the distraction from thoughts of the lost Mr. Hamilton, Mary Ann settled down to ponder this mystery.

Chapter Five

Sarah dug her trowel carefully into the soft earth, prying until she loosened the glistening object. It was a tiny, broken fragment of some metal, hooked and twisted. She wiped it on her already dusty apron, and took out her quizzing glass to study it closer.

It was a warm day. The sun beat down on her head, even through the loose weave of her wide-brimmed straw hat, and tiny, itchy rivulets of sweat ran between her shoulder blades. The other people working on the village, digging and hauling artifacts away to the old stable that was their temporary home, moved slowly, stopping often to wipe at their damp brows. Sarah noticed none of this, though. She was too absorbed in the tiny piece of metal, and in the other objects scattered around her.

This had assuredly been the village smithy, she thought, glancing at the objects laid out on old sheets. There were the blades of knives and swords, a half of an iron cauldron, and even a scamasax in such fine condition she could have used it right now, if she had such a violent inclination. The charcoal kiln she had just uncovered this morning confirmed that this was a smithy.

But what was this new object? She would have to take it back to the hunting box that night and look for something like it in one of her books. It would be so much easier if she knew what it was *now*, though! If only John, or even Mr. Hamilton, were here. They knew what everything was on sight, where she was still a student.

Mary Ann, who was sitting on a low stool behind her, sketching the charcoal kiln, suddenly stood up. She shielded her eyes against the glare of the sun, and announced, "Someone is coming!"

Sarah reluctantly tore her attention from the fragment, and looked to where her sister was pointing. A horse and rider were slowly making their way into the small valley where the village was situated. She couldn't tell from this distance exactly who it was, but, judging from the figure's upright, military posture, and the golden hair gleaming in the sun, she had a good idea.

"Blast!" she cursed under her breath. Why did *he* have to come today, of all days? When she was hot and dirty, wearing her oldest and plainest gray muslin dress and a stained apron! Her face was probably pink from the sun, and she no doubt smelled less than pristine.

When they had met last week, she might have looked like a fool getting stuck in the stream, but at least she had been well dressed doing it. Every day since then, she had remembered his promise to come to see the village, so she had dressed in her best day gowns, and even used rice powder on the freckles across her nose. This morning, she had decided he would surely write before he came, and had gone back to her usual working attire. She could get so much more done in her old dresses and aprons.

Why, oh, why, had she done that?

She stuck the fragment into her apron pocket, and pulled the hat off her head to try in vain to smooth her hair back. Short curls of it clung to her damp temples and brow, resisting all attempts at tidying.

"Is that the new Lord Ransome?" Mary Ann asked. Sarah noticed that, despite the sun, Mary Ann still looked cool and pretty, her pale green gown only a bit dusty around the hem. "He looks handsome, and not nearly as old as I would have thought."

Sarah watched as Lord Ransome reached the edge of the village and dismounted from his horse. He wrapped the reins around a thick branch of a nearby tree, looking about him curiously.

"Come on, Sarah!" Mary Ann urged, hurrying off. "I want to meet him."

Sarah followed her slowly, reluctant to leave the work on the smithy—and even more reluctant to have Lord Ransome see her looking like a street urchin!

But there was nothing for it. It would be rude for her to run away and hide, and not at all the way to persuade him to let her stay on his land. She would just have to *pretend* she was properly dressed and groomed. If she ignored her disarray, then he would have to as well.

This was easier said than done, though, especially since Mary Ann was right, and he *was* looking particularly handsome. Even more so than she remembered from the day he rescued her. The waves of his hair, brushed back carelessly from his face and uncovered by a hat, shimmered gold and copper in the light, and his eyes were as blue and piercing as the sky. He smiled when he saw her coming, and a dimple dented the sun-browned smoothness of his cheek.

"Good afternoon, Lady Iverson," he said. "I hope I have not come at an inconvenient time? If so, just say the word and I will go away again at once."

Sarah smiled at him in return, all thoughts of work and her dusty disarray fleeing away. She held her hand out to him, and he lifted it to his lips.

She had to press down on the urge to laugh like a schoolgirl. Then she remembered that that hand was probably not strictly clean, and snatched it back again, shoving it into her apron pocket. Her fingers touched the metal fragment, and she clutched it in her fist as a lifeline.

"Not at all, Lord Ransome," she answered. "It is almost time for us to stop for luncheon." She noticed Mary Ann still beside her, practically bouncing on her feet in excitement. "May I present my sister, Miss Mary Ann Bellweather? Thanks to your loaning us your carriage, she made it here safely."

"How do you do, Miss Bellweather?" Lord Ransome said, giving Mary Ann an elegant bow.

Mary Ann ceased bouncing long enough to curtsy to him. "How do you do, Lord Ransome? I vow I never had a more comfortable journey than I did in your lovely carriage."

Lord Ransome laughed. "I am very glad to hear it, Miss Bellweather."

"It was most gallant of you to come to Sarah's rescue. Have you come to see her village? It is vastly interesting."

"Mary Ann!" Sarah said, taking her sister's hand to make her stand still, as she had begun bouncing again.

It was obvious that Lord Ransome was trying very hard to keep from laughing at Mary Ann's exuberance. His jaw was tight, but his eyes sparkled. "Indeed, I have come to see the village, if Lady Iverson has time to show me about."

"I will be happy to show you what there is," Sarah said. "There is much we haven't uncovered yet. Mary Ann, perhaps you would gather up some of your sketches to show Lord Ransome?"

Mary Ann nodded eagerly, and hurried off to find her sketchbooks. Sarah was left quite alone with Lord Ransome, since the workers had disappeared somewhere for their luncheon. She smoothed her apron once more, self-consciously, and gestured to him to follow her.

She soon forgot the fact that she was dusty and disheveled in the pleasure of displaying her work. Or, as Mary Ann called it, "her" village. It was not hers, of course—it belonged to the long-dead Vikings who had inhabited it. But sometimes it felt like hers, just for this small span of time. It was coming back to life under the labor of *her* hands. People would know again how those Vikings had lived because of what she was doing.

"This was not an enormously large settlement, since Jorvik—or York—was so near," she said. "It was meant to serve the needs of the nearby farmers, I am sure."

Lord Ransome looked about, a small frown of concentration on his brow. "Do the main streets mostly consist of shops and businesses, as it does in modern towns?"

"Mostly, yes. We have uncovered the shops of wood-workers, leather-workers, and a jeweler. Over there are some small houses, but we have only fully excavated one so far—'House A,' it's called. It is a very simple house, with only the main hall, where the hearth is, and a couple of other small rooms. It should be very interesting, though, with many clues as to how the Vikings lived when they settled in England."

"How do you know what every shop is?" Lord Ransome asked. He gazed around, obviously taking in the veritable sea of ropes and markers and rubbish heaps. "Judging from your markers, I would say that each one is the same size and shape."

"Indeed. We can only know—or rather, can guess—because of the objects we find in each one. I was working in the smithy this morning, where we uncovered a char-coal kiln and many metal objects." Sarah suddenly re-membered the odd little hook she had found, and pulled it out of her pocket. "Including this. I'm not sure what it is."

Lord Ransome took it carefully from her, turning it over in the sunlight. "I fear I know very little about Viking history, Lady Iverson, but if I were to make a guess, I would say it was a link of chain mail."

"Chain mail?" Intrigued, Sarah leaned over to exam-ine the tiny fragment. It lay securely on the capable hand of Lord Ransome, the palm vulnerably pink in contrast to the sun-browned, scarred back. She had to clench her fist to keep from reaching out and tracing the calluses at the base of his fingers. "I do believe you are right. I don't know how I didn't see it before! What a clever antiquarian you would be."

He laughed ruefully. "I doubt I would be intellectual enough to do the work you do, Lady Iverson. I was the despair of my tutors. But my father owned quite an ex-tensive collection of ancient weapons, including a shirt of chain mail. I was fascinated by them, and when my father's back was turned, I often took them down from the wall in order to play with them. I am surprised I never chopped a foot off! But this looks exactly like the links of mail in that shirt."

Sarah had to smile at the image of a young Lord Ransome, towheaded and curious, clambering up to lift swords and maces down from the wall. "You must have been the despair of your poor mother."

"Oh, I was. I believe I still am, since she lives in Bath and London all year, and won't come live here with me."

Sarah was fascinated by this tiny glimpse into his family life. "Do you have any siblings?"

"One sister, but she is married to an officer in an Indian regiment, and she lives with him and their two children in Calcutta. She has plenty of time to worry about me, but fortunately she can only express that worry in long letters." He smiled, and held the link out to her.

Sarah wondered what his sister could possibly find to worry about him. "No, you keep it," she said, pressing it back into his hand. "You were the one who identified it so quickly."

"Are you certain?"

"Of course."

He gave her a smile of such sweetness and humor that Sarah almost melted beneath it. He acted as if she had handed him a diamond. "Thank you, Lady Iverson. It will remind me of my father's collection, until I can unpack it and display it all at Ransome Hall—and it will also remind me of this day."

Sarah smiled in return. "Would you care to see the rest of the objects we have found? We keep them in the old stable up on that hill, until I can find them a more suitable home."

"I would like that very much."

He held his arm out to her, and she slipped her hand into its warm crook. They might almost have been stepping into a ballroom rather than a dusty stable so formal and gallant was he. Sarah wished for one instant that she was wearing a silk gown and diamonds, and that her hair was properly dressed. How would Lord Ransome look at her then? With admiration?

She shook her head, and tried to push those thoughts back. She was not here for such frivolous things as gowns and flirtations! She was here to work.

And *only* work.

Miles followed Lady Iverson into the dim cavern of the old stable, ducking his head to avoid a low-hanging spiderweb. The only light was from sunshine through the chinks of the wooden walls, pale bars where dust motes danced. The floor was covered by a layer of fresh straw, and the air smelled of its sweetness and the warmth of the day. Lady Iverson's skirt stirred the straw when she walked across the building.

He thought again how very different she was from any other lady he had ever met. She worked out under the sun, uncaring of her attire or her complexion, intent only on the nine-hundred-year-old objects she was unearthing. When she spoke of her work, her eyes glowed, and her mobile mouth turned up with eagerness. Her hand, when she reached out to give him the tiny metal link, was tanned and dusty. Her gown was far from fashionable, and covered with a stained apron.

But, for all that—*because* of all that—she was lovely. Miles was drawn to her inexorably. He wanted to be near her brightness, her vitality, and absorb some of it into himself.

He had been so tired since the end of the war, bone-deep tired, but so restless at the same time. On the Peninsula, there had been times of maddening boredom, yet he had always known that he had a purpose there. And he was good at the military life, too. He took care of his men, and won accolades—some perhaps even deserved—for his actions in battle.

He sometimes wondered if he could be half as good being a marquis, if he could find a purpose here, as Lady Iverson obviously had. He was beginning to imagine that helping former soldiers in these difficult times could be that new purpose. He just had to decide how to begin.

There was a rustling sound from the far end of the

stable, and he turned his attention back to Lady Iverson. She had gone to a row of tables, and was pulling canvas covers from them. He moved closer, and saw that the tables were laden with objects of every shape and size, many of them quite unrecognizable, all of them neatly labeled.

"These are items we found in House A," she said. "Mostly domestic items, of course, and things that would have belonged to a lady. Glass beds, soapstone spindles, and bowls—the soapstone would have been imported from Norway, so I assume these people were originally Norwegians. Some pottery storage jars. We found seeds in them, which a friend of my husband's, who is a noted botanist, says are barley, wheat, and dill."

Her gaze softened when she mentioned her late husband. Miles wondered with an odd pang if she still loved him, still longed for him. "What are these?" he asked, trying to shake off those disquieting thoughts by leaning over an array of beautifully decorated silver items. "They're quite lovely."

Lady Iverson smiled softly, as if she had a particular affection for these pieces. "Indeed, they are. These are a pair of silver brooches, which would have fastened a lady's overdress. We found them in House A, along with these amber beads and enameled armbands. Even though the house is small, the inhabitants must have been well-to-do to own such things. There was also this. It is one of my favorites."

She held up an ivory comb, carved with a fantastical, dragonlike creature that writhed along its handle, entwined with flowers and leaves.

Miles suddenly had an odd flash, a picture in his mind of Lady Iverson seated beside a fire, her dark hair spread over her shoulders. She wore only a simple white tunic, and she pulled the pretty ivory comb through her curls. She looked up at him, and gave him a smile so full of passion and sweetness that it pierced right to his heart.

He closed his eyes against this odd, disturbing vision. He barely knew Lady Iverson, and soon they would have to have a serious discussion about her leaving the work she so obviously loved. It would never do to imagine her in such an intimate way, even if it made sense—which it did not.

He pressed his hand to his brow, and his mind went blank.

"Lord Ransome?" he heard her say. Her voice sounded worried, but quite ordinary. It brought him back to the present moment, to the reality of their situation. "Are you ill?"

He opened his eyes, and looked down at her. She stared at him with her almond-shaped, dark eyes. "No, not at all. A mere instant of dizziness."

"It is rather warm in here," she said. "I cannot work in here for very long myself. Shall we go back outside?"

"Yes, of course." Miles watched as she replaced the comb on its labeled spot on the table, then offered her his arm to lead her back out into the sunlight.

Fortunately, the vision or picture or whatever it had been, had quite vanished, as if it were just so much mist. But it left a most odd feeling in its wake, and he could no longer see Lady Iverson in quite the same manner he had before—as a pretty, interesting lady he would like to get to know better. Something new and intense came forward when she laid her hand on his arm, something he did not understand at all.

Perhaps he should speak to her now about the land and his plans for it. It would be better to have that all out in the open, to have honesty and reality between them.

"Lady Iverson," he began.

"Yes, Lord Ransome?" she said, turning her gaze up to him.

Blast, but it was harder than he would have thought to speak to her about such things, when she looked at him so guilelessly.

But he had to do it. "I think I should tell you—"

"Sarah! Lord Ransome!" a voice called, and Mary Ann Bellweather came dashing up the pathway, a leather portfolio in her arms. "There you are. You had quite disappeared."

Lady Iverson turned to her sister with a smile, and Miles could have kissed the girl's cheek for saving him. He *did* have to speak about the land, but he felt a rather deep relief that he wouldn't have to just yet. It was cowardly of him, he knew, but there it was.

Now he could just enjoy the rest of the afternoon in Lady Iverson's company.

Chapter Six

Sarah watched as Lord Ransome examined Mary Ann's sketches. He was obviously not as ignorant as he claimed, because he asked very intelligent questions about the drawings and the site. Mary Ann chatted and laughed, her cheeks pink with delight that someone was looking at her work.

They might have opposing ideas about the best use for this land, Sarah thought, but she could not help but be thankful to him for drawing Mary Ann out. Her sister had been uncharacteristically quiet since she came here, and Sarah knew she was moping over the lost Mr. Hamilton. Sarah had considered taking away the novels she was always reading, and asking Phoebe not to send her any more, because they were giving her false ideas of love and romance.

Today, though, she chattered just like the old Mary Ann, holding up a sketch of a reconstructed Viking house. She pointed out the central hearth, the built-in benches along the walls which would be covered with furs for sleeping at night. Lord Ransome nodded, carefully listening to her.

Sarah pretended to be absorbed in writing in her notebook. She was meant to be taking notes on the newest finds in the smithy, but in reality she was not sure exactly what it was she was writing down. All she could think of was that odd look on Lord Ransome's face when she showed him the ivory comb. He had looked—thunderstruck was the only word for it. He had stared at her as if he had never seen her before in his life, as if she was some strange new life-form.

Or as if he did not see *her,* Sarah Iverson, at all.

Sarah herself sometimes had odd reactions to some of the artifacts. She would hold a brooch or a spindle, and flashes of some other life would come into her mind. That was only because she was so deeply absorbed in the work, though, and the life of centuries past sometimes seemed more real to her than the present day.

The present day seemed very real indeed, however, when she was near Lord Ransome. It was hard to focus on her work, or the Vikings, or anything else when he stood close to her. He smelled delicious, like soap and wool and horses, like the clean autumn breeze. When he leaned over to closely examine the sketch, a lock of sun golden hair fell across his brow, making Sarah long to brush it back, to feel its silk under her fingers. She wondered what it would feel like to lay her finger on the dimple in his cheek. . . .

Fool! she berated herself, and sternly turned her gaze back to her notebook. She was getting quite as silly as Mary Ann, and it would just have to stop.

"Your sister is a very talented artist, Lady Iverson," he said, breaking into her thoughts. His voice was polite and brisk, bringing a much needed reality into this odd day.

Sarah pushed away the notebook, and looked up to see Lord Ransome and her sister watching her. She smiled, hoping she seemed as normal as they did. "Yes, she is. I wish I was half as fine. She does a wonderful job of envisioning what the buildings would have looked like when they were new."

Mary Ann blushed and ducked her head, shuffling the sketches into a neat pile. As Sarah watched her, she realized she should compliment her sister more on her talents. Perhaps then Mary Ann would not dwell so much on her romantical infatuations.

Just as Sarah was beginning to dwell too much on Lord Ransome, after just a short acquaintance.

Lord Ransome drew out one of the sketches, a depiction of the leather-worker's shop. "This is very interesting. Which, er, site is this?"

Sarah looked out from the shady spot under the grove of trees where they sat, out along the sun-drenched village. It was quiet now, all the workers still gone for luncheon, and she was able to see every carefully marked spot on the ancient street. "That one there, at the very end on the left," she said, gesturing toward it.

Lord Ransome studied it for a moment, using his hand to shade his eyes. He looked very serious, and for a moment Sarah could imagine him as he must have appeared before a battle, scanning the enemy's position.

"Why is it so much deeper than the other dwellings?" he asked. "They're quite shallow, especially the ones farther out, while that one appears to be a veritable pit."

"It had a cellar of sorts, which we discovered as we dug into it. It was the first building John—my husband—worked on, where your uncle found the coins. We believe the craftsman kept his shop above, and worked in the cellar."

"I see," Lord Ransome said. "And why are the beams laid across it?"

Before Sarah could answer, Mary Ann blurted, "Because there was a terrible cave-in, caused by the ghost! Sarah doesn't want anyone to fall in."

Lord Ransome looked at Sarah sharply, his blue eyes narrowed. "A cave-in? Mr. Benson told me of it. Was anyone injured?"

"Not at all. It happened at night, not long after my husband passed away," Sarah said. She hadn't wanted to tell him of any of the troubles at the village yet, for fear he would think her a silly, incompetent woman. "And it certainly wasn't *terrible*, Mary Ann; you mustn't exaggerate. It was simply one of those things that happens occasionally, though, of course, we always do our best to be certain everything is properly secured." She sent her sister a stern glance. "It certainly was not caused by a ghost."

Mary Ann made a doubtful moue with her mouth. She loved the legends, and would listen endlessly to the local farmers' tales.

"The Viking witch Thora?" Lord Ransome asked, that hint of laughter back in his voice.

Sarah sighed inwardly. That ridiculous story was always going to haunt her here—so to speak. Even he, who had only been in the neighborhood a short while, knew of it. "Indeed. So you have been told the tale, Lord Ransome?"

"Only a very bare outline. That Thora has a treasure here, and will curse any who touch it." He looked down at her, his eyes sparkling, as if inviting her to share some joke. As if they were some sort of kindred spirits.

Sarah couldn't help but smile in return. She opened her mouth to answer, to dismiss the stories, but Mary Ann leaped in first.

"Oh, no!" Mary Ann said earnestly. "That is not the entire tale. The treasure was left to Thora by her true love, who entrusted it to her before he left on a long voyage back to Norway. But he never returned, and Thora mourned him all the rest of her days. When she died, she put a spell on it saying that only those pure of heart and true of love—her real heirs—can safely touch it." Her dark eyes shone as she recited this.

Sarah stared at her sister in amazement. "Mary Ann, wherever did you hear all that?"

Mary Ann looked away, and shrugged. "Oh, here and there."

"It sounds as though it came directly from one of your Minerva Press novels," Sarah said.

"No!" Mary Ann protested. "Every bit is true."

"Well, I think it sounds quite fascinating, Miss Bellweather," Lord Ransome said, his voice kind and full of a smile. "I would love to hear more about the legend. Which reminds me of my other purpose in coming here today."

"Other purpose, Lord Ransome?" Sarah asked, glad they were moving away from talk of ghosts and curses.

Glad—but also apprehensive. Was he going to say she would have to give up the land now?

"Yes. I almost forgot, since your work here is so interesting, but I am having a supper party on Friday evening. I hope you and Miss Bellweather will be able to attend. It is nothing grand, just supper and cards with some neighbors. I thought I should make myself more social, if I am to live here."

Mary Ann clapped her hands delightedly. "A party! How very grand. Of course, we will come, won't we, Sarah?"

Sarah didn't do anything like clap her hands, but she had to admit an excitement stirred inside her, as well as relief that he had not yet evicted her. It had been quite a while since she had attended an entertainment of any sort. There had been a card party at Lady Eaton's house in Upper Hawton on Phoebe's last evening here, but nothing since. She knew that Mary Ann was easily restless, and she herself enjoyed the company of other people, even when she was absorbed in a project as she was now.

"Thank you very much, Lord Ransome," she said. "We would be happy to accept your invitation."

"I am very glad, Lady Iverson. I'm sure you will know everyone who will be there, and can help me get to know them." He drew his watch from inside his coat, and checked its face. "Now, I fear I must be leaving. Thank you for so graciously showing me about—"

"You can't leave yet, Lord Ransome!" Mary Ann interrupted. She was looking behind them, toward the road. "Someone is arriving."

Sarah turned to see an open landau drawing to a halt. In it was a man, and a woman with a parasol and an elaborate feathered bonnet. The man's hair glinted mahogany-red in the sunlight.

Mr. Hamilton, returned from his wedding trip with the new Mrs. Hamilton. Sarah looked at Mary Ann, praying that her sister was not wearing all her emotions on her pretty face.

Mary Ann's complexion was a trifle pale, and her lips pinched together, but that was all. "It is Mr. Hamilton," she said quietly.

"And *Mrs.* Hamilton," Sarah added, as gently as she could.

"Yes, indeed," said Mary Ann. "What poor taste she has in millinery."

"Friends of yours?" Lord Ransome asked.

Sarah glanced back at him. "Oh, yes. Mr. Hamilton is an antiquarian, a colleague and friend of my husband. He has helped us greatly here, but he has been gone on his wedding trip and is only now returning. As you see."

They watched as Mr. Hamilton alighted from the carriage, then turned back to help his bride. She descended in a great, frothy flurry of pink-and-white ruffles. Her laughter carried even to where Sarah, Mary Ann, and Lord Ransome stood.

"Would you care to meet them?" Sarah asked Lord Ransome.

"I would be delighted to meet any friend of yours, Lady Iverson," he answered. "Perhaps they would like to attend the supper party, too?"

Sarah remembered Mrs. Hamilton's, the former Miss Emmeline Harris of Bath's, patent joy in meeting *anyone* with a title, even one as minor as Sarah's. She would no doubt go into raptures over a marquis. "I am sure they would be most honored to be invited."

She had no time to say anything else, for then the Hamiltons were upon them.

"Dear Lady Iverson!" Mrs. Hamilton trilled, closing her parasol in order to peck a kiss on Sarah's cheek. "We are here at last. It feels as though we have been driving for an age."

Sarah made herself smile. Mrs. Hamilton always seemed very friendly and open, with her giggles and her soft blond curls, but somehow Sarah had never been entirely able to warm up to her. There was always something rather hard and somehow calculating behind those pale blue eyes.

But Neville Hamilton had been a good friend to her and John, and an invaluable help to them in their work. For a time after John's death, Sarah had feared he might harbor feelings warmer than those of friendship for her, and she had *known* he wanted to take over the village entirely. Yet then he had married the well-dowered Miss Harris, and all had gone on as it had before.

For the sake of their friendship, Sarah could be civil to the new Mrs. Hamilton.

"Mrs. Hamilton, Neville," she greeted, with a smile. "It is so good to see you again. You must tell me about your wedding trip."

"It was all quite delightful!" Mrs. Hamilton gushed, before her husband could even open his mouth. "And this must be your *adorable* sister."

"Oh, yes," Sarah said. She took Mary Ann's hand, acutely aware of Lord Ransome standing behind her, still and watchful. She turned her head slightly to glance at him; his face was expressionless. "Miss Mary Ann Bellweather. Mary Ann, of course, you know Mr. Hamilton, and this is the new Mrs. Hamilton."

"How do you do?" Mary Ann murmured. Her fingers curled around Sarah's.

"Hello, Miss Bellweather," Neville said, with a small smile for her.

Mary Ann just nodded, and looked away.

Then Mrs. Hamilton saw Lord Ransome. Her eyes widened, and her lips parted to let out another giggle. "And who might *this* be?"

"This is Lord Ransome." Sarah smiled. "He has only lately moved into Ransome Hall."

Lord Ransome obligingly stepped forward to give the Hamiltons a polite bow. "How do you do, Mrs. Hamilton? Mr. Hamilton. Lady Iverson was just very kindly showing me the work here. She tells me you have done a great deal with the village, Mr. Hamilton."

Neville Hamilton, who had hitherto been looking quiet and rather stunned, showed a spark of interest in his eyes, and opened his mouth to reply. But his wife stepped in front of him to hold her hand out to Lord Ransome, her mouth curved in a flirtatious smile.

"Lord Ransome!" she said, with yet another giggle. "It is very good to meet *you*. I must say you are much more handsome than the previous marquis!"

Lord Ransome looked at Sarah wryly, one golden brow arched. Sarah turned away to hide a laugh.

"Er—thank you, Mrs. Hamilton," he answered, a hint of laughter in his own voice. "And may I wish you much happiness in your new marriage?"

"And charming, too," Mrs. Hamilton cooed. She stepped closer to lay a lace-gloved hand on his sleeve.

Lord Ransome's wry look turned to one of alarm, and Sarah decided she really ought to rescue him. "I fear Lord Ransome was just leaving us," she said. "Perhaps Mary Ann could take you both to the house for tea, and I will join you after I have walked with him to his horse?"

Mrs. Hamilton pouted prettily. "Oh, no! Must you go, Lord Ransome, when we have only just arrived?"

Neville finally took some action, and stepped forward to take his wife's arm and draw her away. "We mustn't keep Lord Ransome from his duties, Emmeline."

"I came here today to invite Lady Iverson and Miss Bellweather to a supper party at Ransome Hall on Friday," Lord Ransome said. "Perhaps you could both join us?"

"Oh, yes!" Mrs. Hamilton cried. "How very delightful! Only here one day and we are invited to a soiree."

She was still rhapsodizing about Lord Ransome, soirees, and the world in general as Mary Ann led her and Neville toward the hunting box.

Sarah watched them go before turning back to Lord Ransome. He appeared a bit—dazed. He shook his head slightly, and smiled at her.

"Mrs. Hamilton is very, er, lively," he said.

"Indeed, she is," Sarah answered. Lord Ransome offered his arm, and she took it to walk with him back to where his horse was tethered. "Well, now you have met our entire party here. It was very good of you to invite them to your supper. I hope it will not make. it too crowded?"

"Not at all. I'm sure they will be very charming additions." He unlooped the reins from the tree branch. "I look forward to seeing you—*all* of you, of course."

Sarah found she looked forward to it, too. Very much.

Chapter Seven

"Lord Ransome is a handsome gentleman, is he not?"

"Hm?" Sarah did not even look up from the book she was perusing, but inside she smiled at Mary Ann's words. Lord Ransome was indeed handsome—more than handsome. It was simply too bad that he was not an antiquarian, did not even show interest in becoming one.

Or perhaps it was all for the best. For if he was as interested in history as she was, then he would be quite perfect. And she had no time right now for such distractions—or for becoming better acquainted with Lord Ransome, not when he could pull her work out from under her at any moment.

Mary Ann, who was curled up next to the fireplace with her sketchbook, repeated, "I said Lord Ransome is very handsome, for an older gentleman."

Sarah laughed aloud at that. "He is hardly *old*, Mary Ann! Though I must say he is probably bit too old for you, if that is what you are thinking of."

"Oh, so now you think I am transferring my 'infatuation,' as you call it, for Mr. Hamilton onto Lord Ransome!" Mary Ann said indignantly. "Well, I am certainly not. I was never infatuated with Mr. Hamilton, and I am not so with Lord Ransome, either. I merely said that he was handsome. It was just an observation."

Sarah gave her sister a conciliatory smile. "I am sorry if I sounded condescending, dear one. I did not mean to imply that you had any sort of feelings for Lord Ransome. And you are right, he *is* handsome. Quite so. Just remember, handsome is as . . ."

". . . handsome does," Mary Ann finished, in a perfect imitation of their mother's "lecturing" voice. "So Mother always says, and she must mean it, since she and the Dowager Lady Lyndon are always giggling like schoolgirls over old Colonel Webster, and he is in no way outwardly handsome."

"And very old, too, eh?" Sarah teased.

Mary Ann gave an embarrassed little laugh. "Oh, all right, so Lord Ransome is not so very old. Not old for having done all the things he did on the Peninsula."

"How do you know what he did on the Peninsula?" Sarah set aside her book. This conversation was proving to be more interesting than the history of Jorvik.

"I was talking to one of the workers, a Mr. Smith, while you showed Lord Ransome the objects in the stable. Mr. Smith's family has lived on Ransome land for simply ages, and he knows all the *on dits*. Lord Ransome was a major in the Forty-first Foot, and fought very bravely at all sorts of battles. He saved many, many lives, and Wellington himself commended him, and his regiment even gave him a medal." Mary Ann's voice was breathless as she recited this litany of gallantry.

Sarah had to admit that even she was impressed. Lord Ransome certainly *looked* the part of the brave officer, but, as Sarah well knew, appearances could often be deceiving. There was many a man who strutted about in his regimentals, bragging to the ladies about exploits they had never performed. It seemed Lord Ransome was no such preening peacock.

"It sounds as if Lord Ransome was very brave," she said.

"Indeed." Mary Ann's wide, dark gaze turned shrewd as she looked at Sarah. "He seemed to like *you* a great deal. He listened very intently to everything you said about the Vikings."

Sarah felt her cheeks grow uncomfortably warm, and

she glanced back down at her book. "Of course, he listened, Mary Ann. This is *his* land we are working on. He is bound to be interested in what happens on it."

Mary Ann shook her head. "No, it is not just that. He was admiring you, not the work."

"Mary Ann! Really," Sarah cried. It had been a long time since she was teased about a gentleman by her girlfriends; so long ago, she could not even remember it. She wasn't sure how she felt about it now, especially from her baby sister. It made her want to squirm.

Ancient Viking relics she was quite comfortable with. Men, especially handsome, young ones, she was not so sure about.

"What?" Mary Ann said innocently. "I merely observed that Lord Ransome seems to admire you. And why should he not? You are very lovely."

"And I am also newly widowed."

"Hardly new! Sir John has been gone for over a year. It is perfectly respectable for Lord Ransome to admire you, and for—for . . ."

Sarah was quite curious against her will. What was Mary Ann going to say? "For what?"

Mary Ann shrugged. "For whatever may happen to happen."

"I am not thinking of marrying again, as I have told you and Phoebe many times. I am far too busy. If I did want to look about for another husband, I would do so among my friends, among other scholars." She gave her sister a rueful smile. "A man like Lord Ransome would not find a woman like me very interesting for very long."

"Fustian!" Mary Ann cried. "How could he not?"

"Well, for one thing, his station is far above mine. The Bellweathers and the Iversons are respectable, but hardly at the level of a marquis. And that is only the beginning of the reasons Lord Ransome and I would not suit. But we don't have time to discuss this now! Mr. and Mrs. Hamilton are coming to supper, and we have to change our gowns."

Mary Ann sighed, and shuffled her sketches back into

their portfolio. "Very well. May we discuss it later, then?"

"No! Later we will have too much work to do to giggle over men."

"Oh, Sarah! You are no fun at all."

"Imagine it, Neville! Only here one day, and we are invited to a *marquis's* supper party!" Emmeline Hamilton peered into her dressing-table mirror, and dusted rice powder over her cheeks. Then she reached for her jewel case and dug inside it for a pair of pearl earrings. "It is absolutely splendid."

Neville Hamilton, who had been staring out the window of his wife's inn bedchamber down to the street below, looked over his shoulder at Emmeline, watching her uncertainly. She appeared happier than he had seen her since the days of their courting. Her pale blue eyes sparkled with life. All because of the prospect of supping with a marquis.

When he first met Emmeline, at an assembly in Bath, where he had gone to visit his old aunt, he had thought her so fun, so fresh. Not at all like the serious, scholarly women he was accustomed to. She flirted with him, and flattered him as no woman ever had. He had always been rather shy with ladies, comfortable only with his studies and his work, but Emmeline had taken no notice of that. She looked at him as if he were the strongest, the most handsome man in all of England.

That had been very reassuring, after his recent disappointment when Lady Iverson had not given him the village project after Sir John's death. He was a man, her husband's colleague, and she was just a woman, albeit an intelligent one. She had known nothing about Vikings, about antiquarian work, until she married Sir John and he taught her. Yet she refused to give it over to him!

Emmeline had thought that was appalling. She had looked at him with wide, sympathetic eyes, and laid her little, white, soft hand on his sleeve. Those eyes, along with the ten thousand pounds of her dowry, convinced him to relinquish his bachelorhood.

So he had married her. And all was well, until their wedding trip to Scotland. He wanted to explore ancient castles and forts, and saw it as a perfect opportunity to teach his bride more about his work. Yet Emmeline saw no interest in marching through the heather to look at ruins. She spent all her time changing into the various elaborate gowns of her trousseau, and talking about the soirees they would have once they were settled into their own house in Bath.

Bath! Neville never wanted to live in Bath. He almost snorted aloud now, as he watched his wife slide jeweled combs into her elaborate coiffure. One would have thought she was going to the Court of St. James, not to supper at Lady Iverson's hunting box home.

No, married life was not at all what he had hoped. Perhaps he should have married pretty little Mary Ann Bellweather, who looked at him with worshipful dark eyes. She seemed malleable to learn anything there was to know about history, but she did not have ten thousand pounds, as Emmeline did.

Not that the ten thousand would last long, with the amount Emmeline spent on clothes and jewels. There would soon be nothing left at all for his studies.

"Papa will be so pleased when I write to him that we have met a marquis!" she went on, giving her hair one last pat. "Perhaps once we have our house in Bath, Lord Ransome will come to a party there. A supper. No, a ball! I would be the envy of all my friends."

"Emmeline!" Neville burst out. His hand crushed the cravat he was trying to tie. "I have told you several times I have no intention of living in Bath, at least not for many years. We must finish the work on the village; then there is that new find in Northumberland to be explored."

Emmeline slapped her hand against the dressing table, rattling glass pots and bottles. The sparkle on her face faded as if it had never been there, and her pink lips flattened. "I do not want to hear another word about Vikings! I refuse to spend my whole life as I did our wedding trip, shivering in the wind while you go dig up some moldy old bits and pieces. When I married you, I thought . . ." Her voice trailed away, and she closed her eyes.

"What?" Neville said, frustrated beyond all belief. "What did you think?"

Emmeline shook her head. "Just that you would *know* people, people who are something in Society, with titles and all—like Lady Iverson. That we would have a fine home, where I could entertain, as I have always dreamed of doing. Instead, we're here at an inn in this pokey old village, and you say we will never live in Bath! It is not what I expected."

"Marriage is not what I expected, either," Neville muttered, so low that Emmeline could not hear. His entire life was not what he expected. It was blighted by women—first by Sarah Iverson, who refused to yield him his rightful place at the Viking village, and now by his silly wife.

It was infuriating.

Emmeline, completely unconscious of his stewing thoughts, reached for her gloves, a new smile forming. "Well," she said, "at least we have met a marquis. It is too bad he won't be at supper tonight! I can hardly wait until the party at Ransome Hall."

Miles sat at his desk in the library at Ransome Hall, reports and plans for the estate spread out before him. But he wasn't really paying attention to any of that. He leaned back in his chair, watching the red-gold flames dance in the grate, sending light piercing into the dark corners of the vast room.

The map on the top of the pile detailed the corner where Lady Iverson's village sat, with notes drawn up by the bailiff. He wrote about soil conditions, possible crops, spots where cottages could be built.

Cottages to house unfortunate ex-soldiers, like the Lieutenant O'Riley Miles had met in London, and their families. It was a grand plan, one that could combat unemployment and hunger, at least for a few. It was all that he could have wanted to accomplish.

But all he could see in his mind was Lady Iverson's face as she showed him the village, the objects so carefully laid out and labeled. Her eyes shone like dark stars, and her wide, mobile, kiss-tempting mouth curved with delight. She loved those dusty fragments as most women loved gowns and jewels. Her tanned, capable little hands were tender as she touched them, and turned them over and over. It made him wonder, beyond all sense, how it would feel if she touched *him* like that, if she looked at him as she did old soapstone spindles.

What would it feel like, if she was to care for him even a quarter as much as she did her village? No man could ask for more, for it was very clear how much she *did* care about her work. It shone from her like an aura.

They had only known each other for a very short time, yet he liked her, felt drawn to her. How could he take away her work? That would be unconscionably caddish of him, and she would probably never speak to him again.

But how could he go against his conscience, when he knew how desperately good men needed the jobs his land could bring? He remembered the vast expanse of ropes and pits where she had been digging, stretching as far as the eye could see, across prime farmland.

Miles buried his face in his hands, pushing back his hair with his fingers. He did not know what to do. Battles and the rigors of camp life on the Peninsula had been simple compared to this. Simple, with no Lady Iverson there, with her dark eyes and bouncing curls to make him forget his duties. He knew what was expected of him there at all times, and what was the right thing to do.

He missed those days.

Miles laughed. No man in his right mind should ever prefer a dusty tent to the splendors of Ransome Hall, the advantages of a title! He must be *out* of his mind!

He reached for the tiny fragment of ancient chain mail that Lady Iverson gave him, and turned it in the firelight. What Viking warrior had once worn it? Had he been driven mad by a Norwegian woman's flashing eyes? Had he sailed away in order to escape new and

unwelcome emotions? Had he drifted out into the un-
known waters?

For that was what Miles felt he was doing. Floating
adrift into something he had never seen before.

Chapter Eight

Sarah examined the gowns laid out on her bed, trying to decide which one to wear at that night's supper party at Ransome Hall. Usually, she just wore whichever gown her maid pressed, or the first one she came across in the wardrobe, but today she could not stop dithering like a young miss on her way to her first ball.

She held up one gown, then another, peering at her reflection in the looking glass. Each dress seemed duller and less fashionable than the last, all of them the grays and lilacs of half-mourning. She didn't want a gown like one of Mrs. Hamilton's fussy pink-and-white creations, but something with a bit more—more dash would be nice. Something with color and shine.

She found a cinnamon brown silk she had worn before John died, and draped it around her shoulders, over her chemise. It would be all right, if only it did not make her look so very *brown* all over! Brown eyes, brown hair, brown dress. Terrible.

Oh, nothing was right, she thought, and threw the gown down on top of all the others. She might as well just wear one of her old work dresses. Lord Ransome had already seen her looking like a ragamuffin in one of them, anyway.

That thought froze her in her agitated tracks. She stood still, and stared down at the gowns. Lord Ransome. Was he the reason she was in such a flurry over her attire? Did she want him to admire her in a fine gown, to forget he had seen her all dusty and dank?

"No," she whispered, sitting down heavily on the nearest chair, which happened to be covered with more gowns and shawls. She had never dressed for men's admiration—she could hardly afford to start now.

Lord Ransome needed to see her as a sensible, capable scholar, one whose work must be completed. That was all.

That was *all*.

There was a quick knock at the door, and Mary Ann popped in without waiting to be summoned. She was already dressed for the party, in a pretty gown of pale pink muslin, her hair tied back with a bandeau of pink ribbons and seed pearls.

"Sarah, what do you think of these gloves? Do they make . . ." Her voice faded as she took in the heaps of discarded garments, the slippers scattered across the carpet. "You aren't dressed yet!"

"I cannot decide what to wear," Sarah answered faintly.

"What do you mean? You are always ready for parties and outings faster than any of us! Where is your maid?"

"She is in the kitchen, no doubt chattering with Rose and the cook. I saw no sense in calling her until I made up my mind."

"Which you just cannot seem to do?" Mary Ann gave her a skeptical look, and walked over to the bed to begin sorting through the gowns. "I don't see anything wrong with these."

"They're dull."

"Hm. Perhaps, just a bit." She threw Sarah a teasing glance over her shoulder. "But that never seemed to bother you before!"

Sarah laughed in spite of herself. "Mary Ann!"

Mary Ann reached to the bottom of the pile, and pulled out a gown. "This one isn't dull at all. And it looks as if you have never worn it!"

"I haven't." Sarah regarded the gown with surprise. She had forgotten she owned it, and hadn't even noticed it when she drew all the gowns out of the wardrobe. It was one of her black ones, purchased to wear to an historical lecture in Brighton when she had a flash of bold feeling, then abandoned on the day for a more staid gown when the boldness faded. It was made of a rich black velvet, so soft and deep that in certain lights it appeared purple or dark blue. The long, fitted sleeves were of sheer black tulle, tied at the wrists with black satin ribbon. More ribbon trimmed the low, rounded neckline.

Mary Ann held it against herself, stroking her hand over the fabric. "It is marvelous, Sarah. You *must* wear it."

Sarah was sorely tempted. It was a gown made for someone totally unlike herself, someone daring and flirtatious, someone unafraid of the world and sure of her place in it. Not someone who always had to be sensible. Not someone who spent her days getting hot and dirty working under the sun.

"I shouldn't wear black," she said. "My year of deep mourning is over."

"Who says you cannot still wear black?" Mary Ann argued. "And this is not just any dull old black, this is— beautiful. Oh, Sarah, you have to wear this one!"

Sarah looked from the black gown to the others still piled on the bed and chairs. They lay there in a jumble of brown and gray, just meant for a sensible lady antiquarian.

She made up her mind.

"Very well," she said. "I will wear it." She stood up, all her fluttering uncertainty gone now. She felt more like her levelheaded self—but a new levelheaded self, one who wore daring gowns. "Now, Mary Ann, be a dear and ring for my maid for me, so she can dress my hair. We will be late, and that would never do."

The drive leading up to Ransome Hall was crowded with carriages when they turned into the gates and took their place in line, a vast array of equipages that held a myriad of guests. Sarah would not have thought there could be so many people in the neighborhood; they must have come from as far away as York, and maybe even London.

She pulled her fur-lined wrap closer about her shoulders, and watched Ransome Hall looming closer. Every window sparkled with welcoming golden light, and the front doors were thrown open to admit the visitors as they were disgorged from their carriages.

Beside her, Mary Ann craned her neck to take it all in, and clutched at Sarah's arm in her excitement. Her young eyes sparkled, and she didn't even seem to notice anymore Mr. and Mrs. Hamilton seated across from them. "Oh, Sarah, isn't it marvelous! There are so many grand people. Mother would be so jealous if she could see us now."

Mrs. Hamilton giggled behind her painted silk fan. "As would my friends in Bath, Miss Bellweather! I cannot wait to write to them and tell them all about my supper with a marquis."

Her husband looked away from her, out the opposite window into the night. "You are hardly having supper with him by yourself, my dear. There are dozens of other people here. You needn't call it *your* supper with the marquis."

Mrs. Hamilton frowned at him. "Of course, I will not be alone with him, Neville! How can you say something so ridiculous? There will be many other people, perhaps even other titled people." She turned to Sarah with one of her bright, brittle smiles. "Do *you* think there will be other titled people, Lady Iverson?"

Sarah made herself smile back. Mrs. Hamilton was not the easiest person to be around, it was true; she giggled, and plucked at her ruffles, and knew nothing about history. But Sarah could not help but feel a bit sorry for her. In the last few days, the strain between the newlywed Hamiltons had been all too obvious, and Sarah feared for their future. She also feared for Mr. Hamilton's scholarly ability. Ever since their return from their wedding trip, he had been short-tempered and forgetful. More than once he had forgotten to label objects from the bakery he was excavating.

He had always been intense and serious, but now he seemed intense and—angry.

Sarah had considered talking to them, but then decided the whole thing was patently none of her business. The Hamiltons would just have to work out their difficulties on their own. But she had resolved to be kinder to Mrs. Hamilton, and she hoped Mary Ann would, too.

She glanced over at Mary Ann. Her sister watched the Hamiltons with a solemn look on her face, and Sarah couldn't help but wonder what she was thinking. Aside from a few glances and sighs, and references to a volume entitled *Miss Anderson's Secret Love,* there had been no signs that her old infatuation had returned. Sarah wanted to keep it that way—she had quite enough to worry about without her sister's romantic sensibilities causing trouble.

"I am sure there will be some titled people," she answered Mrs. Hamilton. "At least Lord Dunston, the nearest neighbor to Ransome Hall, and old Lady Eaton. She is never one to miss a rout."

Mrs. Hamilton smiled, as if satisfied. "Lady Eaton. I shall be sure to mention her in my letters, as well."

There was really nothing Sarah could think of to answer that, and fortunately she did not have to, as their carriage was stopping at the foot of the front steps. With great relief, she took the footman's hand and stepped out onto the gravel drive.

She had been to Ransome Hall several times in the past, even before she had taken tea there after Lord Ransome rescued her from the stream. The late Lord Ransome had been great friends with her husband, and they had often come here for supper and long discussions about the Vikings and ancient Britain. But she had never seen the vast house look like this.

Old Lord Ransome's collections of antiquities and medieval-style furniture were still in place, yet they were lit with tall branches of candelabra, and surrounded by banks of greenery and sweet-smelling white roses. The dark, echoing house was full of laughter and conversation, the clink of champagne crystal.

Mary Ann laid her hand on Sarah's arm, staring around her with amazed eyes. "Oh, Sarah! It is lovely. Like a fairyland."

"Indeed," Sarah murmured. She handed her wrap to the waiting footman, still taking in the light and the flowers. It *was* like a fairyland, not like an ordinary supper party at all.

And not like something a bachelor Army officer would arrange, either, she thought. Her own husband would never, ever have thought of flowers.

She wondered if there was a lady who had helped him with the arrangements. A *special* lady.

She felt a sour pang in her stomach, one that felt suspiciously like—jealousy.

"I am *not* jealous!" she whispered, not even realizing she spoke aloud. "Don't be silly."

"Sarah?" Mary Ann, who had wandered slightly ahead, looked back at her. "Did you say something?"

Sarah smiled at her, and hurried to catch up. The other guests were gathered in the drawing room, and she could feel their merriment, their happy sociability, pulling her in. This was not a night for any conflicted emotions or uncertainties—it was just a night for enjoyment. It had been so long, too long, since she had been to a proper party.

"I was just saying that the champagne looks lovely," she said.

"Could I have some?" Mary Ann begged. "Just a tiny, tiny bit? I *am* sixteen now."

Sarah laughed. "Maybe just a sip, dear, if you behave yourself."

They stepped into the drawing room, and found more flowers, more light and laughter. People, some that Sarah knew and a few that she did not, were gathered there. The ladies' silk and satin gowns, a myriad of stylish colors, shimmered, their jewels sparkled. The gentlemen, though garbed in more somber colors, were no less fashionable.

Sarah was very glad she had worn the black velvet, and the diamond necklace and earrings John had given her when they married. They seemed to shine even brighter after their long confinement in her jewel case. She reached up and touched one of the drop earrings, and smoothed back her upswept hair.

"You look beautiful," Mary Ann whispered. "And I am sure Lord Ransome will think so, too!"

Sarah gave an unladylike little snort. "I hardly tidied myself up specifically for Lord Ransome!" Or whatever lady it was who had helped him arrange this party.

"Of course not," Mary Ann said. She stepped eagerly into the room, pulling Sarah with her.

Lord Ransome waited just inside the doors, greeting his guests. He looked every bit as handsome in a dark blue coat and creamy silk waistcoat, his golden hair brushed back, as he did in casual attire standing about in the sun. He nodded at whatever the people in front of them were saying.

Behind Sarah, the Hamiltons were talking in low, intent voices, obviously quarreling about something. Mrs. Hamilton's lace-edged silk ruffles rustled, releasing waves of a lilac perfume that rivaled the flowers around them with its sweetness. Sarah paid attention to none of this. She only saw Lord Ransome. Even the sounds of conversation around her faded to a mere buzzing drone.

He looked toward her, and smiled. His gloved hand reached for hers, and she released the breath she hadn't even realized she was holding. The voices rushed back onto her, bringing her back into the room.

She hoped fervently that he had not seen her dazed expression, that he did not realize how ridiculous she became every time she saw him.

"Good evening, Lady Iverson. Miss Bellweather," he said. "I am very glad you were able to join us."

"Thank you, Lord Ransome," Sarah answered. Her body leaned toward him infinitesimally, of its own volition, when he raised her hand to his lips, but other than that she thought she remained quite cool. "You have quite transformed Ransome Hall!"

"It looks like an enchanted castle in a book," said Mary Ann.

He laughed. "Thank you very much, Miss Bellweather! I fear I cannot take the credit for the decorations, though. I have little imagination for such things." He turned slightly, and Sarah saw the woman who stood beside him.

She was beautiful, tiny and perfect, with moonlight-colored curls piled on her Grecian head and held by a band of sapphires and diamonds. Her artfully draped blue silk gown made Sarah feel a bit like a crow next to a shining bluebird.

A few faint lines radiated from the corners of her blue eyes, indicating that she was a bit older than Lord Ransome, but surely no one could care about that when she was such an exquisite little doll.

Lord Ransome took the woman's arm in a fond gesture, and said, "This is the person who should be receiving your compliments—my mother, Mrs. Jane Browning. She surprised me with her arrival two days ago, and immediately worked wonders with these arrangements."

Sarah gave an hysterical little laugh, one that escaped before she could catch it. "Y—your mother, Lord Ransome?"

Mrs. Browning smiled at her sweetly, and clasped Sarah's hand in both of her own tiny ones. "My name *is* a surprise, isn't it? Mr. Browning was my second husband, who passed away only three years ago. I see from your gown that you have also lost someone. I *am* sorry."

"Mother, this is Lady Iverson, and her sister, Miss Bellweather," Lord Ransome said. "The ones who are working on the Viking village."

Mrs. Browning's eyes lit up. "Of course! Miles has told me all about you and your work, and I am eager to hear more. I live in Bath, you know, and we have many scholarly lectures and meetings there. I would love to hear more about what you are doing here."

"Of course, Mrs. Browning. I am always happy to talk about my work." To cover the confusion she still felt inside, Sarah turned to the Hamiltons. "Mrs. Browning, this is Mr. and Mrs. Hamilton, who are also working on the village. Mr. Hamilton is a great expert on the Vikings, and Mrs. Hamilton lived in Bath herself until their marriage. Perhaps you will have some mutual friends?"

Sarah stepped back a bit as Lord Ransome and Mrs. Browning greeted the Hamiltons. She felt like such a fool. This had become a feeling she was very accustomed to since she met Lord Ransome—was it only a week ago?

It felt like a year. It felt like forever.

She would just have to keep control of herself, she resolved, for what seemed like the twentieth time. But this time she *meant* it.

Really, she did.

Heavy silver clinked against delicate china as footmen served course after course. Laughter and talk wound down the length of the vast rosewood table, echoing through the arrangements of white flowers and the goblets of wine. Supper was a great success so far.

Miles only realized this as something vague, at the edges of his mind, though. The merriment was like some half-heard conversation. He only saw Sarah, who sat on his right, talking to the man on her own right about the Viking village. Her dark eyes sparkled with enthusiasm as her slender hand sketched the outline of a building in the air. Through the sheer tulle of her sleeve, glimpses of pale skin shimmered. When she turned her head, her earrings shone and swung, tangling in the one long curl that lay against her neck.

She was fascinating, he thought, like some exotic bird who had suddenly alighted in his dining room. He had seen her as the dashing phaeton driver, and the dusty, dedicated antiquarian. Now she was yet something else entirely—a beautiful, sophisticated temptress.

He could not help but wonder what she would appear

as next. It occupied his mind when he should be thinking of other things. Things such as his work, his new duties and responsibilities.

Or, more immediately, his guests.

Miles glanced down the table to where his mother sat at the foot. She gave him a knowing glance, then made a small gesture, as if to say, "Smile! Smile and talk."

She had always told him he did not smile enough, that he looked too serious and frightened people away. So he turned to Lady Iverson and smiled.

She blinked at him, as if startled. Did he really always appear so solemn, that it surprised people when he *did* smile? Smiling had simply not been something one did very often in military camps. There was not the time, or the cause, for it.

But you are *not* in a military camp now, he reminded himself. He was in England, in his own home, among polite society. Sitting beside Lady Iverson. He found himself *wanting* to smile more around her, to laugh and enjoy his life, as he never had before.

He wanted to make her laugh, too, wanted to make her lose that wary tightness about her eyes that she sometimes had when she looked at him. Even when she talked and smiled with him, there was that watchfulness.

Just as there was now. She gave him a tentative little smile, and said, "I was just telling Lord Dunston about the smithy in the village, and how you so quickly identified the link of chain mail."

"Excellent work, Lord Ransome! Your uncle would have been proud," old Lord Dunston said. "Are you becoming a great scholar, as he was?"

Miles almost laughed aloud at the thought of himself as a scholar, as his old tutors no doubt would have if they could have heard Lord Dunston. "I fear not. My uncle was a brilliant man, and I'm just a crusty old Army man. Identifying the chain mail was only a very lucky guess."

"Oh, come now, Lord Ransome, you are being too modest!" Lady Iverson said. "It would have taken me hours to label it, and it was a vital clue to what sort of equipment a Viking warrior might have in battle. You helped add knowledge to *military* history."

Miles had not thought of anything like that. "Really, Lady Iverson?"

"Really." She paused to take a sip of her wine. "Military history is really more Mr. Hamilton's forte than my own—I am more interested in the domestic sphere. But I know that he was very excited by the discovery of chain mail."

Miles could not quite picture the taciturn Mr. Hamilton "excited" about anything, but he was nonetheless ridiculously gratified by the compliment. "I am glad to know I could be of some assistance, Lady Iverson."

Her eyes sparkled at him. "I can see that there is more of your uncle in you than you think, Lord Ransome."

"Perhaps the antiquarian bug will bite you in the end, just as it did him!" Lord Dunston said.

For one instant, Miles had a tantalizing image in his mind of himself and Lady Iverson, happily digging in the dirt together. Her face lit up with joy as he showed her some newfound object, and she put her arms around him in delight and exuberance.

Miles looked down at his plate. He knew that such images, no matter how delightful, could only be fleeting fantasies. Once he talked to Lady Iverson, and established a schedule for her to be off the land so it could be converted to farms, she would never look at him with any delight at all.

Right now, some of her wariness had faded, and she looked comfortable and happy to be talking about her favorite subject—the Viking village.

The blasted Viking village, that would always stand in the way of his knowing her better.

But he also knew that if it was not for the village he would never have met Lady Iverson at all. So really, all he could do was enjoy this evening, this moment. Enjoy her presence next to him, for however long—or short— a time it lasted.

"I doubt there is much of my uncle in me at all," he said. "But I thank you for the compliment."

"Well, you are welcome to visit the village anytime you wish," she answered. "We can use all the help we can find."

"I did hear that you were having some troubles with your workers," Lord Dunston said. "That they were being frightened off by some superstitious nonsense."

Lady Iverson's mouth tightened. "Unfortunately, you heard correctly, Lord Dunston. But we are doing well now. Many of the workers came back after I spoke to them rationally."

"Then you have great powers of persuasion, Lady Iverson," said Lord Dunston. "The tale of Thora's Treasure is one that has been told in this area for many years, long before anyone knew there was an actual Viking site. I've heard that mothers frighten their children into behaving by telling them that Thora will snatch them away if they are naughty. It is difficult to change such thinking, especially among the lower classes. They are so very superstitious."

"Indeed," Lady Iverson murmured. She toyed with her wineglass, but did not take a drink. "But, as I said, we are doing well now. There have been no further incidents at all. There have certainly been no apparitions."

Mrs. Hamilton, who was seated on Miles's other side, and had been chattering to her supper partner, turned to them at the mention of the word "apparitions." "Oh, my dear Lady Iverson!" she cried. "Are you telling them about the ghost of the Viking woman?" She shivered, a small shadow passing over her blue gaze. "I do get such a chill at the tales of her. Sometimes I imagine I see her at night. . . ."

Lady Iverson looked across the table at her, wondering at the obvious fear in her voice. "I was telling them that *some* people tell tales of her, Mrs. Hamilton, but that we have gotten past that nonsense."

Mrs. Hamilton shivered again, setting her rose-colored ruffles to trembling. "Nonsense? Oh, you must not call it that! She may come to haunt you for doubting her."

Miles almost laughed at the earnest expression on Mrs. Hamilton's face. Despite her shivers, her cheeks were pink with delight. She was obviously one of those ladies who took a great interest in spiritual matters; perhaps she even held those newfangled séances in her drawing room.

He just hoped she would never invite *him* to one of them.

"I take it you have some belief in those tales, Mrs. Hamilton?" he said.

She turned her guileless gaze onto him. "Don't you, Lord Ransome?"

"I believe in common sense, in things I can see," he answered slowly. "There are enough things in this world for us to be frightened of without imagining such things as specters and demons. There are things like war and poverty, young men killed in their very prime, families left to grieve. There is carelessness, and good people starving in the streets."

Mrs. Hamilton frowned, as if she hardly knew what to say to that. She turned her attention back to the gentleman on her other side.

Miles looked away from her to find Lady Iverson watching him closely. Her face was expressionless, but her eyes were no longer wary. For just one moment, they were sympathetic.

Then she dropped her gaze down to the table, her sablelike lashes sweeping across her cheeks.

"That was well said, Lord Ransome," she said quietly.

"Not exactly dinner table conversation, though," said Lord Dunston. "Particularly not for the ladies!"

Lady Iverson gave him a small smile, and raised her gaze back up to Miles. Some of the wariness was back, but there was something else, as well. Something Miles could not quite identify.

"Perhaps not," she said. "But it was honest, and all too often honesty is something sorely lacking in our society. We hide behind our politeness, our falsehoods." She shook her head with a little laugh. "Now I am being maudlin! I apologize, Lord Dunston. Now, what shall we discuss? The weather?"

She was saved from saying anything about the weather when Miles's mother rose from her chair and said, "Well, ladies, shall we take our tea in the drawing room?"

Lady Iverson stood up, and, with a last smile for Lord Dunston and himself, departed in a whisper of velvet. Only the faint fragrance of some spicy perfume remained to remind Miles she had sat beside him for a while.

Chapter Nine

The tall French doors in the drawing room that led out to the garden were half open to the cool night air, to the breezes that carried the scent of late-blooming autumn flowers. Sarah drifted toward them, her teacup in hand, glad of the coolness against her skin, the gentle silence to combat the women's chatter behind her. When she was certain no one was paying her any attention, she pushed open one of the doors and slipped outside.

There, she found herself in an enchanted garden.

Someone had strung white and blue Chinese lanterns in the trees and placed them along the edge of the terrace. They glowed with the same silvery, opalescent light as the moon, casting a glow on the trees and shrubs, making the neat flower beds into something exotic.

Enchanted by the unexpected sight, Sarah drifted over to stand by the marble balustrade and look down into the garden. Below her, a fountain sent a spray of water into the air, dancing and murmuring, blending its music with the voices of the women that floated from the open door.

Soothed by the beautiful sight, by the peace of being alone at last, Sarah leaned against the balustrade and closed her eyes. She inhaled deeply of the fresh night air.

What an odd supper it had been. Odd, and disquieting. At least, she had ceased to feel all fluttery and schoolgirlish when Lord Ransome was near! She had begun to be quite annoyed with herself for such ridiculous and unwarranted reactions. She had met handsome men before, and none of them had *ever* made her want to giggle.

Tonight, she had felt more like herself again, even when seated right next to him for the entire length of supper. Yet something even more unsettling had happened, as she listened to him speak of the evils of poverty and war, of how humans had no need to look for imaginary ghosts in their lives. She felt she had seen a tiny glimpse of the *real* Lord Ransome, as he was inside, and not just his golden outer self.

She had a glimpse of a man who saw things, felt things deeply, even as he hid behind a practical military-man facade. She felt that he probably concealed that side even from himself, and it only came out in very small bursts, as it had tonight.

Sarah found herself wanting to know more of that side of him, to talk to him, confide her own thoughts and fears. Such a man as she had glimpsed in Lord Ransome tonight would surely understand those fears.

But then, she might just be imagining all of this. He might truly only be what he chose to show the world—a genial gentleman, who had enjoyed his military life and was settling into one of country gentry.

Sarah prided herself on her practicality, her sensibleness, but she knew that, deep inside, she harbored a kernel of Mary Ann's romanticism. She had found her girlhood refuge not in novels as Mary Ann did, but in historical works. She went away from her irresponsible mother, and the sisters she was often expected to look after, into the worlds of medieval knights and ancient Greek philosophers. She had longed for a life different from her own, and that was what Sir John Iverson offered her when they met.

He had offered her learning, and a work that would benefit people for generations to come. He had told her that history was not dead, but something that lived around them and affected them all the time. Sarah had been fascinated by this, and had come to imagine John as a sort of intellectual white knight, who would rescue her and carry her off into her childhood fantasy world.

It had not proved to be exactly like that, of course. John *had* taught her much, and she loved the work they did together. But he had been so much older than her, so set in his ways and often bewildered by her desire to socialize. Many was the night when he had sent her off to a rout by herself while he stayed home with his books. He had taken her away from the old life, it was true, yet he had scarcely been any sort of white knight.

She had misjudged Sir John because of her girlish fantasies, and she did not want to misjudge Lord Ransome, too. Especially since misjudging him could cost her her work, before she was close to being finished with it. She could not read more into his flash of sadness and wisdom than there had been.

Sarah's teacup clattered in its saucer, and she looked down at it distractedly. She had forgotten it was there, had even forgotten she stood on the night-swept terrace all alone. She lifted up the cup and took a sip of the now cold liquid. It was smoky and strong, bracing, and it brought her back to herself.

"Lady Iverson?" a voice said behind her. "Are you quite all right?"

Sarah turned around to find Lord Ransome's mother, Mrs. Browning, standing in the open doorway. Her pretty face held an expression of concern.

"Oh, yes, Mrs. Browning," Sarah answered. "I am well. I just needed a bit of air; I never meant to stay out here so long."

"I quite understand. It was growing rather stuffy in there." Mrs. Browning came out onto the terrace to stand beside Sarah, her silken skirts rustling and flowing around her. "It is almost time for the gentlemen to rejoin us, and I thought we could set up some tables out here for the cards. Do you think it is warm enough?"

"It's a beautiful evening; I think it's a lovely idea." Sarah looked back out to the garden. "Everything is so perfect tonight, Mrs. Browning."

"I wanted it to be special, for my son's first gathering here at Ransome Hall. That is why I left Bath to come here." Mrs. Browning laughed. "I am not much of a country sort of person! But one must make some sacrifices for one's children."

"How long are you going to be at Ransome Hall?"

"Oh, a week perhaps. There is a ball in Bath I absolutely must return for. But I hope that tonight will help 'launch' Miles, so to speak, into the neighborhood, and encourage him to socialize more." She leaned toward Sarah, and added confidingly, "You would not think it to look at him, but my son is really very shy."

Sarah felt her eyes widen with surprise. "Shy, Mrs. Browning?"

"Yes. Oh, not with his Army friends. With them, he is as voluble as anyone could wish. But with other people, Society people in particular, he is quite shy." Mrs. Browning gave Sarah a speculative glance. "You seem a sensible sort, Lady Iverson, and my son appears to like you. I hope you will help him out a bit when I have returned to Bath?"

Sarah hardly knew what to say. Lord Ransome *liked* her? As far as she could see, he treated her no differently than he did anyone else. "I—will certainly do my best, Mrs. Browning."

Lord Ransome's mother nodded, as if satisfied, and turned around to go summon the footmen to bring out the tables. As they hurried about, carrying chairs and table linens and relighting lanterns that had gone out, Sarah stood still by the balustrade, her mind spinning. Lord Ransome, shy? He genuinely liked her? His mother wanted her to help him?

This evening could scarcely grow any stranger. It was almost like one of those odd dreams that had been plaguing her of late. For a moment, she wished she could run away back to the hunting box where she lived, and crawl under the bedclothes with a book about the Vikings.

But she could not, of course. The party was still young, and she had card games to get through. All too soon, the servants had finished their task and the guests came out onto the terrace in a jeweled horde. There was much laughter and jostling as everyone searched for their places, and flirtatious shrieks and giggles. It was obvious that some people had been imbibing more than tea in there.

Sarah wished that she had some of whatever spirits those had been.

Mary Ann came up to her side, and took her hand. "Here you are, Sarah! I feared you had gone off back home."

Sarah smiled at her. "I could scarcely leave you, now could I? I just came out here for some fresh air."

"I talked to Lord Dunston's granddaughter, Miss Milton, in the drawing room. She enjoys novels, too. Would it be all right if I just sat and talked with her while you play cards? I am such an absolute fool when it comes to cards."

That was all too true, Sarah thought. For such a smart girl, Mary Ann just never could seem to remember if the ace was high or low. "Of course, dear. Just do not go wandering off anywhere."

As soon as Mary Ann hurried off with her new friend, Mrs. Browning took her place. "Lady Iverson, could you make up a whist table with my son, and Mrs. Hamilton, and Lord Dunston? Miles is the only one without a partner."

Sarah glanced past her to see Lord Ransome standing beside a table, with Mrs. Hamilton chattering away beside him. He nodded politely at whatever she was saying, but he watched Sarah and his mother. When she caught his eye, he gave her a faint, almost pleading smile.

And her flutters came right back onto her.

"Of course, Mrs. Browning," she said, careful to keep her expression politely blank. "I would be happy to."

"Oh, dear, Lord Dunston! Never say I have made us lose again," Mrs. Hamilton cried. She tilted her golden-curled head, her face the very picture of consternation.

"Of course not, Mrs. Hamilton," Lord Dunston said gallantly. "My fault entirely."

Miles grinned at them. What a most diverting evening

it had been, he thought, much more than he had imagined it would be when his mother was planning everything out. He had actually enjoyed himself, and ceased to look about for his uncle whenever someone called him "Lord Ransome." It had been—enjoyable.

And that was mostly due to the fact that Lady Iverson was next to him for a good deal of the evening. Supper had moved quickly, as he looked at her, at the way her hair gleamed in the candlelight, the animation on her face when she spoke of the Vikings. When she left the dining room, a great deal of the light and air seemed to depart with her, leaving the evening dull and dry, full of masculine talk of politics and port.

He glanced at her now, sitting across from him at the whist table. She laughed good-naturedly at Mrs. Hamilton's and Lord Dunston's words, and folded her own cards in her hands. "Or perhaps we won because Lord Ransome is such a superior cardplayer?" she said.

"He is certainly that," Lord Dunston agreed.

Lady Iverson smiled across the table at Miles, and he couldn't help but smile back. Her cheeks were flushed with the pleasure of the game, and her wariness had yet to return. She looked relaxed and happy.

Miles wished things could always be just like this. But, of course, they could not; all he could do was enjoy this very moment.

"Where did you learn to play cards so skillfully, Lord Ransome?" she asked. A footman stopped to offer her a glass of sherry from his tray, and she took it and sipped at it. The pinkness in her cheeks brightened and warmed.

Miles found it difficult to concentrate on her question, as he watched her sun-touched throat move when she swallowed. The tiny pulse at the base of her neck fluttered.

He looked back down at the table, at the scattered cards, and reached for his own snifter of brandy. He took a deep drink of it.

"Evenings were long and dull on the Peninsula," he answered. "Cards were often all that lay between us and going mad with boredom. So I became quite adept."

Lady Iverson gave him a sympathetic smile.

Mrs. Hamilton squeaked. "Oh, poor Lord Ransome! How perfectly fearful. You must be so happy to be home in England now, here in this lovely house."

Miles turned to her. She was a pretty woman, if a bit silly and empty-headed, and she seemed kind. It appeared her husband did not appreciate that kindness, though; Mr. Hamilton sat at the table next to theirs, and whenever his wife laughed, he cringed. It was obvious that the Hamilton marriage was a mismatch, and they were only just starting out.

Miles could not help but feel a bit sorry for Mrs. Hamilton, even if it *was* rather disconcerting when she fluttered her lashes at him, or reached out to touch his sleeve with her lace-gloved hand.

"I *am* very grateful to be here, Mrs. Hamilton," he answered. "There are many who were not so fortunate."

Lady Iverson watched him steadily with serious eyes. "You mean—the ones who did not come back at all?"

He looked at her. He had the sudden, irrational urge to tell her of the friends he had lost, the guilt that gripped his heart when he thought of them, left behind in foreign graves. He wanted to tell her of Jack, who had died in his arms on the battlefield, of Will, who had lost his leg, and died in an agony of blood poisoning in a field hospital.

But, of course, he could tell her none of this. They were in a polite social setting, and even if they were not, she was a lady. He could not be such a boor as to tell her of these horrors.

He wasn't even sure why he wanted to. Those were in the past; they were locked up in his memory, and there they would stay.

"The ones who did not return, yes," he said slowly. "And also those who did return, only to find misfortune. But I hope to be able to help some of them, now that I am so fortunate as to be settled here."

Lady Iverson nodded faintly; the wariness crept back into her face, closing her expression. It was as if she knew what his words meant.

"That is very good of you, Lord Ransome, to want to use your position to help others!" Mrs. Hamilton cried. She glanced over at her husband. "Some people only care about themselves and their own situations. They do not even care about their own families, let alone strangers."

Mr. Hamilton appeared not to hear her.

"Indeed," Lady Iverson said. "I am sure we will be hearing more about your plans later, Lord Ransome."

There was no escaping that, no matter how much Miles wished there could be. He never wanted to hurt Lady Iverson, not with these new, strange feelings he had toward her, but he knew that his plans were far too important to abandon. He owed it to all his lost friends.

"I hope that I may tell you more about them very soon, Lady Iverson," he said.

Lady Iverson turned away. "Of course, Lord Ransome. I will be very—interested to hear of any of your plans. Right now, however, I must find Mary Ann. It grows late. If you will excuse me?" Still averting her gaze, she left her cards in a neat pile on the table, and rose in a rustle of fluid black velvet.

Miles and Lord Dunston stood and bowed to her as she left. Only when she had melted into the crowd did Miles sit back down.

As he did so, his gaze caught Mrs. Hamilton's. For one instant, there was a shrewdness, a watchfulness in those pale blue eyes. Then her lashes swept down, and she gave one of her trilling laughs.

"I suppose I ought to go after her," she said. "After all, we came in the same carriage. It would not do for me to be left here overnight!"

Sarah saw that Mary Ann was still sitting with Miss Milton, the two of them deep in some earnest conversation. She decided not to pull her away just yet, and instead turned and went down the marble steps of the terrace into the garden.

As she moved farther away from the noisy affability of the party, the cool quiet of the night wrapped around her. Her spinning thoughts stilled, and she breathed deeply of the peace.

Eventually, the only sounds she heard were the crunch of her own shoes on the gravel pathways, the swish of her skirts as they swept over the lavender borders of the flower beds. Once in a while, a particularly merry burst of laughter made its way to her ears, but other than that, she felt all alone in the enchanted night.

All alone—except for Lord Ransome. Even though she had left him behind on the terrace, he still seemed with her. His words were still in her mind.

She stopped at the edge of the manicured gardens, and leaned back against a sheltering old oak to stare up at the moon. She had known that Lord Ransome was not a frivolous man—no one could fight in a war for years and be frivolous. Even so, his words tonight had surprised and moved her. They had been brief, but full of some pain and despair that was usually hidden. She had wanted to know more, to take his hand in hers, to comfort him if she could.

The urge had been so great, that she had to clutch her fork in her fist until the patterned silver pressed into her skin. It had been so strong that it had frightened her.

Sarah had thought, hoped, that Lord Ransome's visit to the village would show him how important her work there was. Now she knew, from his words tonight, that he still had some other plan for the land. She did not know what that plan could be; no doubt he would tell her "later," as promised.

And that would be the end of her work here. She could find another project, of course; she could write her book with what knowledge she had already gained. But it would not be the same.

"I wanted to finish this for you, John," she whispered aloud. "I wanted to finish it for myself." It had been the first thing in the world that felt like it was *hers*.

Well, who says you cannot finish it? a contrary voice at the back of her mind whispered. *You just have to work harder at persuading Lord Ransome.*

Sarah laughed at herself. How could she ever persuade

him of the importance of her work, when her thoughts grew all jumbled and silly when she was around him? She had never been very good at persuasive arguments at the best of times, and feminine wiles only felt ridiculous.

But the voice was right—she did have to at least try to make him see the importance of her position. She had never given up on anything she cared about, not without a fight. She had refused to give in to her mother, when she tried to stop Sarah from marrying John. She had not given the village over to Neville Hamilton, when everyone expected her to. And now this village was too important to just surrender.

Sarah pushed away from the tree, and turned her steps back toward the house. It was time for her to find Mary Ann, and summon their carriage to go home. She had to plan out carefully what she would say to Lord Ransome.

Mary Ann stood at the top of the terrace steps, peering down into the dark garden. She knew she had seen Sarah go this way quite a while ago, and she was beginning to be a bit worried. It was not like her sister to go wandering away, and besides, it was growing late. Miss Milton and her grandfather had gone home, and Mary Ann was tired.

Her head ached from the effort of laughing and chatting all evening, while she watched Mr. Hamilton and his giggling bride.

Mary Ann glanced back over her shoulder. Many of the guests had departed, and those who were left drifted back through the French doors into the drawing room. Mr. Hamilton was nowhere to be seen, but Mrs. Hamilton was hanging on to Lord Ransome's arm, laughing up at him. In return, he gave her a rather strained smile.

Mary Ann sniffed. Really, some women were terribly shameless! Mrs. Hamilton already had one husband, and now she was flirting with Lord Ransome, just because he was a marquis. And it was quite obvious that *he* preferred her sister, as any sane man would.

Perhaps that was why Mr. Hamilton had looked so

morose and angry ever since he had come back from his wedding trip, she thought. The man she had known before, the one she imagined to be a gallant knight in a story, had been serious to be sure. But he had also told her thrilling tales of ancient Vikings, and taught her how to make charts and sketches of where objects were found at sites.

Now, he could not even seem to care about the work. And he almost never spoke to her.

Thinking about it all made her headache worse. Mary Ann went down the steps into the garden, determined to find her sister. Sarah could not have gone far.

Past the Chinese lantern light of the terrace, it was dark and quiet. Mary Ann moved cautiously down the walkway, past marble fountains and benches. Once, she thought she bumped into someone, and gave a little screech. Then she realized it was just a statue, some stone classical figure, poised to toss a spear.

She laughed nervously, and pressed her hand to her pounding heart. "Silly!" she gasped. "Sarah was right— I *have* been reading too many novels."

It did feel rather like a night in a novel, cool and scented with breezes, lit by the silver glow of the moon. She could only too easily imagine specters gliding about in the garden.

Mary Ann shivered. Spirits and elves suddenly did not seem as romantic as they usually did. She hurried away, now doubly intent on finding her sister.

There was a slight rustle in some bushes behind her, and she spun about. "S-Sarah?" she called, half hopeful, half terrified.

A figure stepped out into the pathway, a man. "I fear it is only me, Miss Bellweather," Mr. Hamilton said.

Mary Ann fell back a step in surprise at his sudden appearance. He held a cigar in one hand, and its faint red glow lit his face, showing her that it was indeed him, and not some ghost.

Yet somehow that did not comfort her a great deal. He looked even less like her old friend, the object of her romantic dreams, than ever. He watched her, unsmiling, intent.

"Mr. Hamilton," she managed to say. "I was just . . ."

"Looking for Lady Iverson?"

"Yes. I saw her come this way earlier. I did not mean to intrude."

"Not at all." He cast away the cigar, leaving them in only the meager light of the moon. "I never had the chance earlier to tell you how pretty you look this evening."

Normally, such a compliment would fill her with a giddy pleasure. Now, though, it was strangely disquieting. "Thank you," she murmured.

"You are quite grown up now, Miss Bellweather. Almost a lady." He took a step toward her.

Mary Ann wanted to step back, away, but she seemed frozen. She shivered, and wished she had her shawl. These feelings were frightening and unwelcome; she had never encountered them before in her books or dreams. Mr. Hamilton was an utter stranger now.

"Mary Ann!" a blessedly familiar voice called. Even though it was full of a tightly controlled anger, Mary Ann turned to it in profound relief.

Sarah came up the walkway, her black gown blending into the night, throwing her face into pale, sharp relief. Mary Ann could see the flush of her sister's cheeks, her pinched-together lips. She came to Mary Ann, and took her arm in a secure clasp.

Mary Ann could not stop herself; she threw her arms around Sarah's neck, and held close to her safe warmth.

Sarah put her own arm around Mary Ann's waist. "What is going on here?"

"I was looking for you!" Mary Ann said.

"With Mr. Hamilton? Alone, in the garden? Mary Ann, you know better than this."

"Miss Bellweather was walking alone," Mr. Hamilton said quietly. "She merely came upon me here. We were only alone for a moment."

"Indeed?" Sarah's voice was low and heavy. Mary

Ann peeked up at her, and saw that her face seemed to be as set in stone as those of the statues around them. She stared unwaveringly, coolly, at Mr. Hamilton.

He shrugged, and gave Sarah an odd little smile. "It is what happened, Lady Iverson."

"I am sure that is so." Sarah's arm tightened on Mary Ann's waist, and drew her away from Mr. Hamilton, back toward the house. "Come, Mary Ann, we should be making our farewells to our host and hostess. Mr. Hamilton, I am certain your wife must be looking for you."

"No doubt she is," Mr. Hamilton answered, his tone suddenly cold.

Mary Ann knew that she was in for a blazing lecture later, and felt that really it was quite unfair, since she was innocent of any mischief—this time. But somehow she did not even care. She would endure any lecture at all, she was so relieved at being taken back to the lights and reality—and safety—of the house.

Her old infatuation for Mr. Hamilton melted away, as if it had never been.

Chapter Ten

Sarah collapsed into a heap on her bed, not even caring that she crushed the fine velvet of her gown. She was too tired to even reach for the bellpull and ring for her maid.

After the silent carriage ride home with the Hamiltons, and then an hour spent lecturing a tearful Mary Ann on propriety and safety, all she wanted was peace and quiet. Chaperoning was such a terrible chore at times, especially on top of the worries she already had about the Viking village and Lord Ransome. She loved Mary Ann so much—she never, ever wanted to see her hurt.

And she did not like that look on Neville Hamilton's face when she came upon him with Mary Ann in the garden. She had never seen him look that way before, so—so predatory. It was as if his marriage had unhinged him.

"Just as this is all going to unhinge *me*," she muttered.

She had been so sad when her marriage proved to be childless, but perhaps it had been for the best after all, she thought. Especially if her daughter had grown up as fanciful and flighty as Mary Ann could be. How did parents ever keep from going mad, when so many pitfalls awaited their precious children in the world?

But, oh, she really would have liked to have had a child. A sturdy little boy, or a girl with dark curls, to toddle behind her and dig with their miniature trowels. Even if they grew up to be ten times as flighty as Mary Ann, she would have loved them with all her heart.

With a sigh, Sarah abandoned her old, impossible visions and rolled off the bed. She reached up behind her, stretching to unfasten her gown. It was not a simple thing to do on her own, and it took some time, but she finally managed to wriggle loose of it. The beautiful velvet gown was tossed into a chair. She shook her hair free of its pins, pulled on her nightdress, and climbed gratefully between the bedclothes.

"Surely all I need is sleep," she whispered into her pillow. "In the morning, all of this will be much clearer. It must be."

In the morning, she would know how to help Mary Ann. She would know how to persuade Lord Ransome to let her keep her village. She would be free of her troublesome attraction to him.

If she could only sleep . . .

It was undeniably the Viking village. The same stream ran alongside it; the same smoky-green hillsides rose above, enclosing it in its snug little valley. But it was not the same as Sarah knew it—not at all.

Buildings, new and fresh, stood around her, their walls of wood and some sort of plaster surrounding the narrow walkways. Doorways were open in the shops, displaying wares of beautiful soapstone bowls, strings of amber beads, silver-chased brooches, and carved chess sets. The metallic "clang" of the smith's hammer rang out amid the laughter and talk of people gathered outside in the bright, warm sunlight. Chickens and geese waddled along the muddy street, and a black-spotted dog raced by, chased by a pack of children.

The street was crowded, humming with life and vitality. Sarah seemed to be right in the midst of it, surrounded by it, yet everyone passed her as if she was not even there. As if she were invisible. But she heard and saw everything they did; she smelled the warm, summery scents of animals and spices and fireplace smoke. The people spoke some strange language, but she understood every word.

It was her village! Her village, as it had been when it

was first built, so very long ago. Even though Sarah knew that this had to be a dream, she felt excited and exhilarated. If only she could remember every, every detail, and write it all down when she woke up.

She knew, though, that dreams never worked like that. It would all be forgotten in the morning; only hazy, floating little bits still clinging to her mind for a while before they, too, drifted away. All she could do was enjoy it now.

She turned in a wide circle to take the whole scene in, to absorb all the little images of it. Laughing at the joy of being there, she swung wider and wider—until she stumbled to a halt, brought up short by a vision.

There was a glimmer of movement in a polished bronze mirror hanging outside the jeweler's shop. A spinning woman. Herself Sarah, she thought, until she peered closer.

It was not her. Not really. This woman had dark hair, like hers, but it spilled to her waist in a thick riot, not like Sarah's own shoulder-length curls. She wore a tight-sleeved white tunic, not unlike the nightdress Sarah had put on before she fell asleep, covered by a dark blue, apronlike overdress. The straps of it were fastened by two beautifully worked silver brooches.

The same silver brooches that now lay, carefully labeled, in the stable with the other artifacts. But now they were shining and whole.

Sarah stepped closer to the mirror, reached up to touch one of the brooches. The reflected figure's hand reached up, too.

"Who am I supposed to be?" she whispered. "What is happening here?"

A movement to her left in the mirror caught her attention, and she turned around. A man stood behind her on the street, tall and handsome, clad in leather leggings and a green tunic edged in white embroidery. A wealth of golden hair fell over his shoulders.

"Miles!" she gasped. That, even more than the whole village, convinced her that this must be a dream. She would never in real life call Lord Ransome by his given name! She hadn't even known that she knew what it was.

Yet it was undoubtedly him, despite the long hair and the strange clothes. He stepped toward her, his eyes as blue and intense as the summer sky above them.

"There you are," he said, reaching out to clasp her arms in his hands. They felt warm and secure, more solid than any dream she had ever had before. "I have been looking for you."

"You have?" she asked, completely bewildered. "But I only saw you a few hours ago. We were playing whist on your terrace."

He frowned, a tiny crease appearing between his eyes. "What is this 'whist' you speak of?"

"Miles, you know what whist is! A card game," Sarah argued. She knew it was futile to try to talk sense to a dream-figure, but she couldn't help it. It was so strange, so deeply disconcerting to be here with someone who was, yet so obviously wasn't, Lord Ransome.

Lord Ransome, of course, would never look at her as this dream-Miles was doing, with affection and a deep sensual understanding.

"Ah, I see," he said, with a deep, stirring laugh. "You are playing one of your tricks, Thora."

"Thora!" Sarah cried. "I am not Thora. I am Sarah, Miles. Sarah."

"You may call yourself whatever name you choose." Miles drew her closer, so close she could feel his warmth through his tunic, could smell his clean pine scent. His mouth dipped toward hers, closer and closer.

By heavens, he was going to kiss her! Sarah found herself longing for that dream-kiss more than she ever had for anything before in her life. To feel his lips on hers, the press of them, the heat and sweetness . . .

"Thora," he whispered.

"I am Sarah," she answered, still aching for that kiss, yet desperate to hear her own name in his voice. Not some Viking witch with a treasure and a curse, but her. *"Sarah. Say it, Miles. I am Sarah."*

Then she felt herself slipping back to consciousness, felt the pull of the real world on her senses. "No!" she cried. "Not yet!" She tried to cling to Miles, but her hands grasped only air. The village shifted and vanished around her, and she fell back and back. . . .

"Sarah! Sarah, wake up. Oh, please, wake up."

Sarah jerked awake with a start, and slowly opened her eyes. She was in her own bedchamber at the hunting box, in her own bed. The blankets were twisted around her, and she felt uncomfortably hot.

Mary Ann knelt beside the bed, her expression worried as she looked down at Sarah. Her one candle cast a faint circle of light on her, making her look like a concerned and very young Madonna.

Sarah pushed herself up against the pillows, trying to take deep breaths and slow her racing heart. "What is it, Mary Ann?"

"You were calling out in your sleep, and I heard you from my room. I was so worried; I didn't know what could be wrong! I came in here, and you were saying, 'I am Sarah,' over and over."

Sarah took her sister's hand, glad of her solid presence beside her. "I was just having a very odd dream, dear. That is all. I'm sorry I woke you."

"I could not sleep anyway." Mary Ann sat down on the edge of the bed with a sigh. "I wanted to tell you again how sorry I am for talking to Mr. Hamilton in the garden. I *do* know better, and I should never have stopped there."

Sarah tried to shake off the remnants of her dream. She slid higher against the pillows, and rubbed at her eyes. "No, Mary Ann, it was not your fault. It was mine for leaving you alone. I was feeling tired, and in some desperate need of fresh air, and it made me careless of my duty."

"No. I am not a child anymore; I can be left alone at a crowded party for a few minutes. Or at least, I usually can. It won't happen again, Sarah, I promise."

"I hope not. I was just thinking, before I went to sleep, that perhaps it would be better for you to go home."

Mary Ann looked utterly horrified. "Oh, Sarah, please, no! I like it here so much more than at home. Mother keeps bothering me about my Season; about how I have to make up for your 'disappointing match' and marry a viscount at least. And Kitty is still such a baby, I cannot talk to her at all. I want to stay here and learn more about your work."

Sarah weakened under her sister's pleading. She had never been truly serious about sending Mary Ann home, anyway. "Of course, I do not want you to go away. It is very lonely here without you, and I can certainly use your help. But you must promise me you will be careful from now on."

"I will. I promise." Mary Ann laid her head down on the pillow next to Sarah's, and said wistfully, "Mr. Hamilton is not as I imagined him, is he?"

"Mr. Hamilton is a very intelligent and learned man," Sarah answered carefully. "He and John were good friends. I think perhaps his marriage is not—not all he hoped for, but I am sure he will be his old self very soon. Tomorrow, I will talk with him."

"Not about me?" Mary Ann said, her tone aghast. "How awful to be *talked* about. It's like something Mother would do."

Sarah laughed. "I must, dear. It is my duty as your older sister. But I also want to see if he will tell me what has been amiss with him."

"Well, if you must, you must," Mary Ann said with a sigh. Then she gave Sarah a mischievous little smile. "Lord Ransome seems like a very nice man."

"Yes," Sarah said, keeping her tone neutral. "He does seem a nice man." She was not sure that "nice" was exactly the correct word, especially after the dream she had just had, but it would do.

"And Ransome Hall is a pretty house. I can see a person being very comfortable in its rooms. And since Mrs. Browning prefers Bath to the country, a lady would never have to worry about her mother-in-law interfering there." Mary Ann's voice was determined, but growing sleepy. She yawned through her next words. "Very comfortable—and happy." Her head drooped on the pillow.

Sarah slid back down onto her pillow, and closed her

eyes. Sleep would not come back, though, and she lay there for a long time, listening to Mary Ann's soft breath and thinking. Always thinking.

Ransome Hall *was* a pretty place, and she could envision herself happy there. Happy with Lord Ransome, maybe. She could see herself sitting at the foot of the table at supper parties, and looking down to see him at the head, smiling at her. She could see herself dancing with him in the ballroom there, walking with him along the garden paths, working on her writing in the library while he went over estate business.

She liked Lord Ransome—far too much. She was attracted to his golden looks, his smile, and laugh. She missed the companionship of being married. She especially missed it on long, dark nights like this. If she were sensible, she would chase after the attractive Lord Ransome and secure him as soon as she could, as no doubt her mother would have advised her to do.

Yet, deep in her heart, even in lonely moments, Sarah knew she could never again be completely happy without her work. It fulfilled a deep yearning within her to learn, to *know,* as nothing else, not even love, could ever do. And Lord Ransome did not seem the sort of man who would understand that, or be able to share in it.

No matter how many strange, alluring dreams she might have about him.

"It was a splendid supper, was it not?" Miles's mother said. She leaned back in the settee before the library fire, sipping at a last cup of tea before retiring.

Miles relaxed in his own chair, a glass of port in his hand. "Yes, indeed. All thanks to you, Mother."

She laughed. "Not at all. It is *your* house, and the guests were your neighbors. I merely lent some of my social expertise to the arrangements. As I will be glad to do again—until the happy day when your wife becomes hostess here."

"I fear that day may be a long while away. What lady would have a sunburnt officer like me?"

"Oh, any single lady you wanted, I would imagine. You are a marquis now, remember, my darling, and a wealthy one. A handsome man, too—and that is not just my maternal prejudice! Any woman would count herself fortunate to have you." She took a sip from her cup, her glance speculative over its china rim. "Lady Iverson is a very interesting lady. I wish I could have had more converse with her. But perhaps she will still be in the neighborhood when next I visit."

"She is very interesting indeed," Miles murmured, thinking of how she had looked over the card game, beautiful and intent.

"Unusual," his mother continued. "And, one might say, very pretty."

Some hopeful tone in her voice caught his attention away from memories of the evening past. He looked over at her. "Are you trying to dabble in matchmaking, Mother?"

She smiled mysteriously. "Of course not! I have never been very successful at that sort of thing. But you *will* have to marry, you know. Lady Iverson, or someone like her, would be far preferable to some silly young miss I could find for you in Bath." She placed her cup back on the tray, and stood up to come and kiss Miles on the cheek. "Well, I am tired, darling. Shall we breakfast together tomorrow, before I depart?"

"Of course. Good night, Mother."

"Good night, Miles. Do not sit up too late thinking."

Miles listened to her soft slipper-steps fade, and the library door click behind her. He did not want to "sit up thinking"; social events were far more exhausting than campaigning had ever been. Yet how could he help it? His mother was right about Lady Iverson—she *was* interesting, and pretty, and so much more besides. He found himself wanting to spend more time with her, to know more about her, to know everything. What her childhood had been like, what drew her to her work, if she had truly loved her husband—if she still loved him.

But he had the distinct sense that she did not feel the

same way about him. She watched him with caution, and a certain reserve. Except when she had shown him the Viking village. Then her eyes lit up, her entire being became animated and glowing.

He dreaded the discussion he would have to have with her, and soon. He dreaded it more than any battle or skirmish he had ever faced.

Chapter Eleven

"So, are we understood, Mr. Hamilton?" Sarah looked across the tea table in her tiny drawing room at Mr. Hamilton. He smiled at her, calmly, politely, as if completely unruffled by anything she had said.

Sarah, though, had shaking hands and a dry mouth. She did so hate quarrels and confrontations—they were such a waste of time, when she could be out in the sunny day, digging. But she had to do her duty as a sister and a chaperone, and so she had summoned Mr. Hamilton and talked to him about what had happened in the Ransome garden.

She was scarcely sure of what she had said—something about impressionable young ladies and reputations and marriages. Now, she had said her part, and she reached for her teacup for a grateful sip.

"Of course, we are understood, Lady Iverson," he answered. "I hope you know that I have the greatest respect for you and your sister. I would never do anything to harm Miss Bellweather. Last night was a mere chance encounter, and it will not happen again."

"I hope not. What would your wife think?"

His jaw tightened at the mention of his wife. "Mrs. Hamilton knows the respectful regard I have for you and your family."

Sarah nodded. "And I hope you know the respect I have for you, Mr. Hamilton—the respect Sir John also had. He always spoke so highly of your abilities. I would hate to lose your excellent assistance here."

For the first time in their conversation, Mr. Hamilton's composure seemed ruffled. He leaned toward her, frowning. "No more than I would hate to leave! The village is a great find, with much potential for education, and valuable treasure. I know that Sir John wanted me to continue here."

Sarah remembered the discussions after her husband's death, Mr. Hamilton's assumption that she would leave the village and let him take it over. He had been very unhappy at her insistence on staying. She had wanted Mr. Hamilton to remain, both for his expertise and in memory of his friendship with John, but she had wanted to be in charge. To handle the work as she saw fit—as a methodical quest for knowledge, not just a tearing about for treasure. He had not been happy at her decision; she had seen that, even though he tried to hide it.

Apparently, he still remembered all that, as well.

"Of course, I hope you will stay here," she said. "As long as there are no more—misunderstandings."

"Certainly not." He sat back in his chair and folded his hands, the unperturbed scholar once again. "Though, really, Lady Iverson, how long will any of us still be here?"

Sarah frowned at the question. "Whatever do you mean?"

"The new Lord Ransome, as worthy as I'm sure he must be, is not his uncle. He does not seem to understand or appreciate what we are doing here. I have heard rumors that he has other plans for the property."

That was exactly what Sarah feared, but she hardly wanted Mr. Hamilton to see her doubts. Keeping her face carefully expressionless, she reached again for her cup and took a sip before replying. "Where did you hear such rumors?"

Mr. Hamilton shrugged. "Here and there. People do talk, you know, and my wife is a great gossiper. She always knows the latest *on dits,* no matter where she happens to be."

"Lord Ransome has not spoken to me about it. We

have not been asked to leave the property. And, until we are, I see no use in worrying about it. We have work to concentrate on." She was lying, of course—she worried about it all the time. But she couldn't quite bring herself to talk about that yet. Especially not with Mr. Hamilton.

"Of course. We should get as much done on the Viking site as we can. Now, Lady Iverson, though this has been a charming meeting, I fear I must depart. I have to fetch my wife, who has gone into Upper Hawton for some shopping."

"Yes." Sarah rose, and walked with him to the front door, where his carriage waited. "Shall we see you at the site this afternoon?"

"Certainly. I have made some real progress on the bakery; I would hate to leave it now."

Sarah watched his carriage drive off down the lane, then went upstairs to her chamber to change from her good morning gown into a work dress. It was quiet in the house, Mary Ann having already gone to the village and the maids being in the kitchen.

Too quiet. It left too much time for thinking.

She hurried to change her gown, then sat down on the edge of the bed to slide off her kid slippers and put on her stout boots. She did not like it that there were rumors abroad about Lord Ransome and his land, she thought as she laced up the boots. She did not like it at all. It seemed to confirm all her fears.

She reached for her straw hat and the bag that held her notebooks. If those fears were indeed about to be confirmed, she had a great deal of work to do. She had to finish as much as possible before she was forced to leave.

She hated to rush the work—valuable artifacts and evidence could be destroyed in the haste. Right now, she did not *have* to hurry; surely, if he asked her to leave, he would give her a few days to pack. Still, that was no reason to waste any time. The morning was already almost gone.

* * *

Mary Ann and the workers were not alone at the village when Sarah arrived. The first thing she saw as she came down the pathway was a horse tethered to a tree. A familiar horse.

"Lord Ransome," she whispered. She froze in her tracks, staring at the horse she had ridden on the day she got her phaeton stuck in the stream. It looked placidly back at her.

There could be only one reason he was here today— to have the promised conversation with her about her continued residency on his land.

Sarah glanced back over her shoulder, but there was no escape. She had no excuse whatsoever for running back to the hunting box. So she continued forward, her back straight and chin up, as if marching into battle.

He was with Mary Ann at the edge of House A; she held an object in her palm, and was pointing to it as she talked. Lord Ransome nodded solemnly, looking down at the item. He asked one short question, and Mary Ann laughed and answered him.

Sarah smiled, despite her trepidation. Mary Ann had the makings of a real antiquarian, and it was wonderful that he listened to her, took her seriously.

Then she frowned. How could he even think of taking this away from Mary Ann, away from *her*?

Mary Ann looked up, and Sarah wiped the frown quickly from her lips. It would never do for anyone to see her doubts, and fears, written across her face.

Lord Ransome turned, too, and smiled when he saw her. She was reminded sharply of her dream, of their almost-kiss there that had so stirred her emotions. "Good morning, Lady Iverson!" he called.

"Good morning, Lord Ransome," she answered, moving forward to greet him. She forced the memory of that dream, of the Viking Miles, to the back of her mind, and shuffled her bag of papers and the lunch hamper to hold her hand out to him. "I am very sorry I wasn't here to greet you when you arrived."

"Miss Bellweather and I were having a very interesting discussion. She was showing me this—this . . ."

"Spindle," Mary Ann said. "A soapstone spindle, probably from Norway."

He smiled at her. "Yes. And she was most kindly explaining to me how it was used."

"Mary Ann has been reading a great deal about this time period," Sarah said. "She's become quite invaluable to me here."

Mary Ann's cheeks became rose-pink with pleasure, and she turned away to place the spindle back on the pile of objects she was accumulating from the house. "I'm going to take these down to the stream and rinse them off," she said, gathering them carefully into a basket.

"I should take the hamper into the stable," Sarah said. "The workers will be wanting their luncheon soon. Would you care to walk with me, Lord Ransome?" She would have to listen to what he had to say, and would have to decide how to deal with it, eventually. So she might as well do it now, she decided.

"Certainly, Lady Iverson. Here, allow me to carry that." He took the large hamper from her and tucked it beneath one arm, as if the heavy container was a mere bauble. It was certainly obvious that, unlike many officers returning from the Peninsula, he had not let himself grow soft.

His other arm he offered to Sarah, and she slid her hand into the crook of his elbow.

As they walked to the stable, Sarah cast about for something, *anything,* to say. The silence seemed to press down on her in the warm air, and she did not want Lord Ransome to fill it.

"Your supper party was lovely," she said. "My sister and I had a most pleasant time."

"Thank you, Lady Iverson," he said, his voice full of some amusement. "But you really should be thanking my mother—she was the one who saved me. I have never had any experience in planning soirees, and I'm sure everyone would have had a most dull evening if I had been left to my own devices."

"Well, I am certain that you will have many opportunities to gain experience now." Sarah paused, and realized how odd her words sounded. "Experience in planning parties, that is."

"Of course," he said with a laugh. "What other experience could you possibly have meant, Lady Iverson?"

Sarah laughed ruefully. "No other experience, of course." She pushed open the doors to the stable, and hurried ahead with great relief. It seemed that every time she opened her mouth to speak around Lord Ransome, something ridiculous came out.

The stable was dim and warm, all the objects in their neat rows gleaming in welcome. She felt some of her apprehension lift when she saw them, the fruits of all her labors. Seeing them there, all perfectly labeled and cleaned, items that someone had used and cherished so long ago, never failed to give her the deepest sense of satisfaction.

She ran her fingertip lightly over a carved chess figure, before going to pull the table they used for eating away from the wall. "I would like to thank your mother, then. Is she still in residence at Ransome Hall?"

He helped her situate the table, and stood back to watch as she took a white cloth out of the hamper and spread it across the smooth wood before he placed the hamper there. "She is packing today. She so hates to be away from a town!"

"My mother is the same," Sarah said, bending to take food out of the hamper. "When Mary Ann, Kitty, and I were children, we only saw the country from carriage windows! We thought trees, *real* trees, were just something that appeared in parks."

"Did you move around a great deal, Lady Iverson?"

Sarah paused in taking bowls of cold ham and salads out of the hamper, thinking back to those restless years. She did not often think, much less speak, about the days of her childhood and youth. The past was gone, finished, and she didn't want to live it again.

But something in Lord Ransome's expression, in his eyes, told her he would understand.

"Oh, yes. My father died when I was just ten, and the girls were even younger. He left us a fortune, and a lovely house in Devonshire—my childhood home. But my mother had always hated the country, hated the time we spent there. As soon as she could, she took us off. We went to London, Bath, Brighton, Wycombe-on-Sea—anyplace there would be people, society. It was always interesting, of course, and I met a great many fascinating individuals. But . . ." Sarah's voice trailed away, and she looked down at the bowl she held in her hands. How could she put into words the feelings she had had back then, the loneliness, the longings?

They were pushed down so far into her heart that she didn't even think she could feel them anymore, let alone speak about them.

Lord Ransome stepped up next to her. "But what, Lady Iverson?"

She looked at him. "It was hard to feel as if I belonged anywhere, except with my sisters. Until I married, I never had a true home."

"I understand entirely," he said quietly. "My father died when I was very young, as well. After that, I was at school, or at my mother's house in Bath for holidays. My mother has always been an excellent parent, but her house there did not feel like a home. I only found a true sense of belonging when I was in the Army."

Sarah swallowed hard, and looked at him. "Did you—*like* the Army, then?"

"Very much indeed." He reached one hand towards hers, then stopped, balling that hand into a fist. But the atmosphere of new sympathy and understanding, of regret, still hovered about them like the dust that floated in the air. "Lady Iverson, you must have some idea of what—"

His words were cut off by a distant, but sharp and urgent, scream. Sarah stood up, her heart leaping in a skipping beat. The jump from one dread to another was almost too much, and she pressed her hand to her throat, looking about frantically as if the solution lay somewhere in the stable.

The scream came again, even more piercing.

"That is Mary Ann!" Sarah cried. She ran for the door, yanking it open and stumbling out into the world. She blinked at the sudden rush of bright light into her eyes, and turned blindly toward the stream where Mary Ann had been going to rinse off the newly found artifacts.

Lord Ransome was right beside her as she dashed away from the stable, down a muddy slope. Some of the workers had also heard the scream, and dropped their tools to follow them.

Mary Ann stood by the stream with some man Sarah had never seen before, a farmer to judge by his rough, dirt-splattered clothes. He was a big man, tall and broad shouldered, and his florid face was suffused with anger as he pulled on Mary Ann's arm.

Mary Ann radiated an equal amount of rage, a hectic red spreading across her cheekbones down to her throat. She yanked back on her arm, and shouted, "How could you! You heartless and wicked man! Give them to me right now."

"They be my property, girl, and none of your affair!" the man growled. "Now go away and tend your own business."

"I will not!"

"That man is assaulting my sister!" Sarah cried, a white-hot fury rising up in her, choking her. She lifted her skirts above her ankles, and ran down the bank toward Mary Ann, Lord Ransome close at her heels. "Release her this instant, you villain!"

As they came closer, the man let go of Mary Ann, and she fell back a step, rubbing at her upper arm. She latched on to Sarah's hand an instant before Sarah could slap the man heartily across his face.

Only then did Sarah see the rough sack on the ground between Mary Ann and the man. It writhed and mewed and wriggled.

Mary Ann turned a tearstained, indignant face to Sarah and Lord Ransome. "This dreadful man was going to drown these kittens."

"I already have plenty of mousers. These would just be nuisances!" the man protested. "I don't need no gentry mort to tell me how to run my own business! Now, go away and let me get on with it."

"Never!" Mary Ann broke away from Sarah, and lunged down to grab the sack.

The man shoved her roughly, and she landed in the mud with a pained cry.

As quick as a lightning flash, Lord Ransome grabbed the front of the man's stained shirt. He twisted hard, raising the man up onto his very toes. The farmer's face turned purple with the effort to breathe, and his eyes bulged.

He was a bigger man than Lord Ransome, but flabby where Lord Ransome was lean. The strong muscles that Sarah had earlier felt beneath her hand corded and bunched under his coat sleeve. His face was utterly blank as he watched the struggling man, his blue eyes like ice or marble. Her warm, laughing companion of only fifteen minutes ago had completely vanished.

Sarah knelt beside Mary Ann and helped her sister sit up, never taking her stare from the horribly fascinating scene before her. She wasn't sure whom she was more frightened of, the bullying farmer or the cold stranger Lord Ransome had suddenly become.

"You will never treat a lady in such a fashion again, or I will thrash you to within an inch of your life," Lord Ransome said, his voice low and emotionless. The man gave a choking sound, and Sarah was just wondering if she should somehow intervene when Lord Ransome released the man's shirtfront and he fell onto the ground. He sucked in a large breath of air, while Lord Ransome watched him dispassionately.

"Do you know who I am?" Lord Ransome said, in that same cold voice.

The man shook his head.

"I am Lord Ransome. You are not a tenant of my land, are you? I have never seen you before."

"I—no, my lord," he said hoarsely. All of his bluster

had vanished. "I live on the other side of York. My name be White."

"You are on my property now, and nobody abuses a lady anywhere in my presence. Now, leave before I have you clapped into irons."

The man scrambled to his feet, and reached for the sack. Mary Ann, despite her pale, shocked expression, gave a protesting cry.

"Leave that," Lord Ransome ordered brusquely.

The man dropped the sack and scurried away. The workers who had gathered about drifted off, muttering amongst themselves. Sarah, Mary Ann, and Lord Ransome were left alone in their frozen tableau. Sarah put her arm about Mary Ann, holding her close, and Lord Ransome stood with his back to them for a long moment.

Gradually, Sarah was able to breathe again, to hear the sounds of the birds and the stream that flowed around her. She watched Lord Ransome, warily waiting for him to turn and look at them.

Mary Ann drew away to pull the sack toward her. She untied the rope around its opening, and three tiny kittens, all of them bundles of black-and-white fur with bright green eyes, tumbled out onto her lap. They mewed softly, stumbling about on Mary Ann's muslin skirt in a sweet tangle.

The sounds of them made Lord Ransome turn around. He looked tired and still expressionless, but slowly the mask cracked, and he smiled at them. It was a weary, strained smile, yet it made him seem a little more like the man Sarah had come to know. She relaxed a bit, her shoulders aching with the stiffness she had not realized she was holding there.

"I—apologize, Lady Iverson, Miss Bellweather," he said. "I should not have behaved in such a way in front of you."

Mary Ann, cuddling one of the kittens against her shoulder, looked up at him with shining eyes. "You saved me, Lord Ransome! You drove that horrid brute away. These darling babies are alive because of you."

"I hardly think you needed 'saving,' Miss Bellweather," he answered. "You seemed to be more than
holding your own; you are a very brave young lady."

Mary Ann giggled, and ducked her head to nuzzle
the kitten.

"Thank you, Lord Ransome," Sarah said. "You were
indeed very gallant."

They all fell into silence, the kittens' mews and the
rush of the stream the only sounds, until a voice behind
them said, "That was quite a scene, your lordship."

Sarah looked back to see a man coming down the
muddy slope toward them. He wasn't one of the workers;
he was a stranger, as the rough farmer had been. But he
looked nothing like the farmer.

He was obviously not very old, though his sun-
browned skin and the deep grooves that lined his mouth
made him seem older. The jet-black hair that waved back
from his face was liberally streaked with silver, and his
green eyes looked out wearily onto the world. He limped
slightly as he walked.

He was very thin; his cheap clothes hung on him as if
made for another man. But he was not at all fearsome,
as the strange farmer had been. He looked at them seriously but kindly, with only the hint of a spark of interest
when he saw Mary Ann.

Lord Ransome's eyes widened with surprise, and he
took a step forward. "Lieutenant O'Riley? What are you
doing here?"

Lieutenant O'Riley laughed, and answered, with a hint
of a lilting brogue in his voice, "Well, now, you said if I
was ever in need of work I should look for you. Here I
am. I should have appeared earlier; I can be a handy
man to have around in a brawl."

Lord Ransome laughed, too. "It was hardly a brawl!
But it is good to have you here nonetheless. You look—
different than when we last met in London."

"Ah, well, I cleaned up a bit before I came here."
Lieutenant O'Riley glanced at Sarah and Mary Ann.

"Forgive me," Lord Ransome said, turning to them. "Lady

Iverson, Miss Bellweather, this is Lieutenant O'Riley. We met some months ago in Town."

Sarah rose to her feet, and drew Mary Ann with her. Mary Ann now held all the kittens in her arms, but she managed to give him a pretty smile over their fur.

"How do you do, Lieutenant O'Riley?" Sarah said. "I am Lady Iverson. I work on the Viking village just over the slope. And this is my younger sister, Miss Bellweather."

"I'm very pleased to meet you. But it's just plain Mr. O'Riley now—I left the Army behind long ago."

Sarah nodded. She wondered just what Lieutenant— Mr. O'Riley had been in Lord Ransome's military life, and what his coming here meant. Perhaps he was the former soldier who was going to turn her village into a farm.

She wasn't sure she quite liked the way Mary Ann was looking at the Irish soldier, either. She took Mary Ann's arm, kittens and all, and said, "We should be going home now. It's muddy and hot here, and I'm sure Mary Ann is tired."

"I need to make the kittens a bed, and find them some milk," Mary Ann said.

"Let us walk back with you, then," Lord Ransome suggested. "Just in case our new friend the kitten-drowner decides to return."

"Thank you," Sarah said. "That is most kind of you."

Sarah was glad of the men's company and strength on the walk back to the hunting box. But, in reality, she was not sure which was more dangerous—kitten-hating farmers, or Lord Ransome himself.

Chapter Twelve

That night, Sarah sat at her desk in the drawing room of the hunting box, ostensibly working on her notes from that day's dig. Her papers and books were spread out, but her pen lay idle in her hand.

She watched Mary Ann, where she sat playing with the kittens beside the fire, and thought about their very strange afternoon. If Mary Ann had not shouted out when she had, what would Lord Ransome have said to her? Would he have given her a time when she must be off Ransome land? And what would she, *could* she, have said to that?

There would have been no choice for her but to acquiesce.

Sarah looked down at her notes, half finished on the page—just like her work. She laid down the pen, and closed her eyes.

In the darkness of her mind, she saw Lord Ransome, not as he usually was, kind and open, but as he had been today when he threatened Mary Ann's assailant. She would not have imagined there could be such violent intent on his handsome face—he had been so very deeply angry with the man. He had been unaware of anything around him but that cold anger. Sarah imagined that was what he must have been like in a battle.

She herself had been angry with the horrid farmer, and would have knocked him to the ground if she had been capable. But she was also taken aback by the new side of Lord Ransome she was seeing.

Taken aback—and maybe just a little frightened. And something else, some dark excitement she could not, or would not, name.

"Sarah?" she heard Mary Ann say. "Are you quite all right?"

Sarah opened her eyes to look at her sister, still sitting on the floor with all the kittens asleep on her lap. Mary Ann frowned in concern.

"Oh, yes," Sarah answered, trying to smile reassuringly. "I just have a bit of a headache."

"Poor Sarah! That is hardly surprising after the long day we have passed." Mary Ann looked down at the jumble of downy kitten bodies on her lap, and rubbed one's head with her fingertip. "I think you ought to marry Lord Ransome."

Unlike her usual outrageous pronouncements on gentlemen, Lord Ransome in particular, this statement was made quietly, hopefully, almost wistfully.

"He was so heroic today, rescuing me and these babies from that horrible man," Mary Ann went on. "Just like a knight in a book. He would be worthy of you, would look after you always. I am sure he would look after all of us, even Mother and Kitty."

Sarah watched Mary Ann in surprise. Mary Ann had been so young when their father died, just an infant really, and she had grown up in a family of only women. But Sarah had not realized she so wanted male influence—not *romantic* influence, but fatherly or brotherly—until now.

She tried to laugh. "Oh, Mary Ann! A lady can hardly marry a man who has not made her an offer. Nor is he likely to."

Mary Ann shook her head. "I am sure he wants to."

Sarah left her desk, and went to sit on the floor beside her sister. She took one of the sleeping kittens onto her own lap, and it sank down into her skirts with a mew and a stretch. "Oh, Mary Ann. We cannot know what he wants. We can only go about our lives the best we can. I have my work, and it makes me happy. One day, you will see that things cannot be as they are in books, but that life can be just as good—or better. You will meet someone, and fall in love, and build a real life with him. A good one, all your own."

Mary Ann looked up at her, tears sparkling in her brown eyes. "Do you think so?"

"Of course. Just be certain that you marry someone you *do* love, not just someone that our mother thinks would be suitable."

"Oh, never!" Mary Ann said with a laugh. "You cannot imagine the truly horrid men Mother thinks are suitable."

Sarah thought she could; they were probably the same men their mother had once tried to foist onto *her*. But she was confident that Mary Ann would not let herself be bullied into an unhappy match, and hopefully her search for her own true love would distract her from Sarah's romantic life, or lack thereof.

There was a knock at the drawing room door, and Rose, Mary Ann's maid, came in. She held a square of expensive-looking vellum on a tray.

"Excuse me, my lady," she said, "but this just came for you by messenger."

"Thank you, Rose." Sarah stood up, and took the letter, breaking the wax seal with her fingernail.

"What is it?" Mary Ann asked worriedly, as Sarah read in silence. "Bad news?"

"Oh, no." Sarah turned to look at her sister. "We are invited, along with the Hamiltons, to dine at Ransome Hall tomorrow evening. So then we may thank Lord Ransome in person for his gallant rescue today, can't we, Mary Ann?"

"Of course." Mary Ann hugged one of the kittens close to her. "Do you suppose that that handsome Mr. O'Riley will be there?"

"It is good to see you again, Lieutenant—Mr. O'Riley," Miles said. He poured out a generous measure of brandy and handed it to his guest.

Mr. O'Riley laughed. "Call me Patrick, please, my lord. I feel all stiff and formal enough in your grand house without looking about for my father or my uncle every time someone says 'Mr. O'Riley.' ''

"Patrick it is, if there will be no more 'my lording.' I am Miles." He poured his own brandy, and sat down in the chair across from Patrick's. The library around them was dark and quiet in the after-supper lull, and, indeed, very grand. "I am glad you are here, but I would have looked for you several weeks ago. I thought perhaps you did not mean to take me up on my offer of a job. I take it you have not mended things with your family in Ireland."

Patrick shrugged, and took a deep, appreciative swallow of his drink. "There is little chance of that, I fear, though it's a pity. That estate was my father's home, as well as his older brother's, my uncle's. And I could not afford to come to the country, until now. I got work, though, building a grand house for some earl or such, despite my bad leg. Then I got this cough. The apothecary I saw told me I should go the country, find work on a farm where there's good, clean air. I remembered your offer, and I had heard one of the earl's friends say you had inherited this place, so here I am." He looked solemnly at Miles. "I wasn't sure you would even remember me."

"Of course, I remember you. You helped me a great deal."

Patrick's dark brows arched in surprise. "I helped you, Lord—Miles? How could that be? We only met so briefly."

"I was quite lost when I came home to England," Miles answered. "I felt useless, with no direction in this new life. A purpose was what I needed, and when I met you, I saw what that purpose could be. I could help men who had returned from brave service in the war only to find poverty and hardship."

"A noble goal."

Miles shook his head. "Hardly noble. It is only a tiny drop in the sea of trouble I have seen here. But when I inherited this title and estate, I saw a way that I could make some of those aspirations a reality. Ransome Hall is vast, and fertile."

"And not used as it should be," Patrick said. "I saw many fields that lay fallow."

"You are quite right. I have been working with the bailiff to develop a plan, one which will call for many more workers."

"The portion that that lady antiquarian—what was her name? Lady Iverson?—is using is a large one. The soil looks rich."

"Indeed, it is." Miles did not want to think of it, did not want to imagine what the scene would be when he asked Lady Iverson to abandon her village. But he knew that the day was coming, and coming soon.

Seeing Patrick O'Riley, remembering what had set him on this course in the first place, only affirmed his conviction that he had to do what was right.

"I hope to have it under cultivation by the spring," he said.

Patrick's green Irish gaze was shrewd. "And what does Lady Iverson say about this plan?"

Miles laughed ruefully. "Well, the truth is I have not yet had a chance to speak to her about it. I have invited her and her party to supper tomorrow evening, and I will make an appointment to speak to her then."

"Ah. I see." Patrick swallowed the last of his brandy, and put the snifter down on a nearby table. "Lady Iverson is very pretty, is she not? And her sister, too. Many people would say they are wasting their charms in digging about in the dirt all day long. Is that not so?"

"Some might say that. Lady Iverson is an attractive lady, and her sister a pretty *young* girl." Miles felt an irrational surge of protectiveness toward Lady Iverson and her family. It made absolutely no sense, as he was the one who would send them away from their work soon.

"Young—and not for a poor Irish ex-lieutenant," Patrick said with a grimace. "And quite right you are. But that does not mean I can't admire her fine dark eyes, eh?"

Miles laughed. "I would say not."

"Well, I am off to my bed. I fear your butler was quite shocked when you told him I was *not* to be housed in the servants' quarters, but in a guest chamber."

"The servants are not yet used to my changes. They think everything should continue as they were in my uncle's time. But we are coming to terms. You are my friend, not a servant, and thus should stay in a guest chamber."

"That is most kind of you, Lord—Miles," Patrick said. "But I insist on working for my keep, friend or no."

"Oh, never fear about that! Tomorrow, I will show you the plans for the farm, and I'd like your opinion on them."

"Of course. Good night."

"Good night, Patrick."

Long after Patrick had gone, and the butler cleared away the brandy tray, Miles sat in the library. He stared into the crumbling sparks of the fire, remembering the day just past.

He had been completely taken by surprise at the force of his fury toward that farmer today. It was true that wanton cruelty, even against animals, always angered him, but this was something more. When he saw the man push Lady Iverson's sister, and the shock and pain in Lady Iverson's eyes, a feeling sharply akin to the rage he had felt in battle rose up in him. He could very well have killed the man, if the ladies had not been watching. Certainly, he would have delivered the thrashing that the bully so richly deserved.

He had thought all that was left far behind him on the battlefield. What could have made it come upon him today, in the safe light of an English day?

He feared that he already knew the answer to that. It was a primitive male drive to protect his woman—one that no doubt the Viking men who had once lived in Lady Iverson's village would understand.

What the devil was he going to do about it?

Chapter Thirteen

Sarah sat before her dressing table, staring at her reflection, yet not really seeing herself there. Her maid had already dressed her hair, and helped her into her evening gown of smoky lavender silk. Now all she had to do was choose her jewelry from the open case, and she would be ready to go to supper at Ransome Hall.

A shiver of anticipation danced up her spine. She wanted to see Lord Ransome again, so much that it frightened her. But something deep inside her dreaded this evening even more. Dreaded what might happen—what might be said.

Running away from troubles solved nothing, she knew that very well. Tonight, though, she would gladly run away, take a ship all the way to Norway. But she could never do something so wild—her life was here, come what may, and she had to stay and face it.

She reached into her jewel case and took out a pair of Viking silver hair ornaments. They had been a gift from her husband when they married, and she loved them, loved their intricate etchings of strange beasts and unreadable runes. Wearing them always gave her confidence, made her feel closer to the history she had devoted her life to. She slid the ornaments into her upswept curls, and reached into the case again to find her earrings. There was a knock at her bedchamber door, and, thinking it was her maid returning or Mary Ann, she called, "Come in."

But it was not Mary Ann—it was Mrs. Hamilton. She wore a stylish if over-elaborate gown of ice-blue satin trimmed in white Belgian lace and ribbon rosettes. Her expression above this confection was hesitant, though, as she stepped through the doorway.

"Mrs. Hamilton," Sarah said. "Is there something amiss?"

"Oh, no!" Mrs. Hamilton said, with a forced little laugh. "I just—just thought I would see if you needed any assistance. I fear we have arrived a bit early."

"Thank you, but I am very nearly ready." Sarah slid pearl-drop earrings into her earlobes, and watched Mrs. Hamilton's reflection in the dressing-table mirror. Mrs. Hamilton sat down on the window seat, and ran her fingers over the velvet cushion, as if restless or nervous.

Sarah wondered what this was all about. She and Mrs. Hamilton were hardly friends, and they almost never had private converse.

"Neville told me what happened at the village site yesterday," Mrs. Hamilton said.

"Did he? How very odd, since he was not even there."

"One of the men who are working with Neville on the bakery site told him about it. *All* about it. Such a shocking scene! Whoever would have thought Lord Ransome to be a violent man?"

Sarah had wondered the same thing yesterday, when she watched him menace that farmer, but today the shock had worn away, and she felt only gratitude at his defense. She felt the strongest urge to defend *him* now. "He was in the Army, Mrs. Hamilton. And I would hardly call his behavior violent. That man was cruel to Mary Ann, and we were fortunate that Lord Ransome was there to make certain he departed without causing any more trouble."

"Fortunate indeed," Mrs. Hamilton said. "Fortunate when his anger is turned against someone else—someone outside our circle. But what if he becomes angry with one of us?" She leaned forward in a rich rustle of satin and lace. "I have heard that he means to send us away from here, with the work undone, in order to use the property for his own purposes."

Sarah turned to peer closely at Mrs. Hamilton. She had always thought that Neville's wife was a silly woman, concerned with fashion and parties to the exclusion of all else. Now she thought perhaps she had underestimated her a bit. Mrs. Hamilton's gaze was deeply serious; her words held a disquieting ring of persuasiveness.

"You seemed to enjoy making Lord Ransome's acquaintance," Sarah said cautiously.

"Of course! He is a marquis. I just think—" Mrs. Hamilton broke off on a ripple of laughter. "I just don't know what I am trying to say. I was simply concerned about what Neville told me."

"Yes, I see. Well, I am certain we have nothing to fear from Lord Ransome. Yesterday was a mere isolated incident, one that was over in an instant. He was defending us."

"I am sure you are right. Then he does *not* mean to send us away from here?"

"I do not know what his plans are," Sarah answered truthfully. She only had suspicions. But she would have thought that Mrs. Hamilton would want to be "sent away" with the way she pined so for Bath. "I thought you preferred town life, anyway, Mrs. Hamilton."

Mrs. Hamilton shrugged. "Of course, I would prefer to live among a wider society! But Neville needs his work, and a good wife supports her husband in all he does."

"Hm." Sarah reached for her gloves and reticule. "Well, Mrs. Hamilton, we really should be going. We do not want to be late for supper." And she had had quite enough of this conversation.

Ransome Hall was quieter than it had been the night of the supper party. There were no banks of flowers, no tall candelabras of light, no crowds sipping champagne. Yet Sarah, despite her earlier trepidations, found that she was enjoying herself. The food was much better than the plain fare the cook turned out of the small kitchen at the hunting box, the wine was fine, and the conversation interesting.

Mostly interesting, anyway. Neville Hamilton looked frankly appalled to be asked to dine with an Irishman, even one as obviously educated as Mr. O'Riley, and his wife chattered on to Mary Ann about the gloves she had bought yesterday. Mary Ann's eyes had a distinctly glazed look about them.

Sarah, however, rather liked Mr. O'Riley. She and John had spent several months on an excavation in Ireland early in their marriage, and Mr. O'Riley had lived on a farm very near the site. He was surprisingly knowledgable about antiquarian methods.

"When I was a boy, I used to go to the ruins with my cousins and clamber all about," he told her. "It made me interested to know more about the history and the objects there."

Sarah laughed. "You probably destroyed valuable historical evidence, 'clambering' about!"

He grinned at her, and for one moment the gaunt, war-haunted man fell away, and she saw the charming man he must have been once. From the corner of her eye, she saw Mary Ann turn away from Mrs. Hamilton and look at Mr. O'Riley, a startled expression on her face.

Sarah sighed inwardly, and hoped that this was not the beginning of another infatuation.

"I am very sorry, Lady Iverson," Mr. O'Riley said. "We had no idea we were destroying anything valuable. We just liked to imagine we were ancient Vikings, pillaging and rampaging."

"Well, I have to reassure you, then. You cannot have destroyed a very great deal, for we made some valuable finds there. My husband wrote a monograph on the site that was very well-received in scholarly circles. But those Vikings did no pillaging or rampaging—not in the period of that site, anyway. By then, they were respectable immigrants, farming and building."

"Ah, but you have destroyed my romantic illusions, Lady Iverson!" Mr. O'Riley laid his hand on his heart, as if wounded. "I can never think of the Vikings the same way again."

Sarah laughed. "The Vikings are really far more complex, and interesting, than those myths. You are welcome to come to the village whenever you like, Mr. O'Riley, and we will show you about. If—" She broke off, and glanced down the table at Lord Ransome. He watched them closely, as if interested in what their conversation could be. Her heart quickened at the expression in his eyes.

She looked back down at her wineglass, her cheeks warm.

"If what, Lady Iverson?" Mr. O'Riley asked.

She had been about to say, "If we are there very much longer"; but, instead, she said, "If you are to be in the neighborhood long enough."

"As to that, I am not certain what my plans are as of yet," said Mr. O'Riley.

"Have to get back to the elves and the bogs, eh?" Mr. Hamilton broke in, his voice slightly slurred, as if he had been imbibing freely of the fine wine. "The Irish are such a superstitious lot, they can't be happy in a civilized place like England for very long."

Sarah stared at him, startled. The Neville Hamilton who used to work with her and John would never have been so rude. This just seemed one more sign of how he had changed of late. His wineglass was nearly empty, not for the first time—had he been drinking heavily?

Mrs. Hamilton giggled, an inordinately loud sound in the sudden hush of the dining room. Perhaps his marriage, and not the drink, was unhinging him.

Mary Ann looked furious, and she half rose from her seat. Sarah gave her a small shake of her head, and Mary Ann sat back down. She still seemed mutinous, though, scowling like a fierce little Valkyrie.

Sarah turned back to Mr. O'Riley, who stared expressionlessly at Mr. Hamilton. "Ireland is a lovely country," she said. "Sir John and I enjoyed our time there a great deal. Indeed, I have never seen anyplace more magical."

Mr. O'Riley looked back to her, and gave her a smile. Unlike his earlier wide grin, though, it was humorless and small. "Thank you, Lady Iverson. It is indeed a beautiful place, but not, I fear, a land of great opportunity. Where else have you and your husband been fortunate enough to see? Have you been to Scandinavia?"

"I have not, but my husband did once, and he often spoke of it." She went on to relate John's anecdotes of Norway, but inside she still thought about the Hamiltons and their eccentric behavior.

She resolved that if Lord Ransome did not ask them to leave his land, if they were fortunate enough to continue their work, she would have to rethink her association with them.

"I want to apologize for Mr. Hamilton's odd behavior at supper," Sarah said to Lord Ransome later, as they strolled on the terrace for a breath of fresh air. Ahead of them walked Mr. O'Riley and Mary Ann; the Hamiltons sat in the drawing room, watching them through the open French doors. "He should never have insulted your guest."

"It is not for you to apologize, Lady Iverson," he answered quietly. "And it seems Mr. O'Riley is quite unconcerned with any insult now, not in your sister's company."

Mr. O'Riley was smiling down at Mary Ann, who laughed up at him.

Sarah was glad to see her sister so happy, but . . .

"Yes. They do seem to enjoy each other's company," she said.

"Do you not approve?"

"How could I *dis*approve? She is merely talking to a gentleman, not twenty steps away from me. But Mary Ann is very young, and she reads a great many novels. She has some—some very romantic notions."

"Unlike her sensible sister?" he said, in a lightly teasing tone.

Sarah laughed. "Quite right!"

"I am sure Mr. O'Riley has enough sense for both of them." They reached the end of the terrace, and Lord Ransome leaned back against the marble balustrade, his arms crossed over his chest. "I hope she has not suffered any ill effects from the—incident yesterday."

"Not at all. In fact, she is very happy with her new pets. Though I doubt our mother will be as happy when she arrives back at home with three cats in tow! It was very kind of you to come to our rescue."

"Kind?" He looked quite surprised.

Sarah had a quick, flashing memory of the fury on his face as he grabbed the farmer. She closed her eyes against it. "Yes. But I fear that all the drama interrupted you when you were about to tell me something." She did not *really* want to know what he had been going to say, yet she knew she would have to face it eventually.

"There was something I wanted to talk to you about," he said. "This hardly seems the time, though. Perhaps I could call on you tomorrow, Lady Iverson? If that would be convenient. It is rather important."

Convenient? Convenient for her to abandon her work? She almost gave a humorless bark of laughter, and pressed her hand to her mouth. "Of course. Tomorrow morning, then?"

He nodded. "Tomorrow morning."

Chapter Fourteen

He was not coming. It was too late in the morning. Surely he would not come; perhaps he had changed his mind.

Sarah paced across the drawing room, peering out the window. It was growing late, almost time for luncheon. She had dressed in one of her plain work dresses, so that she could go to the village and do as much digging as possible after she spoke to Lord Ransome. Mary Ann had already gone ahead.

Now Sarah wondered if she should have worn one of her fine muslin morning gowns. She glanced down at her gray dress; it was hardly attire that inspired confidence and authority. It was faded, and dusty around the hem. And her hair was simply pulled back with a ribbon, up off her neck where it would not be in the way.

But it hardly mattered anyway. She looked over at the clock on the fireplace mantel, and decided it was indeed too late, and he would not come today. She could leave.

Or run away, her mind whispered.

No! she protested. She was not running away. She simply had her work to attend to. That was all.

She caught up her hat and the lunch hamper the cook had packed. As she hurried out the front door, she froze when she saw a horse coming up the lane. A horse with a familiar rider.

Lord Ransome. So he *had* come today, after all.

She thought again of her fine morning gowns, and glanced back into the house. There was no time for changing, though. He was almost to her door. So Sarah stood her ground, and tilted her chin up with what she hoped was a welcoming smile.

"Good day, Lord Ransome!" she said, as he dismounted at the foot of her narrow front steps.

"Good day, Lady Iverson," he answered. He smiled, too, but it seemed tentative. Not his usual open grin at all.

Not the bold, white flash of the Viking in her dreams.

Sarah closed her eyes for an instant, to try to push that dream to the very back of her mind. It would never work to try to converse with Lord Ransome while envisioning him as a Viking, replaying his almost-kiss on a village street that had vanished over eight hundred years ago.

"I hope I am not calling at an inconvenient time," he said.

She opened her eyes and looked back at him, half expecting to find him clad in a tunic, long golden hair flowing to his shoulders. But he was just his ordinary self, cropped hair shining in the sunlight, clad in an ordinary dark blue coat and buckskin breeches. Unfortunately, his own ordinary self was far more disconcerting than any dream-Viking could be. "An inconvenient time?"

"It appears you are on your way out." He gestured towards the hat and hamper in her hands.

"Oh." Sarah stared down at them stupidly. She *had* been going out, hadn't she? "Yes, I was on my way to the village, but I'm sure they can manage without me for a while. Please, do come in."

"Thank you." He followed her into the cool dimness of the hunting box's drawing room. As he looked around him at the small chamber, Sarah truly noticed its shabbiness for the first time. She and John had moved into it with the furnishings that were already there, and had never given them a second thought. They were almost never there, anyway, and scarred wood and frayed upholstery hardly mattered.

But now she saw its untidiness through Lord Ransome's eyes. Her desk in the corner was covered with papers and books, and dirty objects newly discovered in the village. Mary Ann's easel was set up by the window, and surrounded by her sketchbooks and paint pots. Slippers, shawls, baskets of mending, and scholarly publications cluttered up the carpet so that the faded floral pattern could scarcely be seen. The kittens slept in their basket bed by the empty fireplace.

Perhaps he was thinking how very foolish his uncle had been to loan his hunting box to such untidy people. Weren't military men noted for being very orderly and organized?

She nudged some newspapers under the settee with her toe, and said, "I do apologize for the—confusion. We have a very small staff here."

"Not at all," he answered kindly, and with every evidence of sincerity. "It is a most charming space."

"Thank you. Won't you sit down? Shall I ring for some tea?"

Lord Ransome moved a shawl from a chair, and sat down. "Please, don't go to any trouble, Lady Iverson. The cook at Ransome Hall will have a tea waiting when I return." He clasped his hands together, and looked down at them, as if gathering his thoughts before speaking again. "You probably know what I have come to speak to you about,"

So the moment had arrived. The tips of Sarah's fingers grew suddenly numb, and she stared at them as if they did not belong to her at all. "In—indeed?"

"Yes. I imagine that you will hardly be surprised at what I have to say. I would have spoken much sooner, but—"

"Please, Lord Ransome!" Sarah burst out. "Just say it, whatever it is."

He nodded, and glanced back down at his clasped hands. She was grateful not to have the force of that sky blue gaze on her for the moment.

"When I was a child," he said, "my father often spoke to me about responsibility and duty. Those were very important concepts to him; they were the principles he lived by, always. And he impressed this on me, along with the precept that when a person is given much in this world, that person owes a debt in return. A debt that is especially due to those less fortunate."

Sarah hardly saw how this was "just saying it," but she held her tongue. She was drawn in by the quiet, deep sound of his voice, by his words; she wanted to see where his tale was going. So she sat in silence.

"I took his lessons into the war with me. In Spain, I commanded many men, some of them worthless rascals I would hope never to see again in my life, but most of them good men. Men with families, and hopes for the future. I did the very best I could for them, and they sacrificed much for their country." He looked back up at her, his gaze intense and unswerving. "Now so many of those very men, and men just like them, are suffering. There are not enough jobs for all of them, not enough money, and they cannot provide for their families."

Sarah swallowed, caught by his unwavering stare. This was obviously something he cared very, very deeply about. She felt almost as if she was looking into his very heart.

It was difficult to find words to answer him, but she knew she had to try. "Yes, I know, Lord Ransome. I do not live entirely in my own world of books and dusty artifacts; I read newspapers. I see how difficult things are right now, and I think it is admirable that you feel as you do. Many are completely indifferent to the sufferings of others."

"But I cannot just *feel,* Lady Iverson! I must do something—do whatever I can."

Sarah was confused, tangled up in emotions of admiration, attraction, guilt, dread. Her work was slipping away from her somehow, caught up in Lord Ransome's conscience, and politics she could in no way control or even understand. She felt as if she was hanging on to her life by a tiny thread, and she was desperate to keep all she had in her grasp.

At the same time, paradoxically, her regard for Lord

Ransome, the man who was taking it from her, grew. His passion, his compassion, touched her.

She pressed her fingers to her throbbing temples. "What—what then do you intend to do, Lord Ransome?"

"My uncle had many concerns other than his estate, as you know," he answered, his voice quiet again, taut with his effort at calm coolness. "Ransome Hall is a desperately underused resource, and much farmland is uncultivated. Land that could provide jobs and food."

"Including the land my village lies on," she said, looking away from him. Her gaze landed on the painting resting on Mary Ann's easel, a half-finished watercolor of what the Viking house would have looked like when it was newly built. She focused on it as if it were her one piece of reality.

"Yes, I'm afraid so," Lord Ransome said. His tone was not lacking in understanding, but at the same time it was full of resolve. "I have spoken to Mr. Benson, the bailiff, and to many of the tenants and neighboring farmers. They tell me that the soil in that valley is rich, and ripe for crops."

"That is why the Vikings settled there. I am sure that, if we could look further afield, we would find other sites such as farms and homes." Sarah wanted to cry. She wanted to wail, and beat her heels on the floor, as Mary Ann and Kitty had as children. But those tantrums had never gained them a doll or a new hair ribbon, and it would not save her village now. All she could save really was her dignity, and she held on to that with all her strength. "The land is yours, of course, Lord Ransome. You must do with it as you see fit."

Suddenly, much to her shock, he leaned forward and took her hand in his. His clasp was warm and strong.

Sarah's fingers curled instinctively around his, and she peeked up at him through her lashes. He looked every bit as surprised as she felt, as if taking her hand had been an irresistible impulse. But he did not move away—and neither did she. He smelled of sunshine and soap, and she wanted to bury her face in that sweet cleanness and cry.

"I am sorry, Lady Iverson," he said. "But there is no hurry. Surely there is time for you to finish the work?"

Sarah shook her head. "If I worked as other antiquarians do, simply digging for valuable objects and tossing the rest away, perhaps. But my husband believed, as I do, that our work has a greater importance. We are learning about the past, and preserving England's heritage for future generations. My husband's methods of recording and preserving as much as possible are very time consuming; that is why we have been here so long. We would have to stop and cover everything for the winter months, and resume in the spring. There is so much still to be found, that I am sure we would be here until next fall." She stared down at their joined hands, just for a second, then pulled hers back and returned it to her lap. "You will need to be preparing the fields for your farm very soon."

"Lady Iverson, I wish . . ." he began. His voice faded on the words.

"Yes." Sarah did not want to sit there and discuss this any more. If they went on, she would truly start to cry. "Could we perhaps talk about this further at a later time, Lord Ransome? I was expected at the village quite a while ago, and they will wonder where I am."

"Yes, certainly." They rose, and walked back to the front door. There, he turned to her with a strangely wistful expression on his face. "I did so enjoy my afternoon at the village last week, Lady Iverson. I do wish . . ."

A sudden wild impulse seized Sarah, a crazy idea that maybe she could still make him see, make him *know*. If he had really enjoyed his time at the village, then maybe, just maybe . . . "Would you care to come with me, Lord Ransome?"

He gave her a startled look. "You would invite me to your village? Even after what I came here to say today?"

"You are only acting on your own convictions," Sarah answered. "I do see that. And I hope that we have become friends of sorts in these last few days—even if we *are* of conflicting opinions."

He smiled at her slowly. "Yes, Lady Iverson, I would like to think we are friends."

"Good. Because I need as many laborers as possible right now, and if you come with me today, I will be sure to put you to work." Sarah tried to speak in a light tone, even though she felt like her heart was broken in her chest. Tears and pleadings would avail her nothing, and would be tiring besides. She might as well be amiable.

"Of course, Lady Iverson. I hope that you will let me assist you in any way I can."

"May I be of assistance, Miss Bellweather?"

Mary Ann looked up from the object she was prying from the ground at the sound of a lilting voice. Mr. O'Riley stood behind her, a pleasant, inquiring smile on his gauntly good-looking face. His green eyes shone like twin emeralds—or the hills of Ireland.

She suddenly had the oddest sensation that she couldn't feel her fingers, and the trowel fell from them onto the ground. She opened her mouth to answer, but no sound emerged.

Oh, dear! she thought. Was Sarah right? Had reading romantic novels so affected her mind that she would swoon away over any handsome man who looked her way? To be fair, Sarah had not said *exactly* that, but Mary Ann had the feeling that was what she had thought. And Mary Ann feared it might be correct.

She couldn't become infatuated with Mr. O'Riley, just because he was good looking and tragically sad. Not after her embarrassing silliness over Mr. Hamilton.

He picked her trowel up off the ground, and handed it to her.

Mary Ann smiled, and clutched at the tool as if it was a lifeline. "Good morning, Mr. O'Riley. You are looking much . . ." She hesitated. She had been about to say "much better," but perhaps that sounded rude. Even though it was true. Some of the haunted look had faded from the edges of his eyes, and the sun was adding color to his thin cheeks.

His smile widened. "I am feeling *much,* too. Ransome Hall is far more comfortable lodgings than I am accustomed to."

Mary Ann ached to ask what sort of lodgings he *was* accustomed to, what he had done before he came here, what his life in Ireland had been like. Instead, she just nodded, and said, "Indeed, Ransome Hall is a very lovely house."

How perfectly idiotic she sounded. Could she not think of anything more original to say than that? She looked down at the trowel in her hands, unable to bear the amusement she was sure she would see in his eyes.

He stepped up next to her, and knelt to peer at the dirt where she was digging. "So, what are you working on here, Miss Bellweather?"

Grateful to speak of something she actually knew about, something impersonal, Mary Ann slid off her stool and knelt beside him to point to the object with the tip of her trowel. "I am trying to pry this out without breaking anything. I think it may be a drinking horn, but it is trapped under a stone or something."

"May I?' he said, holding out his hand for the trowel. "My cousins and I sometimes dug about at ancient sites when I was a child. I prided myself on never breaking a single object."

Mary Ann handed him the tool, and watched closely as he slid it into the dirt and dug around the horn. The lean muscles of his back lengthened and bunched with the effort of his labors, and he sat down in the dirt, unmindful of his clothes, to get closer to it.

Mary Ann lowered herself onto the low stool she had been sitting on. "You mustn't let my sister hear you say that you used to dig for artifacts! There is nothing that makes her angrier than amateur fortune hunters." She remembered the look on Sarah's face, pale and furious, when that wicked farmer had pushed herself down. "Well, almost nothing."

Mr. O'Riley laughed. "It will be our secret then, eh, Miss Bellweather?" He made one last jab with the trowel, and said, "Have you a handkerchief, or something to brush this dirt off with?"

Mary Ann pulled a large paintbrush from her apron pocket and handed it to him. "I use this."

"Perfect." He carefully pushed all the dirt from the edges of the object, and finally pulled it up gently from the earth. Taking a handkerchief from inside his coat, he used it to wipe the worst of the soil from it, and handed it to her.

Mary Ann turned the ivory drinking horn over in her hands, marveling at the intricate etchings. "It is beautiful."

"Beautiful," agreed Mr. O'Riley. "It should be called the 'Bellweather Horn.' "

Mary Ann peeked up at him. "Why?"

"Because you found it, of course."

"Only with your help." She wrapped the horn in Mr. O'Riley's handkerchief, and placed it carefully in the basket with the other items she had found that morning.

Mr. O'Riley sat back, gazing out over the site. "What is this area? A tavern of some sort?"

"A tavern?"

He gestured towards the basket. "You said this was a drinking horn."

"This place is a house," said Mary Ann. "The only house we have found so far, though Sarah—my sister—is certain there are others about. See that sunken area over there? That is the central hearth, where all the cooking would be done, and where everyone in the family would gather on cold winter nights."

He stared at the hearth she pointed to, and around at the ropes that marked off where the walls would have been. "Your sister seems a most formidable woman," he said musingly.

"She is certainly that. And very clever," Mary Ann answered.

Mr. O'Riley looked at her, the force of his green gaze

taking the breath from her. "As clever as you are, Miss Bellweather?"

Mary Ann giggled. No one had *ever* called her "clever" before. "Oh, I am scarcely that. I only follow Sarah's instructions, or I am sure I would make a great bungle of it."

"You seem to know a great deal about this place, about the Vikings."

"It is just what I've read in books."

"A stupid person wouldn't bother reading books, now would they? No. So you *must* be intelligent."

Mary Ann felt absurdly pleased. People had complimented her on her looks before, and on things such as her gowns and her hats. But no one had ever complimented her on her intelligence. Sarah was the smart one in her family. No one but Sarah had ever so much as suggested that Mary Ann might possess even some intelligence.

She was certain she must be blushing, and her cheeks felt even warmer when he grinned at her.

Over Mr. O'Riley's shoulder she saw Sarah appear on the pathway, Lord Ransome at her side. Sarah's face was cold and expressionless; she stared straight ahead, with no indication of noticing what was about her.

Mary Ann wondered, with a little twinge of panic, what could have caused her sister to look like that. Was someone in their family ill? Had she seen Mary Ann with Mr. O'Riley and been angered by it?

Mary Ann leaped to her feet, feeling unaccountably guilty. She had been doing nothing but sitting here with him, talking about the Vikings. No one could be angry about that.

She hurried down the path toward her sister, followed by Mr. O'Riley. Only when she got near them did she see that Lord Ransome looked as tense and expressionless as her sister. Mary Ann felt her hopes for a happy match between Sarah and Lord Ransome sink as she glanced from one to the other. What could they have quarreled about?

"Sarah! I found the loveliest ivory drinking horn, very nearly intact," she called, hoping to cheer her sister up just a bit.

Sarah gave her a small smile. "That is wonderful, dear. I cannot wait to see it." Her gaze slid past Mary Ann to Mr. O'Riley. "Was Mr. O'Riley assisting you?"

Mary Ann heard no suspicion or anger in the simple question. There wasn't even much curiosity. "Yes. He is an excellent excavator. He helped me dig out the horn."

"That was very kind of you, Mr. O'Riley," Sarah said.

"I enjoyed it very much," answered Mr. O'Riley. "You have a fascinating place here. I would love to see more of it."

Sarah gave a faint smile. "Yes, it is indeed— fascinating."

"You possess hidden talents, then, Patrick?" Lord Ransome said, in an obviously strained attempt at joviality.

Mr. O'Riley grinned. "I suppose I must."

Sarah gave Lord Ransome the merest flicker of a glance. "Perhaps you could deliver the luncheon hamper to the stable, Lord Ransome, while Mary Ann shows me the drinking horn?"

Lord Ransome bowed. "Of course, Lady Iverson."

"And I hope both you and Mr. O'Riley will join us for the meal," Sarah said.

Lord Ransome gazed at her steadily. "If you are certain about that, Lady Iverson."

"Of course, I am. Please, do join us." Then Sarah took Mary Ann's arm and led her back down the path toward the Viking house. "Now, Mary Ann dear, show me all that you have found this morning."

"Certainly, Sarah." Mary Ann glanced back over her shoulder at the two men, Lord Ransome and Mr. O'Riley. Even though she burned with curiosity to know what had happened between her sister and Lord Ransome, one thought floated, unbidden, to the forefront of her mind.

Mr. O'Riley's given name was *Patrick*.

Chapter Fifteen

"He did *what*?" Mr. Hamilton cried. He jumped out of his chair and paced the length of the hunting box's tiny drawing room.

Sarah watched him from her seat behind her desk, feeling strangely removed from the whole scene. Her own anger had burned away, leaving her tired and sad. She looked from Mr. Hamilton's reddened face to Mary Ann, who sat in the corner with her kittens on her lap. She looked as tearful as Sarah herself felt.

"It is his own land," Sarah said. "He has the right to do what he likes with it."

"Even if what he likes is to destroy all our work? He will just plow the village under, and it will never be seen again. You must know that."

Sarah closed her eyes against the appalling images his words conjured up. Of course, she knew that! The knowledge of it, of all that would be lost, twisted her heart into a painful knot.

But she had heard Lord Ransome's reasoning for his actions, and they were hard to argue against. Certainly jobs and crops were important, especially in these difficult times. Sarah might be absorbed in a distant past much of the time, but she was not blind, and she hoped that she was not hard-hearted.

Yet wasn't what she was doing important, as well? Wouldn't her work benefit people, too?

Sarah rubbed at her aching temples. She simply did not know any longer.

"I know that, Mr. Hamilton," she answered quietly. "As I said, though, it is . . ."

"His land," he finished, his shoulders slumping with defeat. "So it is."

"We were fortunate to be allowed to stay for as long as we have."

Mr. Hamilton dropped into a chair next to her desk, and leaned toward her. "You know, Lady Iverson, if you had followed my advice we would have been finished by now, and this would not be a concern."

If she had followed his advice, to dig quickly and salvage only valuable artifacts, more would have been lost than was going to be now. She looked at him coolly. "I had to do what I felt was right. What John would have wanted."

Mr. Hamilton opened his mouth, as if to make an angry retort. He snapped his mouth shut, and said tightly, "When do we have to leave?"

"I do not know. Lord Ransome has not said. Will you stay and help me to finish the site?" Sarah felt it was the very least she could do, in memory of John's friendship with Mr. Hamilton. Then she could part peacefully from him and his silly wife.

He shrugged. "I have been corresponding with other antiquarians, and many of them have interesting work they would like me to share. But I am not one to begin something only to abandon it, so I will stay." He paused, then went on. "Emmeline will be very disappointed to leave this place."

Sarah very much doubted that. Mrs. Hamilton seemed bored and restless here, her only joy in talking about her home in Bath and meeting titled people—like the Marquis of Ransome. "As we all will. But, as you said, there is other work to be found."

"Of course." He stood up, and gave her a stiff little bow. "I must be going—Emmeline will be wondering where I am. I shall see you tomorrow at the village."

"Good night, Mr. Hamilton."

The silence in the room was thick and sad after he

departed, broken only by the sound of the papers Sarah shuffled around aimlessly on her desk. Then she heard a soft sob, and looked up at Mary Ann.

Her sister was bent over the kittens in her lap, tears trailing down her cheeks. "Oh, Sarah! This is terrible."

Sarah went to kneel beside her sister. "Mary Ann, dear, it is not *terrible*! It is disappointing, to be sure, but not terrible. There will always be other work out there." She had to convince herself of this as much as Mary Ann.

"I will have to go home to Mother now."

"Not if you don't want to. You can stay with me, and we will go to . . ." Sarah thought quickly. "To London! I will take a house there, and we'll go to the British Museum, and meet all sorts of interesting people."

Mary Ann sniffled mournfully, and hugged the kittens close to her. "But you will never marry Lord Ransome now."

Sarah almost laughed at the sorrow on her sister's face, despite the sadness in her own heart. "My dear, I never *was* going to marry Lord Ransome. That was just a romantic idea you conjured up in your own mind, and it was not realistic."

"I only want you to be happy. You are the very best person in the world, Sarah, and this is all so unfair!"

"Oh, Mary Ann." Sarah hugged her close, wriggling cats and all. "I *am* happy, whether I'm married or not. How could I not be, with a sister like you?"

Mary Ann leaned her head against Sarah's shoulder. "He seemed so nice, though."

Yes, he had, Sarah thought. *So nice.*

"Lord Ransome is not a bad man. He just has different ways of seeing things than we do."

"It is still not fair." Mary Ann's voice rose on the last word, and Sarah had the sense that she was becoming hysterical.

She gave Mary Ann a small shake, and said, "You must not worry about it any longer. Everything will be well, no matter what happens. You seem very tired, dear. Why don't you go up to bed? I will send Rose up with some warm milk and biscuits."

Mary Ann nodded weakly, and stood up, gathering all her Littens into her arms. "Aren't you going to retire, too, Sarah? You must be just as tired as I am."

"I will be up soon. I just want to finish some work here first."

Sarah watched Mary Ann leave the drawing room, and listened to her go up the stairs and close the door to her chamber. After she rang for Rose and instructed her to take some refreshments to Mary Ann, she sat back down at her desk and stacked her papers around her. She needed to organize her notes, to decide what the most important projects were to complete at the village, but she could not concentrate on them. She kept going over and over that meeting with Lord Ransome, kept seeing his face as he told her she would have to leave.

She closed her eyes, and the image shifted, changing into the Miles she had seen in her dream. His face had not been serious and determined in that fantasy world; it had been tender, and humorous, and, yes, lustful.

She opened her eyes and stared down at the notes and sketches on her desk. If only real life could be like that dream, she thought wistfully. If Thora, the Viking treasure-witch, had actually existed, had she ever faced such a jumble of emotions as this?

Suddenly, something deep inside her insisted that she *had* to see the village, right at that moment. She knew that it was not sensible to go wandering about at night, but it was an urge she could not resist. She wanted to see it, alone and in the moonlight, imagine it one more time as it was hundreds of years ago. Soon, too soon, it would be gone forever, and she needed a memory like this to hold on to.

She fetched her cloak and a lantern, and left a note on her desk for Mary Ann, in case her sister woke and wondered where she was. Then she slipped silently out of the house and walked down the pathway toward the village.

It slept silently beneath the night sky, the moonlight shimmering over the ancient street. The buildings were now only depressions in the ground, bound by ropes that marked off their perimeters, but she could imagine it all as it had been when it was alive. It had never truly been a dead place to her; it had always lived in her mind.

She walked past the leather-worker's shop that still had beams covering its gaping pit. At the jeweler's she stopped, and envisioned the polished bronze mirror that hung there in her dream. With a little laugh, she twirled about, imagining it was still there.

She stopped abruptly, in mid-twirl. The door to the stable where the artifacts were stored looked like it was ajar.

Distinctly, she remembered closing and locking it before they left for the day. She *always* locked it.

She took a step towards the stable, then another and another. She didn't want to see, but she knew she had to.

She wondered if this was yet another dream.

"Don't be silly," she whispered. "Probably the wind knocked the door open."

But there was not a breath of wind that night. The air lay cool and still around her. She shivered at the sensation of the hairs on her neck standing up.

All too soon, she reached the stable, and slowly pushed the door open. She stepped inside, into the familiar scents of dust and antiquities and trapped sunlight. Something crunched under her boot as she stepped inside. She lifted her lantern high—and gave an anguished scream.

Someone had swept all the artifacts from their labeled places on the tables, and pushed the tables themselves over. Combs, hair pins made of animal bone, beads, bowls, knife blades, pottery jars, rune stones, Mary Ann's drinking horn—they were all scattered across the floor in a tangled jumble. Some of them had shattered, surviving hundreds of years only to fall victim to a modern viciousness.

Sarah pressed her hand to her mouth as she stared at the mess. All of her beautiful things, objects she and many others had so laboriously unearthed, cleaned, and labeled, were tossed about and broken like so much trash.

Not since John died had she felt so hollow inside, so wounded and frightened.

She dropped to her knees and began blindly gathering artifacts. She took off her cloak and spread it on the floor to receive them. Some of them, like the chessmen and the silver brooches, were still intact, but many of the more fragile items were damaged beyond repair.

She found the carved ivory comb she had shown Lord Ransome the first day he came to the village. It had a new crack along its handle. Sarah cradled it in her hands, and felt her eyes begin to itch with unshed tears. As she stared down at the precious comb, they fell, trailing in silent, salty tracks down her cheeks and her chin, falling onto her hands.

"Who would do such a thing?" she cried out. She was frightened, surrounded by some miasma of evil she could not see or understand. She loved and treasured beauty; how could anyone destroy it like this?

And *who* would do this? She had no enemies, none that she knew of, anyway.

Perhaps it could be that farmer, the one who had tried to drown the kittens. He had looked so furious when Lord Ransome threatened him. . . .

Lord Ransome. He did not want her here, did not want her work to continue.

"No," she whispered, closing her hand tightly around the comb. "Why would he do that?" This was *his* land; if he wanted her gone from it right now, all he had to do was tell her. He was not the sort to do something cruel like this.

Or was he?

She could not help but remember his face, etched with cold fury, as he held that farmer by the throat. He had been a soldier, had probably done things in battle she could not even imagine. She remembered a man who had lived near their lodgings in Ireland. He had come back from the war almost a lunatic, doing wild, violent things and then having no memory of them after. John had kept her well away from the man until his family sent him away, but she had heard tales of him.

Lord Ransome was nothing like that. He did not rave, or stalk about, or shout. Even when he had been threatening the farmer, his face had been coldly blank.

So cold . . .

Sarah hugged herself around her hollow middle. She did not *want* to think Lord Ransome could do this, but the suspicion had been planted in her mind and would not be dislodged.

She gathered up her cloakful of artifacts, and stumbled out into the night, half blinded by her tears.

"Mr. Hamilton? Sir?"

Neville Hamilton was awakened by a knocking at the door of his chamber at the inn. It sounded like the innkeeper, his voice low but urgent.

"Damnation," Neville said. His head ached from the wine he had consumed at supper, from the news Lady Iverson had given him, and the quarrel he had had with Emmeline. "The inn had better be on fire to warrant this disruption," he muttered, as he stumbled out of bed and reached for his dressing gown. "I am coming!" he shouted.

The connecting door to Emmeline's room opened and she appeared there, blinking sleepily. A fringed Indian shawl covered her nightdress, and her blond hair fell in half-unpinned disarray.

"What is amiss, Neville?" she cried.

"How should I know?" he muttered. He went and opened the door, his wife close behind him. The innkeeper stood out in the corridor, a candle in his hand and a bewildered expression on his face. "Yes? What is it?"

"I am sorry to disturb you, sir, but there is a—a lady belowstairs. She says she must talk to you."

"A lady?" Emmeline said shrilly. "What lady would be calling on you in the middle of the night, Neville?"

His head still ached, and her voice was not helping matters. He could recall no recent indiscretions that might bring a woman to his door, and he could not even try to think with her nattering at him. "How should I know, Emmeline?"

"She seemed upset, if I may say so, sir," the innkeeper said. "She says she won't leave until she talks to you."

"I will be right down, then."

"And I am coming with you, Neville," Emmeline said.

"Very well." Anything to get rid of both of these women, whoever the mysterious lady in the parlor might be, so he could go back to sleep.

Sarah sat silently in the private parlor of the inn, her bundled cloak on her lap. She wasn't sure what she was doing here; she did not even really like the Hamiltons. All she had thought of was that Neville Hamilton knew almost as much about the work as she did, and perhaps he would have some idea of who might have done this.

Who besides Lord Ransome.

Mr. Hamilton burst into the room, his red hair standing on end, his dressing gown hastily fastened over his night shirt. Mrs. Hamilton was close behind him, her eyes wide with curiosity and even a strange excitement.

"Lady Iverson?" Mr. Hamilton said, his tone surprised, as well it might be. "Is something amiss?"

Sarah stood up, her arms wrapped around her bundle. "I'm afraid so. I apologize for waking you both so very late. I just did not know whom else to go to."

Mr. Hamilton pushed his hair back, obviously struggling to stay alert and calm. "That is quite all right, Lady Iverson. We are your friends; of course, you can call on us whenever you are in need."

Mrs. Hamilton hurried forward to take Sarah's arm, and urged her to sit back down. "What has happened, Lady Iverson?"

Sarah glanced from her to her husband, then unfolded the cloak. The sight of the jumble of damaged artifacts gave her another spasm of sadness, and she had to press her hand to her stomach to catch her breath again. "I found—this tonight."

Mrs. Hamilton gasped, and her fingers flew to her lips.

Mr. Hamilton leaned over to examine the items, frowning. He reached out to touch a chess piece that lay in two halves. "These are the objects from the village."

"I had a strange feeling that I needed to go to the village this evening," Sarah said. "The door to the stable was open, and when I went to see what was amiss, I found—well, these. I gathered what I could, but there was so much left. We will have to investigate further in the daylight." She dreaded that very much. The damage had been great enough by the light of the lantern. How much worse would it be in the harsh sun?

"I fear I do not understand," Mr. Hamilton said slowly. "Were they disturbed by a wind?"

Mrs. Hamilton lowered her hand to say, "There was no wind tonight, Neville."

"No," Sarah agreed. "And it would have taken a gale force to cause this damage. This was deliberate. Someone went to the stable and viciously destroyed what we have worked so hard for."

Neville's face blanched beneath his sunburn, and he sat down heavily on a nearby footstool. "Who would do such a thing?"

Who, indeed? "I do not know," Sarah answered. "I was hoping you might have some suggestion. Who could hate us?" She prayed he might have an idea, someone she had not yet thought of.

Mr. Hamilton shrugged, still looking completely bewildered. "We have done nothing to hurt or insult anyone here with our work."

Mrs. Hamilton, who had been sobbing quietly into the fringes of her shawl, glanced up at them. "What about that man who was threatened by Lord Ransome? Could he not have come seeking revenge?"

For the first time since Sarah could remember, Mr. Hamilton looked at his wife with something like gratitude and a grudging respect. "Yes," he said. "Emmeline and I were not there, of course, but we did hear that the man left in a very angry mood. This vandalism reeks of rage, and an ignorant mind."

Sarah nodded in relief. Of course, that made perfect sense. How could she have suspected Lord Ransome for a second, when there was a more convenient culprit at hand? "You are probably right."

"I will go find the man tomorrow, and confront him with this," Mr. Hamilton said angrily. "He will not be allowed to get away with this horrible crime."

His wife gave him a startled glance. "You cannot go there alone, Neville!"

"I will take some of the workers," he said.

"And I will go with you," said Sarah.

"Oh, no! You should not subject yourself to that, Lady Iverson," Mr. Hamilton exclaimed.

Sarah shook her head. "It is my village. I want to hear what this man has to say."

Mr. Hamilton looked away from her, down to the artifacts. A long silence fell in the room as they all grew lost in their own thoughts, broken only when Mrs. Hamilton reached out to touch the drinking horn.

"Since this has happened," she said, "surely there is no need for us to remain here? Lord Ransome wishes us to leave, and there is really no more work for us to do here. We should return to Bath, and you can decide there what is best to do next, Neville."

Her voice was quiet, but stretched taut with some tension or eagerness. Sarah glanced over at her, and saw that Mrs. Hamilton looked suitably subdued and sad, but her pale blue eyes were eager.

Sarah had known that Mrs. Hamilton missed her city, but she had not realized until now just how unhappy she was. Even in the midst of her own confusion and pain, she felt sorry for her.

Even more so when Mr. Hamilton said brusquely, "Don't be silly, Emmeline. Of course, we will stay here. We have more to do than ever."

Mrs. Hamilton's lips thinned, and she turned away from her husband.

Mr. Hamilton tore his attention away from the artifacts, and said, "If you will wait for me to dress properly, Lady Iverson, I will escort you back to the hunting box. You must be exhausted after your ordeal."

"Thank you, Mr. Hamilton." Sarah watched him leave the room, then turned to Mrs. Hamilton. She ran the fringes of her shawl between her fingers, staring off at something in the distance that only she could see.

"I am sorry you have been unhappy here," Sarah said. "If I had known, I would have—" Her words broke off, for she did not know *what* she would have done.

Mrs. Hamilton turned her gaze back to Sarah, and gave her a small smile. "You would have sent Neville away, perhaps? It would have done no good. This work is his life—his whole life. I thought when we married that things would have been different, that we would have a different sort of life."

"I am sorry," Sarah said again, helpless.

Mrs. Hamilton shrugged. "Everything will work out as it must, Lady Iverson. I am sure of it."

"Of course." Sarah hugged her bundle against her, feeling suddenly so, so cold.

Chapter Sixteen

"Open the door, man! We know you are in there."

Sarah stood behind Mr. Hamilton as he pounded on the farmer's door. It had taken them all morning to find out the man's identity and discover where he lived, and she was tired and dizzy from the effort and the sleepless night she had passed. Now that they were here, she dreaded what they might find, what the man might tell them. What if he said it *was* Lord Ransome who did it?

Mr. Hamilton stepped back from the door, and turned to one of the workers who had come with them. "Break the door down," he ordered.

The man looked uncertain. "Sir, I'm not sure . . ."

Mr. Hamilton shook his head impatiently. "This man may have viciously destroyed ancient objects. I want to discover the truth of this. Now, break it down!"

Still uncertain, the worker picked up a chunk of firewood and used it to batter at the door until it swung open on its hinges. Mr. Hamilton pushed it aside, and strode into the dim house.

Sarah followed slowly, her head aching from the noise and violence. She clutched at her reticule, which held a small pistol in its velvet depths. It was an old one that had belonged to John, and had not been fired in years, but it gave her a measure of comfort to have it.

Mr. Hamilton turned into a room ahead of her, and gave a strangled cry. Sarah came up behind him, and reached out to clutch his arm at the sight that greeted her.

The farmer, so large and blustering when he pushed Mary Ann down in the dirt, lay in the middle of the floor, staring up at the ceiling with sightless eyes. His face was wax white, frozen in a rictus of horror. The wooden handle of a plain kitchen knife stood straight up in the center of his chest. A sharp, nasty smell assaulted her nostrils.

Sarah felt a sour pang of nausea in the back of her throat. She choked on it, on the horror of the vision before her. She had seen deceased bodies before, of course, but never a *murdered* one. And somehow the fact that this man had been quite despicable the one time she had met him did not make it any more palatable.

Her gaze fell to her reticule, to her own weapon, and she shuddered.

Mr. Hamilton, his own face white with shock, took her arm and turned her out of the room, away from the body. "Come outdoors, Lady Iverson. This is no place for a lady."

Sarah leaned gratefully on his arm. "It is no place for a human being," she murmured. "Who did this? The same person who destroyed our artifacts?"

He helped her to climb up into the waiting carriage. "I do not know," he said, his own voice faint. "But we *will* discover who is doing these terrible things." He turned away to one of the workers and called, "Fetch the magistrate! Tell him to come here at once."

"Of course, sir," the man said, seizing the reins of his horse.

Mr. Hamilton looked back to Sarah. "You should go home, Lady Iverson. Your sister will be worrying."

Sarah longed for home, for a comforting swallow of brandy and the solace of her own fireside. But she knew that she had to do her duty. "Will the magistrate not want to speak to me about—about what we have found here?"

"If he does, he can just as easily speak to you at your home. I see no reason why he should involve a lady in this matter, though. It will be safer for you at home."

Safer? She stared at him in mounting horror. Did he

think there was some rampaging maniac on the loose, out to kill everyone in the neighborhood? "Do you think that whoever did this will try it again someplace else?"

He gave her a bracing smile. "Of course not. I would just feel more secure if I knew that you and your sister and my wife were safe. Perhaps you would do something for me, Lady Iverson?"

"Of course, Mr. Hamilton."

"Will you look in on Mrs. Hamilton at the inn? Just tell her that I will be back this evening, and that she is not to venture out until then." He looked away, back to the ramshackle farmhouse. "Emmeline can be rather— headstrong at times."

Or spoiled, Sarah thought. She did not voice this aloud, though. She just nodded, and said, "Yes, certainly. I would be glad to look in on Mrs. Hamilton."

"Thank you, Lady Iverson. That is very kind of you."

Sarah nodded, and sat back against the leather cushions as Mr. Hamilton shut the door and the carriage jolted into motion.

She closed her eyes, and wished for once that she was the sort of female who carried hartshorn with her. She could certainly use a whiff of it now.

The Hamiltons had convinced her that it was the irate farmer who had destroyed her artifacts, in a petty act of vengeance for his humiliation at the hands of Lord Ransome. She had been sure it had been him—someone she did not know, someone whose rage was relatively impersonal and therefore not so difficult to understand. The thought that now it was probably someone she knew made her feel sick all over again.

Who could it be? Who could it be?

She pressed her gloved fingers to her temples, trying to force out the images of her shattered objects, the farmer's dead body. She'd faced small jealousies and pettiness before in her life, but never true hatred. It made her feel ill and frightened to be face-to-face with it now— and she disliked feeling frightened.

She shook her head. She would *not* feel frightened

now; she could not afford to. There was too much at stake. She had to find out what was happening, what was causing her world to spin out of control, and put an end to it. Before something even more dreadful, such as someone hurting her sister, could happen.

Sarah lowered the carriage window and leaned out. "Coachman!" she called. "Take me to Ransome Hall, please."

Sarah stood in the drive of Ransome Hall, staring up at the house. It looked quiet and peaceful in the late morning light. It looked as if nothing evil or ugly could ever touch its hallowed stones.

What am I doing here? she thought. She did not know. She only knew that she had to see Lord Ransome, to talk to him, to watch his face as she told him all that had happened.

She did not, *could* not, think that he had anything to do with this horrid business. No man she had ever come to care about, as she had Lord Ransome, could possibly do such things!

Yes, she admitted to herself finally. She *did* care about Lord Ransome, more than was sensible. She could not help it, despite everything that had happened between them, despite the fact that he did not understand the true importance of her work. His kindness, his good nature, the fact that he was concerned about those less fortunate than himself, had touched her deeply, and would not be erased.

No man who had all those things could possibly harbor such cruelty in his heart. Could he?

Sarah wished that instead of studying ancient history all the time she had spent some effort in studying human nature. Perhaps then she would not be so confused, so bewildered.

She did not know what she would say to him when she saw him, but she knew that she could not turn back now. She climbed the front steps, and reached up to lift the polished door knocker and let it drop.

Only a moment had passed when the door opened, and Makepeace, the butler, stood there. She could not run away now.

There was a quick flash of surprise in Makepeace's eyes, but he was too well-trained to let it stay. It was swiftly covered in bland inquiry. "Lady Iverson," he said. "How pleasant to see you this morning." He stepped aside to let her into the house.

"I must see Lord Ransome at once," she said. "It is most urgent."

Makepeace hesitated. "His lordship is in the library, my lady. I will see if—"

"I am sorry, Makepeace, but there is no time for politeness." Sarah turned on her heel, and walked as quickly as she could down the corridor to the library, Makepeace sputtering behind her. There would be gossip about this, she was sure, but somehow she could not care. She just wanted to see him. To watch his face as she told him about what had happened.

She knocked briefly at the library door, and pushed it open before she could be summoned.

He stood behind his desk, a sheaf of papers in his hand. He obviously had not expected company, for he wore no coat and his cravat was loosened. His shirt-sleeves were pushed back, revealing strong, corded forearms, lightly dusted with pale brown hair. His expression, blankly polite when he looked up to see who had interrupted his work, turned startled when he saw that it was she who stood there.

"Lady Iverson," he said, slowly putting the papers he held back down on his desk. "Is something amiss?"

Sarah felt frozen, her hand still on the doorknob. For one instant, she could scarcely remember what she was there for. The seriousness of her mission clouded at the actual sight of him, at being truly in his presence. Attraction, suspicion, exhaustion, it all tangled up in her mind, confusing her, disorienting her. She closed her eyes, swaying dizzily. In the darkness, she saw him as he had been in her dreams—a bold Viking.

She felt a touch on her arm, and opened her eyes to find him next to her. His hand was warm through the sleeve of her spencer; his eyes were kind, deeply concerned.

Could this man have possibly done those terrible things? Sarah, once so sure of all the things in her life, now could be sure of nothing.

"I am sorry, my lord," she heard Makepeace say behind her, his voice distinctly breathless after chasing her down the corridor. She took the opportunity of the distraction to move away from Lord Ransome.

"I wanted to properly announce Lady Iverson," the butler went on.

"It is quite all right, Makepeace," Lord Ransome said. Even though Sarah had moved a few steps across the room, she could feel him watching her. "You may leave us now."

"Of course, my lord."

Sarah listened to the butler's footsteps echo away, and only when she heard the door click shut did she turn around.

Lord Ransome leaned back against the wood of the door, his arms crossed over his chest. He looked most perplexed. "Would you care for some—tea, perhaps?" he said finally.

For one moment, she longed desperately to go to him and lay her head on his shoulder, feel his strong arms about her, keeping her safe. She felt like she had been alone, had been the strong one, for so long, and his shoulder looked sturdy enough to hold all her burdens.

But the memory of her artifacts shattered on the stable floor, the farmer with the knife in his chest, held her where she was.

"I do not need tea," she said.

"You look as if you need something a great deal stronger," he answered. He pushed away from the door and crossed the room to pour her a measure of brandy from the decanter on the desk. When he came back to press the glass into her hand, he said, "What is amiss? Are you ill?"

"No." Sarah stared down into the amber depths of the liquid. Its heady fragrance beckoned her to its warm comfort, and she swallowed it, gasping a bit at the bite at the back of her throat. It helped to steady her, to ground her in the moment.

It also made her dizzy, though. She sat down unsteadily on a nearby settee.

Lord Ransome followed her, kneeling at her side. He took the glass from her hand, and put it down on the carpet. "Then is your sister ill? Please, Lady Iverson, I want to help if I can. There must be a reason you have come here today."

"Yes, there is." Sarah looked at him closely, trying to judge his expression as she talked. "Some terrible things have happened. Last night, someone broke into the stable and vandalized our artifacts."

He looked deeply shocked. His lips parted, but no sound emerged. In the silence, he reached out to touch her arm. Finally, he said, "You were not there when it happened? You were not hurt?"

"No, no. I could not sleep, so I went to check on some of my work, and found the—the destruction." She choked on the remembrance, and wished for more of that brandy. She was grateful at the steady support of his hand.

He *had* to be innocent. Not even Kean himself could be such a fine actor as to appear so shocked. Sarah felt a rush of relief, a warm wave that almost drowned out her terrified doubts.

"I was able to salvage many of the objects," she said. "But some were lost beyond repair. It was a truly vicious act."

A muscle ticked in his jaw, and his mouth tightened. His shock turned to anger, an anger as deep as Sarah's own had been in the stable last night. "Do you know who did this?"

She shook her head. "I could not say. I did have my suspicions." She bit her lip. One of her suspects had been *him*. She could scarcely tell him that.

One of the others had been the dead farmer.

"Who?" he said shortly.

Sarah looked down at her lap, at their hands joined together there. "The vadalism was not the only occurrence, I fear. Do you recall the dreadful man who tried to drown Mary Ann's kittens?"

He gave a short, humorless laugh. "How could I ever forget?" His hand tightened on hers. "Was it that bast— man who did this?"

"I had thought so, at first," she admitted. "But then this morning, when Mr. Hamilton and I went to confront him, we found him . . ." She could not say it. Again, her voice failed her, and she wished for the brandy. For something to make her forget that vision. "Dead. He was dead."

"Dead?"

"Murdered. Someone had stabbed him," she said, all in a rush, to get the words out and send them away.

Lord Ransome rose up from his knees and sat beside her on the settee. He said no words; he just put his arms around her and drew her close.

He *was* strong, and warm, and to be close to him felt like the safe haven Sarah had imagined it would be. She gave in to her longings, and rested her head against his linen-covered chest. She felt his heartbeat, strong and steady.

"You should never have had to see such a thing," he said gently.

Sarah smiled weakly. "I am hardly a sheltered young miss. I have seen bodies before."

"But not, I would wager, one that has been cruelly murdered," he answered, his arms tightening around her. "I should have been there, to help you, to protect you."

Sarah drew back a bit to look up at him. "You could not have known."

"I *should* have known." He framed her face in his hands, looking down into her eyes with a strange, intent glow in his sky-colored eyes. "Lady Iverson—Sarah. This will sound lunatic, but I feel some—connection with you that I have never felt before with anyone. I have tried to deny it, to explain it away, but I cannot. God knows, I would go back onto the most hellish battlefield I have ever known before I would see you have any more pain."

Sarah stared at him, unable to breathe, unable to think, unable to do anything but *feel*. Could this be Lord Ransome, speaking to her so passionately? She could scarce believe it. How could he feel the same way she had, that something very odd connected them, something unexplainable but quite undeniable?

She had felt caught in a dreamworld ever since she opened the stable door last night. Now that nightmare shifted into something sweet, but just as unreal.

She reached up and covered his hand with hers. She had no words, and let her actions be her voice. She rose up, and captured his lips with hers.

They were warm and surprisingly soft, parting beneath hers. How she had missed this intimacy in her life, longed for it from Miles! She had not even known how much until this moment.

His clean, masculine scent enveloped her. She wrapped her arms about his neck, and rose up onto her toes to be closer to him, ever closer. He groaned deep in his throat, a sound that moved through her like a warm bolt of lightning, and drew her against him. They fell back onto the settee in a tangle of limbs and skirts, their kiss deepening, hands reaching desperately, hungrily.

After an eternity—or was it only a moment?—they drifted apart, slowly, sweetly. Sarah rested against his shoulder with a sigh, her senses still humming and alive. Never had she known a kiss like that before!

Miles stroked her tumbled hair back from her temples. "Can you doubt how I feel?"

"No." No more than she could doubt her own feelings. For one more instant, she rested in the golden emotions, until she could hold the outside world at bay no longer. There was still great evil lurking somewhere in her life, waiting for her.

It was not a time for undiluted basking in romance.

She had far too much to worry about to try to puzzle out where their places could be in each other's lives.

But, for this one moment, it felt so delicious to not be alone any longer.

She sat up, feeling suddenly cold at the loss of his closeness. Slowly, she came back into herself. She straightened her hair and clothes in a rather bewildered haze, almost unable to believe that she was the same person who had given in to a passionate impulse only seconds before.

A true wanton, that was what she was. She giggled at the thought.

Miles sat up beside her, looking as dazed as she felt. His hair was adorably tousled, and Sarah reached up to tidy it.

He smiled at her, catching her hand in his and lifting it to his lips for a quick kiss. "We must speak of this later, Sarah."

"Must we?" she said, teasing him for his oh-so-serious tone.

"You know we do. But first, we have to find who has been doing these terrible things."

A little more of the glow faded at the reminder of the awful scenes that had brought her to Ransome Hall today. "You mean *I* must. These are my difficulties. It could cause quite the scandal if Lord Ransome was thought to be involved in a *murder*."

He caught her shoulders, turning her back to him. "*We* must. And I will hear no arguments."

She smiled at him. "I am not arguing."

"Very good. Then you should go home to your sister, while I look into some things. I will call on you later this afternoon."

He sounded quite the officer-in-charge. She almost laughed, but then decided that was not perhaps the most appropriate reaction. And it felt nice to know she did not have to be alone in this confusion any longer. "I do want to be certain that Mary Ann is all right, and that she has obeyed my orders to stay at home today."

He nodded, still serious and distracted, as if plotting out a battle strategy. "Did you come in your carriage? Shall I send some of the footmen to escort you back to the hunting box?"

"I came in the Hamiltons' carriage." She gave him a teasing glance. "Did you think I was driving my phaeton all over the countryside?"

He kissed her forehead, and gave a wry laugh. "With you, one never knows. I will send two of the footmen with you, anyway."

Sarah nodded, and stood up to cross the room and peer into a small mirror that hung on the wall. Her hair was a tousled mess of curls, quite beyond redemption, even as she tried to push it back into its pins. Reflected behind her, she saw Miles take his coat from the back of the chair where it hung and shrug his arms into it.

For a second, it was as if she stood before the polished bronze Viking mirror again. His coat and cravat were gone, replaced by tunic and leather leggings.

She blinked, and the vision vanished.

"You will send a message to me later, will you not, and tell me what you discover? If you cannot make it to the hunting box," she added. Her voice shook, even to her own ears.

"Of course." He came to her, and laid his warm hands on her shoulders. His lips pressed to her temple, all too briefly. "Don't be frightened, my dear. I am certain we will find whoever is behind these terrible acts, and he will be stopped."

Sarah covered one of his hands with hers. "I am not frightened." And truly, she was not. How could she be, with the memory of their kiss glowing in her mind?

Only later, when she was alone in the carriage going home, did she think that perhaps she *should* be frightened. After all, someone—perhaps someone she knew—had destroyed her artifacts and committed a murder. She had been so busy feeling like a giddy schoolgirl over a kiss that she had almost forgotten all that.

She sank back against the cushions with a little frown.

That had been foolish of her, she admitted to herself, and she would not do it again. It was imperative that they find the villain and put a stop to his activities—before anyone else could be harmed.

After he was caught, well, that was a different story. She certainly would not mind another of those kisses then.

But did kisses, no matter how passionate, mean that Lord Ransome—Miles—would allow her to continue her work at the village? In all the confusion, she had misplaced that point.

And that was not something she could afford to forget at all.

Miles watched Sarah's carriage roll away down the drive. He had promised her that he would go and do his best to seek out the villain who had done this, but all he really wanted to do was make certain *she* was safe. Sending her away, even with the escort of two armed footmen, was the most difficult thing he had ever done.

The sight of her pale, frightened face as she told him of the destroyed objects, the murdered man, had aroused such a storm of fury in him! That anyone could hurt her, or frighten her, was unendurable, unforgivable. Every primitive instinct in him, buried for so long under the polite world, screamed out for revenge, for blood.

Not even in Spain had he felt this way. There, battle had been heated but strangely impersonal. Now he wanted to murder someone with his bare hands.

It was frightening—and strangely exhilarating. He felt a great rush of strength, and he knew that he would not rest until he had found his man.

He watched Sarah's carriage until it was lost to sight, then turned and went back into the house, to the library. The first sight that greeted him there was the settee where they had kissed so sweetly, so passionately.

Where he had never wanted to let her go until he made her his completely.

He looked away from the settee. He could not think

of that now. It would distract him from his mission, from what he must accomplish.

He could not even think of what might happen after.

Instead, he crossed over to his desk, opened one of the drawers, and took out a carved and inlaid box. Inside, resting on a bed of blue velvet, was a pair of gleaming pistols.

After, he and Sarah would have to face their differences and their attraction. But now he had a battle to face.

Chapter Seventeen

"Sarah!" Mary Ann ran out of the hunting box before Sarah could even step down from the carriage. The kittens chased after her, batting at her skirt hem with their paws. "Where have you been? What is happening? I received a note from Mr. Hamilton saying I should stay at home today, but there was no explanation." Her glance flickered over to the footmen, both of whom had short swords, and one with a rifle over his saddle. "Something terrible has happened."

Sarah took her arm and turned her back to the house, leading her along the walkway she had just run down. "Come inside, dear, and I will tell you all about it. I am sorry I was gone so long; I went to Ransome Hall, then to the inn to see Mrs. Hamilton for a moment."

Mary Ann's brow creased. "Is there something wrong with Lord Ransome? Or Mrs. Hamilton?"

Sarah remembered the strange call she had just paid on Mrs. Hamilton, dazed from her time with Miles, and was not sure what to say. Mrs. Hamilton had not looked well at all, and had still been clad in her dressing gown when it was past time for luncheon. She had not appeared to understand what Sarah was saying to her. But Sarah just explained the situation as completely as she could (which was not very), and sent her back to her bed with a tisane.

She longed for her own bed now, after all the shocks of the day. That would have to wait, though; right now, she had to talk to Mary Ann. Once settled in the drawing room, she explained the situation yet again. If she had to say the words "artifacts destroyed" and "that man killed" again, she would surely scream.

Mary Ann shook her head, her face bewildered. "How could all this be? What is happening here, Sarah?"

"I am not sure. But you are quite safe, my dear, I assure you. Lord Ransome, Mr. Hamilton, and myself are doing all we can to find out who has done this." Sarah tried to assure herself as much as she did Mary Ann. "But you promise me you will only go about with me, and that you will stay safely here the rest of the time."

"I am not completely bacon brained, Sarah!" Mary Ann protested. "I have no desire to be killed. I only wish I could be of some assistance."

"You are of assistance to me just by being here. I would so hate to be all alone right now." Sarah hugged her sister close, deeply grateful that Mary Ann was here, safe and whole. "Come, now, it is late, and I have not yet eaten. Let's find something to eat, and then perhaps you could help me sort out the remaining artifacts and start to relabel them."

Mary Ann nodded eagerly. "Oh, yes! I've been learning so much lately that I am sure I could do that. Tell me about the objects you found, Sarah. Is my drinking horn among them?"

Sarah nodded, and led the way toward the kitchen, glad to think and speak of something positive. All of their work was not lost, and relabeling would occupy her mind far more agreeably than the doubts and fears of the morning had.

As for the future—well, she would have to face that soon enough. At this moment, she had work to do, and that would be enough.

"What have you discovered?" Miles asked Mr. Hamilton, whom he had finally found at the home of the magistrate, Sir Walter Farnham, in Upper Hawton. They walked along the main street now, in the direction of where their horses were being watched.

Miles thought the other man looked tired and strained, and seemed years older in only one morning. His smirks and rudeness were vanished. Miles couldn't help but feel a bit sorry for him.

"Sir Walter says that farmer—whose name, by the way, was Mr. White—was feuding with a neighbor of his over a property boundary. In fact, Mr. White was apparently feuding with a great many people over a great many things. Sir Walter says he is not at all surprised that he came to a bad end. I do not think he will exert himself too greatly to find the culprit." Mr. Hamilton laughed dryly. "So I do not imagine that Sir Walter will look too closely at your own unfortunate encounter with the man, Lord Ransome."

"That is not what I was concerned about." Miles stopped on the walkway, and turned to face Mr. Hamilton. "What does Sir Walter say of the vandalism of Lady Iverson's artifacts?"

Mr. Hamilton's chuckles died away, leaving him sad and pale again. It was obvious what he considered the true crime; what Miles was ashamed to admit he himself was more concerned about: the vicious destruction of the Viking items.

"I would not say they were exclusively Lady Iverson's artifacts," Mr. Hamilton answered. "But Sir Walter believes it was the work of Mr. White, who then coincidentally, and deservedly, met his own end. Sir Walter knew of Mr. White's—meeting with you, and judges the vandalism to be an act of revenge."

"And what do you think? Do you believe this to be the case?"

Mr. Hamilton shrugged. "I cannot imagine who else it could be."

"It does not strike you as being a great coincidence, that this Mr. White would destroy valuable antiquities, and then go home to immediately be murdered?"

"Are you saying that you do *not* believe that is what happened, Lord Ransome?"

Miles was not sure what he thought. This whole situation was becoming ugly beyond belief, and he just wanted to save Sarah from any more suffering.

He wanted nothing but happiness and light to fill all her days. And he would do anything, find any villain, to do that.

"Was there not some trouble before?" he asked. "A cave-in of the cellar at the leather-worker's shop? Some missing tools?"

"Those were simply accidents!"

"Were they, indeed?"

"Of course. We did not even know of this Mr. White then—no one at our site ever saw him before the day he attacked Miss Bellweather. *I* never saw him until I discovered his dead body. Why would he have caused those mishaps weeks ago?"

"What if it was not Mr. White?"

Mr. Hamilton shook his head. "Who else could it have been?"

"That is what I am trying to discover." Miles turned back around, and continued along the street to reclaim his horse from the urchin who held the reins. He swung up into the saddle and looked down at Mr. Hamilton, who merely stood still beside his own horse, staring blankly off as if trying to comprehend the whole situation. "Are you going to come with me, Mr. Hamilton?"

The man blinked up at him. "Where are you going, Lord Ransome?"

"I am going to speak with those neighbors Mr. White was feuding with. After that . . ." After that—Miles did not know. "I will see what I find."

"I must look in on my wife. I asked Lady Iverson to give her a message earlier, but she has been alone all day, and she is not well." Mr. Hamilton grasped the reins of his horse. "Then I will be happy to lend any assistance I can."

Miles wasn't sure what use Mr. Hamilton could really be, but he just nodded, and said, "I will call on you later, then."

He turned his horse away, and galloped out of the village on his errand. A fool's errand, he feared, but he had to do something, *anything*. No man could possibly sit idly by while the woman he cared about, the woman he loved, was in trouble.

Miles almost fell off his horse in shock at his own thoughts.

Love? He loved Sarah?

Miles reined his horse in beneath a tree and just sat there for a moment, letting the newness of his emotions settle on his mind. Yes, he confessed to himself. He did love her. Their kiss had proved that to him, beyond a doubt. Their surprising kiss that had seemingly come from nowhere to offer passion and comfort in the midst of ugliness. The feeling of her in his arms, of her lips beneath his, had been sweeter than anything he had ever known, ever dreamed of.

The way she laughed and smiled, the serious frown on her face as she concentrated on her work; he could watch her in all her moods, all her ways, and never tire of it. Of *her*. It was all unbearably precious to him.

When he was in Spain, when things were difficult and he was far from certain about the future, he would sit under the stars in the hot, dry night and try to envision a different life in England. A life where he would have a home and a family, a wife who was gentle and soft, who smelled of roses and had a musical laugh.

Those thoughts had been precious, especially when he feared that none of them would ever have the chance to come true. But they had been dreams; the reality of Sarah, of his unique Sarah, was more fine than any dream could ever be.

Even in the middle of this terrible mess they found themselves in, the realization of his love made him smile, made him laugh aloud. Never would he have thought to be given such a glorious gift!

He loved her. *He loved her!* If there had been anyone near, he would have shouted the news at them. The only living creature near to him, though, was a placid cow, who chewed at a mouthful of grass and watched him calmly.

"I am in love with Sarah Iverson," he told the cow.

The creature just turned around and loped back across its meadow.

Miles tugged at his horse's reins and continued down the lane at a slower pace. Yes, he loved her; but did *she* love *him*?

The ardor of her kiss would certainly suggest so. She had held him so tightly, had melted into him with soft sighs.

But their situation was far from mundane. They were surrounded by danger, by a palpable malevolence, and she may have just been reaching out for his comfort. He himself had done such, with Spanish widows and pretty courtesans. Sometimes a person needed the safety, the reality of another person. Sarah had been so unhappy with him before, when he told her of his new plans for the land her village sat on. Perhaps, once this was all past, she would be angry with him again.

He hoped that was not true. He wanted, desperately wanted, her to feel tenderness and perhaps even love for him. If she did, he could never ask for a greater gift.

Only time would tell.

"Emmeline?" Neville Hamilton knocked at his wife's chamber door. It was silent behind the thin wood, but surely it was far too early in the day for her to be asleep. It was scarcely teatime.

Then again, he was never sure what to expect from her anymore.

He knew that she had not been happy for a long time, maybe not since their wedding day. He had his own unhappiness, though, his own disillusionment. He had his work. That did not leave a great deal of time for a wife who was in so many ways a stranger to him.

A stranger whose laugher and gaiety, the qualities that had once drawn him to her, had been growing ever more desperate of late.

She was not what he had sought in a wife at all. She could not help him in his work, could not even understand him. Just as he did not understand her.

That thought renewed all his old anger at the unfairness of fortune, and gave strength to his knock at her door. "Emmeline! I know that you have not gone out. The innkeeper says they have not seen you downstairs all day. Now, let me in, at once!"

A moment passed. Then there was a faint shuffling noise, and the grate of a key being turned in the lock. The door swung open, and Emmeline stood there.

She was still clad in her dressing gown, her hair falling over her shoulders in a tangled tumble, her eyes red rimmed from sleep. Or tears?

"What do you want, Neville?" she asked dully.

Despite his already low expectations, Neville was shocked. Emmeline always slept late, but when she awoke, she attended her toilette and dressed carefully, as if still in Bath. Their quarrel over supper last night had not been an unusual one—Neville could not even recall what it had been about. It was certainly not something to cause *this*.

He pushed past her into the chamber, and saw the unmade bed, the untouched luncheon tray, and a glass of some milky liquid on the bedside table. He turned back to face her, watching as she closed the door and sat down on the nearest chair, moving as if she was too tired to stand any longer.

"Are you ill?" he asked.

"I am just tired," she said. "And you needn't pretend you care."

"Of course, I care. You are my wife."

She laughed, and waved her hand in a listless, dismissive gesture. "And you are my husband. Yet where were you this morning, when, from what I hear, there was a murderer abroad? You were chasing about the countryside, leaving me here alone and unprotected."

Neville raked his hands through his hair in a burst of impatience. "Emmeline! You were hardly unprotected in an inn full of people. I was attempting to find out who has done this, so that we will all be safe again."

"This would never have happened to us at home in

Bath! We are always safe there." She burst into great, gulping sobs, and buried her face in her hands. "I hate it here! I hate everything about it. And then for you to leave me alone . . ."

Neville awkwardly put his arm around her and patted her shoulder. He had never been good with weeping females. "Emmeline, please. Did Lady Iverson not bring my message to you?"

Emmeline nodded, but still cried. "She does not understand how I feel, either. She is an unnatural female, who would rather dig about in the dirt than marry and go out in proper society. If I had the things that she has, a title and money of my own, I would never waste them as she does."

Neville feared that this sort of vituperative outburst could go on for hours, and he remembered his pledge to assist Lord Ransome. He tightened his arm around her, and said, "Come, my dear. Let me help you back to the bed. You are obviously not well."

She went with him willingly enough, letting him tuck the bedclothes around her, but she said, "You are just going to leave me again. To go to Lady Iverson and her ridiculous sister."

"I told Lord Ransome I would join him in the search for the culprit," he said. "I *must* go again, but only for a brief while."

Emmeline sniffled, and looked up with a glimmer of interest. "Lord Ransome?"

"Yes."

"Can I not go with you?" she asked plaintively. "If I could just leave these rooms for a while . . ."

Neville would never have allowed his wife to ride about the countryside with him, even under the best of circumstances. It was out of the question now, especially in light of her current state of mind. But he dared not completely refuse her, for fear she would take to weeping again. "You must rest right now Emmeline. But perhaps this evening I could take you to visit Lady Iverson for a while."

Emmeline nodded weakly, and laid her head back down on the pillow, closing her eyes. Her golden lashes lay in pale relief against the purple shadows lurking there.

Neville stared down at her, remembering Lord Ransome's suspicions that it had not been the brutish farmer who destroyed the Viking artifacts. Obviously, though, it had to have been someone who was desperate and angry about something, something to do with the village or the people who worked there.

Desperate—and angry.

Chapter Eighteen

"How does this look, Sarah?" Mary Ann asked.

"Hm?" Sarah glanced up, startled by the sound of her sister's voice. She had been looking at a pottery storage jar for several minutes, but, in truth, her thoughts had not been on it. She forgot all about her task, all that had happened that day, and thought of only one thing—her kiss with Miles.

Over and over, her mind saw how he looked in his library, his guinea-gold hair tousled, his eyes heavy and intent. Her hands remembered his warmth, the feel of his strong shoulders. Her lips wanted to feel his beneath them again.

Her cheeks grew warm just with the memory, and she pressed her hand to her face. Never would she have thought that she could become a lust-starved widow, but apparently that was what had happened! Nothing, not even the seriousness of their situation, could turn her from that kiss.

She had even forgotten that she was not alone in the drawing room. Mary Ann sat on the floor, next to an old blanket spread out and covered with objects. When Sarah turned to look at her, she saw that her sister had a book open on her lap and held an ivory figure of a warrior in one hand. With her other hand, she gave him a last wipe with a rag.

"I am sorry, Mary Ann. Did you say something?" Sarah asked.

"I asked if this looks all right. I'm afraid he lost part of his spear, but other than that he seems in fine shape. I finished cleaning this bowl, too." She polished at the little ivory face. "They are ready to be labeled. Have you finished with that jar?"

"Jar?" Sarah stared dumbly at the piece of pottery before her. "Oh. No. Not yet."

"Poor Sarah. You look so tired."

"I *am* tired, I fear."

"Why do you not retire?" Mary Ann rose stiffly to her feet, and crossed the room to pull the draperies back from the window. "See, it is full dark outside. You should be in bed."

Sarah was startled that it had grown so very late. When she first arrived back at the hunting box, time had seemed to pass very slowly as she waited impatiently for news. Then she had become engrossed in her work, and in lustful, ridiculous daydreams, and it had slipped away from her.

Darkness had fallen—and she had not yet had any news from Miles.

"No," she said. "I cannot retire yet."

"Not until you hear something. I know. I, too, am anxious." Mary Ann leaned against the window frame, her smooth dark hair limned in moonlight. "Do you suppose Mr. O'Riley is searching with Lord Ransome?"

Sarah did not miss the wistful note in her sister's voice, and knew that it boded ill for a new infatuation. She was too tired, though, and too nervous to speak to her about it now. When everything was resolved, she and Mary Ann would have to have yet another talk about the differences between Minerva Press novels and real life.

For now, all she said was, "I would suppose so. As is Mr. Hamilton."

Mary Ann wrinkled her nose. "Mr. Hamilton is probably at the inn, nursing his ninny of a wife."

"Mary Ann, that is unkind," Sarah protested. "She has had a very unhappy time adjusting to her marriage."

"Is marriage always such an unhappy adjustment?"

Mary Ann asked, her tone full of curiosity. "I have often wondered. Mother just purses up her lips, and says a wife must always do her duty. She is of no help at all."

Sarah imagined that marriage to Miles would not be an onerous adjustment at all. Not that she could say that to Mary Ann, of course. "It is of no surprise that Mother is no help to you. She was not to me, either. After all of this is settled, you and I will have a long conversation, I promise."

Mary Ann sighed. "It is always 'after.'" She straightened up suddenly, peering out the window. "I think someone is coming!"

Sarah's heart seemed to skip a beat, then pattered quickly, too quickly, in anticipation. She carefully put down the jar, and rose from her chair. Could he be here, finally? "Who is it?"

"I cannot tell. It's too dark. A man on horseback."

Sarah went to stand by her sister at the window. There was indeed a man on horseback just turning into their garden from the lane. He was tall and straight backed, but the moonlight caught no gleam of golden hair. He dismounted and strode to the front door. The knock echoed through the house, and they could hear Rose scurrying to answer it.

Mary Ann suddenly clutched at Sarah's arm. "What if it is not someone we know? What if it is the murderer, come to finish his revenge?"

Sarah thought she sounded too deliciously horrified, and gave her a stern look. "Mary Ann. Would a murderer knock at the front door?"

"I do not know *what* a murderer would do, having never met one," Mary Ann answered.

"I am sure it must be Lord Ransome, or one of his men. Hopefully, he will have some news for us." Sarah had just reached up to be sure her hair was tidy when Rose opened the drawing room door.

"Mr. O'Riley, Lady Iverson," the maid announced.

It was not Miles. Sarah's hand fell from her hair.

Mary Ann stepped away from the window, her eyes

shining eagerly. She bounced up on her toes as Mr. O'Riley came into the room, stooping his tall figure a bit in their low doorway.

He looked very serious, no hint of a smile. Why should that be? Sarah wondered, grasping the back of a chair in a sudden wave of dizziness. "What news?" she asked. "Has something—something not pleasant occurred?"

"Oh, no," Mr. O'Riley said quickly. "I did not mean to frighten you, Lady Iverson. Lord Ransome has asked me to stay with you for a time while he finishes some business. He will be here later this evening."

"Oh, I see." Still dizzy, Sarah sat down on the chair, and reached out to take Mary Ann's hand and stop her fidgeting. "Mary Ann, dear, could you go and ask for some refreshments to be brought in?"

"Of course," Mary Ann said. "I will see if there are some of those lemon cakes left that you like so much. You ate almost nothing at supper." With another smile at Mr. O'Riley, she hurried from the room, closing the door halfway behind her.

She had been too full of thoughts and worries to eat at their early supper, Sarah remembered, a fact her stomach was only now reminding her of. It gave a small rumble. She crossed her arms over her midsection, and said, "Won't you please sit down, Mr. O'Riley?"

"Thank you, Lady Iverson." He sat down across from her, still looking very solemn, but his green eyes lit up with interest as he saw the objects spread across the floor. "It appears you and Miss Bellweather have been very busy."

"Yes, I wanted to examine and relabel the objects as soon as possible, so we could judge what was lost."

"Not a great deal, I hope."

"Not as much as I had first feared. Many of the artifacts required only minor repair or some cleaning, which my sister has been taking care of. Some of them, though, are damaged beyond repair, or even recognition. I have had to look at the records to see what is missing." Sarah knew that she was babbling on, but she hoped that talk-

ing about the work would help distract her from everything else that was happening—just as the work itself
had.

That hope was in vain. It was all still there, floating in
her mind.

"I am sorry to hear that," Mr. O'Riley said. "If I could
assist you in any way . . ."

"Oh, yes, if you like. We need to sort this box of knife
blades according to size, so I can reference them in the
records." Sarah stood up, and fetched the boxful of
dented and nicked blades. She spilled them out on her
desk, and pulled a chair up for Mr. O'Riley.

A few silent moments passed companionably, as they
sat and arranged the blades. The only sound was the soft
tick of the clock on the mantel, and the distant hum of
voices from the kitchen. Sarah could feel herself calm as
she went through the routine of the motions. Mr. O'Riley
was a very soothing, understanding companion—she
could see why Mary Ann would choose him for a friend.

"Were you in the same regiment as Lord Ransome?"
she asked, holding one blade up to examine it in the
lantern light. "I do not think I have heard how you met."

"No, we were not in the same regiment," Mr. O'Riley
answered in his light brogue. "Our regiments did fight in
the same battles a time or two, but I never had the privi-
lege of meeting him. We became acquainted after the
war, when I was living on the street in London."

Sarah looked up at him, startled. "You lived on the
street?"

"Aye. I returned from Spain to find that there were
not many positions for limping Irishmen with few skills
aside from soldiering. Nothing on the land, which was all
I knew before I went into the Army. My cousins made
it clear I was not welcome back at my family's estate.
Somehow I found myself in London, doing the odd job
of manual labor. The day I met Lord Ransome, there
were no such jobs to be had."

"I am so sorry," Sarah murmured. She was appalled,
and even a bit ashamed. She had understood the reasons

Miles gave for wanting to use his land for practical purposes, in an intellectual way. But here before her was a living human who was deeply affected by things such as that. Not an abstraction, but a *person*.

She was more confused than ever.

Mr. O'Riley gave her a reassuring smile. "Now, you needn't feel sorry for me, Lady Iverson. I'm here now, aren't I? In this fine country, with good friends and the prospect of work. I have a fine life."

Mary Ann came into the room in time to hear his words. She stood aside as Rose arranged the tray on the table beside the fire. "Work? Sarah, have you put Mr. O'Riley to work already?" She leaned over Sarah's shoulder to examine their tidy piles of blades. "But I see that you have. And I was only gone for five minutes!"

Sarah laughed, pushing aside all doubts and confusions for the moment. "He did volunteer, Mary Ann. And no one should volunteer in here unless they truly want to be given a task."

"And very tidy work he has made of his task, too." Mary Ann reached out to touch one of the artifacts with her fingertip, and smiled at Mr. O'Riley. Her gaze held his for long seconds before turning away.

Mr. O'Riley smiled back at her. Sarah glanced between them, a tiny misgiving taking root in her heart. She could not help but sense the admiration in those smiles, as no one could who saw them. She herself felt that Mary Ann was for once being sensible in her infatuation—Mr. O'Riley was handsome, and intelligent, and obviously right hearted. But would their mother agree?

Sarah was absolutely certain she would not. Mr. O'Riley was estranged from his family, and who knew who they were, anyway? And he was Irish.

She took Mary Ann's arm, and steered her firmly to the tea table, pushing her into a chair as far from Mr. O'Riley's as possible. "Tell us some more of Ireland, Mr. O'Riley," she said, and reached for the teapot to pour. "It is such a fascinating land, and, I think, rich in antiquarian sites that have not yet been properly studied."

They spent the next half hour in conversation about the history and artifacts of Ireland. Almost all of the tea cakes and sandwiches had been consumed when there was another knock at the front door.

Sarah almost dropped her teacup in surprise, having become so immersed in the talk that she had nearly forgotten what was happening outside their cozy drawing room. The china rattled in the saucer, and she set it down carefully on the table.

Rose came in, just as she had earlier to announce Mr. O'Riley, and said, "Lord Ransome, my lady."

And he was there, just as she had hoped for, longed for all afternoon and evening. The firelight glinted on the wheaten waves of his hair, and on the white flash of a smile he gave her. He looked tired, with exhaustion creasing his eyes, and his boots were dusty, but she thought him the most beautiful sight in all the world.

She longed to jump up, to run to him and put her arms around him, to hold him close.

But, of course, she could not. Not with her sister and Mr. O'Riley and Rose looking on. She could smile at him, though, and hold out her hand for him to bow over. "Lord Ransome, it is so good to see you at last! Won't you sit down? I believe there is a drop of tea left in the pot."

"Thank you, Lady Iverson." He sat down in the last empty chair, his expression revealing deep relief at being off his feet. "I would certainly not say no to a cup of tea. I see Mr. O'Riley has been guarding you well."

"Guarding us?" Sarah lifted up the china teapot, praying that her hands would remain steady and not spill any drops of liquid. "If that is what he was meant to be doing, then he has accomplished it very well. We have come to no harm, and he has even assisted me in some of the sorting." The pouring accomplished, she passed the cup to Miles.

His fingertips brushed hers gently, and lingered just for an instant, warmly.

Sarah shivered, and pulled her shawl closer about her shoulders.

"Have you discovered the murderer, Lord Ransome?" Mary Ann asked, leaning forward eagerly.

His jaw tightened, and he shook his head. "Not as yet, I fear, Miss Bellweather. But I have learned a few things, and he will not elude us for long, never fear."

"Oh, I am not afraid!" said Mary Ann. "I know that he will be caught, and that until then my sister will keep me safe."

There was such confidence in her sister's voice that Sarah looked at her in surprise. Mary Ann's face was open, shining with assurance that she was safe and always would be, surrounded by people who would protect her. It gave Sarah a small glow to know that someone had such faith in her, even if she could not have it in herself.

Miles nodded to Mary Ann. "Indeed, she will, Miss Bellweather. You and your sister will both be safe."

"What are you going to do next?" Mary Ann asked.

"Tonight, I will guard the village site," he said. "There will be no more destruction."

"Guard the site?" Sarah cried. "But you must be so very tired! And what if the villain *does* return, and you are alone there?"

"I will not be alone. Some of the footmen from Ransome Hall are stationed there, armed, and Mr. O'Riley will go with me. Enough has been lost there already." He held up his hand as Sarah opened her mouth to protest. "No, I am determined on this."

Sarah could see that he was, and she could not help but love him more for it. Even though he did not value the village as she did, he knew that she loved it, and was willing to safeguard it for that. It gave her a small, unwitting hope for their future.

She nodded. "Very well. Then I will go to the village, too."

"Me, too!" Mary Ann said eagerly, clapping her hands. "Oh, how very exciting! Do you think we will see ghosts while we are there? Perhaps Thora will appear, and show us where her treasure is."

"Mary Ann, I do not think you should be out in the night air," Sarah told her.

Mary Ann crossed her arms stubbornly. "If you do not let me go with you, I will just follow. And if I cannot go, then you should not, either."

Sarah sighed. She knew that Mary Ann would do exactly as she threatened. Probably she would be safer at the village with all of them than alone in the hunting box, anyway. "Very well, but you must stay close to me."

Miles watched them, his expression almost bewildered as the situation slipped out of control. "It will not be a place for ladies."

Sarah turned to him. "It is *my* village. I must help to protect it." When he still looked doubtful, she added, "I know how to fire a pistol, if I need to."

Miles laughed, and held up his hands in mock surrender. "Why am I not surprised by that? Very well, Lady Iverson. You and your sister may come with us. But you, like Miss Bellweather, must promise to stay close."

Sarah gave him a small smile. "Well, I do not think that staying close will prove too onerous a task."

Chapter Nineteen

The moon was bright on the Viking village, shimmering down in silver and pale gold, turning the sea of mundane ropes and holes and trees into something enchanted and otherworldly. It was not an ancient, dead place anymore; it had a pagan aliveness that transcended ordinary time.

Sarah sat on a stool outside the stable door, and watched as the vague figures of the footmen-guards moved in and out of patches of light. She could see Mary Ann and Mr. O'Riley sitting beside the remains of the smithy. Occasionally, a word of their conversation would float to her on the breeze, and then drift away.

Miles stood next to her, leaning back against the door with his arms crossed over his chest, watching and alert. Always alert. She knew he must long to send her away, for her own safety, and she loved him for it, even though she would never, ever go.

Despite the strangeness of their situation, Sarah had truly never felt happier. Never felt more at peace. She wished she could sit here, wrapped in her cloak and the night air, with the village spread out before her and Miles beside her, forever.

She sighed, and closed her eyes to hold it all inside her heart.

"Are you cold?" Miles asked.

She smiled without opening her eyes. "Oh, no. I feel perfect."

She sensed him kneel beside her, and he took her

hands in his, rubbing them gently. "Your hands *feel* cold. Sarah, darling, you really should have been sensible and stayed at the house."

Sarah laughed, and opened her eyes. His head was bent over her hands, his hair shining like a bright beacon in the darkness. She drew one of her hands away to touch the soft waves, unable to resist. It was almost like touching liquid gold, she thought whimsically.

"I do not want to be sensible," she murmured. "I want to be here with you."

He looked up at her, still holding her hand. She slid her hand to the nape of his neck, where the hair tapered away silkily. "I would never want to see you hurt," he said, his voice thick and hoarse. "It would kill me."

Sarah felt just the same about him. "How could I be hurt here tonight? This is an enchanted place, just for this one night, and no wickedness can enter here."

Miles lifted her hand to his lips, pressing a kiss to her fingers. "Any time is enchanted when I can be with you, Sarah."

She smiled at this bit of romanticism, made more precious by the sense she had that he was not usually a poetic man.

He held her hand against his chest, warm through his wool greatcoat. "But this could be a dangerous time. I do not know what will happen, or even who it is we are fighting."

"It is not very much like it was for you in Spain, is it?"

Miles shook his head. "Not at all. There I always knew who the enemy was." He paused, then added softly, "There I did not have you."

She gazed up at him, her heart warmed and soothed by his sweet words. "I fear I am a great burden to you. At a time when you should be enjoying your inheritance, and being back in England, I have brought trouble to you. I am nothing but trouble."

He smiled, a ray of light piercing his so-solemn mien. "You are—a gift. A precious one that I want to keep safe."

"I *am* safe," she said. "If I thought there was any danger here tonight, I would never have let my sister come. There are so many of us about, that unless our foe possesses an army, I doubt he will confront us. I rather wish he would, though, so this could be over."

"It will be over very soon. I promise." He released her hand and sat down on the ground, leaning back against the wooden wall and stretching his long legs out before him.

Sarah half turned to face him. "What did you learn today? I have not had the chance to ask you before now."

He snorted. "Precious little, I fear! The magistrate informed Mr. Hamilton that that farmer was feuding with some of his neighbors. Indeed, he had a nasty habit of annoying almost everyone around him to the point of violence. I spoke to his neighbors, in the hope that it might be one of them who had done for him."

A hope that this could be ended so neatly, with strangers as the culprits, rose up in Sarah's mind. "And was it?"

He shook his head, looking as regretful as she felt. "It could not have been. They were all at a wedding celebration until very late that night, and saw and heard nothing suspicious."

"But you also said he made many enemies. It could have been any of them, could it not?"

"Of course, it could."

"Then perhaps, now that he is dead, they are satisfied. There will be no more—incidents." Sarah was almost desperate to believe this, even though she knew how unlikely it was. Why would someone who only wanted to be revenged on that man also destroy her artifacts?

Miles laid his hand gently against her leg. "Sarah, what is it that you are frightened of? Do you suspect that *I* might be the one who did this?"

"Of course not!" she cried. "I never did, truly. Or only for a moment. But I am not sure what I am frightened of, beyond the obvious of having my sister hurt, my work destroyed. Perhaps I am scared of losing the magic of this place. Of seeing it buried beneath all this ugliness."

Miles's hand tightened. "Nothing can do that. Not truly. This was a place of life, was it not? It will always be a place of life."

Sarah looked at the village, seeing it in her mind as it had been in her dreams. Bustling, moving, brimming with messy, glorious life. "Yes."

"Then it has surely seen ugliness before, to surpass even this. Life is seldom perfect, and sometimes it is hideous and incomprehensible. But sometimes it is beautiful, and sweet. Like this moment here with you." He leaned forward, looking up into her eyes. "Nothing could ever erase this moment from this spot; it will take its place as so many moments have before. And its beauty will take away the brutality." He gave a snap of his fingers. "Just like that."

Sarah laughed, even though she really wanted to cry. No one had ever spoken to her so before, had ever articulated her deepest feelings about the ancient sites she worked on. She loved them—not because of the treasure they could yield, but because of the life they had held. A life that had not, and never would, change in its deepest essentials of love and family.

Thora, with her treasure and her lost love, had not been all that different from Sarah herself, she realized. She, too, must have felt the deep beauty of sitting with her lover in an early autumn night. Felt the quickening of her heart, of her very soul, when he touched her.

Sarah could understand, too, how she could have cursed her treasure in her pain at losing those feelings. She knew, though, that no matter what happened in her own life, what happened to her village, she would never lose the beauty of this night. It was a part of her heart forever.

She leaned over and wrapped her arms around him, holding him close. "Thank you," she whispered.

He drew back a bit and looked at her, his expression surprised. "Thank you for what?"

"For being here with me tonight."

He chuckled deeply, and pulled her against him again. "Believe me, my dear—it is entirely my pleasure."

Mary Ann, from her seat on a stool next to the smithy, smiled to see her sister and Lord Ransome embracing right in front of the whole world.

She had just *known* they were perfect for each other, even when they had seemed most determined to deny that fact. Sarah had been very unhappy when Lord Ransome asked her to leave the village and so had Mary Ann. She enjoyed this work, enjoyed feeling as if she could contribute something to the world besides her prettiness. For a time, her faith that Sarah and Lord Ransome would make a fine couple had been shaken. But only for a time. Now, watching them talk, so close to each other, she saw that her first instinct had been the correct one. Surely, they knew that, too. Surely, everything would work out as it ought to.

Surely, she would not have to go home to her mother. If Sarah married Lord Ransome, perhaps they would even let her stay here with them forever!

"What are you smiling about, Miss Bellweather?" Mr. O'Riley asked.

Startled back from her daydreams, Mary Ann looked away from her sister's romantic tableau and turned to the Irishman. He watched her with an unfathomable expression on his face, serious and curious and something she could not read. His gaze held hers steadily.

Mary Ann, who was seldom flustered by anything, did not know what to think. Her own gaze faltered, and dropped down to the ropes that bound the perimeter of the smithy. "I smile because—well, because I feel like it." Then, not sure she really liked the fluttery, uncertain feeling in her stomach, she tilted up her chin and looked him in the eye. "Why do *you* frown, Mr. O'Riley? Did you consume a poor bit of cheese at supper and it does not agree with you?"

His eyes widened, and he gave a startled-sounding

laugh. "I frown because I do not like not knowing what will happen next. I had hoped to leave that feeling behind when the war was over."

Mary Ann nodded. "I do see what you mean. Uncertainty is seldom pleasant. But it sounds as if your life in England has not been precisely stable, Mr. O'Riley."

"Too true. You are a very blunt young lady, Miss Bellweather."

She shrugged. "I apologize. In the house where I grew up, the real, true thing is almost never spoken. Here, I feel freer. My sister does not care when I speak my mind, and I fear it has sometimes made me forgetful of the way things are outside the privacy of her house. I did not mean to be rude."

"You were not rude. I am hardly a bastion of propriety and civilized society myself. I would hope that you feel like you can say anything that you wanted in my presence."

Mary Ann tilted her head to one side, studying him closely. He still looked serious, but somehow not so grim. She nodded. "I think I do feel that way."

"Have you lived with your sister very long, Miss Bellweather?"

"No, not long. I have tried to visit her as often as I can since she married, but I hope that now . . ." Her words faltered. It was true that she felt quite at ease with Mr. O'Riley, but she did not know if she should share the yearnings of her heart, the deep desire to stay here where she was free to be herself—whoever that self might be.

"You hope what?" he asked. He sounded as if he truly wished to know, and was not simply being polite.

"I hope that I might stay here with her, after—if . . ." Once again, words failed her, and she broke off with a laugh.

"If she stays here herself?" Mr. O'Riley looked to where Sarah and Lord Ransome sat, no longer touching yet still close to each other. "I don't think you need to doubt *that*. Or that your sister would want to have you with her. It is obvious that she loves you at great deal."

"Oh, yes, as I love her. She has really been more a mother to me than our true mother has. I would do anything for her."

He gave her a sad smile. "You are fortunate indeed, Miss Bellweather, to have a family who loves you so."

"What of your own family, Mr. O'Riley?"

"My own family is dead. My parents and my baby sister died when I was quite young. I grew up with aunts and uncles and cousins, so it was scarcely a lonely life."

"Oh!" she cried, her heart aching at the loss she heard in his voice, despite his attempt to shrug it away. "But that is not the same as having your own family—your own place."

"Sometimes we have to make our own place in the world, find our own way." He looked about at the night-cloaked village. "And sometimes we are fortunate enough to find a special place like this, and people with kind hearts."

No one had ever put into words so perfectly Mary Ann's own feelings before. She had nothing of equal worth to say in reply. "We are truly fortunate," she murmured.

"Truly, Miss Bellweather, we are."

Chapter Twenty

"Mary Ann, hold it steady! Don't let it blow away."
Sarah clutched at the corner of a large oiled canvas,
spreading it over the open pit of House A as Mary Ann
struggled to anchor the opposite end.

The day, which had dawned with a hazy brightness,
had turned ominously dark. Thick clouds rolled overhead, and a brisk wind had picked up. She and Mary
Ann had collected the canvases from the stable as
quickly as they could, and tried to cover the open sites.

As Sarah tied the sheet down, she glanced out over
the village, and she thought it looked utterly different
than the enchanted, moonlit realm it had been just last
night. The dark gray sky cast it in gloom and shadows;
the wind stirred the dirt and whipped the canvas. Many
of the workers had abandoned them once again, certain
that the destruction of the artifacts signified Thora's renewed displeasure at their trespassing on her property.
Only a very few people remained to secure the village,
including Miles and Mr. O'Riley, who were tying down
a canvas at the smithy. Even Mr. Hamilton, usually so
very diligent, had not appeared that day.

Despite the gloom and trepidation, Sarah couldn't help
but smile to see the men laboring so seriously and valiantly. From the expressions on their faces, she assumed
they would be cursing most soundly if not for the presence of ladies.

It was all she could do not to run into Miles's arms

and kiss the frown away. The sound of his voice, the clean scent of him, was almost intoxicating. . . .

"Sarah!" Mary Ann cried suddenly.

Sarah, pulled away from her reveries, only then noticed that she had let go of her end of the canvas, and it whipped away. She grabbed for it, and pulled it down to tie the lashings more securely. "Oh, bother! I am sorry, Mary Ann. I must have been woolgathering."

"You were, indeed." Mary Ann finished tying off her end, and stood up. "And you accuse *me* of daydreaming!" She gave Sarah a sly glance. "Whatever could you have been thinking of?"

Sarah looked at her sternly. "I was worried that we would not have the entire village secured before the storm comes, of course. But it appears we have."

"Hm." Mary Ann peered out over the sea of white canvas, and waved at Mr. O'Riley, who let go of his own rope to wave back. "Of course. Will it protect them, do you think?"

"It always has in the past. We will have muddy work tomorrow, but we have faced that before. This will keep some of the earth from sliding back into the pits, and therefore save us a great deal of re-digging. We won't lose as many artifacts." Sarah stood up, too, and brushed off the dusty skirt of her work dress.

"Speaking of artifacts, I ought to take these back to the hunting box before it rains." Mary Ann lifted up the basket of objects they had found that morning before the storm clouds came in, a collection of mostly ladies' toilette items that Sarah couldn't wait to examine closer. "Are you coming?"

"I should check the stable one more time, and be certain there are no fragments we've missed."

Mary Ann giggled. "Perhaps Mr. O'Riley would be so kind as to escort me back to the hunting box, then?"

"Mary Ann . . ." Sarah said warningly.

"What?" Mary Ann's eyes widened innocently. "It would be perfectly proper! We would be outdoors the entire time, and I am sure Rose will be lurking right inside the door when we get there. She is convinced we will all be murdered in our beds if we do not exercise ceaseless vigilance."

"I am not certain she is wrong," Sarah said. "At least about the ceaseless vigilance. I am not at all sure about the being murdered part."

"Then I truly ought to have a gentleman's protection," argued Mary Ann. "Who knows? The villain might be lurking along the pathway, just waiting to snatch away my basket of hairpins and scent bottles and dash them on the ground!"

Sarah had to laugh. It was truly marvelous to see the sparkle back in Mary Ann's eyes, extinguishing the anxiety of the last couple of days. She only hoped there was a new common sense to go along with that exuberance. "Very well. But I shall be along shortly, and I want no hint of mischief."

Mary Ann shook her head. "Not a one. I promise."

"Go along, then. Cook is marketing today, but have her prepare a cold collation for us when she returns, and perhaps Mr. O'Riley and Lord Ransome will join us."

"Of course." Mary Ann kissed her cheek, and hurried off to fetch Mr. O'Riley, seeming to veritably skip over the ground.

Sarah watched her take Mr. O'Riley's arm and turn towards the pathway, the two of them talking and laughing. Then she picked up her own basket and trowel. She walked over to where Miles waited, and smiled up at him.

He gave her a sweet smile in return, one that dissipated the clouds and gloom with the mere upturn of his lips.

He took the basket from her. "Your sister seems very bright and cheerful this morning, Sarah."

"Mary Ann is usually bright and cheerful. I am glad to see that the shocking events of these days have not extinguished that." She slipped her hand into the crook of his arm, and they walked to the open door of the stable. "I think that your friend Mr. O'Riley is partly to thank for that."

"I know that he—admires Miss Bellweather."

"Oh, yes? And what else might you know?"

Inside the cool gloom of the stable, Miles put down the basket and took her in his arms. Sarah melted into the warm, safe haven of his embrace, stretching up on tiptoe to be even closer.

"I know nothing else of your sister and my friend," he answered. "But I do know a bit of *this*."

His lips came down to meet hers, and Sarah clutched at his coat, suddenly dizzy. The entire building tilted in a giddy dance; indeed, the whole world vanished in the heat of their embrace. How she had missed this warmth, this closeness, in her cold year of mourning! But even before that, she had never felt anything like this wild rush of emotions.

When her eyes finally fluttered open, and she went back down flat on her feet, she became aware again of her surroundings. Raindrops pattered softly at the roof in a gentle sprinkle, not yet the deluge it threatened to become. The rain was nothing to the tumult in her heart.

She felt safe when he held her, as if the world outside could not touch her, could hold no horrors for her. She trusted him to hold her secure. Never had she felt this way before, not with her husband, not with anyone.

Sarah leaned her head against his shoulder, the wool of his coat soft-scratchy on her skin. His clasp tightened, and she felt his cool breath stir in her hair, his lips pressing there ever so briefly. She wondered if he felt as she did, if he sensed the beauty of this time. Or if it seemed commonplace to him, a mere diversion.

"Sarah," he said quietly. "We must have a serious conversation."

She closed her eyes. A "serious conversation" was the very last thing she wanted at that moment. Such times of sweetness were rare, and she wanted to hold it against all the storms—real and feared—that waited outside.

But she knew that she could not do that. Miles was right; they did have many things to talk about.

She drew back to look up at him. "You are correct. But not now. Later. Later, we can converse on as many serious topics as you like."

He smiled at her, and bent his head to kiss her lightly on the nose. "Of course. Your sister will be looking for you, and we have stayed here too long as it is. I will remind you of your promise to talk with me later, though."

"I hope that you will." Sarah clung to his hand for just an instant longer before turning to the stable door. "For I have much I want to say to you, Miles."

The wind was brisk as Mary Ann and Mr. O'Riley followed the pathway back to the hunting box. It pulled at Mary Ann's cloak and skirt hem with chill fingers, but she scarcely noticed it. She was laughing too much at a tale Mr. O'Riley was telling her, a wild yarn of a princess and a wily leprechaun.

"Oh, no, it cannot be!" she said, gasping through her giggles. "You are making that story up as you go along."

"I certainly am not!" His tone was stern, but his grin decidedly was not. "It is a very ancient tale, one that my aunt used to tell my cousins and me every night. Though, when I was in Spain, a woman there told me an old *Spanish* story very like it. Of course, in that story the trickster's name was not Sean but Juan, and the princess was a dark-eyed infanta."

"Well, here in England I have never heard anything like it. But I did have a nanny once, a Welsh woman, who had a terribly hair-raising tale of a water spirit she would frighten me with at night." At the bend in the path, where it turned into sight of the house, she stilled her steps. She did not want to go in there just yet, even though a few cool sprinkles of rain were beginning to land on her cheek. She wanted to laugh some more with Mr. O'Riley, to hear more of his outrageous Irish tales, to feel free for just a few more minutes.

"I have enjoyed our conversation today," she said.

Mr. O'Riley slowed his steps to match hers, yet they still moved inexorably to the turn. "As have I, Miss Bellweather. I find the work you and Lady Iverson are doing fascinating."

"Oh, yes!" Mary Ann smiled at him in delight; his

interest in the work here raised him even higher in her estimation. "I am sure you can assist us here any time you like, and I can tell you of what I have been reading—" She broke off suddenly, as she remembered the truth— that she and Sarah might not be working here for very much longer. Not if Lord Ransome carried out his original plans.

Lord Ransome seemed to admire her sister greatly now, and it only stood to reason that he would not take the village away from the woman he cared about. But Mary Ann had learned from her short life of traveling about with her mother that often the world did not conform to reason, and sometimes people did not behave as they ought.

Mr. O'Riley gave her a curious glance. "What you have been reading, Miss Bellweather?" he prompted.

"Yes." Mary Ann looked up at him, and realized she had not finished her sentence. She knew that her family would think her even rasher than they already did if she told her doubts to someone she had only just met. Somehow, though, she felt perfectly at ease with Mr. O'Riley. His green eyes radiated wisdom and understanding quite beyond his young years.

"I have been reading a great deal about the Vikings," she went on. "And I have many ideas for the village. Yet I know that Lord Ransome has other plans for this property."

"I know what his plans have been, and why he made them," he said. "But I do not think he will toss Lady Iverson off of the village site like some evil villain in a cheap play."

Mary Ann felt a small flutter of hope. "I thought so, too. He seems a kind man, yet I can see that he is determined to do what he thinks is right."

"I am sure there must be some other plan. One that can accommodate both you and your sister, and Lord Ransome." He winked at her. "We shall just have to put our heads together and devise something, won't we, Miss Bellweather?"

Mary Ann laughed. Her laughter died, though, when

they came into sight of the hunting box and saw the carriage waiting outside the front door.

"Oh, no," she whispered.

"What is it, Miss Bellweather?"

"It seems the Hamiltons have come to call."

His face froze, its merry smile slipping into a complete blank. "The Hamiltons."

"Yes. I had hoped that when they did not appear at the village this morning that we would not see them today. Sarah said that Mrs. Hamilton did not look well yesterday. But I suppose they have just been waiting here the whole time."

"Well, then." He did not move away, but Mary Ann had the distinct sense that he was withdrawing. Their laughter and fun turned as chill as the rain on her skin. "You should have no more need of my escort, Miss Bellweather. You will be quite safe here in their company."

Mary Ann wanted to reach out, to grab his hand and hold him there. She tangled her hands in the folds of her cloak to keep them still. "Do you mean to say that you will not come inside for some tea?" *That you will leave me?*

He relented a bit, and gave her a smile. "I have suddenly recalled an errand I must perform. But I am sure we will meet again very soon. Your friends will look after you now."

He handed her the basket, and, with a quick kiss on the back of her hand, set off in the direction of Ransome Hall. She wondered what errand he could have *there*.

Men were such cowards sometimes, Mary Ann thought crossly, as she watched him until he disappeared. She hoisted up the basket, straightened her shoulders resolutely, and went into the hunting box.

Only Mrs. Hamilton waited in the drawing room, with an untouched tea tray and no Mr. Hamilton. Mary Ann almost dropped her basket in surprise at the sight of her. Sarah had been quite right when she said Mrs. Hamilton did not seem well. Mary Ann had rarely seen anyone so changed in just a few days as Mrs. Hamilton was. She was properly dressed in one of her overly stylish gowns, a carriage dress of pink wool trimmed with gold braid and a gold-and-red Indian shawl, crowned by a gold-feathered pink hat. Her hair, though, fell in lank curls from beneath that hat, and her face was chalk pale, except for two hectic spots of red over her cheekbones.

Mary Ann glanced behind her. No one had been there to open the front door for her, and she could hear no voices. Sarah had said that Mrs. Taylor, the cook, was gone to do the marketing, but surely Rose at least ought to have been there. It seemed the household was uninhabited today, except for the kittens, two of them sleeping in their basket and one perched on the fireplace mantel.

Mary Ann slowly put her basket down on the floor just inside the doorway, and pasted what she hoped was a welcoming smile on her face.

"Mrs. Hamilton! What a lovely surprise to see you here."

"My dear Miss Bellweather," answered Mrs. Hamilton, her voice full of a strange, tense cheer. "I hope I have not come at an inconvenient time."

"Not at all." Mary Ann came farther into the room, and perched on a chair across from the other woman's. "Though I fear my sister has not yet finished the day's work at the village. She should be here very soon." At least she hoped Sarah would be. The rain seemed to be beginning in earnest now, tapping at the window, and Mary Ann was not at all sure what she should converse about. Mrs. Hamilton really only seemed to enjoy talking about Bath and gowns, two subjects Mary Ann knew little about.

"Oh, that is quite all right," Mrs. Hamilton said. "I was actually hoping to have some time to talk with *you*, Miss Bellweather."

Mary Ann wondered what about. "Indeed, Mrs. Hamilton?"

"Indeed." But, rather than going on to talk, Mrs. Hamilton fell silent, pleating her skirt with nervous fingers.

Mary Ann tried to remember all the polite-hostess manners she had been taught. "I do hope Rose has been looking after you," she said, gesturing to the tea tray that appeared untouched.

"Oh, yes, but she said you have no cream cakes about. So I sent her into the village to fetch some. I do so adore cream cakes with my tea."

So *that* was why it was so silent in the house. Mary Ann felt a small chill of disquiet. She glanced to the window, but there was no sign of her sister and Lord Ransome. How she wished Mr. O'Riley had come inside with her!

"What was it you wished to speak to me about, Mrs. Hamilton?" she asked.

Mrs. Hamilton leaned forward, her eyes strangely bright as she looked at Mary Ann. "My husband thinks so highly of you, Miss Bellweather, you and your sister. He often asks why I cannot be more like you."

Mary Ann was nonplussed. Whatever she might have expected to hear, it was not that. "Well—we think highly of him, as well. He is a very respected antiquarian."

Mrs. Hamilton shook her head. More carelessly pinned curls spilled down onto her shoulders. "No! I mean to say, he respects your opinions—unlike mine. He thinks I am just a silly, uneducated chit."

"Oh, no, I am sure that is not true—"

"Of course, it is true!" Mrs. Hamilton interrupted, her voice so sharply pitched it made the kitten on the mantel cease washing its paw and peer at her. "He thinks I know nothing, and he will not listen to me. But he would listen to you, and to Lady Iverson." She reached out and caught Mary Ann's wrist with her hand, her grip surprisingly strong for such dainty fingers.

For the first time in her life, Mary Ann tasted the faint metallic tang of fear in her mouth. Not even being pushed down by the kitten-drowning farmer had scared her as much as the glow in Mrs. Hamilton's eyes.

She resisted the urge to pull away, to scream out in the empty house. She knew it would only make Mrs.

Hamilton more desperate, so she took a deep breath and tried to speak calmly. "What is it you would want to tell him?"

"That he *must* take me home to Bath!" Mrs. Hamilton cried. "I miss it so. I miss the people, the balls and routs. Here there is nothing but dusty artifacts and country bumpkins." She closed her eyes, and whispered, "There is nothing."

Mary Ann remembered how excited Mrs. Hamilton had been to be invited to Ransome Hall, and said, "You have been to supper twice at Ransome Hall, the home of a *marquis*."

Mrs. Hamilton's eyes flew open. "Yes, and now he is just as obsessed with digging in the dirt as the rest of you! It is an illness here, and it has infected all of you. But it has not infected me! I will escape."

In the blink of an eye, so quickly that Mary Ann had not time to discern what she was about or stop her, Mrs. Hamilton shot to her feet, pulling Mary Ann with her. Mrs. Hamilton's other hand snatched up a sandwich knife from the tea tray, and she drew Mary Ann close against her. The knife pressed to her neck. Even though it was a small thing, it stung when it made a tiny cut to her skin.

Mary Ann almost fainted from the shock; dark spots danced before her eyes. Small, fluffy Mrs. Hamilton was going to stab her right in her own drawing room? It was absurd!

But unfortunately all too real. Mary Ann was not much shorter than Mrs. Hamilton, but the woman had the fierce strength of some bizarre, inhuman anger behind her. Mary Ann could not pull away.

"Well, he will listen to me now," Mrs. Hamilton said, her voice suddenly as calm as if she was discussing the weather. "He will have to, if I have his precious Miss Bellweather."

She pulled Mary Ann toward the drawing room door, and Mary Ann panicked. She cried out, and felt a sharp stick, and the drop of some warm liquid on her flesh.

Suddenly, there was a loud hiss and growl, and a scream from Mrs. Hamilton, who released Mary Ann and fell back a step, clutching at her arm. Mary Ann stumbled and fell at being so hastily freed, and she looked up to see that the kitten on the mantel had launched itself through the air and caught Mrs. Hamilton's arm with its tiny, razor-sharp claws. Her sleeve was torn away to reveal two long, deep scratches, ruby with spots of blood.

Mrs. Hamilton kicked the kitten away, and it mewled piteously once before lying still. She fell against the white-painted wall with a sob, leaving a crimson smear there.

Mary Ann scrambled to try to grab one of the Viking blades laid out in their box, but Mrs. Hamilton was too quick for her. She lunged forward and caught Mary Ann by the hair, pulling her to her feet. She drew her once again to the door, inexorably, and Mary Ann could have cried with the helplessness and the fear of it all. It was Mrs. Hamilton all along, Mrs. Hamilton who had ruined the artifacts, and probably even killed that man. Mrs. Hamilton—who was obviously insane.

"Oh, yes, indeed," Mrs. Hamilton said, as she hid her knife behind the folds of her shawl and forced Mary Ann up into her carriage, slamming the door behind them, before her dozing coachman could see them. "He will listen to me now."

Chapter Twenty-one

"The door is open." Sarah paused at the first sight of the hunting box. She had been laughing at something Miles said to her, and had opened her mouth to reply, but was brought up short by the sight of the front door standing open. Surely Mary Ann and the servants would not be so careless as to leave the door open, not at such a time as this, when there was a murderer roaming about.

It was true that they had been longer at the village than she had thought they would be, but it had not been *very* long. Surely not long enough for some ill to befall Mary Ann in their own house.

Surely not?

She pushed the hood of her cloak back so she could see more clearly. Aside from the open door, the hunting box looked quiet and peaceful. Too quiet, perhaps.

Sarah remembered how she had so blithely allowed Mary Ann to walk off with Mr. O'Riley. Had that been a mistake? Had she put too much trust in that young man?

She pressed her hand to her throbbing temple. How her mind was racing, and all because of an open door! She ought to walk right over there and investigate, but her feet felt frozen to the earth. All the euphoria of only a moment before had vanished, replaced by nerves that screamed out of danger and caution.

She looked at Miles, who stood stiff and straight beside her. His blue eyes no longer shone with laughter. They were narrowed speculatively as he watched her house. "Would one of your servants have left it open?"

Sarah shook her head. "The only one home today is Rose, Mary Ann's maid. It is my own maid's day off, and Cook went to do the marketing. Rose is very protective of Mary Ann; she would never have done such a thing. She knows we must be vigilant right now."

"And Mr. O'Riley would never have allowed such carelessness." Miles put down the basket he carried, and reached out to briefly squeeze her hand. "Stay here, Sarah, and I will go and see what is happening."

"No!" Sarah said. Her cowardly side urged her with all its might to stay where she was, but she knew she could not. "It is my sister, my home. I will come with you."

"I would rather you did not, my dear. There might be—something there that you would not want to see."

Sarah swallowed hard, a sudden horrifying vision flashing in her mind of Mary Ann's lifeless body.

She pushed it away. Surely she would feel it in her heart if her sister was dead. But she could be hurt, she could need her. "I want to go. I will not get in your way, I promise, but I must—must know."

Miles studied her closely for a long moment before he nodded. "Very well. I have learned enough of you to know that I cannot stop you, Sarah. But stay close to me."

"I will."

From the basket he took a sharp obsidian object, probably once used to grind grain, but now might have to serve a more sinister purpose, and walked toward the house. Sarah followed closely, her gaze scanning the windows for any sign of movement. She saw nothing at all.

And heard nothing when they stepped into the tiny foyer. The house was so silent it echoed. One of the doors opening off the foyer, the one to the dining room, was closed, but the drawing room door was ajar.

Holding his chunk of obsidian like a dagger in his hand, Miles nudged the door open farther with the toe of his boot.

"Blast!" he cursed.

"What?" Sarah crowded in next to him, and gasped.

Her drawing room was in a shambles. A tea tray sat on the low table, its silver pot overturned and spilling amber-colored liquid onto the sandwiches and cakes. A chair lay on its side, as if kicked there, and the box of Viking blades was askew. The three kittens huddled in little black-and-white fur balls beneath the settee, one of them licking its left paw in frantic, obsessive motions.

Worst of all, a smear of drying blood stained one of the walls.

Sarah pressed her hand to her mouth, and pushed past Miles into the room. The basket Mary Ann had taken from the village was on the floor, but there were no other signs of her sister. Unless the blood was hers.

Sarah sat down hard on the carpet, momentarily overwhelmed by that terrible possibility. The room spun about her dizzily.

One of the kittens clambered onto her lap, and when she reached down absently to touch it, she saw that there was some blood there, tiny specks of dried-red crust on its white paw.

"What could have happened here?" she whispered.

Miles stared at the overturned chair. "What ever it is, I think it's safe to say they are all gone now. But where is your sister and Mr. O'Riley?"

They stared at each other in silence for a long moment, a moment broken only when they heard footsteps and rustling in the foyer. Miles lifted up his obsidian.

"Oh, my lady, the rain is starting to come down ever so hard!" Rose said, stepping into the drawing room doorway. She shook off her damp cloak while balancing a white box in her other hand. "You will be wanting—" She broke off with a puzzled look when she saw Sarah sitting on the floor. "My lady, whyever are you there on the floor?"

Then she saw Miles with his "weapon," and screamed. The box fell from her hand, breaking open to spill cream cakes all over the carpet. The kittens sprang on them.

"Rose!" Sarah scrambled to her feet and caught the maid before she could swoon. "Rose, it is only Lord Ransome. It is quite all right."

"Lord Ransome?" Rose murmured, daring to peek over at him. "But why does he have that rock thing?" Her eyes widened as she took in the full extent of the wreck of the drawing room. "And what has happened here?"

"Now, Rose, I do not want you to swoon, but I fear someone has broken in here. And Mary Ann is gone." Sarah found that having to keep someone else steady helped to calm her own nerves. She felt an icy clarity clear her mind, leaving only one thought—to find her sister.

"Miss Mary Ann gone! But how could that be?" Rose covered her eyes with her hands. "I left her here not an hour ago. Miss Mary Ann was not here yet, but Mrs. Hamilton said she would wait for her."

Sarah was puzzled. "Mrs. Hamilton?"

"Yes, my lady. She called here to see Miss Mary Ann. She sent me into the village to fetch some cream cakes for tea." Rose let out a wail. "While I was fetching cakes, someone stole my lamb! My poor Miss Mary Ann. And Mrs. Hamilton, too."

Sarah exchanged a look with Miles. She remembered the last time she had seen Mrs. Hamilton, remembered how ill and frantic the woman had looked. She had thought it was because of a quarrel with her husband, but could it have been something more? An insane jealousy, perhaps, festering in her heart?

It was almost impossible to imagine Mrs. Hamilton, with her ruffles and her giggles, as an insane criminal. But Sarah knew it could be possible; anything was possible.

She saw that Miles was probably thinking the same thing. He slowly shook his head. "Mrs. Hamilton?"

"It *could* be," Sarah said.

"But where is her husband? He was not at the site today; he could be a part of this, whatever it is." Miles slapped his hand against the wall, causing Rose and the kittens to jump. "And, blast it, where is Mr. O'Riley? He was meant to be looking after the girl!"

"I—I saw Mr. O'Riley," Rose dared to peep. "When I was walking back here with the cakes, I saw him going toward Ransome Hall. He said he had left Miss Mary Ann here in the company of the Hamiltons, but he would be back later."

"I suppose he did not wish to encounter the Hamiltons' rudeness again," Miles muttered. "The fool. We were all fools."

And she was the greatest one of all, Sarah thought, to have left her sister alone for even a moment. "Where could they have gone?"

Miles frowned. "The inn where the Hamiltons are staying?"

Sarah shook her head. "Far too public. Whatever Mrs. Hamilton is planning, I am sure she does not want witnesses."

She and Miles looked at each other, and said at the same time, "The village."

"Of course," said Miles. "That is it."

Sarah turned to the sobbing maid. "Rose, I know it is terrible to ask you to go back out into the rain, but could you go to Ransome Hall? Find Mr. O'Riley, tell him what has happened, and that he should meet us at the Viking village. And then see if Mr. Hamilton is at the inn."

"Yes, my lady." Rose wiped at her eyes with her sleeve. "I will do anything that could help Miss Mary Ann!"

After the maid dashed off, Sarah closed her own eyes tightly, and pressed her hand to her belly to quell the sour panic lodged there.

She felt Miles's warm hand on her shoulder. She covered it with her hand, holding on to it tightly.

"We will find her," he said quietly. "And she will be safe."

"Yes," Sarah answered. "Oh, yes. She must be." She tried to press her rising panic back down, but it would not be quashed. It still choked her, hard and cold and immutable.

Chapter Twenty-two

Mary Ann huddled in the corner of the stable where the artifacts had once been stored, and pulled her cloak tighter about her shaking shoulders. The rain could not get into the stable, but she heard it pattering on the roof, felt the chill breeze that seeped through cracks in the boards. Thunder clapped overhead.

Her shivering did not come from these things, though. It came from the fear churning deep inside of her.

Across from her, Mrs. Hamilton sat on one of the low wooden stools, her skirts spread about her prettily, as if she was at a tea party in someone's drawing room. She hummed a soft little tune beneath her breath, and occasionally gave Mary Ann a little smile, or waved her knife about like a fan.

Mary Ann watched her warily. She understood social ambitions; her mother had followed them all of Mary Ann's life, pulling her children from one town to another. And she had always seen that same ambition in Mrs. Hamilton. But she could not understand the depths of desperation it must take for someone to threaten another person in order to achieve their ends. There had to be something more than a need for society at work in Mrs. Hamilton's disordered mind.

Mary Ann prayed that her sister would find her—and soon.

"There is a light in the stable," Sarah said, crowding

close to Miles. The storm had gathered momentum during their short journey to the village site, and she had to almost shout at him to be heard over the thunder. Her cloak was soaked with rain, hanging about her in sodden folds, and she could hardly see through the thick mist of the shower. She brushed at her eyes with the back of her hand, and could not tell if she brushed away rain or tears. "Is it them?"

Miles stared at the wooden structure with a grim expression on his face. "It must be. Who else would be out here in such weather?"

Sarah took a rushing step. He grabbed her arm, pulling her back. "My sister is in danger!" she cried, trying to draw away.

"And you will do her no good if you put *yourself* in danger, as well!" He wrapped his arms around her waist, holding her close as she trembled from the anger and the fear.

"She is my baby sister," Sarah sobbed, falling back against him. "She trusts me to protect her."

"I know," he said. "Yet she would not want you to be hurt. We can only do her good if we wait for O'Riley and Hamilton. We are obviously facing a madwoman, and we must be cautious. Everything seems quiet there for now."

Sarah stared out at the stable. Aside from the faint ray of light that flickered between the chinks in the wood, it *was* quiet. Too quiet?

"You do not think that is because—"

"No!" Miles's clasp tightened. "No, my dear."

"But she killed that farmer, did she not?"

He was silent for a long moment, so long that Sarah thought he was not going to reply. Then she felt his nod against her head. "Very probably."

She could do the same to Mary Ann, then, Sarah thought. Her very soul grew numb at the unthinkable thought. Her hands reached for Miles's arm, and clung with fierce tenacity.

They stood in silent watchfulness for what seemed like

a day, but what was truly only moments, when Mr. O'Riley and Mr. Hamilton rode up together. Obviously, they must have met on the road, and Mr. O'Riley had apprised Mr. Hamilton of all that had happened. He looked pale and frantic, completely unmindful of the rain that poured down on his bare head.

Sarah could not help but pity him as she looked into his shocked and opaque eyes, but concern for her sister still flowed hot in her veins. She pulled away from Miles and ran up to Mr. Hamilton, catching him as he dismounted from his horse.

"Your wife is a madwoman!" she cried. "She has seized Mary Ann, and may do her a grave harm."

"Lady Iverson." He stared down at her, yet did not seem to truly see her at all. "How could this be? Emmeline snatching Miss Bellweather away from her home? Mr. O'Riley said as much, but it cannot be."

Miles came up beside Sarah, taking her arm. "I fear it *is* true. It is obvious that your wife is not well."

"I knew that she was—unhappy," Mr. Hamilton went on, in that same distracted voice. It was as if he, like Sarah, felt himself caught in some terrible dreamworld he could not escape. "But I do not understand why she would do something like this."

"You must go and speak with her," Miles said, in a firm, brook-no-nonsense tone that Sarah thought must have worked wonders on soldiers in Spain. "You are the one who is most likely to be able to get through to her."

Mr. Hamilton's jaw tightened, and he turned toward the stable. His coat flared open, and Sarah saw the pistol tucked there. She almost cried out, envisioning a stray ball catching her sister.

"For God's sake, be gentle, man," Mr. O'Riley said, his brogue thick. "If you go rushing in there, your wife is liable to do anything to Miss Bellweather. It is you she is angry with—don't make her even more angry."

Mr. Hamilton turned to look at him in astonishment. "She is angry with *me*? How would *you* know that?"

"Who else could it be?" Mr. O'Riley answered reasonably. "It obviously can't be Miss Bellweather herself. What could an innocent girl do to inspire such insanity? You must have treated your wife very poorly indeed."

Mr. Hamilton's face turned plum red, and he took a step toward Mr. O'Riley. "I don't need some Irishman telling me how to treat my wife—"

"Enough!" Miles shouted. "This is no time for petty quarrels. Miss Bellweather is in danger. Mr. Hamilton, go and speak to your wife, and, as Mr. O'Riley said, go gently. We will wait outside for a sign from you before we come in."

Mr. Hamilton seemed to deflate at this reminder of what was truly happening around them. His shoulders slumped, and he nodded. "Of course. Yes." He took one hesitant step, then another, more resolute.

They watched him until he reached the barn door, barely visible in the driving rain. He glanced back at them before slipping inside.

Sarah pressed her hand to her pounding heart, certain it must be beating louder than the thunder.

"It is my fault," Mr. O'Riley said. "I never should have let Miss Bellweather go into the house alone, just because I was too cowardly to speak to the Hamiltons again. I should have stayed with her every moment."

"If you are at fault, then so am I," Sarah answered, not looking away from the door where Mr. Hamilton had vanished. "I would not have hesitated to leave her alone with Mrs. Hamilton."

"Nor would I," Miles said. "She seemed quite an ordinary society matron."

Yes, Sarah thought bitterly. So ordinary. They were *all* at fault, for being blind and foolish. For seeing what they only expected to see, and not what was before them.

And now Mary Ann was paying the price.

Mary Ann, half dozing against the splintered wooden wall, jerked away at the sudden sound of Mrs. Hamilton's rustling skirts as she stood up. Mary Ann rubbed at her itching eyes, and looked around the dim space. Rain and claps of thunder still sounded outside, and the room was full of a heavy, close humidity, and the smell of something sharp and metallic.

She sat up straight, and watched Mrs. Hamilton turn to the door. Her pale face was tense and watchful, her hands twisting in her shawl. Mary Ann warily flicked her own glance to where Mrs. Hamilton was watching, and saw that the portal was slowly, very slowly, opening.

Mary Ann stood up, trying to stay in the shadows where no one would notice her. She pressed against the wall, and wished she could just melt through it and vanish into the storm. Into the clean rain that would wash the residue of madness off her skin.

Mr. Hamilton stood in the doorway, gripping at its warped frame with gloved hands. He did not look the coolly intelligent scholar she had once admired so much. Like his wife, he was transformed into something other than a civilized human, other than ordinary. His hair was tousled and wet, its disordered ends dripping water onto his shoulders, over his face.

"Emmeline," he said, his voice breaking up in the thickness of the air. "What have you done? What madness is this?"

Hope had flashed over his wife's face for one instant, but it vanished at his words, and she curled her fingers tighter about her knife. "Madness, Neville? You forced me to this! You would not listen to me, no matter what I did. No matter how hard I tried to be a good wife to you."

"A good wife?" Mr. Hamilton stepped into the barn, bringing the storm with him. "When did you ever try to be that? You have always been selfish and demanding; you never wanted to try to help me in my work."

"You took me away from my home!" she wailed. "You took me away from my life! I do not want to be dragged about from one dirty pit to another all my years. I am young, and I want parties and friends!"

He took a step towards her. "Is that why you have done these things, Emmeline? Because you want to go to *parties?* You smashed irreplaceable artifacts, and kidnapped an innocent girl because I took you from Bath Society?"

Mrs. Hamilton tossed back her head in a defiant gesture, her eyes blazing. "Yes! You did nothing you promised you would do. You love these dead things, these objects, more than you ever loved me. So I hired that dreadful man to destroy your precious artifacts. I thought if your work was gone, you would take me home."

Mr. Hamilton stared at his wife as if he had never seen her before in his life. "And you also—"

"I did! When he tried to blackmail me, the pathetic worm, I killed him. Who did he think he was to threaten me?" She slashed at the air with her knife.

Mary Ann's stomach gave a sick heave. Mrs. Hamilton, who had held a knife to her throat, had dragged her from her home, had *killed* a man. She could very well have killed Mary Ann, too.

She was only sixteen! And her life could have ended today, when she hadn't even *lived* yet.

A sharp cry escaped from her before she could catch it, pushed out by her fear and her revulsion.

Mrs. Hamilton turned to her, frowning in confusion, as if she had forgotten Mary Ann was there. Mary Ann ran for the door.

Mrs. Hamilton screamed, and lunged past her husband in a shockingly swift movement, knocking him aside. She grabbed on to Mary Ann's cloak, causing her to stumble against the door. They tripped and tumbled out into the storm.

Mary Ann kicked out at the other woman, struggling to loosen her iron grip on her cloak. But Mrs. Hamilton, who had always seemed so slim and light in her ruffles, was grotesquely strong. She pinned Mary Ann's shoulder into the mud, and lifted up her purloined knife.

Mary Ann heard a cry from her sister, men shouting out, the rumble of thunder. But all she saw was the flash of lightning on the knife blade.

*　　*　　*

Sarah stared across the muddy village at the night-marish sight of Mrs. Hamilton and Mary Ann tumbling to the ground. A knife shone brightly against the gray and brown of the rain and the muck. The two women rolled down the slope from the stable, coming to a stop near the edge of the leather-worker's shop, Mrs. Hamilton rearing up above Mary Ann.

Mr. Hamilton appeared in the doorway of the stable, and called out his wife's name, but he was too far away to do anything to stop the forward momentum of the terrible events. Sarah was also too far away—she knew this truly, but she was possessed with the need to go to her baby sister. She broke away from Miles's arms and raced across the village, her boots slipping in the mud, her tears mingling with the rain on her face.

Miles and Mr. O'Riley were right behind her, all of them running to save Mary Ann, to end this madness. Miles lifted her up when she fell, carrying her forward. But she had the horrible sense that time had slowed down, that she was too leaden and earthbound to change anything. So many things flashed through her mind—Mary Ann as a tiny baby, wrapped in frills and lace, placed in Sarah's small, trembling arms; Mary Ann toddling across a spring meadow, dark curls shining in the light. It was to Sarah she had always run, on her chubby baby legs, not to their mother or the nanny, to Sarah.

"No," she sobbed. "No."

She would *not* let this happen.

Help me. Help me.

A fork of lightning split the air, turning the sky and all their surroundings a purple-blue. Thunder shook the very ruins a second later, deafeningly.

Mrs. Hamilton looked up from Mary Ann's prone figure, past Sarah and Miles and Mr. O'Riley. Sarah was near enough to see her wildly shining eyes widen, her mouth open in a shocked "O."

"What is it?" Mrs. Hamilton cried. "What is it!"

Sarah glanced behind her to see what had so taken

Mrs. Hamilton aback. She squinted, but could discern nothing in the storm.

Then another bolt of lightning split the sky. There, beneath a spreading tree, was a figure. A woman, tall and slim, clad in a white, chemiselike garment. Her gown and her long, wild dark hair blew in the wind. She held up a scamasax, whole and perfect and shining, like the wrath of some god—Thor or Odin.

Another lightning flashed, and Sarah saw the silver bandeau that held the woman's hair back, the unearthly glow in her eyes.

And then she was gone.

"Thora," Sarah whispered.

"No!" Mrs. Hamilton shrieked.

Sarah whipped back around to see that Mrs. Hamilton had stood up, her knife falling from her limp fingers. Mary Ann crawled away from her, and was caught up in Mr. O'Riley's arms, safe.

Mr. Hamilton rushed towards his wife, his hand outstretched. But she screamed again, backing away from him, away from them all.

"Emmeline, please," he shouted.

"She is here to take me away," Mrs. Hamilton said. She pointed her shaking finger toward the tree. "I knew it would happen!"

Her husband took yet another step closer, reaching out for her with both hands. "Emmeline, come to me now! No one will hurt you."

She stepped back from him—and fell into the open pit of the leather-worker's shop with a terrible scream.

Sarah covered her mouth with her hand, feeling ill. She felt Miles's strong hands on her, pulling her closer. She sagged into him, suddenly so weak and cold she could hardly stand.

Mr. Hamilton scrambled into the pit, and called up, "Help me lift her up, please! I beg you! She is still alive, but hurt."

Sarah clung to Miles for one second longer, her fingers numb on his coat collar. "Go, help him," she whispered.

"You look ill," he answered, his face anguished, clearly torn between doing his duty and staying with her.

Sarah would love nothing more than to have him stay beside her, holding her up, sending warmth into her chilled soul. But Sarah knew that, no matter what Mrs. Hamilton had done, she could not let her suffer in the ancient surroundings she so hated.

"I will be fine," she said. "Go now, and assist Mr. Hamilton. I shall just steady myself, and then fetch the carriage. She will need a physician, and so will Mary Ann."

He nodded, and pressed a long kiss to her temple. "My brave one."

As soon as he released her, and scrambled down into the pit with the Hamiltons, Sarah fell to her knees, trembling. She did not know if she could ever stand up again.

Brave, indeed.

Chapter Twenty-three

"Did you see her?" Sarah asked. "Or was I dreaming? Was I truly caught in a nightmare?"

She sat before the fire in her own drawing room, clad in a warm, dry gown, blankets covering her legs and wrapped about her shoulders, a cup of brandy-laced tea clutched in her hand. They chased the rain-chill from her skin, but there was a cold knot at the center of her that she feared might never be warm again.

Upstairs, Mary Ann slept in her bed, lulled into slumber by one of Rose's tisanes. Sarah thought of how very close she had come to losing her sister, and shivered.

Miles sat across from her, wrapped in his own blankets, his own thoughts.

He stared into the crackling flames. "I saw—something. I thought it was the tree, or the rain."

She saw that he, her dear, sensible Miles, *wanted* to believe that was all it had been. Sarah herself had tried to think it was some trick of the storm. But, as she remembered it over and over, she knew that the woman had been real. That she had been real all along.

Sarah shook her head. "No. It was Thora. Her home was here; her love was here. She hasn't left. She guards it still."

Miles sat back in his chair, regarding her seriously. "So, since Thora guards it, I cannot destroy it. Is that what you are saying, my dear?"

Sarah left her seat, and went to kneel beside him, trailing her blankets behind her. She laid her hand over his, and curled her fingers, entwining them with his. They were warm and strong. How she loved these hands, and the man who possessed them. She loved him in a way she had never thought possible before, a way that made her feel safe, yet tingling with an excitement that was wild and free. Her love for him somehow grounded her, and at the same time made her feel as if she could fly.

It must have been the way Thora felt for her voyaging Viking lover. It had been a love that held her here for centuries. Sarah knew because she had seen Thora and felt all her emotions as her own—in her dreams.

And now those dreams had all come to reality, through her love for Miles.

It was a feeling she never, ever wanted to lose.

But she also knew that she owed Thora very much indeed.

"Miles," she said, still looking at his hand and not up into his eyes. "I know how you feel about that land. And you are right, very right, to be concerned about men like Mr. O'Riley, and to want to help them. Your kind heart is one of the things I care about most in you. I was prepared to leave the village. But now . . ."

"Now?"

Sarah raised her gaze to his. His was as blue and blank as the sky. She could read nothing there. "Now I must try to save it for Thora, as she saved my sister. There is something there, something important, and I must find it."

"Oh, Sarah, my dear." He drew his hands from hers and raised them to frame her face. He held her as if she was a pearl of enormous worth and beauty. "I never truly believed that it was the tree. I saw a woman, just as you did—a woman not of this world. If you feel you must preserve the village, then I cannot deny it to you."

Sarah couldn't breathe. The very air seemed lodged in her throat. "Do you truly mean that, Miles?"

"I would not say it to you if I did not."

"But what of your new farms?"

They stared at each other in silence, still caught in their own needs, their tangled emotions.

"I cannot believe that two intelligent people like you haven't seen what is right before you," a voice interrupted.

Sarah looked over her shoulder to see Patrick O'Riley standing in the drawing room doorway. He had fallen asleep on the floor outside Mary Ann's chamber, and he looked tousled and tired. And rather impatient with the pair of them.

She sat back on her heels. "Whatever do you mean, Mr. O'Riley?"

"Indeed, Patrick," Miles said. "If you have a solution, I wish you would share it with us."

Mr. O'Riley sat down in Sarah's vacated chair and yawned, rubbing a hand over his unshaven jaw. "Lady Iverson has learned a great deal from her village, valuable knowledge that the world should know. Yet she still has much work left to do. And you feel a certain responsibility to chaps like me, Miles. Both are quite proper feelings."

Miles frowned at him impatiently. "So . . ."

"So Lady Iverson should open a museum here, one that shows how Vikings truly lived, what crops they grew, how they did their crafts. And who would help Lady Iverson to set up her museum, to work in it?"

"Former soldiers and their families!" Sarah cried. It was a marvelous idea, and one she did indeed feel foolish for not thinking of. It would take a great deal of planning, but it could be a grand place when it was finished, unlike any other in England. She could just envision the learning that would go on here.

Her hands fairly itched for paper and pen so she could start laying down plans. She would have to design displays for the artifacts she had been able to salvage from Mrs. Hamilton's destruction. Displays that could make others see the true beauty of them. They could just seem like dusty, broken old bits to some people, even though they were treasures to her. . . .

Treasure!

Of course.

Sarah leaped to her feet, seized by a new revelation. Her blankets dropped, and she pulled them back up impatiently. "I have to go," she said, hurrying to the door. "Mr. O'Riley, will you stay here and watch after Mary Ann for me? I will not be gone long."

Mr. O'Riley just smiled at her complacently, but Miles frowned in confusion. He stood up and followed her into the foyer.

"What do you mean you have to go out?" he said. "Go out where? You should rest. You have had a terrible ordeal."

"Rest? How could I rest? It was there—all along!" She went up on tiptoe and kissed his cheek, laughing in her exuberance. "I must go to it. There is no time to explain right now, Miles, I must find my cloak."

She went off toward the staircase, still trailing her blankets.

"Wherever you are going, Sarah, I am coming with you," he called after her.

"My darling, that will be even better!"

Chapter Twenty-four

Sarah drew her phaeton to a halt at the edge of the village. She had expected to be alone there, alone with Miles, but apparently that was not to be. Neville Hamilton stood beside the pit of the leather-worker's shop, his head uncovered to the pale gray light, staring out at nothing.

Sarah had hoped she could avoid this meeting for just a short while longer, until she felt stronger, more certain. She and Mr. Hamilton had been friends of a sort once. What could they be now, after all that had happened?

She took Miles's hand when he helped her from the phaeton, and held onto it as she stepped forward and called, "Mr. Hamilton—Neville."

He turned his head slowly to look at her. His face was as gray as the sky, his eyes a blank. "Lady Iverson," he said. "I trust Miss Bellweather has suffered no ill effects from her—experience? That she is well?"

Miles tightened his clasp on her gloved hand, and gave her a small, reassuring smile as they walked together to Mr. Hamilton's side. The mud and debris of last night's storm pulled at her boots and the hem of her gown. She felt none of the wild enchantment, none of the strangeness that had hung here then. Perhaps Thora was gone, not to return, after performing her good deed?

Sarah felt a sad pang at the thought. A sadness that met and mingled with the one she felt when she looked at Mr. Hamilton. "My sister is recovering," she told him. "She was sleeping peacefully when we left her."

Mr. Hamilton gave a regretful smile, one that spoke of a past path he might have taken "I am glad. I must convey to her my deepest apologies."

"And what of your wife?" Sarah asked.

"Oh, I must give her my apologies, as well."

Sarah gave a startled little laugh at his answer. "I meant—how does she fare?"

"Well enough. The physician has given her a strong draught to help her sleep. Tomorrow, when she has rested, I will take her back to Bath, to her parents' home. Perhaps there she can truly recover. Only the five of us know the truth of that farmer—hopefully that can be an end to that?"

"So she returns to Bath after all," Miles said quietly.

Neville raised his gaze to Miles's. "Indeed. She does." Miles nodded.

"Lord Ransome has agreed to let me build a museum here," Sarah said. "One that will preserve the life of the village. I hope that, perhaps one day, you can return and continue the work. John would have wanted you to."

He looked surprised that she would offer this to him. His response was a merest flicker that broke across the despair of his face. "Perhaps I shall. I—thank you, Lady Iverson." He gave her a small bow. "I must go and see about Emmeline. Good-bye, Lady Iverson. Lord Ransome."

"Good-bye." Sarah watched him go and climb into his own carriage, watched the vehicle until it disappeared from view. Then she turned to Miles, reaching again for his hand. "It is truly sad. He is a gifted scholar, one who cares so much for this history."

Miles squeezed her hand. "Perhaps if he had not married the wrong woman . . ."

She laughed. The sound felt good, warm and real after the long night they had passed. "I suppose that is a mistake *you* do not mean to make?"

"Certainly not. For I mean to marry you, Sarah Iverson."

Chapter Twenty-five

Sarah stared up at him, her laughter fading. She was not sure she had heard him correctly. She had imagined hearing words like that from him, of course, had giggled about it into her pillow at night. She had rather imagined it differently, with flowers, a ring, a beautiful gown—not standing in the mud.

But thinking of it here, thinking of marriage and a life with her love here in her village, was sweeter than any imagining could ever have been.

"Did you say—you intend to marry *me*?" she whispered.

"If you will have me," he answered. He lifted her hands to his lips and pressed a kiss to them, and held them against his chest. She could feel his heartbeat, steady and strong and true. How she always loved that feeling. "I am probably a poor choice for you, an old army man with no knowledge of history and antiquities. I am no great scholar, like your first husband. But I promise you, Sarah, that if you accept me, I will love you and take care of you for all my life. I have never known anyone like you, and I know that I never will again. I love you, Sarah Iverson. Will you marry me?"

Sarah felt tears in her eyes, felt their salty warmth spill down her cheeks in a flood of pure happiness. She had spent so long alone, devoted to her work, and had thought herself happy. But she saw now that she had never known true, complete happiness until this very moment. Her heart was full, her soul bursting with joy.

"I love you, too," she said. "I feel like I have known you forever and a day, like we have always been together. And now we always will be." She went up on tiptoe and kissed his lips, softly, lingeringly. "Yes, Miles. I will marry you."

He laughed, and caught her about the waist, lifting her up off her feet. He twirled her about, and she laughed, too, clinging to his shoulders. When he lowered her to her feet at last, she leaned her head on his shoulder. The world swayed around her in a delicious giddiness.

"I will always do everything in my power to make you happy, Sarah," he said. "I do not want you to ever regret becoming my wife."

"You *do* make me happy," she answered. "And I hope that *you* never regret being my husband. I will never be as other fine ladies are. I will probably be a dreadful marchioness, not at all like your lovely mother. She would be perfect."

"You will be the finest marchioness ever." He hugged her close. "Should we tell your sister of our betrothal? I have a feeling she could use some happy news today."

"Oh, yes! She will want to make wedding plans. She was too small to be a bridesmaid at my first wedding."

"Then let us return to your house, my dear. The wind is becoming a bit chill."

"Of course, I . . ." Then Sarah remembered what she had come to the village for in the first place. "We should go home. I am longing for a fire, and some tea. But there is something I must do here first."

"What is it?"

"Come with me, and I will show you. If it is there at all."

She went back to the phaeton, and took out the trowels and picks she had tucked beneath the seat. Wordlessly, she handed some of them to Miles and led him to the tree where she had seen Thora last night.

The tree stood outside the perimeter of the digging, in the area she had not yet been able to excavate. It was towering and ancient, spreading its wide branches in a sheltering arc. The leaves were heavy from the rain, drooping pale green over her head.

Sarah closed her eyes and remembered how Thora had looked in the purple-blue flash of the lightning, brandishing her scamasax.

"She stood just here," she murmured. She opened her eyes, and planted her trowel deep in the soft earth. "This is where we have to dig."

"Show me," Miles said.

Sarah fell to her knees, unmindful of her gown and pelisse, and scooped up dirt in clods and clumps. Miles knelt beside her, using a pick to pry out stones and branches. They worked together in silence. Miles asked her no questions, even though he must have been very puzzled; he just dug.

And she loved him even more for it.

It took a long time, but finally her trowel struck something hollow with a dull thud. She pulled off her gloves and leaned down, digging into the dirt with her bare fingers, scrambling until she touched something solid.

"It's here," she said. "But I can't pull it up."

Miles peered over her shoulder. "I see it. A box of some sort." He took the edge of his pick and used it to lever the object up and pull it to the surface.

It was indeed a box, of rotting wood bound about with iron fastenings. Sarah reached for the clasp, but her hand was trembling, and it fell back to her side.

"What is this, Sarah?" Miles asked, in a hushed voice, as if he felt the same aura of awe that she did.

"I think—I think it is Thora's Treasure," she said, her own voice shaking. "The one everyone has talked of, but that I never believed in. The one that only her true heir can possess. I thought about where I saw her here last night, and I had a great feeling it must be here."

"Then you must be her true heir," he said. "The one it was meant for."

Sarah thought it more likely *he* was the heir, since this was his land, but she just smiled. "Will you open it with me?"

"Of course."

He covered her hand with his, and together they lifted the heavy clasp and pushed the lid back.

"Oh," Sarah breathed.

Inside the box, on a bed of shredded cloth, lay items similar to others they had found in the village, but grander and richer than any Sarah had ever seen. There were hairpins of ivory with rough-cut gemstones set in their heads; ivory combs etched with flowers and studded with more stones. There were silver storage jars, amber beads, and silver brooches, coins, arm rings, bracelets. They shimmered in the dull light of day, light they had not seen in centuries. They seemed to be tokens from someone to a woman he had loved very much.

Sarah *knew* this, just as she knew every one of these items. It would be the perfect centerpiece of her museum.

On the top of the glistening horde was a ring, made of silver twisted into the shape of tree branches and tiny leaves. One perfect spring green gemstone crowned it.

Miles took the ring, and slid it onto her finger. It fit as if made for her; it lay against her skin as if it had come home.

"So there *was* a treasure, after all," she said. "It was here the whole time."

"Yes. A treasure beyond the worth of all others," answered Miles.

Sarah looked up at him to see that he watched not the treasure, but *her*. In his eyes' blue depths, she saw all the love and passion, all the true acceptance, she had longed for. Nothing, no silver, no jewels, could ever equal that.

She threw her arms around his neck and kissed him, putting all her love, all her life into that kiss. And she felt all of *his* love pouring back into her.

Above them, the gray clouds parted, and the sun shone forth.

A Loving Spirit

Chapter One

England, 1811

"Why is it always so *cold* in England?" Cassandra Richards murmured, burrowing deeper into her fur-lined cloak as she watched the Cornwall landscape roll by outside the carriage window.

"I think my toes are frozen," said her friend Antoinette Duvall. "They will never be warm again." Her usually merry coffee-colored face was glum, at odds with her bright red-and-black printed turban.

The two of them sighed, and leaned against each other disconsolately.

Cassie's aunt, Charis, Lady Willowby, called Chat by all her many friends, looked across the carriage at them and shook her head. "You girls! It is only October. There is barely a nip in the air. What are you going to do when it is December and snow is thick on the ground?"

"Snow!" Cassie cried. She had lived for the last fourteen years in hot, sunny Jamaica; she had not seen snow since she was five. All she remembered was that it was very cold and very wet.

And that her father used to make little balls of it, and throw them at her laughing mother.

That memory of her parents, who were now gone and left behind in the small cemetery of their plantation near Negril, gave her a sharp pang. How she missed them! How she missed their life together, a life of sunshine and warm sea.

Even four months in England had not erased her homesickness.

But at least Antoinette had agreed to come with her, she thought, reaching out with the toe of her half boot to nudge the flannel-wrapped brick closer to her friend's feet. Home never seemed quite so far away when she could hear the lilting, musical cadence of Antoinette's voice. And Aunt Chat really *was* trying to make her feel welcome. She had given parties at her house in Bath to introduce Cassie to all her friends, and now she had organized this trip to Cornwall to visit yet another of her friends, the Dowager Lady Royce.

Cassie knew that Aunt Chat hoped that being near the sea would help cheer her up. The least she could do was enjoy it.

She smiled at her aunt. "I cannot wait to see Royce Castle, Aunt Chat! It sounds most intriguing. We don't have buildings that are over five hundred years old in Jamaica."

Chat smiled back. Her pretty, round face was relieved beneath her plumed bonnet. "I am sure you will enjoy it, my dear. My friend Lady Royce is wonderful, and the castle itself most intriguing. There are underground tunnels, secret rooms, and supposedly many ghosts in residence."

Antoinette brightened a bit. "Ghosts, Lady Willowby?"

"Oh, yes. Several, I believe, though I do not know

the details. Melinda or her son should be able to tell you all about it." She shivered a bit. "Though I certainly hope we do not actually *meet* any!"

"Oh, I do!" Cassie said, clapping her gloved hands in delight. "A ghost would be ever so exciting. Did you bring your mother's book of incantations, Antoinette?"

Antoinette was already digging about in her valise. She came up with a thick, worn, brown leather-covered volume. "Of course! I never travel without it. One never knows when one might need an incantation. I also brought some herbs and potions." She pulled a bottle out of the valise, and held it up to the pale sunlight. Small flowers and stems floated about in a clear liquid.

"Wonderful!" Cassie said. "Antoinette's mother was a Yaumumi priestess, Aunt Chat. She taught Antoinette to find all sorts of things that we cannot see. If there *are* any ghosts, she is sure to find them."

Antoinette nodded firmly. "Yes. And if there are unfriendly entities, we shall banish them."

Chat eyed the bottle a bit nervously. "My dears, are you *sure* this is a good idea? Perhaps we should leave the, er, entities alone. We wouldn't like to get them upset, now would we?"

Cassie gave her a reassuring smile. "You mustn't worry, Aunt Chat. Antoinette knows exactly what she is doing. Now, tell me more about your friend. And her son! How very fortunate that they live in such a *spirited* place. They must be terribly interesting people."

"Dearest, I do hope you are going to change your clothes before Lady Willowby and her niece arrive," Melinda Leighton, the Dowager Lady Royce said to her son, when she came into the library on a wave of lilac scent. She proceeded to open the draperies at all the windows, sending sunlight into the gloomy corners of the room.

"What is wrong with what I am wearing, Mother?" Phillip, the Earl of Royce, said distractedly, not even glancing up from the volume he was perusing.

"What is *not* wrong with it? The edges of the coat cuffs are frayed, and is that a hole in the elbow? You should put your new green coat on. And a fresh cravat. You have made ink spots on that one."

Phillip turned over a page. "I will. Later."

"But they will be here at any moment!"

"Surely not. You said they would not be here before teatime."

"It is already past four, dearest."

Phillip did look up then, squinting through his spectacles at the clock on the mantel. "Oh. So it is."

Melinda came over to the desk, and pushed all the piles of books and papers aside to lean over the volume he was reading. "What is it that you find so interesting, Phillip?"

"Thucydides, Mother. It's a very important source for the monograph I'm writing." He marked his place in the volume, closed it, and reached up to remove his spectacles.

"The Pelo-Pelo . . ." Melinda murmured, running one finger over the gilt letters on the book's cover.

"The Peloponnisian War," Phillip said, rubbing at his eyes. He had been working for hours, since just after breakfast, but had not realized at all how late it was growing.

"It sounds horribly depressing," Melinda said. "I am truly glad we are to have some company. You spend far too much time in this room, Phillip. A little society will be good for you."

Phillip leaned back in his chair and smiled up at

her. "Poor Mother. I know it's terribly dull for you here in the wilds of Cornwall, with only my sorry company." ·

"We were not speaking of me! We were speaking of *you*. Of how excellent it will be for you to be around people for a while."

"I am happy with the way things are. It's very important that I finish my work on the Peloponnesian War; it is a very vital part of my series on ancient Greece."

Melinda shrugged, as usual not listening to her son's obsession with the order and rationality of the ancient world. She was always far more interested in the confusion of the modern world—gossipy letters from her friends, good works at the church, *soirées* on the rare occasions she was in Town.

She went to a mirror on the wall and straightened her cap and her lace shawl. "Nevertheless, dearest, you can take the time to be polite to my friend." She laid her palm against her still-smooth cheek. "I wonder what Chat will think of me. It has been a long time since we saw each other, though I get a letter from her every month. I was much younger then."

"She will think you have not aged a day, because you haven't," Phillip said, coming around to kiss her cheek. "But didn't you say she is also bringing a child with her? I shouldn't think there would be much here to amuse a child."

Melinda laughed. "Her niece is not a child, Phillip! She is eighteen or nineteen, I believe, and she has only just come here from Jamaica. Or maybe Barbados."

Phillip drew back suspiciously. "Eighteen or nineteen? Mother."

She gave him a wide-eyed, innocent look. "What, dearest?"

"You are not matchmaking again, are you?"

"Certainly not! When did I ever play match-maker?"

"When you invited Mrs. Meecham and her daughter to visit. When you invited Lady Bryson and her *four* daughters . . ."

"Oh, well, that. But this is different, Phillip, I assure you. I did not even know that Chat had a niece when I invited her to come here. I am sure the young lady would not be quite suitable, having been out in the West Indies for so long. There is no telling what odd habits she acquired there. Chat writes that she is bringing a very *unusual* companion with her—a native woman! I have never seen a native woman before. And she probably cares nothing for ancient Greece."

"If you say so, Mother," Phillip said, not entirely convinced of her innocence.

Melinda patted his arm reassuringly. "Do not worry, dear. We are going to have a very nice time. Now, I want to go check on the guest chambers just one more time and be sure things are in order. Please, *do* go change your clothes." She turned away to leave the library, then suddenly shivered and drew her shawl closer about her shoulders. "Such a chill! It must be one of the ghosts."

"Mother!" Phillip called after her, exasperated, as she walked away. "I have told you over and over that there is no such thing as ghosts."

"Change your clothes, dear!" she called back blithely.

Phillip watched his mother go, and turned his attention back to his books with a sigh.

He was glad his mother was excited about having guests, truly he was. But why did they have to come to the castle *now*? His work on the new book was only just beginning. There was so much to be done, and time spent socializing was time wasted away from his work.

And, as his mother pointed out, his wardrobe was hardly up to the fastidious standards of ladies. He ruefully examined a spot of ink on his shirt cuff.

They would just have to take him as he was, he thought as he closed up his books. Perhaps he would not have to see them so very often, after all. Supper and the occasional outing ought to suffice.

Chapter Two

"It *is* very grand, Aunt Chat. Just what a five-hundred-year-old castle ought to look like," Cassie commented, leaning against the carriage window to watch as Royce Castle drew closer and closer.

It was set high above the roiling sea, a great, dark stone sentinel on a craggy bluff. Towers and turrets loomed; windows glinted in the fading sunlight like eyes watching their approach. Not a very welcoming place, certainly. Not at all like the low, bright yellow terraced house she had left in Jamaica. But it was very intriguing.

And it became even more so when Antoinette said, "I feel a great many presences in this house."

Cassie settled back onto the seat. "Truly, Antoinette? All the way from here?"

Antoinette closed her eyes and nodded. "It is very powerful. So many emotions—love, hate, anger, laughter, jealousy. Sudden death."

"How grand," Cassie said happily. "I cannot wait until we arrive and can start our explorations. If, of course, Lady Royce does not mind."

Chat still regarded them rather doubtfully, but she

nodded. "I am sure Melinda will not mind whatever you do. She was always interested in—spiritual inquiry. And I wrote her about Miss Duvall and her unusual activities! But I am not certain about her son."

Cassie laughed. "Oh, yes! The classical scholar. I am very glad you warned us about him, Aunt Chat. Anyone with such a passion for—how did you say it?—order and accuracy would not appreciate our kind of explorations. We shall simply have to be discreet, then, won't we, Antoinette?"

Antoinette gave a warm chuckle.

"Cassandra, my dear, Lord Royce is a brilliant man," Chat admonished. "Everyone in my Philosophical Society says so. His work on the economy and society of ancient Greece is much appreciated."

"Perhaps," Cassandra said doubtfully. "I am sorry, Aunt Chat, but he sounds a rather dull old fellow. One who would not appreciate the great romance of the very house he lives in."

Chat gave an odd little smile. "I think you will not find him to be a dull *old* fellow at all."

Before Cassie could question her aunt about this rather strange statement, the carriage drew to a halt outside the massive front doors of the castle. As they stepped down onto the gravel drive, one of the enormous, nail-studded doors opened and a tiny woman came hurrying out.

She looked like a little Dresden shepherdess in her pink-striped gown and lacy shawl, with silver curls that sprang free from beneath her cap. Her small hands, swathed in lace mitts, fluttered in excitement as she rushed down the stone steps to kiss Chat's cheek.

"My dear friend!" she cried. "Here you are at last. Oh, it has been too long."

"Far too long, Melinda," Chat answered. "I will never forgive myself for not coming to Cornwall sooner."

"Nonsense! You have been so busy, with your niece coming and everything. And this must be her!" Lady Royce turned her fairy-smile onto Cassie. "How do you do, Miss Richards? Why, you are the very image of your aunt when she was a girl!"

Cassie very much doubted that. Aunt Chat was reputed to have been a great beauty, and she was still very handsome. Cassie knew herself to be not much above the ordinary, being short and dark where blonde and willowy was the fashion.

But it was a nice compliment for Lady Royce to pay. Cassie smiled at her in return, and bobbed a small curtsy. "I am very pleased to meet you, Lady Royce. My aunt has told me ever so much about you."

Lady Royce laughed merrily. "Not *too* much, I hope! We did have some larks together when we were girls, didn't we, Chat?" Then her bright eyes slid curiously to Antoinette, who stood a bit behind Cassie, uncharacteristically shy.

"Oh!" Cassie said, reaching for Antoinette's hand to draw her around. "Lady Royce, may I present my companion, Miss Antoinette Duvall?"

"The lady that I wrote to you about," Chat added.

Antoinette curtsied and said in her musical voice, "You have a lovely home, Lady Royce. Very *active*."

Lady Royce clasped her hands together in delight. "Do you mean *spiritually* active, Miss Duvall?"

"Miss Duvall's mother was a, er, priestess," Chat offered. "In Jamaica."

"A Yaumumi priestess," Antoinette answered. "Her gifts were very great. Mine are only a small part of hers, but I sense many entities here."

"Good or bad ones?" Lady Royce asked eagerly.

"I cannot say as of yet," Antoinette said.

Lady Royce nodded. "I have often felt things here, as well, but my son insists there are no ghosts. Oh, but here I have kept you standing about outside when there is a chill in the air! You must all come inside and have some tea. I am very eager to discuss this subject further!"

Lady Royce took Chat's arm and led her through the front doors, the two of them laughing and talking. As Cassie moved to follow them, she glanced up at the house. She thought she saw a movement at one of the upstairs windows, but when she blinked there was no one there. Only a small movement of the draperies.

Phillip watched from his bedroom window as their guests arrived. It was the first time they had had company since Lady Bryson and her daughters almost a year ago, and the household was abuzz with excitement. Most of the servants were gathered in the foyer on one pretext or another, eager to see his mother's friend and her niece and strange companion from the islands.

Phillip was feeling rather reluctantly curious himself.

He had not really wanted them to come. His work was progressing so well, and guests could sometimes be a confounding, demanding nuisance. But his mother had looked so happy when Lady Willowby's letter arrived that he had not had the heart to refuse her.

Now he wondered about these people who were going to be living in his house for the next several weeks.

Lady Willowby was just as his mother had described. Tall, dark-haired, impeccably fashionable in a purple pelisse and feathered bonnet, a printed India shawl about her shoulders. She looked a sensible sort.

A woman stepped out of the carriage after her, swathed from head to toe in a hooded red cloak. This had to be the niece from the West Indies. Phillip had wondered what a girl who had lived most of her life on a tropical island might look like, but it seemed he was not to find out just yet. She was as well-wrapped as any Saracen lady would be.

But then she tipped her head to look up at the house, and her hood fell back.

"Oh!" he said involuntarily. His hands stilled on the cravat he had been attempting to tie.

He wasn't sure what he had been expecting, but not this pretty woman. Her hair was black and shining as a raven's wing, parted sleekly in the middle and drawn back to a simple low knot at the nape of her neck. No fashionable curls or whorls marred the sheen of it, and its only ornament was a carved comb of some dark wood.

Her skin was smooth and faintly sun-touched, over high cheekbones and a slightly pointed chin. A pair of long, sparkling earrings swung against her cheeks and caught in the rich sable lining of her hood.

She smiled as she surveyed the house, as if pleased with its aspect, and Phillip found himself quite pleased himself that she should like it. He wondered if she would like *him* as well . . .

Then he realized what he was thinking and frowned. "Fool!" he muttered, his hand crushing his cravat.

He was meant to be thinking of his work, not watching a pretty lady out of windows and wondering if she would like him. That was for men who had nothing better to do, society fribbles who just sat about at their clubs and danced at balls.

Even as he thought this, he could not stop himself from looking at the elf-girl again. She was half-turned away, talking to another woman. This other woman was a very interesting vision, indeed. She was quite tall, perhaps as tall as his own six feet, with dark, gleaming skin. She wore an odd pelisse-robe of crimson and black, with a matching turban concealing her hair. She, too, surveyed the house, with narrowed, assessing eyes. Then she said something to the woman in the cloak and nodded.

Well, this *was* quite interesting. Phillip's scholarly mind was turning, coming up with countless questions he would like to ask these ladies about their lives in the West Indies. It must have been a fascinating existence, full of old-fashioned superstitions and myths.

It was simply too bad they were not Greek. What a great help *that* would have been to his work.

"My lord?" his long-suffering valet said from behind him.

Phillip turned to see that he held out his best coat, the dark green superfine his mother had insisted he wear, the one with only one small hole on the sleeve. "Yes, Jones?"

"Your mother has sent a message saying the guests have arrived," Jones said, holding the coat out farther with a rather hopeful air. "She asks that you join them in the drawing room, my lord, at your earliest convenience."

"Yes, of course. Mustn't be late," Phillip murmured. He glanced back out the window, but everyone had already gone inside.

Chapter Three

Cassie munched on a tea cake and examined all the portraits lining the walls of the vast drawing room. They were varied and very fascinating, ranging from a Renaissance gentleman in a velvet cap and cloak to a picture hung over the fireplace of the present Lady Royce as a young bride. She cocked her head to one side to examine the portrait of a Restoration lady with blond curls and a blue satin gown.

The lady in turn seemed to move her head to examine Cassie.

"Such an engaging family you have, Lady Royce," Cassie said, straightening her head. Now the lady appeared to be staring out vacantly into space. "I would love to hear about each and every portrait."

Lady Royce gave a pleased little laugh. "I will be happy to tell you all you wish to know, my dear Miss Richards! Though of course they are not exactly *my* family, I feel as if they are, since I married into the Leighton family when I was only sixteen." She paused to refill Antoinette's teacup and pass Chat another sandwich, then went on, "That portrait you are looking at is Louisa, Lady Royce. She came to a rather bad end. She fell off the cliffs into the sea."

Antoinette examined the painting. "I believe she still dwells in the East Tower."

Lady Royce looked at her with wide, wondering eyes. "So I have heard. I personally have not seen her, or the knight who walks about in his armor. And then there is our most famous ghost, Louisa's husband's great-grandmother Lady Lettice."

Cassie looked over where Lady Royce indicated to see a painting of a woman in Elizabethan regalia, ruff, drum farthingale, and ropes of pearls and rubies.

Antoinette frowned. "I cannot sense her presence."

"No one has seen her in quite a long time," Lady Royce said regretfully. "Not since before I came to live here. But there are many legends about her. They say she cannot find peace because she was betrayed by her true love."

"We shall just have to find her, then, won't we, Antoinette?" Cassie said.

Antoinette nodded slowly. "Perhaps."

"Well, if I can be of any help, do let me know," said Lady Royce. Then she looked past the settee where Cassie and Antoinette sat, and smiled. "Phillip, dear, here you are at last! Do come and greet our guests."

Cassie put down her teacup and placed a polite smile on her face, preparing to greet the shambling scholar, whom she still pictured as old despite his mother's youthful appearance. She didn't hear any tap of a cane on the floor, or smell any camphor to warn of his approach.

She stood and turned around, and felt the polite smile freeze on her lips.

Why, Lord Royce was not old at all! In fact, he did

not look much like her idea of a scholar, as he was quite good-looking. He was a trifle thin, true, especially compared to the burly, broad-shouldered planters she was accustomed to at home. And his complexion was rather pale, probably from spending a great deal of time studying indoors. His eyes were an intense, stormy gray, that seemed to pierce right through to her innermost soul.

But she would have thought him a poet, not a student of antique civilizations. His hair was not just in need of a bit of a trim, it was truly unfashionably long, falling almost to his shoulders in thick dark brown waves, as if he could not be bothered to cut it. It was damp, as if he had just washed it and hastily combed it back, but it was rich and soft-looking. She actually lifted her hand a bit, wanting to touch it, before she realized what she was doing and dropped her arm back to her side.

No, Lord Royce was not at all what she had been expecting!

Then Lady Royce's voice came to her through the haze, and she realized that things had been going on about her. Things she ought to pay attention to, such as introductions.

". . . and this is her niece, Miss Cassandra Richards," Lady Royce was saying.

Cassie stared dumbly at Lord Royce as he reached for the hand she had dropped to her side, and lifted it to his lips for a brief salute.

His breath was warm on her fingers, and she had to fight down the strong urge to giggle. She scarcely even noticed the small hole in his green sleeve.

"I am pleased to make your acquaintance, Miss Richards," he said. "I suppose you must always speak the truth?" His voice was dark and rich, like Jamaican rum.

Cassie blinked at him. What on earth was the man talking about? "Ex-excuse me, Lord Royce?"

He smiled at her as one would to a rather slow child. "Your name. Cassandra. 'Disbelieved by men.' Are you named after the great prophetess of Troy?"

Cassie vaguely remembered her mother telling her the story of the Trojan Cassandra, who was doomed to always tell the truth of her prophecies and never be believed. Her mother had loved the old myths. "I suppose I must be," she answered.

He gave her another smile, and went to sit beside his mother. Cassie slowly sat back down, her mind screaming one word at her. "Fool, fool, fool!"

She could feel her face flaming. What a thorough idiot he must think her!

"Miss Richards was just asking me about the history of the castle," Lady Royce said, pouring out a cup of tea for her son. "She is very interested in it."

Lord Royce raised his dark brow at Cassie. "Indeed, Miss Richards?"

Cassie seized on the topic. Surely she could converse more easily about a haunted castle than ancient Troy. "Oh, yes! It is truly fascinating. There must be much to learn about it."

"It *is* an interesting place," he agreed. "I plan to someday write a history of it. It was built in 1320, by the first Earl of Royce . . ."

"I believe she is more interested in Lady Lettice, the knight, and Louisa, dear," interrupted Lady Royce.

That dark brow rose again. "Is that what you are interested in, Miss Richards? The so-called ghosts?"

Cassie frowned, but before she could reply, Antoinette said, "You are a disbeliever, Lord Royce."

"I suppose I am," answered Lord Royce. "I prefer

the logic and rationality of ancient Greece to spooks and haunts."

"Hmm," Antoinette murmured, surveying him through narrowed ebony eyes.

Lord Royce fidgeted a bit under her steady gaze, and turned away to address a question to Aunt Chat.

Cassie studied him over the rim of her teacup. Well, he might be handsome as a poet, but he was obviously quite as obnoxiously *logical* as she had feared he might be.

Chapter Four

"I liked Lady Royce, didn't you, Cassie?" Antoinette
asked. The two of them were in Cassie's room before
they retired, to brush each other's hair and talk over
the day. After they had convinced some rather
snooty upper servants that Antoinette was Cassie's
friend and not her maid, she had been given the
chamber next door to Cassie's. Just like at the house
in Jamaica.

"Yes, very much," Cassie answered, reaching for
a strand of her freshly brushed hair to braid. "She
was all that was charming. And she agreed to give
us a tour of the castle tomorrow. That should be
most interesting."

"Perhaps we can find Lady Lettice!"

"Perhaps so. And Louisa and the armored knight.
I don't think Lady Royce's son would very much
appreciate us going on a ghost hunt, though," Cassie
murmured. She thought of Lord Royce, of his poet's
hair and his mysterious gray eyes, of the smoky
roughness of his voice.

Of that obnoxious raised brow, proclaiming how
silly he thought her.

She frowned.

"Oh, yes. Lord Royce," Antoinette said. "He does not believe. He does not sense all that is around him. It is very sad."

Cassie felt a strange urge to defend Lord Royce, even with the memory of his scoffing in her mind. "Not everyone is as sensitive as you, Antoinette. Not everyone can so easily believe in things they cannot touch or see. Or read in dusty books, as Lord Royce does."

"*You* believe."

"I am different from most of the English we have met. I lived in Jamaica, where things are very—different." Cassie turned her head to look out the uncurtained window, where all the autumn stars shimmered.

Usually she was happy enough here in England. Her aunt had been all that was kind, and life at Chat's house in Bath was very comfortable. But sometimes, especially in unguarded moments like these, she felt like such an outsider. Like she could never possibly understand the people around her, nor they her. She did not understand the things they took for granted, and they often thought her an oddity.

Just as Lord Royce had.

She would feel completely alone all the time, were it not for Antoinette. But she sometimes felt guilty for bringing her here, where, if Cassie felt like an oddity, Antoinette must feel ten times more so. She had faced shocked looks and fierce whispers ever since they reached England.

She turned to Antoinette, and asked, as she had a dozen times before, "Do you not miss home?"

Antoinette paused in braiding her thick mane of wavy hair, and gave the same answer she always gave. "Of course I do. Just as you do, Cassie. It is the only home I have ever known. But I would have missed you far more, if you had left without me."

"Truly?"

"What did I have left in Jamaica? My mother is dead. Since I grew up with you and was educated, I do not fit in with my own people. You are like a sister to me. How could I let you go off into the world alone?"

Cassie blinked at the sudden prickle of tears at her eyes. She wiped at them with the sleeve of her dressing gown. "Just as you are like my sister! I only hope you will never be sorry for your decision."

Antoinette dabbed at her own tears. "I will not. But if I do, I can always go back. It is a long way, but not impossible. Just as you could go back, Cassie, and marry that awful Mr. Bates. He did offer for you before we left."

Cassie laughed at the memory of Mr. Bates, pressing his suit on her just as she was about to board the ship to England. "So he did! Though I daresay life at Aunt Chat's home in Bath is far preferable to life as Mrs. Bates. And we would have missed seeing this lovely castle!"

"Indeed we would have," Antoinette said, the lilting humor back in her voice. "Speaking of which, we have much to do tomorrow. Shall we retire?"

Cassie shook her head. "You go ahead. I am not tired yet."

Antoinette frowned in concern. "Do you want me to find you some warm milk?" Cassie had had some trouble sleeping since coming to England, and Antoinette and Aunt Chat tried everything to help her. Nothing really seemed to work.

"No, I think I'll go to the library and look for a book," Cassie answered. "Lady Royce said I could

w any of them I like, though I must say her son
ked rather doubtful about it. He probably thinks
will put all his precious volumes out of order!"

Antoinette laughed. "Very well," she said, walking
toward the door. "Just be certain you don't choose
one of those horrid novels you are so fond of. They
always give you bad dreams."

"I won't. Good night, Antoinette."

"Good night, Cassie."

Once her friend was gone, Cassie slid her feet into
her bedroom slippers and lit a candle to carry down
to the library.

Royce Castle seemed different in the lonely night
darkness, eerie and echoing. The main staircase, a
winding, wide expanse of stone, had been covered
with a long Aubusson carpet runner and decorated
with tall candelabra and statuary, but it was still cold
and dark. Her candle flickered in a sudden draft,
sending shadows dancing on the walls. The wind
whistled around the edges of the narrow windows,
and made the tapestries flutter.

It sounded like high-pitched laughter. And did that
portrait just *wink* at her?

Cassie cautiously lifted her candle higher to peer
at the painted image. Obviously the wink had just
been a trick of the light, thank goodness. She did
want to see a ghost, but maybe not when she was
all alone.

She hurried her steps along. Once she reached the
library, she was so relieved to be there that she
slammed the door behind her and leaned back
against it. She closed her eyes, listening to the swift
patter of her heart.

"May I help you?" a deep voice said.

Cassie's eyes flew open, and she stood up perfectly
straight. Lord Royce sat behind a massive, carved

desk set half in the shadows, books and papers piled around him in untidy heaps. Light from the blazing fire in the hearth fell across him in a red-gold glow, burnishing his rich fall of hair and glinting off the spectacles he wore.

Cassie felt oddly breathless, and she had the sneaking suspicion that it had nothing to do with ghosts or shadows.

"L—Lord Royce," she managed to gasp. "I had no idea anyone would be here. The lateness of the hour . . ."

"It *is* rather late. I would have thought you would be quite tired, Miss Richards, after your journey." He rose from behind the desk, and Cassie saw that he was in his shirtsleeves, his waistcoat unbuttoned and his cravat untied and carelessly dangling. She even had a glimpse of his strong throat, and the hollow at its base where his pulse beat, as he walked toward her.

She had lived a rather casual life in Jamaica, had seen her father and other planters come in from the fields dressed in very similar fashion. But she had never been so disconcerted by it before. She was not quite certain where to look as he moved closer and closer.

He stopped what seemed like mere inches from her, so close that she could feel his warmth, could smell the faint scent of some spicy soap on his skin. She forgot to breathe entirely when he reached his arm behind her, the fine cambric of his sleeve brushing against her hair.

He took his coat from the hook that was on the door she had just been leaning against, and slid his arms into the sleeves. He stepped away from her, pulling his hair from under the collar in one smooth motion.

"Are you not, Miss Richards?" he said.

The sound of his voice seemed to shake her from some sort of dream state. Then she realized that the entire process of him moving across the library, which had seemed to take hours, had only taken a moment.

"Am I not what?" she murmured, confused.

And there went that blasted eyebrow. "Tired after your journey."

"Not at all." She moved away from him, crossing the wide expanse of the room to be closer to the fireplace. She was suddenly all-too-aware that she was clad in her nightclothes. She pulled the edges of her velvet dressing gown closer together and wished she was still in her dinner gown. "I wanted to find something to read."

"Well, we certainly have plenty of that," he said, gesturing to the massive bookcases. "What do you care for, Miss Richards? History? Biography? Sermons?"

"Do you have any novels? Recent novels," she said without thinking, then immediately regretted it. She felt like a fool asking a classical scholar for novels.

But his brow did not arch at all. "Of course. I believe you will find most of them here. Many of them are my mother's, which she orders from London every month." He showed her a smaller case, placed against the wall near the desk.

As Cassie came closer to inspect them, her attention was caught by the clutter on the desk. A large sheaf of paper, closely written in a small, neat hand, balanced beside a stack of leather-bound volumes. *His* handwriting, *his* work, she realized.

She was suddenly intensely curious as to what it was that so preoccupied this strange, beautiful man. She veered off her course and went over to gently touch one of the books.

"What is it you are working on, Lord Royce?" she asked. "My aunt and her Philosophical Society in Bath are great admirers of your writing."

"I am flattered," he said, moving closer. "I am working on a series about the wars of ancient Greece, which will follow my series on society and economy. This one concerns the Peloponnesian War, between Athens and Sparta."

Cassie nodded and turned some of the books over in her hands, reading the titles by Aristotle, Pausanias, Xenophon.

They made her feel terribly ignorant.

Then she saw something a bit more familiar, a slim volume titled *The Gods and Goddesses of Ancient Greece.* She picked it up and flicked through the illustrated pages.

"My mother adored the myths and tales of Greece and Rome," she said. "She died when I was eleven, but I remember her telling me some of these stories."

She looked up to find Lord Royce watching her intently with his gray eyes, uncovered now by the spectacles. She gave a nervous little laugh and placed the book carefully back on its stack. "I am sorry," she said. "I did not mean to mess about with your books."

He shrugged. "It is of no matter. You can read any of them you choose, Miss Richards. So your mother was a scholar of the classics?"

Cassie laughed to think of her sociable, party-loving mother as any kind of scholar. "Oh, no! Not a bit. She was far too busy with routs and fetes to study. She just enjoyed the stories. Perhaps because the ancient gods so enjoyed a good party themselves!"

He laughed at her little quip, and she found herself grinning like an idiot that she could make him laugh.

"Then I am surprised she did not name you after someone more lighthearted than Cassandra," he said. "Aphrodite, perhaps, or Psyche."

He leaned forward to straighten the pile of books, and a long lock of dark hair fell forward over his face. Cassandra had the strangest urge to brush it back, to see if it was as silky as it looked.

"There must have been something about Cassandra that appealed to her darker side," she answered distractedly. "What did you say it meant? Disbelieved by men?"

He smiled at her wryly. "Much to the men's peril."

She smiled at him in return, feeling a faint warm glow. Perhaps he was not such a stuffy prig after all, she mused. "I should like to hear more of Cassandra's story."

"Then I shall tell it to you one day soon. It is a very good tale."

"I would like that."

"And perhaps in return you could answer a few questions about Jamaica, Miss Richards? One in particular, though I fear it is rather prying."

Cassie positively burned with curiosity to know what it might be. "Yes, Lord Royce?"

"Your friend Miss Duvall. Is she your slave?"

She stared at him, more deeply offended than she could ever remember being before. All the warm camaraderie of only moments before blew away like so many cold ashes. "Of course she is not my slave! She is a free woman, as was her mother. Her mother came to work as my mother's lady's maid soon after we arrived in Jamaica, and she became a dear friend. When she died, Antoinette stayed with us, as my companion. We grew up together, and she is like my sister." She glared at him, daring him to contradict her.

He held up his hands, as if in surrender. "Miss Richards! My deepest apologies. I never meant to offend."

Cassie looked at him rather suspiciously, but he seemed sincere. She nodded and said, "My father owned no slaves. All his workers were freed men whom he paid wages. It meant that his endeavors were not as profitable as those of some of his neighbors, but he did the right thing, and I was very proud of him."

"As well you should be, Miss Richards," he said in a soft, respectful tone she had not heard him use before. "He sounds quite admirable, and I am truly sorry for being so flippant."

"Apology accepted, then, Lord Royce."

"How can I make amends for being such a dolt?"

"Well . . ." Cassie said, pondering this question carefully. "You can tell me about the castle's ghosts, as well as about Cassandra."

He shook his head. "I fear my mother is the expert on ghosts. I know little about the stories."

"But you live right here in the castle!" Cassie said, unable to fathom that someone could be so completely uninterested in the spirits around them. "Aren't you the least bit curious about them?"

"I have more important work to do, Miss Richards, than chase 'ghosts' about." He picked up a book from a nearby shelf, *Letter to a Member of the National Assembly* by Edmund Burke. "Burke says, 'Superstition is the religion of feeble minds.' "

Cassie wrinkled her nose. "He sounds a most dull fellow."

"He was one of the greatest thinkers of the last century."

"Was he indeed?" she murmured, unconvinced. "Perhaps I should read him, then, after I have toured the castle and met every spirit in residence."

"Perhaps you should, Miss Richards. Perhaps you should."

Cassie felt faintly disappointed. Their conversation had been going so well, until he asked her about Antoinette and then dismissed the ghost stories out of hand. Now he only seemed the stuffy scholar again, watching her with that doubtful look on his face. As if he had some reservations about her sanity.

She pulled a couple of novels off the shelf in order to fulfill her original errand, and, clutching them against her, turned toward the door. "It is getting very late, Lord Royce. I will say good night."

"Good night, Miss Richards," he replied, giving her a small bow. "It was a most interesting conversation."

"Indeed it was," she said quietly. Then she hurried out of the dimly lit haven of the library and back up the cold stone stairs.

She was so distracted that she did not even notice the drafts and the portraits this time. Indeed, she thought of nothing but the strange Lord Royce until her head fell onto her pillow and she dropped into a dream-filled sleep.

Chapter Five

Phillip sat alone in the library long after Cassandra left, long after the embers faded in the fireplace and a late-night chill crept in from the tall windows.

What a very odd young woman Miss Cassandra Richards was. She did not behave as any other young lady of his acquaintance did. She did not shriek and scurry away when she found him there in the library, even though it was quite an improper situation. She did not back away from his questions about life in Jamaica. Instead, she faced him directly and unflinchingly, not at all awed by his title or position.

Very unusual.

Phillip gave a little, self-mocking laugh. His experience with well-bred young ladies was admittedly not wide. He escorted his mother to Town when the occasion warranted. He squired her about to stultifying Society balls, and met with his publisher and other scholars. He enjoyed the discussions and debates, but could distinctly do without the balls.

All the young ladies there would cluster about him like so many pastel-clad butterflies, giggling and chattering on about fashions and parties. It gave him a headache just thinking about the superficial chaos of it all.

He always felt such an outsider at those occasions, as if he were speaking a different language from the people around him, and he longed to be home at Royce Castle, with his books and studies.

He knew very well that one day he would have to marry, to carry on the family line and add to the portraits that clustered on every wall. But he had always imagined he would find a sensible woman when the time came, a widow or spinster bluestocking, who could share his interest in antiquity and bring up equally sensible children.

Miss Richards was obviously *not* a sensible bluestocking by any stretch of the imagination. She did not know much about classical history, nor did she scruple to admit her interest in the so-called supernatural. She had worn a most daring gown of canaryyellow satin to supper, along with dazzling beaded earrings and a carved stone pendant. She had chattered brightly with his mother about ghosts and popular novels.

All the things he usually so disliked. But he had *not* been bored in the least. Rather, he had been quite fascinated and had wanted to listen to her more, to lean closer to her and breathe deeply of her exotic perfume.

It was all most odd. It he were to subscribe to the ideas of Miss Richards, her enigmatic friend Miss Duvall, and his mother, he would say he was under a spell.

But more likely it was the lateness of the hour, he thought, as the clock struck three. And the fact that he had been working so hard of late. It was making him tired and distracted. Perhaps his mother was right. Company would do him some good.

He would just have to spend more time with Miss Richards—and Lady Willowby and Miss Duvall, of course—and see if that helped cure these fancies. No doubt once he spent more time with Cassandra Richards, her exotic appeal would wear off and his life would return completely to normal. No more talk of ghosts, no more rich perfumes, just ancient wars and philosophy.

On that comforting thought, he closed his books, blew out the candles, and left the library for bed.

Two unseen "people," perched atop the rolling library ladders, watched him go with great interest.

"Oh, this *is* going to be amusing!" said Louisa, twisting one long, golden ringlet about her finger. "He is infatuated with that girl already and will not admit it."

"He cannot admit it," Sir Belvedere said, his armor clanking as he turned a page over in the book he was perusing. If Phillip had still been in the library, he might have looked up to see a volume floating about in midair, but he would have put it down to fatigue or a bad cheese at dinner. Just as he always did.

This amused Sir Belvedere and Louisa to no end, brightening their endless days and nights in the castle. And now it looked as if the amusement was about to increase.

"I like that Miss Richards and her tall, strange friend. I should not have been so mischievous about making the portrait move, when they are so very nice!" said Louisa in a most chagrined tone. "They believe in us; they know we are here."

"Not as of yet, my fair lady. But they will know when we reveal ourselves to them." Sir Belvedere's visor fell with a loud thud over his face, and he pushed it aside impatiently.

"Oh, no!" Louisa answered, fluffing up her lace-trimmed blue satin skirts. "They already know, I am certain. And they will soon make that stubborn Lord Royce see. Why, he is every bit as obstinate as my husband was!"

Sir Belvedere chuckled. "It will be vastly amusing to watch them try to make him see, Louisa. *Vastly* amusing. 'Twill be the most enjoyment I have had since I overran castles in my mortal life!"

"It is simply too bad Lady Lettice is not here to see this. She was always so wonderful at match-making, at helping people to see how perfect they are for each other. Do you remember what she did for this Lord Royce's grandfather and that Miss Sutcliffe?" Louisa smiled at the memory. "I think Lord Royce and Miss Richards will need a great deal of help as well."

"I, too, miss Lady Lettice," said Sir Belvedere. "It has been a long while since we saw her. But if anything can bring her back, it is two people falling reluctantly in love."

Chapter Six

Cassie awoke from a dream of Jamaica, of walking along a warm, sandy shore with the bright morning sun shining down on her, to find herself not sunbathed and cozy but chilled and shivering. Sometime during the restless night she had thrown off the bedclothes, and her bare feet stuck out into the cold room.

"Wretched!" she muttered, yanking the blankets back up over her shoulders and rolling over onto her side. The fire was long-dead in the grate, but the draperies at the window were drawn partially back, letting a bar of yellow-white sunlight fall across the floor.

The room was so quiet that she could hear, very faintly, the rush and roar of the sea, far below the cliffs. It reminded her of her dream, and drew her out from the warm cave of the bed. She slid her feet into her slippers and padded over to look out the window.

She *could* see the sea, but it was not like the violet-blue waters of the island. It was gray, almost black, roiling angrily against the steep cliffs beyond the castle's manicured gardens. The sun that was struggling so valiantly through the slate-colored clouds did not even seem to penetrate them at all. Scrubby trees grew along the cliffs, bending gaunt limbs toward the sea like hands in the wind.

Cassie had never felt so far from home before. She shivered and crossed her arms tightly in front of her.

Then, out of the starkness, she saw a flash of movement. A figure on horseback riding along the cliffs, sweeping past the trees and creating a veritable whirlwind of energy.

He was quite a distance away, but she could see the banner of dark hair that flowed in the wind.

Lord Royce.

Cassie had decided when she went to bed that he was just a fusty scholar after all, interested only in his books, but he certainly did not look *fusty* this morning.

He looked like a dashing poet. Or a pirate, against the backdrop of that dark sea. He rode along fast and furious, his horse's hooves churning up the earth. His white shirt billowed, adding to the illusion of piracy.

Cassie smiled. Perhaps her strange fascination with him was not so odd after all.

There was a quick knock at the door, dashing these fanciful thoughts. Cassie turned away from the window and called, "Come in."

Antoinette entered the room, majestic in a blue-and-green swirl of a gown and a matching turban. Despite the early hour, she looked rested and regal, as usual.

"Cassie!" she tsked. "Here it is time for breakfast, and you're not dressed."

"I did not sleep restfully," Cassie said with a little shrug. "I had such odd dreams."

Antoinette came up beside her and peered over

her shoulder out the window. Lord Royce was just disappearing from view, his hair still flowing in the wind. "Um-hm," she murmured. "And I see what those dreams were about."

"Antoinette!" Cassie cried, jerking the draperies closed. "It was not like that at all. Lord Royce is not even my sort of gentleman. He is—is narrow-minded, and cares only for books, and . . ." She struggled to remember what it was she had not liked about him, but the image of him riding along the cliffs kept interfering.

Antoinette laughed. "And just what *is* your sort of gentleman? Men like the ones back in Jamaica?"

"Yes!" Cassie said firmly. She went over to the dressing table and picked up her hairbrush, pulling it through her hair and detangling the night's plait.

"Planter sorts?" Antoinette's voice was sardonic, her accent thick.

"Yes," Cassie repeated, but more doubtful this time. Antoinette made her remember how some of those men had truly been, careless and unrefined, caring only about getting foxed on rum.

"Then why did you not accept Mr. Bates' proposal?" Antoinette teased. "With his big plantation and all. Why, he would be just your sort."

Cassie laughed, acknowledging the truth of her friend's words. "Oh, all right! So they were *not* my sort. But neither is Lord Royce."

"Is he not?"

"No. I wouldn't think *you* would like him, either; he doubts your sight. And why are we talking about this at all? I'm not interested in finding a suitor here. I am interested only in the ghosts."

Antoinette nodded. "Then you should hurry up and get dressed. Lady Royce is going to give us a tour of the castle after breakfast, and tell us all the tales."

"What fun!" Cassie cried, and ran over to the armoire to find a morning dress. "I presume her son will *not* be joining us."

So she would be able to enjoy herself without the distraction of his presence.

"Presumably," Antoinette agreed. "But you must bear up under the disappointment, Cassie. I am sure you will see him at supper; I foresaw it in the cards."

Cassie threw a pillow at Antoinette, who just ducked and laughed.

"That particular Lady Royce, Louisa was her name, had a very sad history," Lady Royce said, enthusiastically spreading marmalade on her toast. "Very sad indeed. Her husband left her alone here at Royce Castle while he fought in the Civil War, and even when the king came back he was away at Court often. They say Louisa took a lover in her loneliness, but he betrayed her, and she threw herself off the cliffs in despair."

"What fustian!" Louisa muttered, peering down from her perch atop a decorative cornice in the breakfast room. "I was in my cups after that ball, and *fell* off the cliffs."

"Ha!" scoffed Lord Belvedere, his armor clanking. "It is true! No lover ever betrayed me."

"Methinks, fair lady, that the years have clouded your memory. I was right here, as I have been for almost five hundred years, and I saw you that night. You were indeed 'in your cups,' but if you had not quarreled with that Lord Ponsonby and gone running down to the cliffs . . ."

"Oh, hush!" Louisa interrupted, reaching out a hand and shoving him off his own cornice. "I want to hear what else she has to say."

"What was that clattering noise?" said Lady Royce, her toast held up halfway to her mouth.

Antoinette looked directly at Sir Belvedere, causing him to gasp and vanish altogether, leaving only Louisa high on her perch.

"Probably only one of your footmen," said Chat. "Now, what were you saying about the sad Louisa?"

"Sad, hmph," whispered Louisa. "I am *happy*."

"Oh, she is not sad," said Antoinette, taking a serene sip of her chocolate.

"Exactly," Louisa agreed.

"Perhaps once she was, but now she enjoys her existence here."

"She is here, then?" Cassie said eagerly. "You can feel her presence? Can we find her?"

"Really, Cassie," said Chat. "It is too early in the morning for hauntings and ghosts and such."

"And everyone knows that midnight is the time for such endeavors," a deep male voice said from the doorway.

Everyone's gaze, including Louisa's, turned to Lord Royce. She eyed him with some approval; he looked a bit like her husband, William, who had not been an unhandsome man by any means. But this Lord Royce, like her William, was bent on his own ends, which left little time for romance. With William it had been advancement at Court, with this man it was his studies.

Oh, the great folly of men! They never learned, not even in over a hundred years. With a rueful shake of her head, Louisa vanished, gone to seek other amusement in the East Tower.

Antoinette watched her go with narrowed eyes, but Cassie was far too distracted by the presence of Lord Royce to notice any ghostly doings.

He had obviously bathed and changed after his

ride, for he was respectably, albeit a bit shabbily, attired in a blue morning coat and buff breeches, his hair tied neatly back. The wild pirate was gone, and the scholar/earl firmly in his place.

But Cassie still felt flustered and flushed when he looked at her.

"Good morning, ladies," he said, sitting down in the last vacant chair, the one across from Cassie.

Her fork clattered against her plate, and she had to catch it before it fell to the floor.

He smiled at her. "I trust you all found your first evening at Royce Castle to be comfortable?"

"Yes, quite," Chat answered. "It was all that Melinda has written me over the years. Splendid."

"I slept quite soundly," said Antoinette. "Although next door there were some rather restless noises . . ."

Cassie kicked her under the table.

"The butler told me you went riding this morning, dear," said Lady Royce. "You were awake unusually early." She turned to Chat and added, "Ordinarily my son is up quite late with his studies and doesn't join me for breakfast."

"It must be the bracing autumn air," he answered, spearing one of the sausages on his plate. "It was a lovely morning for a ride."

"Indeed," said Lady Royce. "Do *you* ride, Miss Richards?"

Cassie blinked at her, startled to be suddenly addressed. "Yes, Lady Royce. A bit. But I fear I have not had much opportunity for it since I came to England."

"Bath is rather restrictive for poor Cassandra," said Chat.

Cassie smiled at her aunt. "Now, Aunt Chat! I *like* living in Bath. The theater, the concerts . . ."

"But very few places for riding," said Chat.

"Perhaps you would care to ride while you are here, then," Lady Royce said. "We have such a nice stable, and Phillip knows all the best paths. I am sure he would enjoy showing them to you."

Then, Lady Royce and Chat exchanged little smiles, and simultaneously lifted their teacups to their lips for demure sips.

Cassie clasped her hands tightly on her lap, twisting her napkin, and looked across the table at Lord Royce. Surely he would refuse to go riding with her, would scoff at his mother's obvious scheming. What would they ever find to talk about on their ride? What could they have in common?

But, to her surprise, he looked rather—amenable.

"*Would* you care to go riding with me, Miss Richards?" he said, his face smoothly polite.

Would she? Cassie remembered the vision of him she had seen from her window, all dashing and piratical. Then she imagined herself by his side, riding free in the wind, just as she had at home.

Of course she would *like* to go riding with him, but whether she *should* was something else. It would be far too easy to forget their differences out there in the sunshine.

And, as she had no intention of falling in love with a man so very serious-minded, forgetting those differences would not be good. She ought to refuse . . .

"Yes, thank you, Lord Royce," she heard herself say. "I would enjoy that."

He gave her a startled little smile, as if surprised that she had agreed. "Very good. Perhaps we could inspect the stables later and find you a suitable horse."

"After I show them the East Tower, dear," said Lady Royce. "They want to see where poor Louisa's chambers are."

He rolled his eyes a bit. "Of course. And you can play a game of piquet with her while you are there. Do you think she would care for a sherry? There is a fine Amontillado in the cellar."

Obnoxious man! Cassie fumed in her mind, turning her attention back to her plate. And to think she had agreed to go riding with him.

Chapter Seven

"This is the East Tower, where Louisa lived," Lady Royce said, unlocking a door and leading them up a narrow staircase. "I seldom come here; with just Phillip and myself in residence there are many rooms that are unused. But I promised you a look at them, so here we are! What do you all think?"

"Very pretty," Chat said.

"Very," agreed Cassie, looking about her. The round tower room was large and high-ceilinged, furnished in the style of almost two hundred years ago, with a massive carved bed and looped draperies at the tall windows. Another portrait hung over the marble fireplace of Louisa and a stern-faced man with long dark hair.

He looked a bit like the current Lord Royce, Cassie thought. She went over to take a closer look.

There was a gilt-framed mirror next to the painting, and Cassie thought she saw a brief flash of blue in the glass. But when she glanced over her shoulder, there was no one there who should not be. Only Aunt Chat and Antoinette, examining some little china figurines while Lady Royce pulled the elaborate draperies back from the windows. None of them were wearing blue.

Oh, really! she thought, with a little irritated tap of her foot. If there *was* a ghost in here, she wanted very much to see it. Why would it keep running away?

Then she looked back to the portrait, to the man who looked so much like the doubting Lord Royce.

Maybe Louisa had a good reason for hiding after all, if her husband had been half as pigheaded as this Lord Royce. She probably felt one lifetime tolerating him was quite enough.

"Yes, Louisa *did* have a sad history," Lady Royce sighed, tying back the last of the draperies with their gold cords. "So very lonely, out here all alone."

There was a small sound that echoed in the air like an irritated huff.

"I am surprised she would wish to stay here, then, at the site of her unhappiness," Chat commented uncertainly. "I certainly would wish to move on."

Cassie smiled at her aunt. Chat did not always believe all this business about ghosts, but at least she tried. She did not scoff and make fun, like *some* people.

Antoinette, who stood beside the bed with one hand on the satin hangings, said, "Perhaps she cannot move on. Perhaps the sad events of her life keep her here. But she is not sad now. And she is interested in our activities."

"She is here, then? In this room?" Lady Royce asked eagerly.

"Oh, yes. Most assuredly." Antoinette closed her eyes and placed her fingertips lightly at her temples. "But she is not sure about showing herself yet. She doesn't wish to be misunderstood, as she was in her life."

The others crowded in closer around her.

"What was misunderstood about her?" Lady Royce whispered.

Antoinette shook her head. "I do not know. My powers are limited without my books and guides, unlike my mother, who could see things very clearly. And the daylight is too harsh."

"But I want to know!" Lady Royce cried. "I *want* to understand her."

Cassie quite agreed. They only wanted to talk to Louisa, to understand her. And anyone else who might be about.

She thought Louisa was behaving like a little brat.

Antoinette touched Lady Royce's arm reassuringly. "We will soon find out. If you like, we can come back here at night, with my mother's book of incantations. We will discover more then."

Lady Royce and Cassie enthusiastically agreed, even though Chat still looked doubtful. As they left the East Tower and walked back to the inhabited sections of the castle, Antoinette said, "Tell me about Lady Lettice, Lady Royce. The one who has not been seen here of late."

"I fear I do not know much about her," Lady Royce said in a regretful tone. "She has not been seen since my husband's parents' time. She was the daughter of the earl, and served as a maid of honor to Queen Elizabeth. She never married or had children. I do not know why she would come back here after her death, or why she would leave."

"Hmm," Antoinette said, tapping her finger thoughtfully on her chin.

"Do you sense *her* presence?" Cassie asked.

"Not now," Antoinette answered. "But perhaps later . . ."

"Oh, there you are," a voice interrupted as they walked past the open door of the library. Lord Royce emerged from the dim depths of the room, like Merlin exiting his cave, and gave them all a polite smile. "You were certainly on your tour a long while."

"There is much to see in the castle, dear," his mother said. "As you would know, if you did not spend all your time in just this one room."

He laughed. "Well, Mother, you will be glad to know I am going to remedy that. I was just going down to the stables, and wanted to see if Miss Richards would care to accompany me, now that your tour is finished." He turned his lingering smile onto Cassie.

Cassie examined him carefully, his smile and his coolly polite eyes. So, the Doubting Thomas wanted to be hospitable now, did he?

Well, no one could accuse Cassandra Richards of forgetting the lessons her mother had taught her about not being a rude houseguest. She nodded and gave him a smile of her own.

"Thank you, Lord Royce," she said. "I would be happy to come."

Chapter Eight

Cassie followed Lord Royce down the pathway that led to the stables. He was very quiet on their walk, and so was she; she wasn't exactly sure what to say to him.

She wondered if he felt like his mother was forcing him into taking her riding, and it made her feel rather awkward.

Awkwardness had been an unaccustomed feeling until she came here. At home, in Jamaica, she had had her share of admirers. Her dance card was always full, and she never seemed to lack for conversation. And even at Aunt Chat's house in Bath, where she often felt shy and strange, she enjoyed the company of the card parties and concerts.

Why did she always feel so tongue-tied and awkward around Lord Royce in particular? He was just a scoffing scholar.

Albeit a handsome one.

Then they turned a bend in the path, and she lost any awkward feeling at the surprise of the beautiful view.

They were at a lower level here than they were at

the castle, nearer to the sea. A low stone wall lined the edge of the pathway, where it veered closer to the cliff. Cassie went to lean on the crumbling stone, wide-eyed, as she looked at the vista.

From the castle, the sea was undeniably lovely, but here it was more elemental. She could hear the rush of the waves as they hit the pebbly shore and then receded.

"Beautiful, isn't it?" Lord Royce said, coming to stand beside her at the wall.

Cassie smiled up at him, bringing her hand up to shield her eyes from the afternoon sun. "Very beautiful," she answered. At least *that* they could agree on.

"You sound rather surprised," he said amiably, propping his hip against the wall so that he was half-turned to face her. "I don't spend all my time immured in the library, you know. I do get out once in a while to breathe fresh air."

"And go riding along the cliffs," Cassie murmured. She remembered her vision of him from this morning, galloping along like a wild pirate.

"Yes. Of course." He turned his gaze away from her, back to the sea. "Miss Richards, my mother looks very sweet and harmless, but she can be quite ruthless when she wants something. And she is not above using someone's politeness as a guest to further her own ends. If you really *don't* want to go riding with me, I will understand. We could tell her you did not find a horse to your liking. I am sure you would prefer to be looking for your ghosts rather than spending time with me."

Cassie turned to him, surprised. "Oh, no! I *would* like to go riding with you. Unless . . ." Her voice faltered as a thought struck her. Was he trying to get rid of her? "Unless you have work you must be doing. I would hate to keep you from it."

He gave her a startlingly charming smile. "Nonsense. No one in their right mind would rather be inside working than out in the sunshine with such a lovely companion. The Peloponnesian War can wait until later."

She smiled at him tentatively in return. "Why, Lord Royce. Was that a compliment?"

He laughed. "Shocking, I know. But, despite what my mother may think, I am not completely socially inept. I can pay compliments as well as the next gentleman, when they are sincere."

"*I* never thought you were socially inept," Cassie said, almost truthfully. Emboldened by his new, more comfortable presence, she said, "Do you know what I would really like to do today?"

"No, Miss Richards. Look for spirits, mayhap?"

Cassie peered at him suspiciously, but his smile was only teasing, not mocking. "I would like to take a walk down by the shore."

"Really? Well, that is easily done. The stables will always wait. But I fear it is rather chilly down by the water."

Cassie held out a handful of her heavy red cloak. "Oh, I am always prepared for the chill here!"

"Then there are some steps just a little further down that way, that lead to the shore." He straightened from leaning on the wall, and offered her his arm. "Shall we, Miss Richards?"

Cassie eyed his proffered arm for a moment, half-afraid he might pull away and laugh at her. But when he just held it out a little farther and smiled at her expectantly, she slowly slid her hand into the warm crook of his elbow and let him lead her onward.

The steps to the shore, made of stone at the lowest part of the cliffs, were steep and weathered. Cassie moved carefully on the thin soles of her half boots, but Lord Royce's arm beneath her hand was steady and strong as he helped her down.

Surely he did not spend *all* his time in the library, or the muscles that bunched and moved under her touch would not be so—so *hard*.

Finally she was distracted from her very improper thoughts about Lord Royce's musculature when they reached the shore, and her face was sprayed with a light mist from the sea. She inhaled deeply of the salty tang in the air, so strange but so familiar and sweet. Her footsteps crunched on the pebbles of the beach.

She could not help herself. She let go of Lord Royce's arm and rushed toward the water, until the waves lapped at the very toes of her half boots and dampened the hems of her dress and cloak.

Cassie did not even notice. She was far too enthralled with being so close to the sea again. She gave a little laugh and knelt down to trail her fingertips in a receding wave. The water was much colder than in Jamaica, but it felt delicious on her skin.

She stood back up and glanced over her shoulder at Lord Royce. She expected to find him disapproving of her impulsive behavior, perhaps ready to demand that they return to the castle at once. She was all ready to stiffen her resolve not to let him spoil her joy.

Instead, she found that he watched her almost as if he had never seen her before in his life. His expression was quite startled, his eyes wide. He was frowning a bit, but not in a disapproving way. Rather, he looked—puzzled.

Cassie was not sure what to make of this. She moved one small step closer to him. "The sea is very beautiful, is it not?" she said slowly.

"Oh, yes," he answered in a quiet voice, the sound almost lost in the murmur of the waves. "Very beautiful."

Phillip watched Cassie run toward the water, her laughter echoing on the autumn air, and thought that she looked a bit like a clothed Aphrodite, emerging newborn from the waves. If Aphrodite had chosen chilly Cornwall to emerge from instead of the warm Mediterranean at Sicily, of course.

At the castle, Cassie seemed happy and sociable, but also strangely uncomfortable at times. Almost as if she was afraid of saying or doing something that was in some way wrong. Here there was none of that in her demeanor. She ran toward the water, laughing, her hand stretched out.

As she bent down to touch a receding wave, a lock of black hair fell from her carved ebony combs and brushed against her cheek.

She looked so—so *joyful*. Phillip longed to join her, to feel that way again. To feel free, childlike, to not worry about books and logic and always being in strictest control. He wanted to absorb all her laughter and wonder into himself.

Even to believe in spirits and fairies, perhaps?

Then she looked back at him with her rich, dark eyes. "The sea is beautiful, is it not?" she said, looking at him with a rather puzzled air.

"Oh, yes," he murmured hoarsely. "Very beautiful."

Her eyes widened, as if startled, and he suddenly realized he was gaping at her like a moonstruck schoolboy. A small frown formed on her brow, and his longings of only a moment before vanished like so much mist on the water. He was recalled to himself, to where they were, to *who* they were.

"There are underground tunnels near here," he said, grasping for something, anything, to talk about. Anything that did not involve how lovely her eyes were. "They are said to have been used by pirates long ago, but they are mostly blocked up now to discourage smuggling. Except for one."

"Pirates! How very intriguing," she said. She looked away from him, breaking the last vestiges of the strange spell. "I should like to see them."

"There is not much to see. The one that is still open is just used for storage. Local fishermen keep their boats there."

"I should still like to see it, and imagine the pirates that used to shelter there. I am sure Aunt Chat and Antoinette would like to see it, too."

"Maybe we could all have a picnic near there, one day soon," Phillip said. He found himself grasping at the excuse to spend more time with this strange, intriguing woman. Even leaving his books yet again for a picnic by the sea.

She smiled at him, quite as if they were almost friends. "Yes. I would enjoy that very much. *We* would enjoy that."

Chapter Nine

Cassie was awakened in the middle of the night by the unmistakable tingling sensation of someone staring at her. She opened her eyes—and promptly gave a shriek. Quick as a flash, she scrambled up against the pillows.

"Hello," said the woman who perched on the edge of the bed. "I am sorry I frightened you."

Cassie pulled the sheet up to her chin and stared over it at the woman. She appeared quite solid: a real person, with long blond ringlets and a blue satin gown in the style of the Restoration. Only a faint, white glow around the edges betrayed her as something not *quite* human.

Cassie recognized her face from the portraits. "You—you are Louisa, aren't you?" she managed to stammer out. She wasn't exactly sure how one should address a ghost. Should she have called her Lady Royce?

But Louisa didn't seem to mind the informality of being addressed by her given name. She just nodded, and lounged back on her elbow. "I am! I saw all of you in my tower today and thought I ought to introduce myself. I truly did not mean to scare you."

Cassie lowered the sheet slowly. "You did not scare me. I was simply startled. It is not every day a ghost comes and sits on my bed."

Louisa laughed, a rather strange, echoing sound. "Then I did not mean to *startle* you. I just wanted to talk."

"Then you don't mind that we were in your tower?"

"Mind? Certainly not. It makes a nice change from having only old Sir Belvedere to talk to."

Cassie relaxed back against the pillows. It was beginning to feel almost *normal* to converse with a slightly glowing, long-dead person. "Who is Sir Belvedere?"

"He lives here, too. He was a knight who served the first Earl of Royce, in the fourteenth century. He was killed when the castle was being built, so he has been here for a *very* long time. Much longer than me."

"Killed? How?"

"He tripped on some building materials and fell from the tower. He never talks about it, not in all the years I have known him. He was wearing his silly armor at the time. Truth to tell, he can be a bit of a bore, but he is better company than none. It has been rather quiet around here for a long time."

There was a clanking noise from the corridor. Cassie startled and looked toward the door. "What was that?"

"Oh, that was just Sir Belvedere. He is hovering about in the corridor. He thinks it is improper for him to enter a lady's chamber, but he is just as curious as I am."

There was another clanking sound.

"If he does not cease doing that, he will wake the whole household," Louisa said, but she did not really seem terribly concerned by the prospect.

"Perhaps I could meet him later," Cassie said hopefully. She thought it would be quite interesting to see a ghost in armor.

Louisa gave her a secretive little smile. "Perhaps."

"Is he the only other ghost in residence here?"

"At the moment, yes. There have been others, but they come and go. The only other people who have stayed as long as Sir Belvedere and myself were Lady Lettice and Angelo. We have not seen them for several years, though, so we think they must have moved across."

"Moved across?"

"That is when the ghosts leave to go on to the next plane, a place I have not seen yet. I don't know why some of us get trapped here and some move on right away. It's a mystery."

"But if there are so many of you, why do the people living in the castle never see you?"

"Oh, they do sometimes!" She laughed lightly. "You see, though, there is one great advantage to being a ghost, once you learn the trick of it, and that is that we can be visible or invisible as we choose. Just as I choose to be visible to you right now."

Cassie thought that must be quite an advantage. "And you choose to be *invisible* to Lord Royce?"

Louisa shrugged. "It makes it more fun that way."

"So you and this Sir Belvedere have been the only ones here for a long time, except for Lady Lettice and this—Angelo?" Cassie had heard about Lady Lettice, but never of any Angelo. "Who is, or was, he?"

Before Louisa could answer, the door connecting Cassie's room to Antoinette's opened, and Antoinette stood there, holding a candle and a bunch of herbs. She looked every bit the Yaumumi priestess her mother had been, in a flowing red dressing gown, with her thick, waving black hair falling over her shoulders.

"I thought I heard voices." She held up the bundle in her hand, eyeing Louisa carefully. "I brought herbs, in case there were evil spirits to be sent away. But I see they won't be needed."

Louisa laughed, obviously quite pleased to be suspected of being an evil spirit.

"Indeed not," Cassie said. "Louisa isn't the least bit evil. Come and meet her. She has been telling me the most interesting things."

Antoinette tucked the herbs away in the pocket of her robe and hurried over to sit down on the bed across from Louisa. She placed her candle on the bedside table, and its golden glow made Louisa appear slightly more transparent.

"How do you do," said Antoinette.

"So you are the one with all the spells and potions," Louisa said, her eyes wide with wonder. "Sir Belvedere thinks you might be able to find what became of Lady Lettice for us."

There was more clanking and knocking from the corridor.

"That is Sir Belvedere," Cassie explained. "He thinks it is improper for him to come in here."

"Very polite of him," Antoinette answered. She tapped one long finger thoughtfully on her chin. "I could certainly *try* to summon up Lady Lettice for you, if you would like to see her again. It would be an interesting challenge."

Louisa leaned forward eagerly. "Sir Belvedere and I would help you. Oh, it would be so *nice* to have some excitement here again! I end up playing chess in the East Tower with Sir Belvedere every night, and he cheats horribly."

"Vile slander!" a voice cried in the corridor.

"It is an incantation I have never tried before," Antoinette warned.

"But I have every faith in your powers, dear Antoinette," Cassie said with a thrill of excitement and apprehension at the thought of a new incantation.

"We would have to try it this Friday, when the moon is in the right phase."

"Could we invite Lady Royce and Aunt Chat?" Cassie said. "I am sure they would not want to miss it."

Antoinette gave her a sly little smile. "And Lord Royce, too? Perhaps we could make a believer of him."

Louisa snorted in a most unladylike fashion. "Nay, not him! He is too much like my own husband. Cynical and doubting. William never saw the truth of what was before him, either." She looked away, but before she did, Cassie saw her glowing blue eyes turn sad.

"I think we *should* invite him," Cassie said. "It might be quite interesting to have him there." She laughed, but she could not forget that flash of sadness in Louisa's eyes. Cassie wondered how *she* would feel if her own husband did not understand her. But then she shook her head. That would never happen, since she had no plans to ever take a husband!

"Very well," said Antoinette. "We shall make a party of it, then. This Friday, in the East Tower, I think. We will make a believer of Lord Royce if it is the last thing we do."

Chapter Ten

"I think we should have a ball," Lady Royce announced the next morning as they all walked along the cliffs on their way to a picnic.

"A ball, Mother?" Lord Royce said, shifting the large hamper under his arm. "Who would we invite?"

"Why, all the neighbors, of course! They are all back from Town, and from their holidays in Brighton and Bath, and they haven't been invited to the castle in a very long time. We should do *something* to entertain our guests properly."

"Oh, don't go to any trouble on our account, Melinda," said Chat. "We are quite happy just being here. Are we not, girls?"

Cassie and Antoinette murmured in agreement, but secretly Cassie thought a ball sounded splendid.

"Nonsense!" Lady Royce cried. "We will have a ball. A masked ball! There is a dressmaker in the village who can do our costumes for us. I will have her come to the castle this week!" It was obvious that she had thought about this ball idea quite a bit.

"A masked ball?" Lord Royce said, his handsome face the picture of dismay.

"Yes! A masked ball. You can wear a toga, dear, or whatever it was Greeks wore. You don't need to worry about a thing, Phillip. I will plan it all." Then Lady Royce took Chat's arm and led her ahead on the pathway, saying, "Now, Chat dear, you do so much entertaining in Bath, I would like your opinion on the menu for the ball . . ."

Antoinette walked ahead with them, leaving Cassie alone with Lord Royce. They followed the three women slowly.

"You do not seem very enthusiastic about the idea of a ball, Lord Royce," Cassie said.

"It would be very—interesting. You can tell a great deal about people by what they choose to dress as at a masked ball," he answered, but his expression was still doubtful.

"Indeed." Then, since she was rather excited by the idea of the dance and didn't want him dampening her enthusiasm, she changed the topic. "My aunt tells us that your work on ancient Greece is very well known. I've already told you that you are quite admired by the members of her Philosophical Society."

He tilted his head as he looked at her, as if puzzled by her words. "I have had some modest success," he said quietly. "Though some say it is not proper for an earl to write and publish, I feel that the knowledge is too important not to share, no matter what the gossip."

"Quite right. And how is it you became so interested in Greece?"

"Do you truly wish to know, Miss Richards?" he asked, taking her elbow in his free hand to help her down the steps to the shore. Even through the thick wool of her pelisse, his touch was warm and reassuring. "Or are you just being polite?"

Cassie would never have thought she would truly

be interested in the intricacies of ancient Greece. But she found that, strangely enough, she was. Very much. "I am interested."

"When I was a child, my father had a book about the wonders of ancient Greece. I read it over and over until it fell apart. It inspired me to study the classics at Oxford," he said. "But other than that one book, I did not know much about the ancient world. My tutors, and the school I attended, were much more concerned with the running of estates and playing cricket. It was at Oxford that I first read Socrates and Plato and Aristotle, and they opened my eyes to so many things."

"Things such as what?" Cassie asked, intrigued.

"Well, for a beginning, they emphasized logic and the meanings of words. They based their beliefs on empirical knowledge rather than religion or rituals or myth. They sought natural explanations for natural phenomena. Our own world seems so very chaotic at times, do you not agree? With the wars, and Prinny in charge, and all these poets running about."

"Hmm," Cassie answered slowly, going over his words in her mind. "Order *can* be comforting. It was a great relief to me to be in Aunt Chat's safe, comfortable home after the confusion of my father's death. But the Greeks were not always so reasonable, were they? I mean, the Delphic Oracle was not such a sensible idea, was it, yet they believed it. And they had plenty of poets of their own 'running about.'"

She expected him to quarrel with her, and stiffened her shoulders in preparation to retort. After all, it was rather intimidating to argue with a scholar when one knew almost nothing about the subject.

But, to her surprise, Lord Royce just laughed, and said, "Touché, Miss Richards! And quite right, too.

There are some things about human nature that never change. I should know that, from all the reading I have done of late on the foolishness of the Greek wars."

"Exactly so. The horrors of war do not change. Neither does family, or honor, or—or love."

Lord Royce looked at her, and, for one long, sweet moment, Cassie felt that they were in accord with one another. She wanted so much to go on talking of these things, things she had never really stopped to think about before, but Lady Royce called out to them.

"Come along, you two!" she cried over the sound of the waves. "What are you dawdling about for? We have found the perfect place for our picnic, here behind these rocks."

Lord Royce smiled at Cassie, and led the way over to where the others were waiting. Chat had already spread the blanket out carefully on the sand, and they waited only for the hamper Lord Royce carried.

It *was* the perfect place, Cassie thought as she settled herself on the blanket next to Antoinette and leaned back against a large rock. The crash of the waves was muffled here, and the wind turned away. She would *almost* have thought herself warm, with the pale sunlight beaming down on her uncovered head. It held all the promise of a perfect afternoon, with good friends and the sea.

Yet she almost wished she was alone with Lord Royce, so they could just go on and on talking, with him watching her with his lovely gray eyes.

"What were you two speaking of?" Lady Royce asked, unpacking the bounty of pork pies, cold chicken, and apple tarts from the hamper. "You were talking so *intently*."

"Your son was telling me about his work, Lady

Royce," Cassie said. "About the philosophy of ancient Greece."

"You poor dear! Here, you must be in need of some sherry." Lady Royce poured out a generous measure of the dark gold liquid and passed it over the hamper to Cassie.

"Mother! I am hardly in the habit of boring guests so deeply that they require potent drinks to stay conscious," Lord Royce muttered.

Cassie laughed and sipped her sherry. "Indeed, I was not bored, Lady Royce! I found it quite fascinating."

"After the exciting life you must have lived in the Indies?" Lady Royce sounded most disbelieving.

"Jamaica was not always as exciting as all that," Cassie said, thinking back on the long, hot, lazy days, and the flower-scented nights, when the distant sounds of drums and the ocean would come through her open window.

No, not terribly exciting. But very sweet.

"Not exciting at all?" Lady Royce said in a disappointed voice.

"Well, there *were* a lot of parties. Especially when my mother was alive. How she loved to dance!" Cassie smiled at the memory.

"My brother's wife was a beautiful woman," Chat offered. "And a vivacious spirit."

"Indeed? What of *your* mother, Miss Duvall? Was she also a—vivacious spirit?" Lady Royce asked Antoinette.

"My mother was devoted to her studies, Lady Royce," Antoinette answered. "Just as your son is."

"People came from all over the island to hear her wisdom," said Cassie.

"Just like the Delphic Oracle," Lord Royce murmured. "I should very much like to hear about it sometime."

"Would you truly? Or are you just being polite?" Cassie teased, echoing his earlier words to her.

He laughed. "I assure you, Miss Richards, I am never 'just polite.' "

After they finished eating, Cassie, Antoinette, and Lord Royce set off to look at the tunnels, leaving Chat and Lady Royce to their gossip and the last of the sherry.

The passages were mostly blocked up, just as Lord Royce had said they would be, and what was left was drafty and damp. Sand and pebbles had blown in to form a thin layer on the hard-packed floor. There were crates piled up along the cold walls, and a few upturned fishing boats.

Cassie thought, with a small thrill, that it looked like a smuggler's lair. She leaned back against one of the boats and looked around, wondering what sort of daring adventures had once happened in these tunnels.

Suddenly, her reverie was broken when Antoinette gave a scream and collapsed into a heap on the dirty floor. Her green cloak spread about her in a dark pool.

"Antoinette!" Cassie cried, running across the tunnel to fall down on her knees at her friend's side. "Antoinette, what is it?" She placed Antoinette's head carefully on her lap and rubbed at her cold wrists, wishing desperately that she was the sort to carry smelling salts around with her.

"What happened?" Lord Royce said, his voice hoarse with concern, as he knelt down beside them. "Is Miss Duvall ill?"

"She was perfectly well before," Cassie answered, frantically waving her hand in front of Antoinette's face. "Perhaps it was something she ate!"

"But we all ate the same things. Do *you* feel ill, Miss Richards?"

"Not a bit. Oh, Antoinette, do wake up, please!"

As if in answer to Cassie's panicked entreaties, Antoinette's ebony eyes fluttered open, and she glanced quickly about. "Cassie? What has happened?"

"Thank heaven you are conscious!" Cassie said in great relief. "You fainted."

"Did I? How very odd." She struggled to sit up, with Cassie and Lord Royce's help. Her turban was askew, and she pressed her palm to her forehead as if in pain. "I would like some water, please, if there is any."

"I will just fetch it, then," said Lord Royce. "Miss Richards, you stay here with Miss Duvall and lower her head to her knees if she feels faint again. I will not be gone long." Then he hurried off on his errand.

As soon as he was gone, Antoinette clutched at Cassie's hand and whispered, "We must come *here* on Friday night, not the East Tower. I feel that Lady Lettice's presence is very strong here."

"Is that why you fainted?" Cassie whispered back. "You sense something frightening here?"

Antoinette shook her head slowly. "Not frightening. Just—strong. We must come back here."

"Of course we will come back. On Friday. But you mustn't worry about it now. Are you feeling better?"

"Oh, yes, quite. I must have just been overwhelmed. Here, help me to stand, and we will wait for Lord Royce outside."

"How is Miss Duvall feeling, Miss Richards?"

Cassie, who was hurrying past the open door of the library with a basin of lavender water in her hands, paused to peer into the dimly lit room. Phillip came to stand in the doorway, his gray gaze inscrutable behind his spectacles.

"Much better, thank you, Lord Royce," Cassie answered, thinking how odd it was that he should care. All the men in Jamaica, and even in Bath, had seen Antoinette as nothing but a servant and an oddity. They would never have inquired after her health.

But Phillip appeared truly concerned.

"I was just taking this to her," Cassie added, holding up the basin. "Lavender water is very good for headaches."

"Does Miss Duvall care for wine?" he asked. "I have some very nice German wine put away in the cellar. I could send it up to her."

"How kind of you!" Cassie said with a smile. "So thoughtful . . ."

Phillip waved away her thanks with an awkward gesture. "Not at all, Miss Richards. I am only sorry that your day, and Miss Duvall's, was marred by illness."

"Yes. It was such a lovely day."

He nodded. "Lovely," he murmured. Then, looking rather abashed by that one word he had spoken, he backed up into the library. "I will send that wine up to Miss Duvall. Please let me know if there is anything else I can do."

"Thank you, Lord Royce." Cassie went on her way with her basin, thoroughly bemused by the mystifying Lord Royce. It seemed like every day she found that there was much more to him than books and studies and logic.

Chapter Eleven

"Don't they make a charming picture?" Lady Royce said, looking up from her embroidery to smile fondly across the drawing room at her son and Cassandra.

Antoinette had retired after supper with a lingering headache, but the others had gathered in the drawing room. Phillip and Cassandra were seated together at the pianoforte, attempting a duet. Unfortunately, neither of them was particularly musical, and the discordant plonking noise echoed in the large room.

Chat winced at an especially strident note, and laid down another card in her game of Patience. "Charming. But do you suppose they could engage in something *quiet*, like cards? Or reading?"

"Then we could not admire your niece's talent at the pianoforte!" Lady Royce protested. "Every young lady should play a musical instrument, do you not agree, Chat?"

"Almost every young lady," Chat murmured. She had to agree that Cassie looked very pretty bent over the ivory keys, her dark pink silk skirts spread about her. Chat only hoped that, with all the ghosts floating about the castle, Mozart did not choose to join them, full of wrath at the mangling of his concerto.

"Miss Richards is a very pretty girl indeed," Lady Royce continued. "I must confess I had no idea what to expect, since she had spent so long away from England."

Chat gave a little smile and laid down another card. "Did you think she would wear grass skirts or some such, Melinda?"

Lady Royce blushed, ducking her head over her sewing. "Of course not! I just—wasn't sure."

"Yes. Her parents were not precisely conventional, not like my older brother the viscount. I am not sure Cassandra would pass muster with the high sticklers at Almack's! But she has her own charms."

"Oh, assuredly! She is very pretty, as I said. And obviously kindhearted." Lady Royce gave Chat a sly smile. "Phillip seems to like her a great deal."

Chat looked back over at the young couple. They appeared to be quarreling over a piece of sheet music, with Cassie attempting to pull it out of his hands. "Oh, yes," she said wryly. "You can tell how much they like each other just by looking at them."

"She seems just the sort who could make him come out of his library and into the world. He never would have left his books to go on a picnic before Miss Richards came here, let alone agree to a masked ball!" Lady Royce nodded decisively. "Yes, she is *very* good for him."

But would *he* be good for *her*, Chat wondered. He did have a title and a tidy fortune. But Cassie had her own fortune and was such a free spirit. Could someone like Lord Royce make her happy?

Chat's own comfortable marriage to Lord Willowby, which had lasted twenty harmonious years before his death, made her want nothing less for her niece. A title could not make deep incompatibilities just disappear.

Still, she had to admit that they did look very handsome together.

"You are playing it all wrong!" Cassie said, taking the piece of now rather tattered music from Lord Royce's hand and putting it on the stand. "See these notes here and here? All wrong!"

"My dear Miss Richards, *I* am not the one who is tone-deaf," he muttered.

Cassie stared at him. "Look at the tin ear calling *me* tone-deaf! I thought earls were supposed to be gallant, or at the very least polite."

"Very well! I am very sorry, Miss Richards. Please forgive me for my rudeness. Why don't you play the solo part, and I will turn the pages?"

Cassie looked from him to the music doubtfully. The truth was, she *was* a bit tone-deaf, and had always detested the music lessons her father made her take. Only politeness to Lady Royce, who had asked her to play for them, had made her sit down at the pianoforte. She had not thought Lord Royce would join her there, and now her self-consciousness was making her rather testy.

She gave him an apologetic little smile and said, "I do not really feel like playing anymore. Perhaps *you* would favor us with a song, and I will just go and sit down by the fire for a while."

"As you wish, Miss Richards," he answered. "But I really do apologize for what I said. I am sure you are truly a masterful musician."

"Apology accepted," she said with a laugh. "But flattery denied. I am really a horrible musician."

"That cannot be true."

Oh, but it *was* true. And what was worse, Cassie

found as she went to sit down beside Lady Royce, Lord Royce was quite a competent musician. Not a Mozart, by any means, but tuneful and regular. Only trying to keep up with her had made him play in the wrong key.

She had to laugh inwardly at herself, for always behaving like such a silly goose around him.

"Your aunt and I were just talking about what your life must have been like before you came to England, my dear Miss Richards," Lady Royce said. "How interesting it must have been in Jamaica! And how very different from here."

That was certainly undeniable. "It is rather different, yes."

"But you did say that your parents gave a great many entertainments. There must have been some society there."

"There were the families from the neighboring plantations, like Mr. Bates and his sister, and the Smith-Thompkins, and several people who lived in Negril. They came quite often to our house, and we went into town frequently. After Mother died, Father and I kept to ourselves more, but we still went to card parties and musicales, and even the occasional ball. No, there was no lack of society in Jamaica, Lady Royce."

"You must have had a good many suitors, too," Lady Royce said, pretending great absorption in her embroidery.

"A few," Cassie answered, thinking especially of the persistent Mr. Bates, who had come to the docks to propose one last time before she left.

He had certainly been very different from Lord Royce, loud and boastful. He had probably never opened a book in his life.

"But you accepted none of them?" Lady Royce persisted.

"I did not care for any of them in that way."

"Oh, yes, I see." Lady Royce chuckled. "Yes, I *do* see."

Chat laughed.

Cassie wondered what they were up to, but she was just too tired to puzzle it out at present. "I think I will just go check on Antoinette before I retire, if you will excuse me."

"Oh, yes, dear, do," said Chat. "Make sure she has drunk the brandy and warm milk we sent up."

"I will. Good night, Aunt Chat, Lady Royce." Cassie kissed her aunt's cheek, and left the drawing room with the strains of Mozart floating behind her.

Antoinette was not alone in her chamber. Sitting across from her at a small table, playing what appeared to be a game of Beggar My Neighbor, was Louisa. She was wearing a cloak tonight, a puffy blue satin affair, with the hood pushed back and her golden ringlets spilling free.

"There you are," said Antoinette, studying the cards in her hand. "We've been waiting for you."

Cassie went and sat down in the empty chair at the table. "Have you? For what?"

"I thought you might like to meet Sir Belvedere tonight." Louisa laid down another card and crowed, "I win again! I suppose my card-playing skills are not so dormant as I thought."

Antoinette shook her head. "It is not fair! You have had almost two hundred years to practice."

"You've had practice, too, Antoinette," said Cassie. "We did nothing but play cards all those weeks on the ship from Jamaica. Now, tell me, is Sir Belvedere coming here to meet us?"

"Oh, no," answered Louisa. "He still thinks it is

improper to come to a living lady's chamber. We will go to the East Tower."

"When? Now?"

"Of course, if you are ready." Louisa pulled her hood up over her head, and glided toward the door. "Just follow me!"

Then she disappeared through the solid door, leaving only a faint shimmer behind her.

"We can scarcely follow you that way, now, can we?" Antoinette called, standing up and reaching with her stockinged feet for the slippers she had discarded.

A merry laugh echoed, and Louisa stuck her head back through the door. "So sorry, my dears! Just a bit of ghost humor. Sometimes I simply cannot help myself."

The East Tower was dark and chilly, since the maids did not go there to light fires or adjust the draperies. Only Antoinette's and Cassie's candles cast light into the shadows of the corners.

Louisa settled herself in a chair next to the window and called out, "Sir Belvedere! Where are you? You have callers. I hope you have polished your armor up for them."

There was a faint clattering noise, which grew louder and louder as they listened. Cassie could not tell where the sound was coming from, even though she twisted her head this way and that, peering into the gloom. Then there was one last, deafening clank, and a tall figure in armor appeared next to Louisa's chair.

He pushed the visor back on his helmet, and Cassie saw that he was a rather handsome, if very pale, gentleman.

"Fair ladies!" he cried, giving them a noisy, stiff

little bow. "I am honored you came all this way to make my humble acquaintance."

Cassie glanced at Antoinette, but her friend appeared to be as much at a loss as she was. What did one do with a ghost knight? Curtsy? Shake hands?

She was every bit as puzzled as she had been when she first met Louisa.

She ended up giving a small bob and saying, "How do you do? I am Miss Cassandra Richards, and this is Miss Antoinette Duvall."

"Miss Duvall is going to find Lady Lettice for us," Louisa said.

"Indeed! I have heard you have great powers, Miss Duvall," said Sir Belvedere, holding up his slipping visor to look at Antoinette. "Very great."

Antoinette demurred. "Not *very* great. Not at all like my mother. But I will help you in any way I can. And I know that we would very much like to hear *your* story, Sir Belvedere."

"Ah, my tale. 'Tis a sad one." Sir Belvedere sighed and lowered himself into the chair next to Louisa's. His legs stuck out stiffly in front of him.

Louisa twisted one of her ringlets around her finger. "It is not as sad as all that. Not nearly as sad as *my* story."

Sir Belvedere gave an indignant huff. "Getting drunk and falling down the cliff is not *sad*."

"Neither is tripping on a loose stone and falling off the tower into the moat," Louisa retorted.

Cassie watched them bickering, and wondered if there was something in the air of Royce Castle that caused silly arguments, like the one she and Lord Royce had had over the music.

Then again, did ghosts even breathe air? She had no idea.

And it appeared that this was a long-standing conversation between Louisa and Sir Belvedere. They just shook their heads and looked away from each other to smile at Cassie and Antoinette.

Antoinette perched herself on the edge of the high bed. "I don't remember seeing a moat here," she said.

"It was filled in after Louisa's time," Sir Belvedere explained.

"My husband's brother's wife, who was Lady Royce after me, thought it smelled too foul," Louisa sniffed. "I rather miss it, though."

Cassie sat down on the bed next to Antoinette, listening as Sir Belvedere went on to tell some tales of life at Royce Castle in the Middle Ages, and marveling at the entire strange scene. She had grown up surrounded by tales of spells and spirits, and had never doubted the existence of an unseen world. But she had never thought she would be sitting about casually conversing with two ghosts.

And she would never have thought it would be so very *ordinary*. They chatted about all the other generations Sir Belvedere and Louisa had seen come and go, the ghosts that had stayed for a while and then gone on to nobody knew where. They talked of Cassie's and Antoinette's lives in Jamaica, about Antoinette's mother and Cassie's parents.

It really could have been any tea party anywhere, if their fellow conversants had not been slightly glowing about the edges.

Then the talk turned to the current living inhabitants of Royce Castle.

"We quite like Lady Royce, don't we, Sir Belvedere?" Louisa said. "She's always trying to talk to us."

"A fine lady indeed. Much better than her mother-in-law ever was," Sir Belvedere agreed. "You would have thought that a lady whose marriage was arranged by Lady Lettice would be more receptive to spirits, but no."

"But Lady Royce's son is very different. Always so *logical*," said Louisa. She made "logical" sound like a rather dirty little word. "Always buried in a book. But he is fun to tease a bit."

"We switch his papers about all the time," Sir Belvedere added. "He just thinks it is the housemaids, and asks his mother not to let them tidy in there anymore."

Louisa laughed. "He always forgets that no one *does* clean in there! They stopped months ago." Then she turned a shrewd look onto Cassie. "I think Miss Richards rather *likes* Lord Royce, though."

"Does she indeed?" Sir Belvedere said in a highly interested tone.

"She thinks he looks like a dashing poet," Antoinette offered.

"*Antoinette!*" Cassie cried, feeling her face grow warm. She pressed her palms to her cheeks. "Please."

"Well, do you not think that?" Antoinette said innocently.

"We could assist you," said Sir Belvedere. "Put some suggestions into his head, that sort of thing."

"Oh, no! Thank you, but no," Cassie said hurriedly. That was the very last thing she needed; ghosts matchmaking for her.

Antoinette then said, "He is not really her 'sort of gentleman,' you see."

And, without explaining who she *did* think of as her sort of gentleman, Cassie said good night and retired back to her own chamber.

Chapter Twelve

Once in her bed, though, Cassie found she simply could not sleep. The excitement of talking to the ghosts still hummed in her mind, and she tossed about for a long while remembering it.

Finally, she gave up any attempt to fall asleep, pushed back the bedclothes, found her slippers and dressing gown, and went downstairs to the library.

There she bypassed the shelf of novels and found the neat row of leather-bound books that bore Lord Royce's name on the spines. She pulled out the first volume and took it over to the desk.

She sat in the thick silence of the night. Time stood still as she turned over the pages of the book. She wasn't sure what she had expected when she opened the volume, but not this complete absorption into another world.

She had thought Lord Royce's work would be dry and academic, and it was certainly very learned. But it was also warm and vivid; it brought scenes of an ancient, long-dead place to life. She could almost see the public squares of Greece, where philosophers taught rapt young students and servants hurried to the marketplace bearing amphorae of olives and wine. It almost made her think of Jamaica.

Cassie did not see the logic that Lord Royce claimed to hold so dear, but she did see much more. And she also saw that Lord Royce saw more, too. Probably more than even he realized. He saw the true vividness of life. Why, then, would he deny the richness of what was in his own home?

Cassie was very puzzled. Both by Lord Royce and by herself.

Then, as she eagerly turned over another page, she heard the soft click of the library door opening. She looked up and noticed, without much surprise, Lord Royce himself standing there, a pile of papers in his arms.

Despite the slight chill in the air, he was in his shirtsleeves, his hair falling in a rumpled mass to his shoulders. He looked startled to see her there, and, for one second, the candle in his hand wavered.

"Lord Royce," she said with a smile. "We really must stop meeting like this."

"Miss Richards," he answered slowly. "I did not expect anyone to be about at this hour."

"I could not sleep, so I came down here to find something to read."

"And what did you find? A novel?" He came closer to the desk, put his candle down next to hers and the papers atop some books, and sat in the chair beside her. He smelled of clean soap and night air; his warmth and nearness was natural, comforting.

"No. It is the first volume of your series on ancient Greece."

"Indeed?" His dark brow arched. "What do you think of my work, Miss Richards? Too stuffy and academic?"

Cassie shook her head. "You are a very talented

writer, Lord Royce," she said quietly. "I could almost imagine myself there."

"That is a very kind thing for you to say."

"It is not kindness. It is the truth. Through your words, I can see the marketplace in my mind. Smell the wine and olive oil, feel the Grecian sun on my face, and hear all the chatter and laughter." Cassie looked back down at the open book. "In a strange way, it reminded me of—of Jamaica."

"Of Jamaica? Ancient Greece? In what way?"

She wondered if he was making fun of her. After all, ancient Greece and Jamaica were really nothing alike. But when she glanced up at him, she saw only interest written on his face. "In the way so much of life is lived outdoors. In the warmth of the sun, and the diet of fish and fruit and wine. When I was a child, Antoinette's mother would take us to the market in Negril with her. I remember how much I loved that, how I loved the sights and smells, being surrounded by all the *life* . . ."

Her throat grew tight, and she lapsed into silence.

"You miss it very much, don't you?" he said quietly.

"England is not so very bad," Cassie answered. "It has its own sort of life. But yes, I do sometimes get homesick, even now."

"Why did you not stay on there?"

"My parents were gone; Antoinette was all I had left. And Aunt Chat wrote so often, urging me to come stay with her. It seemed the best thing to do." Cassie ran her hand over the cool smoothness of the paper. "There *are* women who can run their own plantations and succeed. But I do not think I could be one of them."

"I think you could do anything you set your mind to," he said.

Cassie looked up at him, startled. No one had ever said anything like that to her before. No one had ever thought her capable, or sensible, or able to do much of anything. Even her parents and Antoinette, who loved her, never had. "You do? Truly?"

"Truly."

"Then I shall have to set my mind to something." She closed the book and looked down at his name embossed on the cover. "I wish I could write a book, like you."

"You could probably write a grand horrid novel," he suggested. "Strange noises in the night, mysterious servants. Exotic ceremonies in seaside tunnels."

Cassie grinned at him. "Oh, so you have heard about that scheme, have you?"

He grinned back. "My mother said something to me about it. She also said I could come along, if I like."

"Of course you can come along. They are your tunnels, after all. But no cynical comments, if you please."

"The spirits won't appear if there is an unfriendly presence, eh?"

"Something of the sort."

"Then I promise, no comments of any sort. You read my book; the least I can do is be polite at your—ceremony."

"I learned a great deal from your book, Lord Royce," Cassie said. "Perhaps you can learn something from me."

He looked at her steadily, his eyes serious. "I am sure I can, Miss Richards."

Cassie returned his regard for a long, still moment. The room around them seemed to disappear. Books, ghosts, castles, Jamaica—nothing else existed in the world for that one instant. Nothing but him and herself, held together in a strange accord.

It should have been an uncomfortable moment, a nervous thing. Yet it was not. It just felt—right. Completely right, to be here with this man, in this moment, alone in the quiet of the night.

Then he looked away, and the odd enchantment was broken. Cassie, too, glanced away, afraid she might be overcome with this strange emotion, these vague yearnings, and start to cry.

"Why must we go specifically to the tunnels on Friday?" he asked in a strained voice. Then he leaned back casually in his chair, his arms crossed, and Cassie thought she must have imagined that hoarse tone, that moment of intimacy. "Why not the drawing room or the breakfast room?"

He could not be feeling the same way she was. He was logical and rational; she was prone to flights of romance and fancy.

She tried to focus her mind on his question. "Antoinette says that the phase of the moon will be just right on Friday, and somehow her fainting episode told her that the tunnels are the right place. I fear I have not studied these things as she has, so I could not tell you why that is. You will just have to come and see for yourself."

"Oh, I shall. I am quite looking forward to it." The old tone of doubt was back in his voice, in his expression.

Cassie could feel them falling back into what was already a familiar pattern, and she was grateful for it. She would need time alone, time when she was not so confused, to examine these strange new feelings. "And so am I, Lord Royce. Very much."

"You know, 'Lord Royce' sounds terribly formal, considering our circumstances. Perhaps you could call me Phillip? Just when we are alone?" He sounded quite endearingly shy and hesitant as he asked this, not at all like his usual self.

Cassie's eyes widened in surprise at this informality. "Call you—Phillip?"

"Well, you do not have to, of course. It just sounds ridiculous for you to be calling me Lord Royce all the time."

"I should like to call you Phillip. When we are— informal like this. Perhaps you could also call me Cassandra."

He smiled at her. "Very well, then, it is a bargain—Cassandra."

She smiled, too. Her name on his lips sounded different than when anyone else had ever said it. It sounded exotic and elegant, and very sweet.

"Would you care to go riding with me tomorrow, Cassandra?" he continued. "Mother has assigned me to deliver some invitations to the masked ball to her friends in the village. You could meet some of them."

"I would like that very much, Phillip. Thank you." Then the little clock on the fireplace mantel struck two. Cassie looked at it in surprise. "Is it so late already? I should retire."

"Yes," he answered. "So should I."

Cassie stood up, still holding the book in her hands. "Would you mind if I borrowed this? I would like to finish reading it."

"Not at all. Keep it as long as you like."

"Well, then. Good night." Then she hurried off to her own chamber, the book clutched very tightly against her.

Phillip watched Cassie leave, then sat down in her vacated chair behind the desk.

The faint scent of her perfume still clung to the

air. Phillip shook his head to try to clear it of the enchantment of that fragrance.

What a very odd night it had been. He had been unable to sleep, unable even to stay still in his bed. Something in his mind had kept urging him to get up, to go to the library. He had thought it was just an urge to work, something that came on him rather often late at night.

Then he walked into the library and saw Miss Richards—Cassandra—sitting there. Her black hair fell loose from where she had tied it back carelessly with a ribbon, and the candlelight gave it the sheen of the ocean at night. Her eyes were wide and dark and startled as she looked up at him.

Phillip usually disliked it when people came into the library, a place he regarded as his own sanctuary. But it seemed strangely *right* to see her there.

It seemed right to see her anywhere in his home. In the short time she had been there, the place had become a brighter and more cheerful place. A place full of interest and variety. He found himself looking forward to going to the tunnels on Friday night, and even to his mother's silly masked ball.

And he did *not* look forward to the day Cassandra would leave Royce Castle, and his old routine of staying in the library almost all day would return.

"You will just have to find a way to keep her here!" a voice echoed in his head. A voice that sounded oddly—feminine.

Was he hearing things now? First he was feeling sentimental about Cassandra Richards, and now this. He was losing his mind. That was all there was to it.

He rubbed his hands over his face wearily. "I am just tired," he muttered. "This is all just a strange dream."

He blew out the candles and went up to bed, deter-

mined to call on the physician if these strange feelings did not go away in the next few days.

Louisa, perched atop the rolling ladder, shook her
head in exasperation. "Men!" she sighed. "Thick as
a plank, every single one of them."

Chapter Thirteen

For once, Cassie was warm in chilly old England as she galloped along a narrow pathway next to Lord Royce.

No, she reminded herself. Not Lord Royce. Phillip.

She laughed aloud as her horse charged ahead, its hooves churning at the soft ground. They jumped over a fallen log, and she ducked under a tree limb that arched overhead.

The limb missed her head, but snatched her hat away. The hat pins pulled through her hair, disarranging the knot, and Cassie reined her horse in.

"Oh, dear me!" she cried, still gasping with laughter. "I am quite sure I would have won the race, if this silly tree had not gotten in my way." She reached up and tried to smooth her hair back into place.

Phillip rose up in his stirrups to snatch the hat off the limb. "It is easy for you to say that now, but I very nearly overtook you. I am sure *I* would have won."

"Ha! You were miles back." Cassie took the hat from his gloved hand. The jaunty little veil was pulled askew, but otherwise it looked in fair shape. "But we shall call it a draw."

"Done. A draw it is. But I thought you said you had not ridden for a long while?"

"I haven't," Cassie answered, placing the hat back on her head and trying to adjust it back to its former rakish angle. "Not since I came to England."

"Then you are a fine horsewoman indeed. I would hate to see you when you are in practice."

"Why, thank you, Lord R—Phillip! What a nice compliment. Your mother would be very proud to see you doing the pretty."

Phillip laughed ruefully. "I would not say it if I did not mean it! I fear I am not very good at 'doing the pretty,' as you call it." He pointed ahead on the path with his riding crop. "The village is just right over that hill."

"Then I am glad our race came to an end," said Cassie. "I would not want people to think I am some hoyden who gallops carelessly along."

"Oh, no, never that." Phillip drew his horse back onto the path at a sedate walk, and Cassie fell in beside him. "There may not be anyone about who could have seen you come galloping in, anyway. The village is rather small, just the church and a few shops, and some of Mother's friends who live at the far end of the road."

"It sounds lovely," said Cassie. "Bath is so very crowded all of the time. It's always exciting, but sometimes . . ." She paused, not sure of the exact word she was looking for.

"Overwhelming?" Phillip suggested.

"Yes, exactly."

"I often feel the same way in cities. Perhaps that is why I usually stay at the castle, though I know Mother would prefer more society."

"She is so looking forward to this masked ball!"

"Indeed she is. And that reminds me of my other errand. I am to take you to the dressmaker so you

can order your costume. I think Mother and your
aunt have already ordered theirs."

"How grand!" Cassie said with a smile. She already had about fifty ideas for costumes.

They paused at the crest of the hill and looked
down at the village. It seemed like a little fairy-tale
hamlet from this distance, neat rows of half-timbered
buildings and thatched-roofed cottages. Blue-gray
smoke curled out of several chimneys, and, despite
what Phillip had said, there *were* people about. They
strolled along the narrow walkways, and went in and
out of shop doors. She could see the square stone
tower of the church, and what looked like an inn,
and maybe a tea shop.

"It is larger than I expected," she said, smoothing
the high collar of her dark green riding habit.

"It has everything we need," Phillip answered.

"Including a bookshop?"

"Especially a bookshop! And, as you can tell, it is
not very far from the castle."

Cassie looked back over the way they had come.
She could see the castle rising up in the distance,
over fields and trees. It seemed a vast expanse of
green and gray ground. "Who does all that land belong to?" she asked.

"To me, of course," Phillip answered. "Or rather,
to my family."

"Such a lot. My father would have been so envi-
ous," she said thoughtfully.

"Did your father not have land in Jamaica?"

"Oh, yes. A great deal, of which I have kept a
small parcel, just in case. But he only went out to the
West Indies because he was a younger son and had
no land here."

"I sometimes wish *I* had an older brother," Phillip
said, guiding his horse down the hill.

Cassie followed him. "Do you? Why?"

"Perhaps then I would not have to spend any time with bailiffs and secretaries and lawyers. That would have been my older brother's responsibility."

"And you could spend every bit of your time on writing?"

Phillip smiled at her. "Oh, I don't think I would spend *every* bit of my time writing. Not anymore."

Cassie laughed and had just opened her mouth to answer him, when a voice called, "Lord Royce! What a pleasure to see you in the village on such a fine day."

Cassie turned her head to see a tall, reed-thin man in a neat black coat hurrying toward them.

"Good morning, Mr. Lewisham," Phillip replied, pulling his horse to a halt. He dismounted and reached up to assist Cassie. "Miss Richards, this is our good vicar, Mr. Lewisham, who shepherds the flock at St. Anne's Church most admirably. Mr. Lewisham, this is one of our guests at the castle, Miss Cassandra Richards."

"How do you do, Mr. Lewisham," Cassie said politely.

"A pleasure to meet you, Miss Richards!" Mr. Lewisham replied with a wide smile. "You are the one from Jamaica, are you not?"

"I—well, yes, I am," Cassie said, rather nonplused. She had never seen this man in her life; how did he know where she was from?

Mr. Lewisham laughed. "I did not mean to surprise you, Miss Richards! News travels fast in such a small, isolated place. We have heard all about you and your very unusual companion. And my wife and I have been reading about the West Indies. It is a dream of ours to do missionary work there. You must come and have tea with us, if you have the time before returning to the castle."

"Thank you, Mr. Lewisham," Cassie said. "I should be honored."

"We are to have luncheon with Lady Paige," added Phillip. "But we would be happy to call on Mrs. Lewisham this afternoon."

Mr. Lewisham rubbed his thin hands together in delight. "Excellent! Well, I must be hurrying on now, but I look forward to seeing you later, Lord Royce, Miss Richards." Then he bowed and continued on down the pathway to the road.

"What a nice man," Cassie commented as Phillip led her off toward the livery stable where they could leave their horses. Several other people bowed and smiled as they passed by.

"People in Cornwall have the reputation for being wary of strangers," Phillip answered. "But here you can see that is scarcely the case. I am sure you will be very warmly welcomed everywhere. Or at least *almost* anywhere."

And so she was. Cassie went to visit Mrs. Brown, the dressmaker, while Phillip waited for her at the bookshop. There, in Mrs. Brown's cozy front room, she met four other young ladies. They became so caught up in poring over fashion plates and examining fabrics that she quite lost track of time. Until the bells at the church tolled the hour and she remembered that they were to have luncheon with Lady Royce's friend Lady Paige.

She hastily decided on a blue-and-yellow fabric for her shepherdess's costume, gathered up her other purchases, and hurried out of the shop.

Lord Royce was pacing about on the walkway, a square, book-shaped parcel tucked under his arm.

"Why did you not come inside to fetch me?" Cassie asked, falling into step beside him as they set off down the street. "I met some other ladies, and we started talking, and, well, we rather lost track of time."

Phillip looked back at the pleasant little shop, a look almost of horror on his handsome face. "Me? Go into a—a lady's dressmaker shop?"

Cassie laughed. "Oh, Lord Royce! It is hardly the portal of doom. It is really quite a nice place. I found these delightful blue ribbons . . ."

"Please, my dear Miss Richards," he said in a pained voice. "No talk of ribbons. I beg you."

Cassie laughed again, and tucked her hand in the crook of his arm as they strolled along, meeting other people and glancing into shop windows.

She thought it felt rather odd, as if they were some old married couple.

"My dear Lord Royce! How kind of you to come see me. It has been much too long since I've seen you." Lady Paige, a round little matron in elegant gray silk and a lace cap, went up on tiptoe to peck a kiss on Phillip's cheek.

Phillip bent down, accepting the salute with good grace, and Cassie discerned a hint of a blush on his cheeks. She almost laughed as she hung back in the doorway of Lady Paige's drawing room, waiting to be introduced.

"Far too long, Lady Paige," he answered.

"Pish! You used to call me Aunt Lydia. Now, who is this lovely young lady? The houseguest your mother has told me so much about?" Lady Paige turned her curious gaze onto Cassie.

"Yes, indeed. This is Miss Richards. Miss Richards, may I present my mother's dear friend, Lady Paige?"

"How do you do?" Cassie said politely.

"Oh, Miss Richards, what a delight to meet you! You

are every bit as pretty as Melinda said. You have both chosen a perfect day to come for luncheon, as well."

"Have we, La—Aunt Lydia?" Phillip inquired. "How so?"

"Because my nephew, Mr. Neville Vickery, is here from Town!" Lady Paige clapped her hands together. "He so seldom visits his poor auntie, you know, and he has such vastly amusing stories to tell." She leaned toward Cassie and whispered confidingly, "He is quite the beau, you know. The joy of every young lady's eye! I am sure you will like him, Miss Richards."

Phillip gave her an alarmed look, and Cassie again had the urge to laugh. "I am sure I shall, Lady Paige," she said.

Then they went into Lady Paige's drawing room, a small space crowded with figurines, paintings, and embroidered cushions—and one extraordinary "tulip of fashion."

Cassie giggled behind her hand to think that the young man standing by the window could be the joy of any young lady's eye. He was tall, true, and had pleasing, regular features. But his golden hair was pomaded to such a high gloss that it glowed, his cravat was so elaborately tied that it resembled nothing so much as a wedding cake, and his yellow coat was nearly blinding.

Cassie could not help but glance at Phillip, and compare his plain, serviceable garments and carelessly long hair to the yellow coat and embroidered orange waistcoat. It was all too obvious which man came out with the advantage.

But Lady Paige beamed at her nephew as if he were a veritable Apollo come to earth. "Lord Royce, Miss Richards, may I present my nephew, Mr. Vickery?"

Mr. Vickery moved across the crowded room with a stylish languor, and took Cassie's hand in his. As he raised it to his lips, his many rings cut into Cassie's skin.

"Charmed, I'm sure," he said in a low, drawling voice. "Aunt Lydia, you never told me that there were hidden charms in this pokey old village. I would have come to visit an age ago."

Lady Paige tittered as if he had uttered a great witticism. "Oh, Neville! How you do tease."

Mr. Vickery gave Cassie what he obviously considered a soulful, Byronic look. "I am completely serious. You never said an angel resided in this remote corner."

Laughter threatened to bubble up to Cassie's lips again, and she feared that if she let even another giggle escape she would not be able to stop. Did ladies in London really *enjoy* this sort of ridiculous flattery?

It was amusing, to be sure, but she found that she much preferred Phillip's sensible conversation.

"How very kind you are, Mr. Vickery," she said, carefully extracting her hand from his grasp.

"It is not kindness at all, Miss Richards—merely the truth. Please, let me escort you into the dining room. I am so eager to hear what you think of this bleak corner of the world." Without even waiting for her leave, he took her arm and tugged her out of the room, brushing past Lord Royce and his aunt. "I do hope your cook has not burned the soup today, Aunt Lydia," was his only careless comment to her, tossed back over his shoulder.

"Oh, yes! I mean, no," Lady Paige cried, obviously distressed. "I am sure she has not, after your unhappiness with the fish yesterday, Neville."

"Quite," Mr. Vickery said curtly. He leaned closer

to Cassie and murmured, "It is so very difficult here to maintain proper standards, Miss Richards. Not at all like my house in London. You must allow me to tell you all about it . . ."

Cassie only listened with half an ear as Mr. Vickery, the joy of every young lady's eye, went on about his house in London and all his highborn friends. She watched as Lord Royce seated the slighted Lady Paige in her chair at the head of the table and conversed with her about various village doings. Slowly, the hurt look in her eyes over her nephew's carelessness faded, and a new sparkle took its place. Lord Royce nodded understandingly at her words and smiled.

All traces of the impatient, unsocial scholar vanished. He was all patience and kindness—just as he always was with his mother and Aunt Chat and even Antoinette, who most people treated as a mere curiosity.

As hard as he tried to hide it, Lord Royce was a very kind and thoughtful man. Not even his shabby coats could hide that, just as Mr. Vickery's yellow satin could not hide his shallowness.

Cassie smiled at the revelation, but unfortunately that small lifting of her lips encouraged Mr. Vickery to even greater heights of bragging about his barouche.

Phillip half listened to Lady Paige as he watched Mr. Vickery charming Miss Richards.

A sour, unaccustomed pang ached somewhere in his stomach as he looked at the fashionable man leaning close to her, speaking into her ear. She gave a small, almost intimate smile at whatever it was he was saying.

Mr. Vickery must be a riveting conversationalist,

Phillip thought, as well as a sparkling dresser. His yellow coat, though a bilious color, was perfectly cut, his linen impeccably free of ink stains. No doubt he could converse on many subjects other than the ancient Greeks. How could a lady help but be impressed with him?

Phillip ruefully inspected the frayed cuff of his coat. Perhaps, just perhaps, he should visit the tailor and have some new ones made up. Not in yellow, to be sure, but maybe a sensible blue or brown. What would Miss Richards think of him then?

Phillip brusquely dismissed that thought just as it flitted through his mind. He did not have time for such frivolities! His coats had been good enough for months.

But still, a small voice whispered at the back of his mind, if a new coat could make her smile at him as she was smiling now, it could be worth it.

It could be worth it, indeed.

"How did you find my old friend Lady Paige and her nephew?" Lady Royce asked over supper that night at Royce Castle. "Is she enjoying living in the village? Did she accept the invitation to the masked ball?"

"She was very well, Mother, and of course she accepted the invitation," answered Phillip. "Everyone we invited accepted, did they not, Miss Richards?"

"Oh, yes," Cassie said, happy for the excuse to abandon her fillet of sole. The fish was excellent, but after an unusually large luncheon at Lady Paige's house, and tea and cakes with the Lewishams, she was quite stuffed. "All the people we met were so very kind! I had a wonderful day." And she had. Even Mr. Vickery, in his own way, had been very amusing. Cassie laughed, recalling his attempts at flirtation over luncheon.

Lady Royce beamed. "Yes, it is a very nice neighborhood. We should have everyone to the castle more often, should we not, Phillip?"

He looked at his mother suspiciously, as if he thought she might be up to something. "Of course, Mother."

Lady Royce nodded. "And did you get to go to Mrs. Brown's shop, my dear Miss Richards? She does such lovely work. I really think she could go to London."

"She did have some very pretty samples," Cassie agreed. "I ordered a couple of gowns as well as my costume."

"Did you decide on something, then, Cassie?" Antoinette asked.

"I am going to be a shepherdess," Cassie answered. "Have *you* decided on something?"

Antoinette shook her head. "I told you. It is a surprise."

"I am going to be Queen Elizabeth," Lady Royce offered. "And Chat will be Eleanor of Aquitaine. But Phillip still will not tell me what his costume is to be."

Phillip smiled. "That is because I do not know yet. I would rather not wear a costume at all."

"Of course you must wear a costume! That is the fun of it." Lady Royce sighed happily. "Oh, I *am* looking forward to this so very much!"

Chapter Fourteen

"Tell me, Louisa, why do you want to find Lady
Lettice so much? I mean, why her in particular?"
Cassie asked. They were walking along the shore
toward the tunnels, on their way to Antoinette's ceremony. Antoinette, Chat, and Lady Royce hurried
ahead, carrying Antoinette's books, herbs, and candles, while Lord Royce trailed far behind.

He did not even appear to see Louisa at all, but
Cassie thought it seemed quite normal to be in her
company now. It could have been any evening stroll,
really, if only her companion did not float above the
sand rather than walk on it.

Louisa paused for a moment, then answered, "We
want to know where they go."

"Where they go?"

"The ghosts who only stay for a brief while, and
the people who die and do not become ghosts at all,
like my husband. Sir Belvedere and I are the only
ones who have stayed here so long, and we often
wonder why. We just thought Lady Lettice might be
the most likely to return, since she was here a rather
long time as well."

Cassie nodded. She, too, would like to know where they had all gone. Perhaps then she would know about her parents.

Louisa paused and turned her head to look out at the moonlit sea. The hood of her cloak hid her face. "I just want to *know,*" she whispered.

Cassie reached out to squeeze her hand, but felt only cool air. "If anyone can find out, it is Antoinette."

"Yes. Of course," said Louisa, her voice cheerful in a rather determined way. Then she looked ahead and gave a little, glowing wave. "Look! There is Sir Belvedere, waiting at the tunnel." She floated away, leaving Cassie standing alone on the shore.

She shivered a bit and pulled her red cloak closer about her. She *did* want to know, just as much as Louisa did. If she could just know that her parents were at peace, that they were together again . . .

But there was also a part of her that didn't really want to know at all. A very tiny part that was afraid.

Phillip came up beside her and gently touched her arm. "Having second thoughts?" he said softly.

Cassie looked up at him. The moonlight gave a silvery cast to his handsome face, making him look even more beautiful and rather otherworldly. Everything seemed cast in unreality tonight, even this solid, logical man.

She drew herself up to her full height, only to find that she still barely came to his shoulder. "Of course not," she said stoutly. "Are you? Oh, no, *you* would not be. You think nothing is going to happen tonight."

"I never said that. I simply do not *know* what is going to happen."

He looked to the tunnels, where the others had already gone in. The light of their lanterns and candles sent a golden wash out of the entrance onto the rocks and sand.

Cassie studied him carefully. Did he feel it, too, then? This sense that tonight was—special.

He smiled down at her and held out his arm. "Shall we, then?"

She nodded and slipped her hand onto the sleeve of his greatcoat, grateful for its warm solidity beneath her touch. And she knew then that, no matter what happened, she would be safe with him at her side.

"Oh, spirits of the night, of the sea and air! Hear my summons. Come to me!"

Antoinette's voice, deep and resonant, echoed in the dim, shallow tunnel. They had put out their lanterns, and the smoke from the circle of candles stung Cassie's eyes. She rubbed them before opening them again to look around her.

Antoinette stood in the middle of the circle of lights, her eyes half-closed, her mother's book open at her feet. She swayed slightly as she murmured, her green robe shimmering in the light. The others were gathered in a ragged oval outside the lights, holding hands and watching Antoinette with wide eyes.

There was a palpable air of tension and expectation in the still, cold air. No one knew what was going to happen next, and everyone looked about with nervous, darting little glances before looking at Antoinette again.

Cassie saw Aunt Chat look toward the tunnel entrance, her expression full of longing. Her hand tugged slightly in Cassie's grasp, but Cassie gave it a reassuring squeeze and she turned back to the group.

Phillip's hand lay still and warm in Cassie's other hand, his palm slightly rough against her skin. He, too, watched Antoinette closely, with a small, puzzled frown on his face. He looked as if he was listening to a rather fascinating lecture at Oxford.

Cassie wished she could be as calm as he was, as clinical. Her stomach felt fluttery and tight, and her hands were cold. As Antoinette's voice became louder, her words faster, Cassie longed to throw herself into Phillip's arms and shout out for her to stop.

She had even moved a step closer to him, tugging Aunt Chat with her, when a loud explosion echoed from the back of the tunnel. Bright blue-green light flashed, followed by a shower of sparks.

Cassie screamed and really did fall into Phillip's arms. He held her tightly against him, and she buried her face in the starchy, clean scent of his shirtfront.

But she couldn't help peeking back at the tunnel.

Antoinette ceased her chanting, and stared, mouth agape, at the darkness beyond the candles. Chat and Lady Royce clung to each other, also staring. Chat, unflappable Aunt Chat, trembled under her Indian print shawl. Louisa and Sir Belvedere, hovering near the entrance, watched with avid eyes.

In the wake of the brilliant explosion, the back of the tunnel seemed even darker than before. A faint drift of smoke floated to the ceiling.

Then a woman stepped forward, with a little, childlike man holding on to her hand. She was quite an amazing vision, tall and slim, with dark red hair coiled atop her head and crowned with a red velvet, pearl-trimmed cap. She wore a red satin gown in the Elizabethan style, richly embroidered, spread wide over a drum farthingale, with a tall, lacy ruff framing her pale, glowing face.

She stared back at them, faintly bewildered. It was deeply quiet in the tunnel.

Phillip pulled Cassie closer to him, and her hands

tightened on the wool of his greatcoat. She couldn't breathe from wondering what might happen next.

The little man-child the woman held by the hand leaped up and down, the bells on his blue velvet cap and doublet jingling discordantly. He tugged at the woman's beringed hand and cried, "What is happening, Lady Lettice? Angelo is confused!"

"Hush, Angelo," the woman said quietly, taking in their gaping gathering with one sweeping glance. Then she saw Louisa and Sir Belvedere, and her eyes widened.

"Louisa," she said, her voice low and calm. "Sir Belvedere. So lovely to see you again. Have you moved on, or have I returned to Royce Castle?" Before they could answer, she glided forward, her skirts rustling silkily, the little man tugged in her wake. "But I can see that I am back at the castle. I remember these tunnels. Oh, indeed I do."

"Hello, Lettice," said Louisa.

"Fair Lady Lettice," Sir Belvedere said, then did one of his clanking bows. "We are very happy to see you again."

"Are you?" Lettice murmured. She looked at Antoinette, who still stood in her circle of lights. "And I suppose *you* are the one who brought me here?"

Antoinette tilted her chin back, her eyes narrowed as she examined Lettice. "I am Miss Antoinette Duvall," she answered. "I *am* the one who summoned you."

Lettice frowned, her pale forehead puckering under the widow's peak of her hair. "But whatever for?"

"It was at our request," Louisa said. "We wanted to see you again."

"Did you?" Lettice asked, still looking most puzzled. Then Angelo pulled at her hand again and squealed, "Angelo is hungry, my lady! They took me away from my cakes and ale."

"Hush, Angelo. You are always hungry." Lettice pressed one hand on her throat, clattering the long strands of pearls and rubies there. "I need to leave these tunnels!"

She floated quickly out into the night, along with the noisy Angelo. Louisa and Sir Belvedere followed her, leaving the humans alone.

Cassie pulled away from Phillip to look up at his face. She expected to see him scornful and doubting, perhaps with his brow raised or a cynical little smile on his lips.

Instead, he was almost as pale as Lady Lettice. He stared unseeing into the depths of the tunnel, where the ghosts had appeared.

Cassie reached up and gently touched his cheek, bringing his gaze back to her. His skin was cold. "Phillip?" she whispered.

He placed his hand over hers, holding it to his cheek. "This is some sort of dream, is it not, Cassandra? A dream that has you in it, as well. I knew I should not have eaten that mushroom tart at supper."

"It is not a dream," Cassie answered. "I told you Antoinette has powers, but you did not believe me. Now you can see that there really *are* spirits, right here in your very home."

He frowned. "How do I know that these people are not actors you have hired to play out this little scene?"

His mother heard his words. She pulled away from Chat and straightened her cloak over her shoulders. She, too, was a bit pale, but her eyes were bright with excitement. "Don't be so ridiculous, Phillip! How could we get them to fly? To glow? And why would we go to so much trouble just to play a joke on *you*? My dear, you are just going to have to face the fact that there are things in this world that your books cannot explain. That logic cannot dismiss."

With a decisive little nod, she hurried out of the tunnel in search of the ghosts. Chat followed her.

Antoinette was gathering up her book and herbs, her dark face suffused with joy. "I did it!" she murmured as she blew out most of the candles. "I truly did it. Oh, I wish Mama could see this!"

And, she, too, left the tunnel, not even seeing Phillip and Cassie still standing there.

In the cold gloom, Phillip staggered over to an old upturned crate and sat down on it heavily. "So it was not a dream?" he muttered. "How can that be? What was it?"

Cassie was very worried. He did not sound at all like his usual scholarly self. He sounded, and looked, like a little lost boy.

She thought with a fright that perhaps the shock had undone him. She hurried over to his side and pulled the collar of his coat closer about his throat.

"It is all right," she soothed. "Quite all right. Spirits have always been with us, even in ancient Greece. *They* believed in spirits, too, did they not?" She wasn't exactly sure if they had or not, but she certainly hoped it was so. If only she had finished reading his book!

"Rational thinkers rejected such superstitions," he said uncertainly.

"Would you doubt the rationality of your own eyes?" Cassie argued. "Did you not see them yourself? Right here? And they cannot be a dream or hallucination, because we all saw them."

Phillip took her hand and looked up steadily into

her eyes. "But what *are* they? Tell me, Cassandra. I must know."

Cassie shook her head. This was something she had wondered herself, but then she had come to the conclusion that it was simply unknowable. "I do not know exactly. They are the spirits of people who have lived here before, but I don't know why they are still here. *They* do not even know. But perhaps Lady Lettice can tell us something."

He shook his head and pulled away from her. The color had returned to his face, but now he looked angry and confused. He stood up and paced across the tunnel, his arms crossed. "Then if you cannot tell me the purpose, the truth, of this, why have you done it?"

"Because we do *not* know, of course!" Cassie said, confused. She had seen him cynical and doubting, and stuffy and smart, but never angry. Now he strolled the narrow periphery of the tunnel, kicking out at the extinguished candles, the spent piles of herbs. "We—we thought we might learn something . . ."

"Did you have to do it here?" he said, staring at her with burning eyes. "Perhaps things of this sort are usual in Jamaica, but we are in England. This has no place in a civilized, ordered society." He gave her one more glare for good measure. "No place."

Then he turned and stormed out of the tunnel.

Cassie was stunned. She would not have guessed that Phillip had such depths of temper in him. She had disrupted the calm, unruffled order of his life, and now he was unsure. She completely understood his feelings.

But *why* did he have to take out his anger on her? She had meant no harm at all. She had only wanted to help him see beyond his blasted logic, to expand his horizons.

It appeared she had made a great mistake. After all, some people did not want their horizons expanded. She would not have thought that Phillip, a scholar, would be one of them.

Her eyes stung with unshed tears. She wiped at them fiercely with the back of her hand, squared her shoulders, and marched out of the tunnel. Standing about feeling sorry for herself would do no one any good at all.

And she was not about to let such an old fusty-musty as Lord Royce ruin her pleasure in the successful ceremony!

On the beach, the four ghosts were gathered near the water, whispering and gesturing. The only thing that could be heard from them was the clatter of Sir Belvedere's armor and the jingle of Angelo's bells.

Antoinette was sitting down on a large rock, looking thoroughly exhausted but also exultant. She held her mother's book against her, stroking her hand over the worn leather cover.

Chat and Lady Royce hovered near her, talking excitedly. When Cassie emerged into the moonlight, they hurried over to her.

"Cassie, dear, are you quite all right?" Chat said worriedly. "We saw Lord Royce come stomping past earlier. Did you quarrel?"

Cassie gave them a weak smile. "He is rather angry over what happened tonight. I tried to talk to him, but . . ."

"Of course he is angry!" Lady Royce cried. "He would never listen to me before, never even consider that the castle might be haunted. Now he has been proven wrong, proven wrong by *women*, and he is upset. Such a man. I cannot believe I raised him."

Cassie thought there was probably more to it than

that, but she was too tired to talk about it, or even think about it any more tonight.

"I am sure you are right, Lady Royce," she answered.

"We will all talk to him tomorrow," Lady Royce said. "I am sure he will see sense in the clear light of day." She did not seem to realize the irony of having ghosts be "sense."

"You should be in your bed, dear," said Chat. "You and Antoinette both look thoroughly exhausted."

Cassie let herself be led away along the shore; her feet felt like lead in her boots. It *had* been a long, eventful, tiring evening.

Before they turned away to climb the steps up the cliff, she looked back over her shoulder at the gathering of ghosts. Louisa caught her eye and gave her a cheerful little wave.

Cassie waved back. At least *someone* seemed happy about the proceedings.

Chapter Fifteen

"So you know nothing of what happens when we leave here?" Louisa asked Lady Lettice. "Nothing at all?"

Lady Lettice shook her head. "Only what I have told you. Angelo and I were in a sort of sitting room the entire time. It was rather pleasant. There were always people to play cards with, especially that nice Roman gentleman, Didius."

"There was ale and cakes!" Angelo cried. "And roast beef and peacock . . ."

Lady Lettice tugged impatiently at his hand, and he lapsed into quiet mutters. "And sugared almonds and stewed quail and puddings . . ." he whispered, kicking at the pebbles with the upturned toe of his shoe.

"There *was* plenty of food," Lady Lettice said. "Sometimes a man would come and ask us very impertinent questions, and write things down. But I do not know why I was there, or why I returned, except that you summoned me."

"And you did not see—well, anyone *interesting* there?" Louisa asked haltingly.

Lady Lettice gave her a knowing look. "Someone like your William, perhaps?"

"He was not *my* William," Louisa cried indignantly. "Not even when he was alive."

Lady Lettice nodded. "Be that as it may, I did not see him. Or indeed anyone I knew except Angelo. It was sometimes rather dull, despite the food and cards and Didius, so I cannot say I am completely sorry to be back at Royce Castle. Especially with such interesting people in residence. Who is the dark-skinned female who summoned me here? Does she live in the castle?"

Louisa looked over to where the humans had disappeared over the crest of the cliffs. Their figures could be seen faintly, moving up the path to the castle. "That is Miss Antoinette Duvall, from Jamaica. She is visiting here with Miss Cassandra Richards and Lady Willowby, Miss Richards' aunt. Miss Richards is also from Jamaica; we have had interesting discussions about it. I wish that ghosts could choose where they travel, so I could see it for myself. They *believe* in ghosts there!"

"Does anyone really live in such a wild place as that?" Lady Lettice asked coolly, lifting up a small feathered fan from where it dangled on her belt and waving it languidly. "I heard in my lifetime that there was nothing but savages there. I would rather still be in the sitting room of the afterlife than go to Jamaica."

As Louisa looked at her, she remembered what a snobbish wench Lady Lettice could be at times. She wondered why she had ever wanted her summoned back.

"Angelo would like to see Jamaica," Lady Lettice's dwarf piped up. "There is fruit there as big as your head! And fish to be cooked in spices and rum . . ."

Lady Lettice smiled down at him fondly and patted the top of his head. "Angelo, my chuck, you think far too much about food. Ghosts cannot even eat here on earth!"

"Angelo can *remember* eating," he mumbled. "We *could* eat in the sitting room of the afterlife."

"Well, we are here now, and it is impossible to eat in our present form. Now, Louisa, Sir Belvedere," Lady Lettice said decisively, dropping her fan and turning to face them. "It appears I have arrived just in time. Things at Royce Castle seem to be getting completely unruly. Let us go up to my chamber, which I hope has been aired and cleaned properly, and you may tell me all about what has been going on here." Then her voice changed from its usual strident tones to a soft purr. "Especially about that handsome gentleman with the long, dark hair . . ."

Phillip locked the door to the library behind him and hurried over to the table, where the butler left various decanters and glasses every evening. Usually he did not touch them at all, but tonight was a marked exception. He poured himself a generous measure of brandy and gulped it down as if it was water. Then he poured out another one.

What was happening to him? Here, in his very home, the place he regarded as a haven from the insanity of the outside world! Now it seemed that that very hysteria, the wildness of the so-called Romantics, had reached between the stones of Royce Castle and grabbed onto him.

Clutching at his brandy, he sat down in the chair behind the desk and looked about at the library. It all seemed the same; the same neat rows of books, the same dark furniture, the same painting over the fireplace. His notes and volumes were all in tidy little piles on the desk. But he felt dazed, disturbed. Completely out of sorts.

These were feelings he disliked intensely. He liked to know his purpose, his place in the world. He liked his household to be in order, to know what he could expect from every day.

That was gone now, vanished in that blast of blue-green light. If he was to be honest with himself, he would have to admit that it had been gone before that, since the day Cassandra Richards stepped past his threshold. She was making him doubt things he had always believed—things such as logic, order, rationality. She had made unfamiliar feelings rise up inside him—desires for picnics, wild rides, and myths and stories.

And now he had actually engaged in some sort of mass hysteria in the tunnel. The fact that they *all* believed they saw a ghost had infected his own mind and made him believe it, as well.

That had to be all there was to it.

He could not have actually seen some supernatural being. He shook his head stubbornly. That could not be.

He took another sip of the brandy and reflected that soon he would have his peaceful, scholarly life back again. After the blasted masked ball, Cassie and her aunt and her strange friend would surely return to Bath, leaving him to get on with his work.

Through the warm brandy haze, he wondered why that thought did not comfort him as it should. In fact, it did not comfort him at all.

"Handsome but stupid, I see," Lady Lettice commented, watching him from atop the rolling ladder next to Louisa. "Some of the best men are, of course. Sir Francis Drake, for one, was really very thick. But one does hope for more from someone who is meant to be a scholar. Now, if you had known Sir Phillip Sidney . . ."

"Yes, yes," Louisa interrupted impatiently. She had forgotten how Lady Lettice tended to go on and on about all the famous people she had once known. "But what do you think of my idea, Lady Lettice?"

"Of matching up this man with your Miss Richards from Jamaica?" Lady Lettice tapped at her chin thoughtfully with her feather fan. One thing she had always been rather fond of was making matches; Louisa knew that very well. She thought perhaps it was to compensate for having never been married herself. And now Louisa hoped to engage her in this mission.

"The free spirit and the stuffy scholar," Lady Lettice went on. "I think it has great potential, my dear Louisa. Very amusing potential, indeed. Now, all we have to do is come up with a plan."

Louisa grinned. "Oh, yes. Sir Belvedere and I have been thinking on that . . ."

Chapter Sixteen

"Oh, how marvelous!" Lady Royce cried. She had been reading the morning post over breakfast, and now held up a sheet of parchment with a pleased exclamation.

"What is it, Melinda?" asked Chat, picking a piece of toast out of the rack.

"My dear friend Lady Paige, the one Miss Richards met on her excursion into the village, is having a small supper tonight to bid farewell to her nephew, who is returning to Town. We are all invited." Lady Royce refolded the invitation carefully and smiled. "This *is* splendid, is it not? I have not been out to dine in ever so long."

"Will there be many people there?" Chat asked. "Is it very formal?"

"Oh, no, not at all. Lady Paige's dining room is not big enough for a large party. I am certain Viscount and Viscountess Rockley will be there, and Mrs. Sattler and her daughter, and perhaps the Lewishams."

"It sounds delightful. Does it not, girls?" Chat said,

and glanced down the table to where Cassie and Antoinette sat quietly.

Antoinette, whose dark eyes were heavy with weariness after the exertions of the night before, nodded and murmured her assent.

Cassie looked over at Phillip, who just continued eating his sausages and said nothing. He just barely nodded in his mother's direction. He, too, seemed weary, with dark circles beneath his eyes. Cassie had wondered all night and morning what his reaction might be to the night's occurrences.

Now she knew. He was not taking it at all well.

He had greeted them politely when he entered the breakfast room, but had said barely a word since. He had scarcely even glanced at Cassie.

Perhaps he was just tired, as they all were, she tried to reassure herself. But she still wished he would at least smile at her and talk with her as they had that night in the library. They could discuss what had happened in the tunnels, try to figure out what it all meant.

But it was all too clear that he did not want to talk with her about anything right now, least of all what had happened. He appeared intent on denying it.

Cassie turned her attention back to her plate, listening as Lady Royce planned what she would wear to the supper party. Later, when Phillip was not so tired, she would seek him out and talk to him.

They had so many things to discuss.

"Hm. I do see what Louisa means," Lady Lettice muttered as she watched the scene in the breakfast room. Rather than perch on one of the cornices, as Louisa and Sir Belvedere liked to do, she peered out from one of the portraits. It was much more dignified in a farthingale. "He is a terribly stubborn man. He does not believe in us, even though he saw us with his own eyes, and he blames the poor girl for making him see the truth he will not acknowledge. She certainly has a streak of stubbornness, as well." She peered at them closer. "Yes, indeed, this will be a challenge. Much more so than when I matched up Lettice Knollys and Robert Dudley."

Angelo tugged at her skirts. "Angelo wants some of those sausages! They smell so wonderful."

"Hush, Angelo! I told you yesterday, ghosts cannot eat. You do not really feel hungry, you just think you do," she said distractedly.

"No! Angelo is *really* hungry."

Lady Lettice did not answer; she was too busy listening to the humans' conversation. "They are going to a supper tonight. An excellent opportunity. There are far too many of them for just one carriage; we shall have to see that Lord Royce and Miss Richards are alone in one."

"Angelo does not think a well-bred girl would be alone in a carriage with a man," he said thoughtfully. "Look at what happened to Katherine Throckmorton."

"Then we shall just have to see to it that they are *made* to be alone," Lady Lettice answered impatiently. She took hold of Angelo's hand and floated off. "Now we must find Louisa and Sir Belvedere. They are probably lazing the morning away, playing chess in that East Tower, when there is work to be done!"

"And maybe we will run into Jean-Pierre on the way," Angelo said slyly. His dark eyes flashed with a usually hidden intelligence.

Lady Lettice reached out with her free hand and cuffed him soundly on the head. "Never mention that name to me again! Jean-Pierre is—was a toad.

And he is not a ghost, anyway. He has moved on. We shall never see him here."

But her mind whispered doubtfully, *Will you indeed?*

"What will you wear to Lady Paige's supper, Cassie?" Antoinette said, riffling through the contents of Cassie's wardrobe.

"I don't know," Cassie murmured indifferently, turning over a page of the poetry book she was ostensibly reading. In truth, she had not even read a single word in fully half an hour. "What are you going to wear?"

"Probably that yellow gown your aunt bought for me in Bath. I would not want to go frightening all the guests in my robes!" Antoinette laughed. "They will be frightened enough of me as it is!"

Cassie also laughed and put aside her book. "Well, I do not care what I wear. You choose something for me."

"What about this one?" Antoinette pulled out a sapphire-blue silk. "You loved it when you ordered it from the modiste, and you haven't worn it yet."

"Perhaps."

"Perhaps? Don't you want to look pretty for Lord Royce?" Antoinette held the gown up to herself, even though it was a foot too short, and danced about the room. "Oh, Lord Royce, you are *so* handsome," she cooed in a strange, high-pitched Jamaican accent. "Won't you please, please dance with me?"

Cassie tossed a cushion at her, laughing helplessly. "Antoinette, stop! There won't *be* any dancing tonight. It is just supper and maybe some cards."

"But you will still want to look nice, no? So you should wear this." Antoinette laid the gown out on the bed and smoothed the shimmering folds.

Cassie sighed. "I do not think Lord Royce would notice me if I showed up in my chemise."

"Oh, I do think he would notice *that*." Antoinette came and sat down at the end of the chaise where Cassie lay. Cassie slid her feet back to make room for her. "What is the matter, Cassie? Did you and Lord Royce quarrel?"

"Of course not. You cannot quarrel with a person when they won't speak to you. He was so very quiet at breakfast and would not even look at me. Then, when I went to the library to talk to him, the door was locked. The butler said he had orders that no one was to go in today." Cassie felt her chin wobble and clenched her teeth together. "Probably especially me."

"Oh, Cassie dear," Antoinette replied. "Lord Royce has had a shock. He has spent so many years denying the existence of the supernatural, and last night he came face-to-face with it. Of course he does not feel well. He is probably still denying the whole thing. We have seen this many times, remember?"

Cassie nodded. She remembered some of the people they had known in Jamaica, people who had been there for a long time and had seen much. They lived in fear of voodoo rituals and slave revolts.

"At least that fear is not as dangerous here as it was there," Antoinette finished.

"Yes. But what should I do about Lord Royce? If I could just talk to him . . ."

"Give him time. He will come around, probably sooner than you would think. After all, he is falling in love with you. He will listen to you."

Cassie stared at her friend, shocked. "In—in love with me? Of course he is not! He can barely be civil with me."

"A sure sign that he is in love, then." Antoinette

smiled and stood up to cross the room to the door of her own chamber. "We should be getting changed. We have to leave for Lady Paige's house in an hour."

Almost an hour later, they all stood about in the drive, waiting for the carriages to be brought around. Cassie shivered in her cloak as a chill wind swept across her, and she looked over to where Lord Royce—she could no longer think of him as Phillip—stood, slightly apart from the others.

He did not look angry or upset at all. Merely distantly polite and distracted, as if he was thinking of something else and did not see them.

And looking so handsome in his evening clothes, with his hair sleekly tied back.

Cassie sighed and looked away from him, trying to attend to the conversation of Lady Royce, Aunt Chat, and Antoinette. But all she could hear were Antoinette's previous words echoing in her mind—"He is falling in love with you, you know."

Well, if he *was* he had a very funny way of showing it! Being argumentative and cool by turns was not Cassie's idea of falling in love.

She firmly turned her back to him, determined to enjoy her evening despite him.

"Ah, here come the carriages now!" Lady Royce said, gathering her fur-trimmed wrap around her. "I have ordered two carriages for tonight, so we needn't all be squashed together and crush our gowns. Chat and I will take the first one, and, Phillip, you may escort Miss Richards and Miss Duvall in the other."

Cassie thought she heard a soft giggle in her ear, but when she turned to look, Antoinette stood some distance away, and Aunt Chat and Lady Royce were already climbing into their carriage.

"Louisa?" she whispered, wondering if the ghosts were playing some sort of joke that involved being invisible.

"Did you say something, miss?" asked the footman, who had just stepped forward to help her into the carriage.

Cassie looked around one more time, but saw only Lord Royce, who watched her quizzically. "No," she said, taking the footman's arm and stepping up into the dim interior of the equipage. "Not at all."

She had just settled herself on the soft leather cushion, when there was a strange sort of yell, and Lord Royce tumbled headfirst into the carriage. He landed with a hard thud on the floor at her feet.

"Lord Royce!" she cried. "Whatever is the . . ."

Her exclamations were interrupted when the door slammed shut behind him and the carriage jolted into motion. It gathered speed quickly as it set off down the drive.

Cassie heard muffled shouts from outside. After making sure Phillip was not hurt, she lowered the window and stuck her head out to see the footman, Antoinette, and—oh, horrors!—the coachman chasing after them. Antoinette's expression was frantic as she pointed at the carriage.

Cassie twisted about and saw there was no one sitting on the box at all. The horses were running off on their own.

Her heart lifted into her throat with a cold, frightened leap. She fell back against the seat, gasping. They were going to go right over the cliffs in this runaway carriage and become ghosts who were trapped at Royce Castle forever!

Phillip hauled himself up off the floor and onto the seat opposite her, his hair falling loose onto his shoulders and his cravat askew. "Someone pushed me in here!" he muttered indignantly, as if not even aware that they were moving at a dangerous speed.

"We have worse troubles than that!" Cassie practically screamed, lunging across the space between them to grab onto his coat. "No one is driving this carriage!"

"What?" he said, frowning in confusion. "That cannot be."

"Of course it is! I saw it with my own eyes. No one is on the box."

He pressed her gently back onto her seat and stuck his head out the window. Then he fell back beside her, his expression unreadable. "You are right," he shouted over the rush of cold wind that swirled around them from the open window. "No one is driving this carriage."

"What are we going to do?" Cassie asked frantically.

"I have to try to get up onto the box myself and slow the horses." Phillip looked back out the window. "But I do wonder one thing."

Cassie wondered one thing, too—she wondered how he could be so calm in the face of impending doom. "What?"

"Why is our carriage running away so perfectly down the road? Why are we not crashing through the woods?"

Cassie peered past his shoulder to the flashing-by scenery. He was right. They were going in a straight line down the road, away from the village and the castle.

She frowned. *Louisa!* Of course it had to be Louisa and Sir Belvedere and probably that new Lady Lettice and her dwarf friend.

No one had ever told her that dead people could be so mischievous.

She leaned out the window again, and this time she saw Sir Belvedere sitting up on the box, his armored legs held stiffly before him, wielding the reins. Louisa sat beside him, her blue cloak billowing in the wind.

"What are you doing?" Cassie shouted. "Are you trying to get us all killed?" Then she remembered the incontestable fact that those two were already dead, and amended, "Are you trying to get Lord Royce and me killed?"

"Certainly not, fair lady!" answered Sir Belvedere.

"Do not worry, Cassie," added Louisa. "We have a plan."

That was what Cassie was worried about, them and their *plans*. She retreated back into the carriage, where Lord Royce had already stripped off his coat in preparation of trying to take back control of the carriage.

Cassie allowed herself one instant of watching him appreciatively, then said, "I do not think you will have to perform any death-defying heroics today. It is only Louisa and Sir Belvedere playing some sort of joke. They say they have a plan."

He frowned fiercely. "*Ghosts*? Ghosts are absconding with this carriage?"

She nodded, feeling suddenly very tired after her great rush of fear. "I am afraid so."

He pushed past her to look out the window.

"Good evening, my lord!" Cassie heard Louisa and Sir Belvedere chorus.

Then Lord Royce—looking much more like Phillip again—came back inside, and sat down beside Cassie quietly.

"So they *are* real," he said.

Cassie nodded sympathetically, remembering how bewildered she had been the first time she woke up to find Louisa at her bedside. "Yes. Did you think that they were just a dream?"

Phillip gave a short little bark of laughter. "*Hoped* they were, perhaps. It is never easy to admit that one is wrong."

"No, it never is." She knew *that* all too well.

"But what do they want of us?" he said in an unsettled tone.

"I'm not sure. Just for us to be their friends, I suppose, and help them to understand. They are just as confused about why they are here as we are." She paused for a moment, then went on, "I have no idea why they would want to push us into a runaway carriage, though. That seems mean, and they are not *mean* at all."

Phillip still seemed unnaturally still and calm, as if stunned by the proceedings. "You have talked with them a great deal?"

"We have become friends. I do not know this Lady Lettice at all, though, having just met her last night. Perhaps this was all her idea."

"You must think me a terribly stubborn fool, Miss Richards," he said, raising his gaze to meet hers at last. "For denying all this so strenuously and for so long."

"Stubborn, perhaps," Cassie answered slowly, with the realization that this was a great turning point for him and for *them* as well. A Lord Royce willing to admit he might share his house and now his carriage with some long-dead ancestors was a momentous thing.

The least she could do was not crow in triumph.

"But not a fool," she went on. "This is all very hard for anyone to understand, especially someone who has devoted their life to history and philosophy. I, myself, do not fully understand it at all, and I doubt I ever will."

Phillip took her gloved hand in his and lifted it to his lips for a warm, lingering kiss. "Thank you, Cassandra. For not thinking me *too* great a fool."

She smiled at him. "Did you not tell me that my name means 'disbelieved by men'?"

He laughed against her fingers, and it echoed sweetly to the very heart of her. Cassie leaned toward him, drawn to him by an inexorable force . . .

But then there was a great jolt, and the carriage was thrown off balance. Cassie slid against the leather-padded wall, still holding onto Phillip, who fell heavily against her.

"Oof!" she gasped as the carriage ground to a halt, still askew.

Phillip pulled himself away from her. "Cassandra! Are you hurt?"

She was just breathless and a bit sore where her shoulder had landed against the wall. But she *so* wished he would come closer to her again!

"Not at all," she answered, letting him help her up. "But what has happened?"

"I'm not sure." Phillip pushed the door open and climbed down into the road. "It appears your friends have gone, though."

Cassie clambered after him and looked up to the box to see that he was absolutely right. Louisa and Sir Belvedere had vanished, leaving them all alone on a deserted stretch of road with a lopsided vehicle and winded horses.

No one had ever told her ghosts were so unreliable! They had probably floated right back to the East Tower, where they were warm and cozy.

Cassie pulled her cloak closer around her and turned back to see Phillip kneeling down in the road, examining the carriage wheel. "It appears that this wheel is stuck in a rut," he said.

"Can you loose it?"

"Not by myself." He looked up at her and grinned. "I'm just a weak scholar, you know."

Cassie gave a disbelieving little snort. She remembered the lean, strong feel of his body as he fell against her. "I am sure somebody will come along and find us soon. Surely the others will have followed us."

"No doubt. We can start walking back toward the castle, and meet them on the way."

"Yes, a fine idea." Maybe walking would keep her warm, she reflected, even though her thin evening slippers were hardly made for the road.

Phillip reached back into the carriage to retrieve his coat, slid it over his shoulders, then offered her his arm. "Shall we?"

"Thank you," Cassie said. She took his arm and off they went, as if for a pleasant afternoon's stroll.

But they had not gone far before Cassie realized just how impractical her shoes were. She stumbled over a stone in the road.

"What is it?" Phillip asked in concern.

"Oh, these silly shoes! They are supposed to be able to dance all night, but they cannot walk down a simple country lane." Leaning on him, she lifted up her foot and peered wryly down at the thin blue satin. What she wouldn't give for a nice, sturdy pair of boots right now!

With no warning, Phillip reached down behind her knees and swept her up into his arms. He continued walking down the road as if she weighed no more than a quill pen.

"What are you doing?" Cassie cried, twisting about to look at him.

"Carrying you, of course," he answered matter-of-factly. "You are obviously in no condition to be walking. Stop wriggling about so, or I'll have to drop you."

Cassie immediately stilled—and realized how very *nice* it was to be held so. His arms were strong and secure about her, his warm breath stirring in her hair. She leaned her head against his shoulder, and just gave herself over to those lovely feelings.

He hummed a soft little tune as he walked. "You seem quite contented," she commented, marveling at how this seemingly happy-go-lucky man had been so quiet and angry only hours before.

"Oh, I am," he answered, shifting her slightly in his arms. "Just think of all the marvelous new avenues of philosophy that are open to my study now! That is something to look forward to. Best of all, I have a very pretty girl in my arms, and I am strolling along in the evening air rather than sitting at some dull supper party. Do you not agree that this is more fun than being at Lady Paige's house, as worthy as that lady is?"

Cassie thought this was more fun than anything she had ever done before. She was cold and her feet hurt, but she wanted to giggle giddily. What a very good thing it was that the ghosts were so fond of mischief!

"Oh, yes," she agreed. "Much better."

"You do realize, of course, that I have hopelessly compromised you," he said in a genial tone.

Cassie's eyes flew wide open, and she stared up at him. He just smiled blandly back at her.

Was this what it felt like to be compromised? If so, it was not too bad, though perhaps not *quite* as exciting as one would have imagined. "Have you indeed?"

"Oh, yes. I shall probably have to marry you." He sounded singularly unconcerned by the prospect.

Cassie felt an undeniable thrill at the thought of marrying Phillip. But at the same time she felt a stubborn niggling of doubt. She had always fantasized that she would marry for love, as her parents had. She had a sneaking suspicion that she *did* love Phillip, or at least was beginning to.

But did he love her? She rather doubted it. He probably still thought her a silly, flighty girl.

She wanted him to truly *want* to marry her. Not *have* to marry her because the ghosts had pulled a prank for some reason.

And, if they were to wed, she would have to give up any idea of ever going back to Jamaica. Only true love could make her give that up.

She made herself laugh lightly and said, "I hardly think it will come to that! Only my aunt, your mother, and Antoinette know we are out here alone. They will not gossip about it, surely, and the ghosts cannot. They are never invited to dine anywhere."

"Oh, you never know about my mother. She has been so eager to get me married off, she may even be willing to cause a scandal to do it."

Cassie peered up at him suspiciously, not sure if he was joking or not. She had never known anyone with such a *dry* sense of humor before.

He just had that same little, maddening half smile on his face.

"But you needn't fear being leg-shackled to me just yet," he said. "I think I hear a carriage. We are rescued."

Indeed they were. The first carriage from Royce Castle, the one that had *not* run away, rounded a bend in the road just ahead and came barreling toward them, driven by a human coachman. Antoinette, Lady Royce, and Chat all hung out of the windows, the wind disarranging their careful coiffures.

"There they are!" Antoinette shouted, and the carriage pulled to a halt. The women tumbled out and ran across the road to them.

"Cassie!" Aunt Chat cried out. "Are you hurt, my dear? What has happened?"

Lady Royce, too, expressed her concern, but Antoinette looked suspiciously sanguine as she took in the scene of Cassie in Lord Royce's arms.

He slowly lowered her to the ground, still holding onto her arm.

"I am not hurt at all, Aunt Chat," Cassie assured her. "But, oh, you will not believe what has happened!"

For a man whose entire worldview had been turned tip over tail, Phillip was feeling strangely jolly.

They were all crowded into the one carriage now, on their way to Lady Paige's supper at last. Cassie sat beside him, wedged against him as she and Antoinette tried to fix each other's hair into some semblance of tidiness. Even after traipsing about outdoors, her sweet, exotic perfume was still discernible, and she occasionally fell against him as the carriage bounced along the road. She would smile up at him apologetically, then go back to assuring her aunt that no, she was not injured, and yes, she did feel up to going to the supper party.

Her gaze would sometimes meet his, with a little puzzled frown on her brow, but then she would quickly look away. It was clear that his earlier words about being compromised and having to marry were still on her mind. And not necessarily in a good way.

He had tried to convince her he was merely joking when he said that—he tried to convince *himself* he was merely joking. But the truth was he wouldn't half mind marrying Cassandra Richards.

He wouldn't half mind it at all.

He looked down at the top of her dark, shining hair. She laughed at something Antoinette said, and her head tilted back onto his shoulder for the merest second. Her long sapphire drop earrings shimmered in the light from the carriage lamps, then lay still against her white neck.

She was truly the first woman who the thought of marrying did not fill him with some sense of dread. Rather, it filled him with a sense of—anticipation and warmth.

He finally acknowledged to himself that, yes, he was very fond of Cassandra Richards. In fact, he could very well be falling in love with her.

When she first came to Royce Castle, full of fancy and island exoticism, he had been drawn to her, but not at all sure of her. Now he knew that not only was she pretty and vivacious, but she was smart, and caring, and kind to everyone around her.

Even to stubborn old homebodies like himself.

She was also full of life, and she spread that joy in living all about her. He had not realized just how dull and dusty his life had become until she burst into it. Now he never wanted to give up that feeling of being gloriously alive.

He never wanted to give *her* up.

But it was obvious that she could never be happy with the sort of life he could give her, the sort of person he was.

If there was only some way to persuade her otherwise . . .

"Are *you* quite all right, dear?" his mother said, breaking into his thoughts. "You have been very quiet, and you are rather pale."

He looked back down at Cassie, who now watched

him worriedly. "I am quite all right, Mother," he answered. "Quite all right indeed."

"Oh, that was truly splendid!" Lady Lettice said happily as the ghosts gathered in the East Tower to gloat over the evening's triumph. She clapped her beringed hands as she floated over the floor, her skirts barely brushing the carpet. "I must say I had my doubts about the two of you managing things with the carriage, but you did a fine job."

Louisa bristled indignantly. "What do you mean, you had your *doubts*? This entire thing was our doing, Sir Belvedere's and mine. All you did was give Lord Royce that tiny little push into the carriage."

Lady Lettice planted her hands on her hips. "I was the one who orchestrated the entire thing! You would never have even tried it if not for me. Apparently, all the two of you have been doing in the years of my absence is playing chess and pulling tricks on Lord Royce. Very childish!"

If Louisa had not been a ghost, and therefore pale by nature, her face would have flamed with indignation. "I beg your pardon, lady high-and-mighty, but it was *my* idea. . . ."

"Dear ladies, please!" Sir Belvedere interrupted, stepping between them with a loud clatter, as Angelo laughed in delight at the blossoming quarrel. "We all worked on this scheme, and the triumph belongs to all of us. We must concentrate on Lord Royce and Miss Richards, and not squabble among ourselves. Or all our effort will be for naught."

"You are right, of course, Sir Belvedere," Lady Lettice said slowly. Then she went and sat down in the chair beside the window.

Louisa nodded. Sir Belvedere *was* completely right.

They were dead, after all; their troubles should all be behind them, along with human pettiness. This was all about Lord Royce and Cassie, and helping them to not make the mistakes in life that the ghosts had. Cassie had been so very kind to them, so helpful, that it was only right that they should help her in return.

And *someone* deserved to be happy as Lady Royce in this place, even if that someone had never been Louisa.

Chapter Seventeen

"Psst! Cassie! Are you awake?"

Cassie vaguely heard Antoinette's whispering voice through the haze of sleep. She was still muzzy-headed from the wine at Lady Paige's supper, and from the strange excitement of being carried down the road in Phillip's arms. It felt like she had only just fallen asleep, and now here was Antoinette hissing in her ear and poking at her shoulder.

She rolled over and opened one eye to peer up at Antoinette's silhouette in the darkness. "What is it? It cannot be time to get up. It's still dark outside."

"I just realized I left something in the tunnel last night when we were summoning Lady Lettice," Antoinette said. "I cannot sleep for thinking about it. I just wanted to see if you would go with me to fetch it."

"Now? It's been there all this time. Can't it stay just a little longer, until morning?"

Antoinette shook her head. She wore no cap, and her long, thick mane of hair undulated in the shadows. "No, I really think I should fetch it now."

"Why do I have to go with you?"

"Because I don't want to go alone!" Antoinette burst out.

Cassie sat up at that. "You are *scared*," she said, amazed. She had always thought Antoinette could not be frightened of anything.

"I am not scared," Antoinette protested. "Merely— wary. I saw just how mischievous those ghosts can be tonight, when they took off with you in that carriage."

"They meant no real harm. I think they must get bored, stuck here in the castle all the time."

"Well, I don't want to be walking about by myself in the dark, anyway."

"All right, then, I will go with you. If I can come right back to bed after. I have had enough excitement for one night."

So Cassie found herself leaving her snug, warm room in the middle of the night, following Antoinette down the cliff steps to the shore. The pale silver moon was half-obscured by clouds, sending a diffuse, mysterious light across the sky. It was chilly out, but still, with no wind stirring.

She looked up at the moon and the stars, and thought how romantic it all was. How lovely it would be if Phillip was here, with his arms around her. Perhaps he would even kiss her . . .

"No!" she whispered, shaking her head to try to clear it of such silly thoughts. It was only the beauty of the night making her feel all romantical again. If he had not kissed her as they walked alone down the deserted lane, he never would. "I will not think of that right now."

Antoinette, several steps ahead, stopped and looked back at her. "Did you say something, Cassie?"

"No. Must be the wind," Cassie answered.

"Hmm." Antoinette walked on.

Cassie waited at the mouth of the tunnel while Antoinette went in and found her lost item. There were rustlings and knockings, and it was several moments before she emerged again, a small muslin packet clutched in her hand.

"All right, I have it now," Antoinette said. "You can go back to your bed."

"Thank goodness!" Cassie said, pulling her cloak hood up. The night, so romantic only moments before, now seemed just cold and rather lonely.

But when they emerged into the moonlight, they found they were no longer alone. Lady Lettice stood on the shore, staring out over the purple-black sea. Angelo, her little dwarf, sat on a large rock nearby, drawing designs in the pebbly sand with a long stick.

Cassie was caught by the sadness on Lady Lettice's pale face. No wonder the night had suddenly turned so melancholy!

"Good evening, Lady Lettice, Angelo," Antoinette said softly.

Lady Lettice looked over at them and gave a little smile. "Good evening." Her gaze dropped to the little packet Antoinette held. "Is that part of the—apparatus you used to summon me here, Miss Duvall?"

"Yes," Antoinette answered, tucking the packet away inside her robes. "I am sorry if you are unhappy here. I could try to send you back, if you like."

Lady Lettice waved her hand in a dismissive little gesture. "It is of no matter. I like it here as well as I did there, in that strange little sitting room. I just went out for a walk, to think about some things without Louisa and Sir Belvedere yammering at me."

Antoinette walked toward Lady Lettice, the scared young woman who came to Cassie's room gone and the Yaumumi priestess in her place. Cassie followed

slowly, warily watching the supposedly harmless
Angelo. But he paid no attention to her at all, just
went on pulling his stick through the sand and muttering something about spiced wine and roast beef.

"What are you thinking about, Lady Lettice?" Antoinette asked.

"Nothing of any import," Lady Lettice replied in
a don't-be-impertinent tone of voice.

"She is thinking about Jean-Pierre," Angelo piped
up.

"Indeed? Jean-Pierre?" said Antoinette. "Is he the
reason we had to look for you in the tunnel and not
in the castle? Is Jean-Pierre in the tunnels?"

"Of course not! Jean-Pierre is not anywhere. I have
looked and looked . . ." Then Lady Lettice seemed
to realize what she was saying and snapped her
mouth shut. Her lips formed a thin little line.

Cassie stared at her, feeling the night become even
colder around her. So Lady Lettice had been thwarted
in love, just as Louisa had. It was all too sad.

Lady Lettice looked down at them, her head tilted
back haughtily. Cassie did not feel as comfortable
with her as she did with Louisa. Lady Lettice seemed
proud and reserved, not fun-loving and chatty as
Louisa was. But now Cassie could see the lurking
sadness in her eyes, and she felt sorry for her.

Finally, Lady Lettice looked away from them and
said, "Oh, very well. I may as well tell you the tale.
Jean-Pierre has been dead for centuries. And so have
I, I suppose!" she added with a brittle laugh.

Cassie settled down on the rock next to Angelo to
listen to her tale. This was even better than a novel!

"Jean-Pierre was a French nobleman, attached to
the retinue of the Duc d'Alencon when he came to
England to woo Queen Elizabeth. We sat next to each
other often at banquets, and danced, and walked in

the gardens." Lady Lettice's harsh features softened as she talked, absorbed in her memories. "He was so very handsome. So witty and so accomplished!"

"So perfidious," Angelo added softly, his eyes flashing.

Lady Lettice shot him a harsh glare. "Hush, Angelo! How was I to know that at the time? He said he loved me, and I was a silly young girl. I believed him."

"What happened then?" Cassie asked.

"I received word that my father was very ill, perhaps dying. I left the Court and came back here to Royce Castle to nurse him. A few weeks later, I had a message from Jean-Pierre, saying he had come to Cornwall and could I meet him in the tunnels. They had not been filled in at all then, and were much larger." Lady Lettice's voice became rushed then, as if she wanted to speed quickly through the rest of her tale and downplay the end of it. "Of course I met him. But I thought it odd that he would not come to the castle; he would only meet me here. Later, I discovered why."

"Why?" Cassie breathed, deeply in suspense.

Lady Lettice's hands nervously toyed with the fan at her belt. "He had stupidly become involved in a plot against the Queen. He needed to escape, to return to France, and he needed me to help him. That was all he wanted of me."

It was very clear how pained this proud lady was to admit such a thing, even hundreds of years after it happened. She would not look at them, just stared out to sea. Angelo slid off his rock and hurried over to her, slipping his arms around her waist for a comforting hug. She laid her hand gently atop his head.

"And did you help him?" Antoinette asked quietly.

"Of course not!" Lady Lettice snapped. "How could I have? I was loyal to the Queen. He somehow found a way and left on his own. I never saw him again, not in the years left of my life and not in the centuries since." She looked down at Angelo and said, almost to herself, "And the moldwort did not even ask me to go with him."

Cassie, suddenly cold again, closed her eyes, and wondered if there was some sort of a curse on this place that made love turn sour.

Well, if there *was* such a curse, Cassie was very determined not to fall victim to it!

Chapter Eighteen

"Oh, this *is* a splendid tale!" Cassie enthused, turning over a page in the volume of *The Iliad* she was reading. The morning sun fell from the library windows across the illustrations, making the ancient mayhem and blood seem to come alive. And the bright light made last night, and Lady Lettice's sad tale, seem nothing but a strange dream. "I don't know why I have never read it before."

Phillip looked up from his own work and smiled at her. They seemed in a great accord this morning, Cassie thought, each of them engrossed in their books, but always aware of each other's presence. It felt—comfortable, cozy. *Right*. It seemed that with the adventure of the runaway carriage things had fallen into place for them.

She wished the morning could just go on and on forever. She smiled back at him happily.

"It is a splendid tale," he agreed. "One of my favorites. Though I would have thought it rather bloodthirsty in parts for a lady's taste."

"Oh, it is the people I find most interesting," Cassie said. "Though the battle scenes do have their own, er, charm about them. Achilles, Agamemnon, Helen, Athena—they are all so flawed, but so great. As all true heroes are."

"And Cassandra? How do you find her?"

"Poor Cassandra! To be so cursed, and all because of a man's treachery. Apollo was terribly fickle, was he not?" Just like Lady Lettice's Jean-Pierre and Louisa's husband, she reflected.

Phillip laughed. "I suppose he was, a bit."

"More than a bit. It must have been terrible for Cassandra, to always know what was going to happen and yet have no one believe her." Cassie wondered if she should tell him about her and Antoinette's midnight encounter with Lady Lettice, but then decided to take a lesson from the Trojan Cassandra and keep silent. He claimed to believe her now, but it was early days yet. Their new accord was still too fresh.

Later, she would tell him. There would be plenty of time later. Right now she just wanted to be happy. In the bright day, her nighttime fancies of cursed love seemed silly in the extreme.

She looked back down at her book, but had only been reading for a few minutes when Phillip said, "Do you like it here at Royce Castle, Cassandra?"

He sounded so uncharacteristically uncertain that she looked up at him in surprise. "Like it here?"

"Yes. Do you feel—comfortable here? As if you could stay for a while?"

Cassie wondered what it was he was asking. He could not be trying to find out if she would like to be mistress of Royce Castle! Could he?

And what would she say, if that *was* what he was asking?

She felt very confused.

"I am sure Aunt Chat would be happy to extend

our visit here, if your mother was to invite us," she answered carefully.

Phillip took off his reading spectacles, and rubbed at the bridge of his nose. "Cassandra, about yesterday evening . . ." he began.

But he did not finish. Antoinette burst through the library door, her expression flushed and startled. "Oh, Cassie!" she cried. "You must come now, at once!"

Cassie looked at her in bewilderment, her mind momentarily unable to make the switch from Phillip's puzzling words to Antoinette's frantic and mysterious summons. "What is it?" she asked.

"A caller has arrived."

"Who? Someone for Lady Royce?"

"Oh, no. Someone for *you*. You will never guess who it is!"

Cassie glanced at Phillip, who, self-possessed once again, replaced his spectacles and said calmly, "Go on, Miss Richards. Our conversation can wait."

She nodded, marked her place in her book, and left the library with Antoinette.

"A caller for *me*?" she said, still confused. It seemed she was nearly always confused since coming to Royce Castle.

Antoinette just hurried off down the corridor, forcing Cassie to almost run to keep up with her. When they reached the drawing room, Antoinette opened the door and practically pushed Cassie inside.

Cassie took one look and froze with shock. Sitting there, chatting with Lady Royce and Aunt Chat, was Mr. Paul Bates, her erstwhile suitor from Jamaica. The one who had come to the docks to propose to her one last time before she set sail for England.

When he saw her, a wide grin spread across his sun-browned face, and he came over to take her suddenly cold hands into his.

"My dear Miss Richards!" he said fondly, lifting her frozen fingers to his lips. "My very dear Miss Richards! How splendid to see you again."

As Cassie looked up at his familiar face, the face she had seen so often across a card table or a dance floor in Jamaica, all of her old life came rushing back to her. For one moment, it was as if no time had passed at all. She had never come to England, to Royce Castle, had never met Phillip. She was just Miss Richards of Fair Winds Plantation again.

Oh, dear heaven! Phillip. They were just becoming so close. What would this look like to him, an old suitor suddenly appearing from across the ocean? Would it look like she did not care for Phillip at all, that she had been pining for Mr. Bates all this time?

"Mr. Bates," she managed to whisper. "Whatever are you doing here?"

"Cassie!" Aunt Chat said with a strained little laugh. "What a way to greet someone who has come such a long way to see you."

"Of course not," Cassie answered politely. "It is very good to see someone from home, Mr. Bates. Very good indeed."

She peered closer at him. He *was* rather handsome; she had forgotten that in the months she had been in England. He was tall, broad-shouldered, with very blue eyes and sun-streaked blond hair. She had enjoyed flirting with him and talking to him when they were neighbors in Jamaica. It was nice to see him again, to remember that old life.

But she also remembered exactly why it was she had turned down his offer of marriage, even when it would have solved many of her troubles and allowed her to stay in Jamaica. She felt nothing when she looked at him, when he took her hand. She felt no warmth, no quick tingle of excitement, as she did when she was with Phillip.

And *why* was Mr. Bates here at all? They had never been such good friends as all that, and her refusal at the docks had been decisive. She had not received so much as a letter from him since, though she had corresponded once or twice with his sister, her friend Mrs. Bishop. There was absolutely no reason for him to have undertaken such a long, deeply inconvenient journey.

Was there?

"Mr. Bates. Why are you here?" she repeated quietly.

He shrugged and gave one of his hearty laughs. But she thought she detected a flash of irritation in his expression, before he covered it in joviality. "I haven't been to England in years! Thought I should come and visit my grandfather in London. The old fellow can't have much longer to go, y'know, and he's quite flush in the pockets. My sister told me you're living in Bath now, so I thought I'd just pop over and say hello to an old friend."

"I'm not in Bath right now," Cassie said, pointing out the obvious.

"The housekeeper at Lady Willowby's house told us we could find you here," a languid male voice said from over by the fireplace. "Paul said we couldn't possibly leave England without seeing you, so here we came."

Cassie peered past Mr. Bates to see a young man lolling on the settee there, a veritable tulip of fashion in a pink coat and primrose waistcoat. She recognized Mr. Albert Morland, Mr. Bates' cousin, who had been generally acknowledged to be the most useless man in Jamaica. All he had ever cared about was rum and wagering and fashion. Now here he was, being equally useless in England.

She sighed, feeling the idyll of these last few days at Royce Castle slipping further away by the second.

She dreaded having Phillip meet these men. Seeing these people from her past, one of them an old suitor, might make him think she did not care for him. When she *did* care, so very much.

But she could not think of that just yet. She had to be polite.

Her smile felt brittle on her lips as she turned to Mr. Bates' cousin. "Mr. Morland. Here you are, too. Why, I would almost think myself home again."

"How do you do, dear lady?" he drawled. "You are looking as lovely as ever. This dreadful cold climate obviously agrees with you." He came over to her and bowed politely over her hand.

"Thank you," she replied.

"And looking as—democratic as ever," Mr. Bates said, giving a disapproving look toward Antoinette, who still stood beside the door. She looked steadily back at him with narrowed ebony eyes.

His gaze fell away, but he went on in a discontented mutter, "Not very many would allow their maids to come into the drawing room and mingle with guests."

Antoinette whirled about and left the room in a flurry of emerald-green robes.

Cassie gave him a cold glare. Her discomfort and confusion gave way to sheer dislike and anger. "Miss Duvall is not my maid, Mr. Bates, as you well know." She walked over and sat down beside her aunt, leaving Mr. Bates standing in the middle of the room.

Mr. Morland snickered, and Mr. Bates' blue eyes flashed with anger, though his careful smile stayed in place. He came and sat down in a chair next to Lady Royce, who was watching the entire proceedings with a distinctly uncertain air.

"How long are you planning to stay in England, Mr. Bates?" Cassie asked.

"We had planned to return to London immediately after we saw you," Mr. Bates answered. "But your good hostess, Lady Royce, has invited us to stay for a masked ball. Is that not kind of her? We will have plenty of time to reminisce about our long friendship."

Cassie was aghast, but she struggled to cover it with an expression of polite blandness. The masked ball was still five days away! And Mr. Bates and Mr. Morland were going to stay for that whole time?

She would never find any more time to spend with Phillip.

"I thought you would enjoy that, my dear Miss Richards," Lady Royce said uncertainly. "It will give you more time with your friends, and allow them to see your charming shepherdess costume."

Cassie smiled at her. Lady Royce was a dear, considerate woman. It was not her fault that Cassie was only just remembering how much she had disliked some of the people she had known in Jamaica.

She remembered the conversation she and Antoinette had had about "planter sorts" when they first arrived at Royce Castle, and almost laughed aloud.

Laughed bitterly, for it had been funny when she had thought herself done with planters forever. It was not so funny now that there was one here before her.

"Of course, Lady Royce," she said. "It was very kind of you. Now, is there any tea left in that pot? I would dearly love a cup."

They went on conversing for another half hour, time Cassie filled with questions about friends and acquaintances, about the family who had bought most of her father's land, and Mrs. Bishop who lived in Negril. Mr. Bates often sent her "meaningful" glances, and she strongly suspected he had some purpose in coming here to see her. A purpose beyond paying respects to a former neighbor.

She did not want to know what that purpose was, did not want to deal with it. Not just now, anyway, while her emotions were in such disarray.

Her suspicions were confirmed when, as they all left the drawing room to change for luncheon, Mr. Bates caught her arm and drew her into a quiet corner of the foyer.

"I must speak with you, Miss Richards," he whispered.

"We *have* been speaking," Cassie said, feigning confusion. She tried to pull her arm from his grasp.

He gave her his condescending "dear little woman" smile, the one she remembered him giving his sister all the time. "We must speak alone. There is something I want to ask you."

Cassie repressed an irritated sigh. She had known this was coming, a renewal of his "suit." Perhaps a few months ago, when she was racked with homesickness, she might have accepted, out of sheer desperation. But not now.

This was her home now, she realized in one flash of consciousness. England was her home. And even if nothing ever happened between Phillip and herself, as she so hoped it would, she would never leave it.

But Mr. Bates *had* come a long way to see her. The least she could do was hear him out.

"Very well," she said. "Meet me in the drawing room this evening. Before supper. We should have a few moments before the others come down."

"Thank you, Miss Richards! You will not be sorry." Mr. Bates lifted her hand to his lips.

They felt dry and cold against her skin. Cassie shivered and pulled away, turning to go up the stairs. As she did so, she saw Phillip, standing silently in the library doorway.

His handsome face was utterly expressionless as he looked at her. Cassie took one step toward him, her mouth open to call his name. But he turned away from her, going back into the library and closing the door quietly.

Dejected, and more confused than ever, Cassie went on up the stairs to the silent haven of her chamber.

"I do not like that Mr. Bates at all," Louisa said, watching out the window of the East Tower as Mr. Bates and his colorful cousin walked about the castle gardens. "Why has he suddenly come here, making calf's eyes at Cassie and throwing all our good work into disarray?"

Lady Lettice, who sat by the empty fireplace grate with a book in her hands, nodded in agreement. She seemed oddly content this morning, not at all her usual acerbic self. Instead, she went about with a serene smile, as if a great weight had been lifted from her. Even Angelo was quieter. He had ceased complaining about food all the time, and now sat on the carpet at Lady Lettice's feet, playing a quiet game of Patience.

"I do not like him, either," Lady Lettice answered. "He seems—desperate. Slippery. He is here for something, *needs* something. And I fear it is not Miss Richards' heart he is after."

"What could it be?"

Lady Lettice shrugged. "Money, mayhaps? He seems just the sort to be a terrible gamester. Is Miss Richards wealthy?"

"I do not know," said Louisa. "She has some lovely clothes and some nice jewelry. I am not sure I would say she is *hugely* wealthy, though. Otherwise why would she live with her aunt and not in her own establishment?"

There was a great knocking and banging on the stairs, and Sir Belvedere emerged through the door. He pushed his visor back and said, "Have you *seen* those dreadful new visitors, my dear ladies? They are not gentlemen at all, I would say. They are assuredly up to something dastardly."

"How do you know?" Louisa asked him. "Did you discover something about them?"

"Not yet. I have not had the time."

"We do not like them, either," said Lady Lettice. She tapped one jewel-bedecked hand thoughtfully on the arm of her chair. "We shall just have to go spy on them! Discover what they are about."

Louisa's eyes sparkled. She truly loved nothing better than a spot of intrigue! "Yes! Let us go right now and search their rooms, while they are out in the garden. Or perhaps we should eavesdrop on them while they are unaware."

So the four of them joined hands and vanished in a flash from the East Tower, only to emerge a moment later behind the tall hedges of the garden maze.

Mr. Bates and Mr. Morland, completely unaware that they were being watched, sat on the marble benches at the center of the maze, placidly smoking and chatting, feeling quite pleased with themselves indeed.

"She is as good as mine, and her land with her," Mr. Bates said, flicking some of his cheroot ashes into the gardener's carefully tended chrysanthemums. "All I have to do is reach out and scoop her up."

Mr. Morland laughed and brushed some imaginary dust from the sleeve of his pink coat. "I must say, Paul, she did not look exactly ecstatic to see you. She didn't run right into your arms, or anything like that. In fact, I thought she was going to faint there for a moment."

Mr. Bates frowned. He had noticed that, as well. "She was just surprised, that is all. She was hardly expecting me, now, was she? She was overcome by the emotion of it." That had to be it, he assured himself. The silly gel had been giddy over him ever since they first met. She was ripe for falling into his arms—for handing over what he wanted.

He conveniently forgot the fact that she had turned down his ardent proposal on the docks in Jamaica and had gotten on the ship without a backward glance. It had just been shock, he thought, and perhaps a belief that he, the most sought-after bachelor of the West Indies, could not possibly be interested in *her*. She was small and dark, and the whole island knew she was a strange one. Look at her friendship with that native woman!

But now he would have to *make* her believe he was attracted to her. His future depended on it.

"She has agreed to see me this evening before supper," he said.

"Indeed?" his cousin drawled. "And what are you going to do? Clasp her in your arms, declare undying devotion? Beg her to elope with you? Say that you will die without her in your life?"

"I will ask her calmly to sell me the land at first. That would be the most sensible thing. And if that does not work . . . I will do whatever will be necessary." Why, he wondered, did upper-class girls have to be such a lot of trouble, anyway?

Mr. Morland shook his head mockingly. "Not your

usual style of wooing at all. Usually you just snatch onto a woman and shout 'Brace yourself, m'dear.'" He had a hearty laugh at his own joke.

Mr. Bates scowled at him. "Well, that's not going to work with this particular female, now is it?"

Mr. Morland slowly sobered. "No. Not if you want to keep your plantation."

"That is the whole reason for this ridiculous excursion! She must agree to give me that land of hers. One way or another."

There was a sudden, sharp rustling in the hedges. Mr. Bates jumped up, looking frantically around. "Who is there?" he shouted. "Show yourself!"

But everything was silent; the only sound was the distant rush of the sea.

"Cousin," Mr. Morland said. "You are growing paranoid. This is not good at all."

"I am *not* paranoid," he murmured, sitting slowly back down on the bench. Yet he could not quite let go of the feeling that *someone* was watching him.

This whole place gave him the shivers and had ever since they first walked in the front door. There was just something not quite right about it.

The sooner he had Miss Richards' land and possibly her person, and they could leave, the better.

Chapter Nineteen

"What do you suppose he wants, then?" Antoinette asked, helping Cassie dress her hair before supper, as Cassie was too nervous to do it herself.

"I have no idea." Cassie was just as puzzled as she had been when she first walked into the drawing room and saw Mr. Bates. She could think of no reason at all for him to come visit her, even if he *was* in England to see his grandfather. She had thought they said everything there was to say that day at the docks.

It was true that she had been rather good friends with his sister, and he had occasionally flirted with her, in a halfhearted way. His behavior had sometimes been flattering, but there was always *something* she could not quite like about him. Something evasive and odd.

That *something* seemed even stronger now than it had then.

For one moment, when she had first seen him, she had let herself indulge in the dream that he had come to declare his love for her, marry her, and take her back to her old life in Jamaica. Was that not what she had wanted ever since she came to England? To go back to Jamaica?

But now she found that that was no longer what she wanted at all. Her life there had been a good one, but it was behind her now.

And, even if it were not, she could not bear the thought of marrying a man like Mr. Bates. Not when she now knew the truth of what a man could be— honest, caring, strong without making others weak, intelligent, and willing to change when situations warranted.

Someone like Phillip.

Phillip, who had seen her in the corridor having her hand kissed by Mr. Bates. And just when things were going so well between them!

She would just have to talk to him, make him understand who Mr. Bates was. But not just yet. First she had to talk to Mr. Bates, and she only had enough strength for one thing at a time.

She reached for the carved ebony comb that had been her mother's, and placed it carefully in the low, braided twist of her hair Antoinette had finished. "Do I look all right?"

"All right for what?" Antoinette asked, peering in the mirror to straighten her own lavender-colored turban. "For running into Mr. Bates' arms and accepting his oh-so-romantic declarations?"

Cassie laughed. "Hardly! I am just praying he makes no declarations whatsoever tonight. I want to find out why he is here and send him on his way as soon as possible."

"On his way—alone?"

"Of course alone! What do you think, that I want to go with him? What fustian!"

Antoinette shrugged. "He would take you back to Jamaica."

"*Nothing* would be worth being married to him. His hands are cold, and his eyes are—are empty."

"Just be careful, Cassie dear," Antoinette said, bending down to give her a quick, reassuring hug. "Are you certain you don't want me to come with you?"

Cassie shook her head, clinging to her friend. "I will only speak with him for a few minutes, and we will be in the drawing room, with the butler within calling distance."

"Very well. I will let you go down alone for a little while, but then I am going to come stand outside the drawing room door until I see him leave."

Cassie laughed. "My dear friend! What would I do without you?" She stood up, and straightened the folds of her emerald-green satin gown. "This will not take long at all, I am sure."

Soon after Cassie left her chamber, Louisa, Lady Lettice, Angelo, and Sir Belvedere appeared there, finding Antoinette alone, trying to read a book and biding her time until she could hurry downstairs.

"Where is Cassie?" Louisa asked.

"She has gone to meet with Mr. Bates," Antoinette answered.

"Oh, no! She cannot be alone with that dreadful man," Sir Belvedere cried. He paced the length of the floor, his armor rattling even more than usual in his agitation.

Lady Lettice said nothing, but twisted one long strand of pearls around her finger nervously.

"I agree that he is truly dreadful," Antoinette said. "But they are hardly alone with all the servants around." Not alone at all, she silently reassured herself.

"Nonetheless, it is not good," said Louisa. "We do not like that man at all."

"He is after Miss Richards' land!" Angelo cried. "Bad, bad man! Angelo hates him."

"Her land?" Antoinette said, puzzled. "She has no—oh, you mean the land she still owns in Jamaica?"

"That must be it. Land in England could scarcely do a planter in Jamaica any good," said Louisa.

Antoinette shook her head. "But it is not a great amount. Cassie sold most of her father's plantation to a new family there. She kept only a plot big enough for a house and a small garden, in case she ever wanted to go back. Of course, it *does* border Mr. Bates' land."

"Then that is it!" Sir Belvedere said. "He wants to marry her to expand his holdings."

"But his own plantation is huge," said Antoinette. "Why would he go to so much trouble for Cassie's piece of land?"

"Greed, my dear lady," Sir Belvedere answered. "Some men will do anything out of greed."

"He is certainly greedy enough," Antoinette agreed. "And the sort of man who will stop at nothing to get what he wants. But what should we do?"

"Just wait," Lady Lettice advised. "Perhaps after Cassandra turns him down he will leave quietly, and we will not have to worry about him anymore."

"What if he does *not* go away?" Louisa murmured.

"Then, Louisa, *he* will be the one to worry about *us.*"

"So who is this Mr. Bates, Mother?" Phillip asked. It was growing darker in the library; he really should have been thinking of going upstairs to change for supper. But all he could keep replaying in his mind was the image of Cassandra standing in the foyer having her hand kissed by some strange man.

A man who was tall, broad, and sun-browned. A man who looked as if he had never spent an hour bent over dusty books in his life. A man who appeared to know her very well.

"He says he knew Miss Richards in Jamaica," his mother said, fussing about with some of the ornaments on the fireplace mantel. She had ostensibly come in to tell him it was nearing time for supper, but as usual she could not resist changing his arrangements about. "He told us he was in England to see his grandfather, and wanted to see Miss Richards before he returned home."

He *would*. "Oh, just happened to be in the neighborhood, eh?"

"I suppose. He seems quite fond of Miss Richards." She gave him a meaningful glance. "I would not be surprised if he was here to ask her to marry him." Then, her point seemingly made, she ceased moving the ornaments and walked to the door. "Supper will be soon, dear. Don't stay here too much longer with your books."

"I won't, Mother," he answered.

As the door shut behind her, he looked back down at the book that lay open beneath his hand. His mother had been repeating that admonition to him for as long as he could remember. "Don't stay up reading too long, Phillip." Even as a child, he had found a new and engrossing world in books, one that was difficult to tear himself away from. It had been the only world he needed.

Until now.

Cassandra had shown him a whole world outside the library, one that was full of color and mystery and light. It was not always neat and rational; it was sometimes messy and unexplainable, and very, very exciting. When he was with her, he felt like anything at all could be possible. He wanted to spend so much more time with her, to learn everything there was to know about her.

And, miracle of miracles, she had seemed to enjoy his company, too.

Until now.

Now there was a man from her home, a home he knew she missed, here to try to reclaim her for that past life.

Phillip laid his hand flat on the crackling pages of the book. Was he back to living only in books, without her color and vividness in his life?

Or could he find it within himself to fight for her?

Mr. Bates was waiting when Cassie slipped into the drawing room. There was a fire in the grate, but the maids had not yet been in to light the candles, so there were shadows lurking in the corners of the room. Mr. Bates almost seemed to be one of them, a large mass in evening clothes outlined by the fire.

"So here you are!" he said with a jovial grin. "I was beginning to think our talk was going to have to take place another time."

Cassie was not put at her ease. His smile seemed too—too forced. She cautiously came farther into the room and sat down on the edge of a chair. "You came so far to see me. The least I could do is meet with you as soon as I could."

"And I am so happy you did." He sat down in the chair beside hers, and Cassie sensed that he would have taken her hand, but she kept them firmly clasped in her lap. "But I did not come all that far. I was already in England, you know, to see my grandfather."

"But he is in London, is he not? That is a great distance from here."

"No distance is too great to see *you*, Miss Richards. Weren't we good friends in Jamaica?"

Cassie would never have gone so far as to say *that*. "Well, I . . ." she began.

He interrupted her by suddenly clasping at the arm of her chair. His rough fingers brushed against the bare skin above her glove and below her short, puffed sleeve, and she drew away from him.

"Of course we were!" he said heartily. "Almost betrothed, some would have said."

No one had ever said that, as far as Cassie knew. "We didn't know each other that well," she managed to say past the growing lump of trepidation in her throat.

"You know I was always fond of you," he said, leaning closer. "That is why I felt I could come to you and ask you something."

"Wh-what?"

"I need to ask you to sell me your land in Jamaica."

Cassie, who had just opened her mouth to refuse a proposal of marriage, looked at him sharply. "My land?"

"Yes. It would be so convenient for me to have it, seeing that it borders my own plantation, and you seem quite settled here."

She almost laughed in profound relief. He did not want *her*—he wanted her land!

But once the relief had passed, questions popped up in her mind. Her land was not very great; it seemed almost as strange that he would come this far to buy it as it had for him to propose to her.

She looked away from him, into the light of the fire. It made sense to sell it to him, certainly. She had no need of it. But something very strong held her back.

That land was her last link to her father. She did not want to let it go to a man who unsettled and alarmed her in such a way.

She turned back to Mr. Bates. He still smiled amiably, but there was such desperation in his eyes. Desperation, and—and something she could not name, but that frightened her.

"I will think about your offer," she said carefully. "But I must tell you I have no plans to sell that land. Not to anyone."

His smile faded, replaced by a puzzled scowl. "You are refusing to sell me the land?"

"I said I would think about it . . ." she began, but her words became a squeak when he suddenly grabbed her arm.

"You also said you have no plans to sell!" he growled. "You were never going to hear me out at all. Just like a woman—stubborn and two-faced! You don't even need that land. You are just keeping it to spite me."

"Let go of me!" Cassie cried, pulling at her arm.

She managed to yank away from him, but part of her sleeve came off with a loud tear. It echoed in the room, and the door was thrown open.

Phillip stood there, tall and still. He frowned as he took in the scene before him, the firelight glinting like the flames of Hades on his dark hair.

"What is the meaning of this?" he said in a frighteningly calm voice.

Cassie gave a small cry and leaped off her chair to run toward him. Never had she been so glad to see anyone in all her life!

He caught her in his arms, and she held tightly to him, trembling and wordless. Usually she felt so confident, so safe in her world; all that had fled before the anger she saw in Mr. Bates' eyes.

But now her world was slowly righting itself as she held onto Phillip.

He looked calmly at Mr. Bates over the top of her head. "I ought to call you out, sir, for frightening a guest in my own home," he said quietly. "As it is, I ask you to leave at once."

Mr. Bates stood up, his polite mask sliding back into place to conceal that quick flash of fury. "You must be Lord Royce."

"I am."

"Well, Lord Royce, Miss Richards and I were just having a bit of a chat about old times in Jamaica. She became rather emotional, as women are wont to do." He gave a jovial between-us-men smile. "You know how women can be. Especially women as—imaginative as Miss Richards. I certainly meant no offense."

"That is not . . ." Cassie began.

Phillip hushed her with a gentle hand on her hair. "I ask you once more to leave my house. I will not ask again."

Mr. Bates drew himself up with a frown and stalked past them to the door. "You will be sorry," he said. Cassie was not sure if he meant her, or Phillip, or the entire world.

As Mr. Bates pushed into the foyer, he nearly knocked Antoinette to the floor. Without even acknowledging her presence, he continued up the staircase.

Antoinette glared at his back, then came on into the drawing room. "Cassie!" she cried. "What has happened? Did that beast hurt you?"

Cassie shook her head mutely. Her voice seemed to have deserted her in the unsettling proceedings.

"I think she is more scared than hurt," Phillip said. "Miss Duvall, would you be so kind as to ask the butler and some of the footmen to make certain Mr. Bates and his cousin leave the castle immediately?"

Antoinette nodded. "Yes, of course! Right away." She patted Cassie's arm once soothingly and hurried away to find the servants.

Phillip led Cassie back to the fire and made her sit down. Then he knelt down beside her, holding her cold hands in his. "Do you feel up to telling me what happened, Cassandra?" he asked gently.

"I am not sure," she answered. "It all happened so very quickly."

A muscle ticked along Phillip's jaw. "He attacked you?"

"Not *attacked* exactly. He grabbed my arm. But I had been feeling so very uncomfortable with him, that when he did that I—I screamed."

"You were very surprised to see him here, then," he said, more as a statement than a question. "He was not an invited caller."

Cassie studied him quizzically. Could that possibly be a small note of *jealousy* in his voice? That made her feel slightly better, even in the midst of all her confusion and fear. Things could not possibly be all bad if Phillip cared enough to be jealous.

She longed to throw her arms around him and swear to him that he should never need to feel jealous of anyone. That there was no one in the world who could possibly compare to him.

Instead, she just nodded her head and said, "Very surprised indeed. He has never written to me since I have been in England. I have heard from his sister, but she has only mentioned him in passing. She did not even say her brother was coming here." Cassie paused to take a deep, steadying breath. "I confess I was a bit glad to see him when first he arrived. He was a familiar face from home. But I soon realized that something was amiss. He wants to buy my land in Jamaica. Very badly."

Phillip, who had been quietly listening and holding her hands, said, "Is there something—special about your land?"

"To me, yes, but surely not to anyone else. It is a small parcel. The only thing I can think of is that it borders Mr. Bates' own plantation, though surely *that* would not have brought him so far to see me. He could have just written with an offer." She shook her head, confused and exhausted, and she could feel the tears starting again. "I just do not know!"

"Sh," Phillip answered. He rose up on his knees and put his arms around her, drawing her close.

Cassie buried her face in the clean, starched scent of his cravat. She had never felt safer or more cherished in all her life.

He rested his cheek against her hair. "You needn't be frightened, my dear Cassandra. No matter what he wants, he cannot get close to you ever again, I promise."

She wound her arms about his neck and held on as if he were the most precious jewel and she feared someone would snatch him away.

Suddenly, the drawing room door was flung open, breaking into the perfect stillness of the moment. Cassie pulled away from Phillip and looked over to see Lady Royce and Aunt Chat watching them with wide, interested eyes.

"Oh! Er . . ." stammered Lady Royce, looking away.

"Perhaps we should go out and come back in again," Aunt Chat suggested.

"Of course not," said Phillip, standing up slowly. His face was utterly expressionless. "Miss Richards has had an unpleasant experience. I'm sure she is very glad to see you."

She *would* have been glad to see them, if only they

had come in just a little later. But she gave them a quavering smile and just said, "Yes, indeed."

Aunt Chat hurried across the room to put her arm around Cassie. "Antoinette told us something of it. My poor dear! Are you quite all right now?"

"That dreadful Mr. Bates," said Lady Royce. She regained her composure and came to take Cassie's other hand in hers. "I cannot believe I let him and his foppish cousin eat some of Cook's best seedcake."

"Now that you are both here, I will just go and make certain Mr. Bates and his cousin are leaving," Phillip said. He bowed to the ladies and went out the door with a resolute set to his shoulders.

"You needn't worry about a thing now, my dear," Lady Royce said, patting Cassie's hand. "My son will take care of everything. That Mr. Bates shall never bother us again!"

Phillip did not bother to knock on Mr. Bates' door. He merely pushed the wood aside and stood in the portal with his arms crossed across his chest.

He did not trust himself to do anything else, such as speak or walk across the room, not with the memory of Cassie's tearstained face in his mind. And anger, sharp and white-hot, unlike anything he had ever felt before, coursed through his veins. If he came within ten feet of Mr. Bates, he knew that he would kill him with his bare hands.

And that would be the height of rudeness, to murder someone beneath his mother's roof.

He stood there, watching Mr. Bates and his cousin as they hurried about the room, tossing things into valises. His expression, his entire being, felt as if it had been turned to stone.

Mr. Bates straightened up from his valise to glare at Phillip, his sun-browned face red.

"The least you could do is send a servant to do the repacking," Mr. Bates said, coming closer to Phillip than was strictly prudent on his part.

Phillip set his jaw. "I fear all the servants are otherwise occupied. Some of the footmen will be here shortly to be certain you depart, though."

"We have never been treated in such a fashion in our lives!" Mr. Bates growled, taking another step closer. "If this is English hospitality . . ."

That did it. Phillip's fragile hold on his temper snapped, and his hands shot out to grab Mr. Bates by his coat front. "How dare you come to my home, uninvited, and insult a young lady in my drawing room? You're a lout and a bully, and I ought to thrash you within an inch of your life." Strength Phillip did not know he possessed flowed into his fists, giving him a viselike grip on the larger man.

Phillip wasn't the only one who was surprised. Mr. Bates' eyes widened, as he struggled to release himself. Behind him, his cousin fluttered about ineffectually, his face pale above his pink coat.

"It—it was not like that," Mr. Bates managed to gasp. "That stupid chit . . ."

Phillip shook Mr. Bates by his coat until the man's head wobbled on his thick neck.

"Phillip!" his mother's shocked voice cried, breaking into his haze of anger.

He glanced back over his shoulder to see her standing in the doorway, her eyes wide.

"Phillip, please," she said quietly. "Come away, now. These—people are not worth it."

Phillip gave Mr. Bates one last shake, and released him. Mr. Bates fell back, trembling. "If you ever come near Miss Richards again, thrash you is exactly what I will do," he warned. "Now, leave my house."

Without another word, he turned, took his mother's arm, and left the room, not even glancing back.

Mr. Bates watched him go with fury blazing in his eyes.

Chapter Twenty

"Well, you certainly made a mess of *that*, cousin," Mr. Morland said, lolling back against the squabs of the carriage as they raced down the road, away from Royce Castle. "Such a wasted journey. We could have been halfway back across the ocean by now!"

Mr. Bates stared fixedly out the carriage window, his sun-browned face red with the force of his anger. His hands clasped and unclasped into fists. "It was not wasted," he growled. "I *will* get what I came here for."

"How? You frightened Miss Richards out of her wits, and we were not even there four hours. You should have listened to me when I tried to give you some advice about wooing a lady. And that Lord Royce will never let you past the gates again!" Mr. Morland gingerly reached up to touch his shoulder, where Lord Royce had grasped it to push him into the carriage.

"I was perhaps too—overeager with Miss Richards," Mr. Bates acknowledged in a grudging tone. "The stupid girl wanted poetry, I suppose, and pretty words instead of plain honesty. But this is not finished, by any means!"

Mr. Morland looked at him curiously. "Do you mean to say that you *told* her what is truly going on? That our grandfather thinks you are an irresponsible lout—which you are—and that your inheritance from him depends on your making a success of your plantation? And that you have gambled away over half your land, and need Miss Richards' property to begin replacing it?"

Mr. Bates glared. "I did not tell her any of that! But if she had just sold me that land, my troubles would be over. I could recoup before the old man finds out anything! He would think I was the most responsible man in the West Indies."

"But Miss Richards will not sell you so much as a blade of grass, especially since you behaved like such a boor."

Mr. Bates' eyes narrowed. "The land will be mine anyway, once she is my wife. And I will not have to pay a farthing for it."

Mr. Morland sat straight up in surprise, forgetting his stylish languor. "Your wife! She is going to marry you?"

"She will, once I put my new plan into action. Listen to this, cousin . . ." He leaned forward and outlined his ideas to the ever-more incredulous Mr. Morland.

Neither of them saw the small, pale figure huddled beneath one of the seats. Angelo clasped his velvet cap over his mouth, giggling merrily in his mind.

Oh, just wait until Lady Lettice hears of this! he thought. He would be set up with sugared almonds for all eternity.

"Are you feeling better, Cassie?" Antoinette asked, putting a tray holding a glass of milk and some biscuits down on Cassie's bedside table.

Cassie leaned back against her pillows and smiled up at Antoinette. She had been trying to find distraction in a new novel, but the events of the evening kept overshadowing the plot of the book, and so she laid it aside.

"I *am* feeling better," she said, reaching for one of the biscuits. "It is good to know that Mr. Bates is gone and we will not see him here again."

Antoinette sat down on the edge of the bed. "I should never have let you go alone to meet with him, no matter what you said. I was not a very good friend."

"No, Antoinette!" Cassie cried. "You are the best of friends. I was simply foolish. I thought I could deal alone with whatever Mr. Bates had to say. Clearly I was wrong."

"And very fortunate that Lord Royce came along when he did."

Cassie smiled at the memory of Phillip appearing in the drawing room, like a knight of old defending his lady fair. "As you say."

Antoinette fell silent, and for a long moment the only sound in the room was the crackling of flames in the grate. Then she said, "What really happened with Mr. Bates, Cassie?"

"I am not exactly sure. He seemed all right at first—friendly, and full of reminiscences about Jamaica. Then I heard what he had really come here for."

"Your land."

"Yes. My land. It would have been the sensible thing to sell it to him, of course. I will not need it. Yet the thought of him owning something that had once been my father's . . ." Cassie shuddered. "It did not seem right. I tried to be diplomatic in my answer, but he became extremely angry very quickly. There was a look in his eyes that frightened me, and when he tore my sleeve I—I screamed. That was when Phillip, I mean Lord Royce, came in."

Antoinette nodded. "It is a very good thing he came when he did."

"Indeed. I would not have thought that Mr. Bates would attack me in the very midst of a crowded house, but I knew from that look in his eyes that he was capable of anything. I do not know why I welcomed him for even a moment!"

Antoinette reached over and squeezed her hand. "Mr. Bates is obviously accustomed to getting what he wants, and he is ruthless." She looked down, a dull red flush spreading across her coffee-colored cheekbones. "Do you remember Henriette, who was a house slave at his plantation?"

"The one who drowned a couple of years ago?"

"There were whispers that it was not an accident."

Cassie frowned. "I do not remember hearing that!"

"Of course you would not have. I heard it among my mother's people. They do not approve of my living with you, but they will still gossip with me. But the point is that I knew of the rumor, and that is why I am at fault for letting you meet with him. I should never have let my distaste for the man keep me from protecting you."

Cassie felt very shaken and fragile. She clung to Antoinette's hand. "I still say it is not your fault at all. Not one whit! He would not have attempted anything here. And besides, he is gone now. Is he not?"

"Yes. He is gone." Antoinette kissed her cheek and stood up. "Drink your milk, now, Cassie, and try to sleep. We are to go have the final fittings on our costumes tomorrow afternoon, and you do not want to look tired and pale for that!" She gave a light laugh that was obviously meant to be reassuring, but was just as obviously false.

Cassie responded with a weak smile and pulled the bedclothes up to her chin. "I promise I will sleep, if you will, too. Good night, Antoinette."

After her friend left, Cassie lay awake, staring out at her firelit chamber. She was *not* afraid of Mr. Bates, not here in Royce Castle, with Phillip and all her friends, both human and spirit, around her. But she did feel very angry that he had come here and disturbed this happy time. He had no right to frighten her and Antoinette, or to come into her life at all.

For this had been a very happy time indeed, she realized, the happiest she had known since coming to England. Maybe the happiest she had known ever. She loved Royce Castle and the wild landscape of Cornwall. She liked having her aunt and her friends all around her, and walking on the shore, and having books to read and horses to ride.

Most of all, she loved being with Phillip. Walking with him, talking to him, and even just sitting in the library being quiet with him filled her with a warm, secure sense of well-being and joy.

When she had first met him, she never would have imagined she could feel this way! She had thought him a stuffy, cynical scholar, nothing like the hearty outdoorsmen she was used to in Jamaica. But now she saw the truth so clearly, both about Phillip and about Mr. Bates and the men like him. *They* had to make the people around them, especially the women, be weak so that they could feel strong. Yet Phillip *was* strong, innately so, and in such a quiet way that he never had to prove with bluster or violence. His kindness—to his mother, his servants, to Antoinette, and to Cassie—was the largest part of that strength.

She did not know why she had not been able to see that from the very beginning.

But she could acknowledge now that she loved him, that there could be no other man like him in all the world. If he could return even a portion of her affection, she could never ask for anything more.

Cassie smiled and closed her eyes, finally feeling that she was at peace and could sleep. She was warm and secure here.

As she was just about to drift into slumber, though, she heard a rattle in the corridor outside her room. Then there was a short silence and another rattle.

She felt no fear; Mr. Bates could not possibly have gotten into the castle. But she did feel quite curious. She slipped out of bed, put on her dressing gown and slippers, and went out into the corridor.

Sir Belvedere was there, marching smartly up and down past her door in his armor. When he saw her, he stopped and gave her a salute.

"Sir Belvedere!" Cassie said quietly, trying not to wake anyone else, though how they could have slept through the rattling was a mystery. "What are you doing?"

"I am guarding your door, fair lady," he answered.

"Guarding my door?"

"In case those Jamaican ruffians return." Sir Belvedere shook his head. "Those two are most untrustworthy, my lady."

"I certainly agree! It is very kind of you to keep a watch for me."

"I am most happy to do it."

"Where are Louisa and Lady Lettice tonight?"

"They are in the East Tower, talking about shoes and jewels. They have been chattering on about them for hours." He pulled a very masculine mystified face. "How can ladies talk about such things as shoes for so long?"

Cassie shrugged. There was just no way to explain to a man, even one who had been dead for five hundred years, the deep fascination a pair of new shoes could hold. "Well, good night, Sir Belvedere. And thank you again."

"You may rest easily, dear lady. I am ever vigilant!" Then he set off on his march again.

Cassie went back into her chamber and crossed the room to close the draperies at the window. A glimpse of a figure in the garden below stopped her, and she paused with her hand on the cool satin.

It was Phillip, standing in the garden within sight of her window, his tall figure limned in silvery moonlight. He waved up at her, and she blew him a kiss, laughing.

She opened up the casement and leaned out to call, "How very secure I will feel tonight, Phillip, with both my window *and* my door guarded!"

He came closer, until he stood just under her window. "Your door?"

"I just found Sir Belvedere marching up and down in the corridor."

"The ghost?" Phillip's tone was rather doubtful.

"He *does* have a sword."

"A real one? Or a phantom one?"

"I have no idea. It looks rather substantial." Cassie feared she was grinning like a simpleton at this silly conversation.

"Well, I just wanted to make sure you were quite all right and that you were able to sleep."

"I was a bit anxious at first," she admitted. "But I feel fine now. Better than fine, in fact. I am sure that I will sleep very well."

"Mr. Bates cannot come back," Phillip said. "There are guards all around the castle."

"I am not afraid," Cassie answered truthfully.

"Good. I would never want you to be afraid."

They watched each other in sweet silence for a moment, a moment that seemed to stretch into eternity yet was over in an instant. Then Phillip smiled and waved at her once more. "Shall we go riding tomorrow after breakfast?"

"Oh, yes. I would like that."

"I would, too. There are some—things I would like to discuss with you. Good night, Cassandra."

"Good night." *My love*, she added silently.

"And you are certain that is what Mr. Bates said?" Lady Lettice asked Angelo, leaning over him intently.

"He is coming back during the masked ball to kidnap Cassie?" Louisa said, appalled.

Angelo nodded firmly, the bells on his cap tinkling. "That is what he told that overdressed cousin of his. His grandfather will take away Mr. Bates' inheritance, which is a very large one, unless Mr. Bates can prove he is a reformed, responsible character by making a success of his plantation. And gambling away a portion of that plantation is decidedly *not* responsible."

"No, indeed," Lady Lettice murmured. "So he wants Cassie's land to begin to replace what he lost."

"He will kidnap her and force her to marry him in order to get it. And to have his revenge on her for refusing him, as well," Angelo said. Then he burst into tears, wiping at his streaming eyes with the velvet sleeve of his doublet. "Angelo doesn't want the evil man to kidnap Cassie!"

"Oh, do cease crying, Angelo," Lady Lettice said. "He will not kidnap her. We will see to that. It was very clever of you to get into the carriage with them."

Angelo sniffled, his tears dissolving into a rather pleased expression. "It was?"

"Indeed it was," Louisa agreed. "Now, it is five days until the masked ball. Plenty of time to come up with a plan of our own." She gave a merry little peal of laughter. "It is certain that Mr. Bates will never darken *our* door again after that night!"

Late that night, when the castle was quiet and dark, Lettice slipped into Antoinette's chamber. She moved quickly and silently, careful not to wake the woman who slept peacefully in the curtained bed. This would be much easier with Antoinette's help, Lettice knew, but she did not want to involve the humans. It could be too dangerous.

She selected one of the leather-bound volumes from Antoinette's bookshelf, and leafed through it until she found what she was looking for. A solidifying spell for spirits.

Lettice smiled as she read it. Sir Belvedere and Louisa were very blithe about the whole matter, not at all considering in practical terms how it might be brought off. But Lettice knew they had to have a plan, and that being able to mingle freely with the humans had to be part of it.

As she read over the spell again, memorizing it, Lettice tried to reassure herself.

"All will be well," she whispered, trying to maintain her hard-won confidence.

Deep inside, though, were the stirrings of doubt and fear. Lettice had not had very many people to care about in all her existence. Just her father, and Angelo, and, for a brief while, Jean-Pierre. Now she had all these fragile humans, who did not even realize the danger they were in.

She never wanted any evil to befall them.

Chapter Twenty-One

It was a bright, cool morning when Cassie and Phillip rode out from the stables and galloped along the cliff-top paths. White-gold sunlight shone down on the blue and foam-white sea below, and a light breeze ruffled the treetops and sent autumn leaves skittering across the path.

Cassie tilted back her head and breathed deeply of the fresh, salty air. She laughed aloud at the glory of the morning.

"You are looking very well today," Phillip commented with a smile.

Cassie gave him an answering grin. "I *feel* well today. And you are looking quite—refreshed yourself."

"Well, I have had a realization of late, and it has lightened my mind considerably."

"A realization?" Cassie thought of her own realizations of the night before. "What, pray tell, was it?"

He just shook his head, and gave her the little half smile she had once disliked so much, but now found adorable. "Shall we walk?" he said, drawing his horse to the side of the path.

"What a good idea. It's such a lovely day." Cassie pulled her own horse to a halt, then waited for Phillip to dismount and come to her assistance.

His hands lingered at her waist as he lowered her to the ground, holding her warm and safe. Cassie leaned against him, her palm laid lightly against his shoulder. His scent of starch and soap and ink was sweet in the cool air.

"So," she whispered, "what was your realization?"

In answer, he shook his head again and took her arm, leading her along the path. The sun was warm on her head, so warm that she took off her hat and carried it in her hand, letting the breeze ruffle her hair.

It *was* a lovely day, and she was content to walk along next to Phillip in silence. The peaceful moments were most welcome after the shock of Mr. Bates' sudden appearance and just as swift exit. Under this sky, with this man beside her, nothing could hurt her.

They walked until they reached a scenic spot overlooking the cliffs and the sea, where there was a weathered old bench. Cassie and Phillip sat down, but he did not remove his hand from her arm.

"So much has happened in the short time you've been at Royce Castle, Cassandra," he said. "More than ever happened in the years before I met you, I vow!"

"Is this your revelation?" Cassie teased. "Never to have houseguests again?"

Phillip laughed. "Or perhaps to have *more* houseguests?"

"Was that it, then? That you ought to expand your social engagements?"

"Something of the sort." His hand slid down her velvet sleeve to her gloved hand, which he held between both of his. "As I said, so many things have happened since you came here. Most of them to the good."

"*Most* of them?"

"Very well, *all* of them. Or almost all. But they have all conspired to make me think. To make me realize that my life of study, while satisfying in many ways, is not enough."

"Is it not?" Cassie said softly, not daring to hope what he might be saying.

"No. I will always love my books and my work, but they are meant to be part of my life, not the whole of it. There must be time for things such as family, and fun, and wonder at the mysteries of life. Things are not always rational—nor should they be."

"You have taught me many things, too!" Cassie said, curling her fingers tighter around his.

"Have I? I've no idea what they could be."

"I have discovered that our lives are *now*. The past is gone from us, and the future unknowable. I loved my life in Jamaica, but it was over when my father died. I could never have it back, no matter what, and I would not choose it if I could. My memories will always be with me, but my home, my life, is here now. I am where I am meant to be." She looked past him, out to where the sea lay blue-gray under the sun. "Life cannot be built on a foundation of all dreams and fancies. There has to be logic and solidity, as well. And family."

"So we have learned from each other," Phillip said thoughtfully.

"I think we have. My time here at Royce Castle has been the best of my life."

"I hope that time is not over yet."

"Of course not. There is still the ball."

"I mean—oh, I am saying this badly. I mean that I hope it will not be over, ever."

Cassie's gaze swung back to him, her hand tightening on his. He watched her seriously, almost warily. "Wh—what do you mean?"

Phillip took a deep breath. "I mean, will you do me the great honor of becoming my wife?"

She stared at him, trying to decide if she had actually heard what she thought she had. Had he actually said those words?

The silence lengthened, and he looked away from her. His hands began to slide from hers, but she grabbed onto them and held them tightly.

"Do you truly want me to marry you?" she whispered.

"More than anything else," he whispered back.

"Then, yes. I will marry you."

"Cassandra!" he said, his voice ringing with triumph. His arms came around her, drawing her against him, and she tilted her face for his kiss.

It was sweet, and ardent, and filled with all the promise of their life to come. All the passion, all the laughter, all the uncertainty—and all the logic, too.

Cassie's hand crept to his cheek, which was warm beneath the thin leather of her glove. The wind blew a lock of his hair loose, and it fell like a piece of silk across her neck.

He drew back, but his arms stayed around her. She rested her head on his shoulder and sighed in contentment. "I thought you would *never* ask," she said.

He laughed, stirring the curls at her temple with his sweet breath. "Never? Dearest, we have only known each other a short time. I moved as quickly as I could."

"But I knew the first time I saw you that I loved you."

"You hated me the first time you saw me!"

She gave a little shrug. "So I mistook one strong emotion for another. I knew I felt *something* for you, something I would not be able to let go of."

"And I knew I felt something for you, as well. Something I could never feel for anyone else."

"Love?"

He paused just an instant too long before saying, "Yes. That must have been it."

Cassie hit him on the arm, laughing. "So sincere you are! Well, no matter what, that is all behind us now. We have found our love, and I am deeply grateful for it."

"As am I. There is just one more detail to decide."

"What is that?"

"When shall we announce our betrothal? At the masked ball?"

"Oh, that would be perfect!" Cassie said in delight. "But . . ."

"But what? You are not changing your mind!"

"Never! I just want to wait until the day of the ball to tell your mother and my aunt."

"Whatever for?"

Cassie was not quite sure, herself. She only knew that she wanted this to be a secret for just a little while longer; she wanted it to be her own happiness. Then, the day of the ball, she would joyfully shout it from the rooftops, and draw everyone else into the pink glow of her contentment.

"I just want to be *quietly* happy about it for a while," she answered. "And your mother is so very busy with the preparations for the ball."

"Hm. You are quite right," Phillip said. "I am sure that the moment she hears the news she will begin planning the wedding. *Two* festive occasions might be too much for her."

"Then we are agreed?"

"Agreed. It will be our secret until the day of the ball."

Then he drew her back into his arms for another kiss, one to seal their betrothal. It was very late indeed when they arrived back at the castle.

"You are getting *married*?" Antoinette cried, staring at Cassie in a stunned manner. "Truly?"

Cassie laughed and tossed her hat and riding crop onto her bed. As soon as they returned from their ride, she had gone to tell Antoinette the news. She might be able to keep a secret from Lady Royce and Aunt Chat for a short time, but she could never keep a secret from Antoinette.

"I am truly getting married," she said. "Are you not happy for me?"

Antoinette finally managed to close her mouth and rushed over to hug Cassie. "I am more than happy for you, my dearest friend! Lord Royce is a good man and deserving of your love." She drew back to peer closely into Cassie's face. "You do love him, don't you?"

"Of course I love him," Cassie said. "I would not marry him otherwise."

"I know you would not. It is just that when we first met him, you were not—overly fond of him."

Cassie smiled at her and went over to the dressing table to let her hair down and start brushing the tangles out. "That was then. And you did not care for him at first, either."

"He has proven himself to be a man of open mind and great intelligence, and not just intelligent from books, either. He has a kind heart, and he loves you a great deal. I could ask for nothing more for you." Antoinette's reflection in the mirror smiled, but her

eyes looked sad and distant. She turned away and
sat down in a chair beside the fire.

Cassie wanted no sadness from anyone she loved
on this day. She wanted everyone to feel as joyful as
she did! She put down the brush and swung around
to face Antoinette. "Is something amiss? Did something happen while I was gone?" A terrible thought
struck her. "Is Mr. Bates . . ."

"No, no!" Antoinette answered quickly. "He has
not been seen again. It is just—well, I have been
thinking perhaps I should go back to Jamaica. After
your wedding would be a good time."

Cassie was absolutely appalled. She ran across the
room to kneel down beside Antoinette's chair, and
took her friend's hands in hers. "No! You cannot
leave me."

"Cassie, you know I would miss you horribly. But
you are beginning a new life now, a new circle. Perhaps it is time for me to go back."

Cassie shook her head violently. "You said when
we left that there was nothing for you in Jamaica.
That your mother's family, well, that they did
not . . ." Her voice trailed away.

"That they did not approve of my closeness to a
white family," Antoinette finished gently. "No, they
did not, and they chose not to let me be a true part
of their community any longer. You were all my family, and I was happy to come here with you."

"Are you not content here in England? Do we not
have a good life?"

"A very good life, and I am quite content here. I
was looking for a new beginning of my own, you
know. But we both know that it is highly unlikely I
will ever marry. I can't stay under your feet forever."

"You are hardly 'under my feet'!" Cassie protested
stubbornly. "I need you. The ghosts need you, and

Aunt Chat needs you. One day, my children will need you. If you grow bored here at the castle, you can always go see Aunt Chat in Bath. But I will *not* hear another word about your returning to Jamaica! And that is that."

Antoinette smiled. "No one could ever argue with you when your mind is made up."

"No, indeed. So, you will stay?"

"I will stay. Only for as long as you need me, though."

"Then you will be here forever!" Cassie cried happily. "Oh, Antoinette! We are going to be so happy here. I can just feel it."

Chapter Twenty-Two

The next few days passed very quickly, in a blur of social engagements and preparations for the masked ball. Under Lady Royce's careful supervision, the ballroom was cleaned and polished from the frescoed ceiling to the parquet floor. Musicians were hired, new draperies were hung at the windows, and potted palms in unheard-of quantities were brought in.

The costumes were delivered by the dressmaker, and tried on amid much laughter and posing. Guests from far away arrived to stay at the castle and at the inn in the village. They were entertained with suppers, and card parties, and picnics on the shore. There was tea at the Lewishams' vicarage, where they were invited to help plan the annual parish bazaar, and a musicale at Lady Paige's house.

With all the activity swirling around them, Cassie and Phillip could not find a great deal of time to spend quietly together. But they would take their books to the garden in the mornings and stroll the paths and talk about their readings. It was all perfectly proper, and if they occasionally crept behind a hedge to exchange a quick, stolen kiss, who was to know?

At night, Cassie would lie in her bed and hug all the warm happiness of the day close to her. She had truly never been more content than she was now at Royce Castle, and every moment was precious to her, a perfect pearl she could take out and marvel over again in the darkness of her room. She was surrounded by friends, by warm security, and the shining promise of love and a good future.

She clung to these things, as if a small part of her feared they might be snatched away.

"You are certain this is what they mean to do, Angelo?" Lady Lettice said, kneeling down to place her hands on the dwarf's small shoulders.

He nodded vehemently. "Very certain! I snuck into their lodgings again tonight. Mr. Bates is very angry. Very angry indeed. He wants revenge on Miss Richards and Lord Royce. Angelo does *not* like him!"

Lady Lettice patted his shoulder and stood up. "We will not have to worry about him at all after tomorrow night. Is everyone ready?"

Louisa and Sir Belvedere nodded.

"Cassie's costume is a shepherdess, which Mr. Bates knows since Lady Royce mentioned it when they first arrived here," said Louisa. "I have discovered she keeps it in the dressmaker's box at the bottom of her wardrobe."

"And I have examined the 'gentlemen's' carriage," said Sir Belvedere. "There will be no trouble at all."

"Excellent," Lady Lettice said with a smile. "Then we need only wait for tomorrow night. When they make their move, we shall make our own."

* * *

The day of the masked ball was a cold one, with a gray sky and an angry, frothy sea. This put an end to the planned luncheon picnic, and all the houesguests at Royce Castle had to stay indoors. There were card games in the drawing room and charades in the gallery. Servants hurried to and fro, carrying costumes to be pressed, trays of tea, and, as the preparations for the ball itself commenced, hot water for baths.

Laughter and chatter echoed through the ancient castle, as they had not for so many years.

Lady Royce went once more to examine the ballroom before she went to dress. It looked as it had when she had first danced there as a young bride, so very long ago. Footmen were lighting candles in the sconces, casting a golden glow over the cream brocade upholstery of the chairs and the deep yellow-green leaves of the palms. The musicians were practicing on their dais, a sweet, old-fashioned minuet.

If she closed her eyes, she could almost imagine herself swirling about the dance floor with her husband again . . .

A gentle hand touched her arm. "Edward," she whispered, without thinking. When she turned around to look, she found not her husband, but her son, who was his very image.

"No, Mother. It is me," Phillip said gently.

She laughed. "Oh! I am very silly. I was thinking of my first ball here. Your father was so very handsome!" She laid her hand against his cheek, and he covered it with his own warm palm. "You look so much like him."

"I miss him, too, Mother," he said. "I remember how much he enjoyed a ball! He would like this tonight."

"Indeed he would. But you are not yet dressed in your costume, dear! We should be getting ready."

"We will, Mother, but I wanted to speak with you about something first."

"Of course. What is it? Is there something you do not like about the arrangements? I know that you prefer your quiet . . ."

"It is not that at all. I am sure the ball will be perfect." He took her arm and led her to some chairs arranged in a quiet corner, out of the way of the hurrying servants. "I have some news for you."

"*Good* news?" she asked worriedly. She wanted nothing to spoil this night.

Phillip laughed. "Of course it is good news! I have spoken to Lady Willowby this afternoon, and have been given 'official' permission to make it public. I asked Cassandra Richards to marry me, and she accepted."

She stared at him in stunned silence. Was her fondest hope, the one she had thought could never come true, happening? Had her son found love?

"You and—and Miss Richards are to be married?" she whispered.

His hopeful smile flickered at her wide-eyed shock. "Yes. I love her, Mother. And, amazingly enough, she returns my feelings. I would like to announce the betrothal tonight at the ball."

Pure, perfect joy, unlike any she had felt since the night of that long-ago ball, burst through her. She flung her arms around him, sobbing against his neck.

"Mother!" he said, startled. "Are you not happy?"

"I am beyond happy! All my prayers are answered, my dear Phillip. I am to have a daughter at last!"

If either of them had looked up to the portrait of Edward Leighton that hung on the wall, they might have noticed a suspicious brightness about the painted blue eyes. But the sparkle turned back to matte emptiness before they even quit laughing.

"What do you think about my new coiffure, Antoinette?" Cassie asked, twisting about to examine her reflection in the dressing table mirror. Long, carefully formed dark curls bounced and danced over her shoulders. "I think it may be a bit—silly."

"Not at all!" Antoinette answered, adjusting her own costume around her tall figure. She was dressed as Cleopatra, in long pleats of white muslin, cinched in at the waist with gold cord and with a collar of turquoise and coral beads over her shoulders. A gold headdress in the shape of a serpent sat atop her upswept hair. She looked exotic and regal. Cassie only wished she had thought of being Cleopatra first. "You are a shepherdess, Cassie. You are meant to look a bit silly."

Cassie *wanted* to be elegant, as Antoinette was. This was not a night for "silly"!

Yet her happiness at the prospect of dancing with Phillip, as well as the announcement he wanted to make, overcame everything. She laughed, gave her curls one last shake, and went to take the dressmaker's box containing her costume out of the wardrobe.

She lifted the lid—and paused, puzzled. "Antoinette."

"Yes?" Antoinette said, fussing with her headdress.

"This is not the costume the dressmaker delivered the other day, is it?"

Antoinette came to peer over her shoulder. "Not at all! You tried it on, remember? It was not like that one bit. Is this a joke?"

"I am not sure." Cassie unfolded the costume in the box. It was assuredly *not* the blue-and-yellow shepherdess dress. The straw, ribbon-trimmed bonnet and the crook were missing, too.

This was a gown in the style of the Restoration era, and, despite its obvious age, it was in beautiful condition. The pale blue satin was whole and unfaded, and the copious ruffles of white lace were only slightly yellowed. All the pearl beadwork on the bodice was intact.

Cassie unfolded it, spreading it over her lap. It was the most beautiful gown she had ever seen.

Antoinette reached out to touch some of the lace. "It looks like one of Louisa's gowns."

"Why would she take my shepherdess costume away and leave this?" Whatever the ghost's strange reasons, though, Cassie was glad she had done it. She would feel like a queen in this glorious satin.

Antoinette shrugged. "Maybe she wishes *she* could dance at the ball tonight. Here, let me help you put it on."

It fit perfectly once Antoinette had tightened Cassie's corset strings. The satin lay smooth against her, the ruffles frothing about her like the foam of the sea.

Cassie took her mother's pearl necklace out of the jewel case and clasped it around her throat. Now she felt absolutely perfect.

"Is it time now, Lady Lettice? Is the ball starting?" Angelo said excitedly, dancing about the East Tower until the bells sewn on his doublet jangled.

"Very nearly." Lettice peered closely at herself in the mirror, straightening her headdress atop her upswept red hair. The solidifying spell had worked beautifully, and Sir Belvedere and Louisa were off on their last-minute errands. Her plan was falling carefully into place. She should be satisfied and excited.

She felt nervous, though, and almost—almost afraid.

Lettice had never been afraid in her life, or her death! But she was now. Fear hovered around the edges of her mind, and caused her high lace ruff to flutter with the force of her trembling.

Angelo paused at her side, peering up at her with his wizened little face. "What is wrong, Lady Lettice?" he asked, tugging at her skirts.

Lettice forced herself to smile carelessly. "Not a thing! Our plan is coming together."

Angelo smiled. "And soon we will be completely rid of Mr. Bates! Angelo can hardly wait."

Neither could Lettice. If she could just as easily rid herself of these fearful premonitions . . .

Chapter Twenty-Three

"Remember, she is dressed as a shepherdess," Mr. Bates hissed. He and his cousin sat in the darkened recesses of their carriage, parked out of sight just inside the gates of Royce Castle.

For the first time, the languid Mr. Morland looked uncertain. He peered out the window as guests' horses and carriages processed through the gates and up the drive. "Will there not be many shepherdesses there? Ladies seem dashed fond of that sort of thing."

"None of them will have hair like hers," Mr. Bates muttered.

"Are you certain this is a good idea, Paul?"

Mr. Bates shot him a glare. "We have no choice! Are you turning coward on me now?"

"Of course not! It is just . . ."

"Just nothing. This is the plan. If you have no stomach for it, you can start walking back to our lodgings. And keep walking all the way to Jamaica. But don't expect to have a home with *me* when you get there."

Mr. Morland lapsed back into silence.

"Right," said Mr. Bates. "Well, I am off, then. You wait here and keep an eye out for my signal."

He drew the hood of his domino up over his head and slipped out of the carriage, blending in with the stream of guests heading toward the castle. Soon, very soon, Miss Richards and Lord Royce would be deeply sorry they had crossed him.

Cassie stood outside the ballroom doors, watching the dancers move through the patterns of the dance. Beneath the rich glow of the lights, they were a blur of many colors and many time periods. There were knights and their damsels, Harlequin and Columbine, Renaissance poets, Lucrezia Borgia, Henry VIII and Anne Boleyn, Aphrodite, Marie Antoinette. And there were also several gentlemen who had obviously thought it beneath their dignity to wear a costume, and had appeared in evening dress and masks.

The rich fabrics and the ladies' jewels shimmered, and champagne sparkled in heavy crystal.

Cassie's foot tapped lightly to the bright music, and she felt a thrill of excitement as she examined the magical scene. It truly looked like a fairyland, an enchanted place. The perfect spot to announce her new happiness to all the world.

If only she could see her would-be betrothed!

She saw Antoinette-Cleopatra talking to the Lewishams over by the window, and Aunt Chat, in her deep green velvet Eleanor of Aquitaine gown, dancing. And Lady Royce was greeting her guests, looking magnificent in black satin and pearls as Queen Elizabeth.

From the corner of her eye, Cassie saw a flash of white. She turned her head to watch as Lady Lettice, with Angelo close behind her, made her majestic way across the room. Obviously other people saw her, too, as they made way for her wide white silk skirts. She paused to speak with a cluster of guests, peering close at their masked faces as they talked. Then she looked at Angelo, shook her head, and continued on to the next group.

Whatever was she about?

Cassie did not have long to puzzle over Lady Lettice, though. A gentle hand touched one of the lace ruffles of her sleeve, and she looked over her shoulder.

"Phillip!" she said happily, putting her arms around him in a quick embrace, after she ascertained that no one was paying any attention to them. "There you are. I couldn't see anyone in there who looked the least bit like you." She stepped back to examine his costume. "But why are you dressed like a monk, of all things?"

His long brown robe covered him from the top of his hooded head to his feet. He glanced quickly around, then whispered, "This is not actually my costume."

Cassie was puzzled. "It isn't? Then why are you wearing it?"

"To cover up my real costume, of course."

"Don't be silly! Let me see it."

"I think I would prefer to wear the robe."

Cassie laughed. "It is absolutely drab! And that fabric is scratchy. How can we dance if you keep scratching me?"

"You are most persuasive, my dear. If I have to take it off in order to dance with you, then I shall." He looked around once more, then loosened his rope belt and pulled the garment off.

Beneath it, he wore the most amazing thing Cassie had ever seen. She clapped her hand to her mouth to hold her giggles in. They would not be contained, though; they burst forth in a merry torrent. "Oh, Phillip! You look—incredible."

His Greek chiton fell in white silk folds almost to his knees and was trimmed in gold embroidery worked in a Greek key pattern, and held in with a gold sash. The gold sandals on his feet laced up to meet the hem. Even behind his gold mask he looked most disgruntled.

"Incredibly foolish, you mean," he muttered, tugging the embroidered hem lower. "I never should have listened to my mother when she suggested I wear a Grecian costume."

"Not foolish at all," Cassie said, going up on tiptoe to kiss his cheek. "You look very handsome. The most handsome gentleman at the ball, I would vow."

He smiled down at her. "And you are the most beautiful lady. This is an exquisite gown. But I thought you were meant to be a shepherdess."

Cassie preened for him in her blue satin. "I was, but someone took that costume and left this in its place."

"Someone?"

"I suspect Louisa. This looks like one of her gowns." She paused, remembering Lady Lettice and Angelo walking about the ballroom. "Speaking of ghosts . . ."

Phillip gave a long-suffering sigh. "What about the ghosts? What mischief have they done now? I swear, my life was far easier before I believed in them."

"They have done no mischief that I know of—yet. But I just saw Lady Lettice and Angelo mingling among the guests. And where they are, Louisa and Sir Belvedere are sure to follow."

Phillip peered past her into the ballroom, his gaze searching through the company. His expression was wary and surprised. "The guests could see them, then?"

Cassie took her white satin half mask out of her

reticule and tied it over her face. "Oh, yes. She was talking to them and everything. You are not angry, are you?"

Phillip laughed. "Of course not! Surprised, perhaps. I find it so strange and amazing that they have been a part of my life all these years and I am only now seeing them. But I would imagine they get rather bored. A masked ball is the perfect opportunity for them to get out; no one will think their clothes odd at all."

"Exactly! I am sure they are up to no mischief at all." But Cassie bit her lip uncertainly.

"I think my mother has seen us. Are you ready to go in?"

"More than ready."

She took his arm, and swept into the ballroom to join the swirl of color, music, and excitement.

Louisa twirled about in the middle of Cassie's bedroom floor, enjoying the way her skirts belled out around her ankles. It had been decades since she had changed her gown, and the shepherdess costume was very different from her usual heavy satin and silk skirts. It was made of light muslin, with a yellow-and-blue-striped skirt, and a bodice and panniers of blue flowers on a yellow background.

She straightened the blue satin bow at the low, square neckline and smoothed the ruffles of the elbow-length sleeves. It was very fortunate that she and Cassie were almost the same size, and that she was able to change clothes at all. She hadn't been certain she could solidify, having never tried it before, but the spell Lady Lettice had taught her worked. But she knew that it would not last long, and that she would be very tired when it was all over.

The dress looked quite fetching, and she was rather fond of the adorable little shepherd's crook, with its cluster of blue and yellow ribbons. But the hair was all wrong. Louisa twisted one of her ringlets around her finger, examining its silvery-blond color. Cassie's hair was as dark as night.

She would just have to try to will it to change. She had never done that before, either. If solidifying would leave her exhausted, she had no idea what a change of hair color would do.

Ah, well. There was only one way to find out. Louisa closed her eyes, clutched the ringlet tightly in her fist, and filled her mind with the color black.

When she opened her eyes, the curl she held out was coal-colored. She pulled the thick mass of her hair over her shoulder, and saw that it had all turned brunette.

"Oh, I *am* good!" she cried, doing a happy little dance.

Lady Lettice came into the room then, opening the door and closing it behind her like a real human being. "Are you ready yet, Louisa? I think . . ." She paused, tilting her head back to examine Louisa. "Oh! You look just like Cassie with that dark hair."

"Thank you," Louisa said, and reached for the yellow half mask with blue ribbons. "Is Mr. Bates here yet?"

"Not at present. I looked at every guest in that ballroom, and none of them looked like Mr. Bates or his cousin. I left Angelo there to keep a sharp eye on things—if he can tear himself away from staring at the refreshments." Lady Lettice peered into the dressing table mirror and straightened her jeweled headdress with its long white and silver veil.

"I am ready," Louisa said, picking up Cassie's bonnet and the shepherd's crook.

"I do hope Mr. Bates appears soon. We can remain in this solid state for only a few hours."

"Oh, we will be done with this business long before that," Louisa answered confidently. "We will even have time for dancing after!"

"That is my costume!" Cassie whispered in Phillip's ear as they waltzed around the dance floor. She looked over his shoulder at the edge of the ballroom, where a slender figure in a blue-and-yellow shepherdess costume stood. The figure waved the crook at Cassie, then turned and disappeared back into the crowd, dark curls bouncing.

"Someone else is wearing your costume?" Phillip asked, spinning her jauntily around a corner.

"The shepherdess one I told you about. I think it is Louisa, but she has black hair now. She looks just like me!"

"Well, people do say imitation is the sincerest form of flattery."

Cassie laughed. "Who says that?"

"I am not sure. I think it was my mother, when she saw Lady Paige wearing a new bonnet in church that was almost exactly like her own."

She glanced once more over at where the shepherdess had stood, but she was quite gone. Cassie still thought it was very odd, but then she smiled up at Phillip and determined to concentrate on him, and him alone, for tonight. After all, this was their magical night, one they would tell their grandchildren about one day.

And it was certainly proving memorable so far. The music, the laughter of the guests, and the wonderful sensation of twirling about in the dance with Phillip, conspired to create a glittering entertainment. Cassie could not seem to cease smiling.

Yes, this was their night. Nothing, not even mischievous ghosts, could ruin it.

Louisa moved through the crowd, reveling in the feeling of being at a ball again. Usually Royce Castle was so quiet, with only the other ghosts for company. In her life, Louisa had been so fond of parties, just like this one. She hummed along with the music as she walked, smiling at the other guests and eyeing the bubbling, golden champagne enviously. But being solid only went so far. It probably did not permit drinking.

Even if it had, she needed to keep her wits about her if she was to foil Mr. Bates' plan. She looked over at Lady Lettice, who shook her head slightly. No, Mr. Bates was not there yet. Then she turned to Sir Belvedere, who was talking with Cassie's aunt. He also shook his head.

Where could the villain be? Louisa frowned. If he did not appear soon, their plan would have to change. They *could* foil him in their usual forms, but it would be harder.

She scanned over the rest of the company, carefully scrutinizing every man's disguise. A cardinal, a Louis XIV, a medieval prince, Shakespeare, a Cavalier . . .

She paused and looked back at that last one. He *was* dressed as a Cavalier from her own lifetime, his blue satin and white lace a perfect coordinate to the gown she had given Cassie. His long, dark hair fell from beneath a wide-brimmed, plumed hat, which concealed his features.

Then he turned his head and looked directly at her.

"No!" Louisa gasped aloud, startling the people who stood beside her. "It cannot be."

She took one step toward him, but he vanished.

And someone grabbed her shoulder from behind, pulling her away from the crowd. She twisted around to look, half-hoping, half-fearing . . .

It was not *him*, though. It was Mr. Bates. He wore a hooded domino, yet it was still easy to see who it was. His eyes burned through the eyeholes of his mask, and his grip on her was strong and angry.

Louisa longed to bash him on the head with her crook, but then she remembered she was meant to be Cassie, who had no idea about this plan. She put a look of confusion on her face and hoped her old skills at amateur theatricals had not left her.

"What is this?" she said softly, with a quiver of fear in her voice. She remembered to keep it pitched low and soft to disguise it. She made her shoulders shake beneath his hands. It should be easy to lull this thickheaded man into thinking he had a poor, weak female in his grasp. He was the sort who always underestimated women. "Who are you?"

"What, Miss Richards? You do not recognize me?" He sneered at her. "I suppose you thought you would never see me again."

"Mr. Bates?" she gasped. "Lord Royce told you never to come back here!"

"That *scholar*? He couldn't stop me, now, could he? Here I am." He laughed, a soft, humorless, chilling sound. Even Louisa, who had nothing to fear from him, shivered. "I see he has abandoned you to waltz with someone else. How ungallant."

"That is a friend of mine he is dancing with! And if you think . . ."

"Hush!" Mr. Bates squeezed her shoulder cruelly, and showed her a glimpse of a gleaming dagger hidden beneath his domino. "Stop chattering, woman. I do not have all night to stand here listening to you. Come along." He slid a hard arm around her waist, and tugged her along the short distance to the French doors leading to the terrace.

Louisa pretended to dig her heels in, while waving her crook in a signal to Lady Lettice and Sir Belvedere. "Where are you going? Do not do this, Mr. Bates, I beg you!"

"Be quiet!" he hissed, pulling her across the terrace and down the stone steps. "You will see soon enough."

Louisa feigned sobbing and protestations, but behind her mask she was secretly smiling. This was all turning out even better than she had hoped!

In all the excitement of her abduction, she quite forgot the Cavalier she had glimpsed so briefly in the ballroom.

Chapter Twenty-Four

Mr. Bates pulled Louisa inexorably along the dark drive, leaving the lights and noise of the ball farther behind with every step. Louisa, though inwardly highly amused by the proceedings, did her very best to appear frightened and unsure. It was not hard to do; in her life, Louisa had been fond of amateur theatricals and had often acted in plays during house parties at Royce Castle. She was just happy to try the skill again.

In that vein, she gave a little whimper and said, "Why are you doing this? I do not understand! I thought we were friends."

His arm tightened on her waist as he half dragged, half carried her across the gravel. "Friends? A *friend* would have sold me the land. A *friend* would not have been so stubborn and unkind."

"Why do you need the land, anyway?" Louisa said, feigning confusion. "It is all I have left in Jamaica, while you possess so very much."

"So you think," he muttered.

"What do you mean?"

"Never mind. Just come along and quit chattering at me. There is the carriage just ahead."

The black, closed vehicle was half-hidden in the shadows at the edge of the drive, just outside the tall gates. A coachman, muffled in a dark cloak and a hat pulled low over his brow, sat on the box.

As they moved closer, the door opened, and Mr. Bates' cousin stuck his head out. "There you are at last! I thought I was going to have to come fetch you. Did you stop to indulge in some of the champagne?" He snickered.

"Very funny indeed. Our little guest here was late coming to the party." Mr. Bates lifted her off her feet and pushed her toward the carriage door.

As he did so, a voice called, "Here! What do you think you're doing?"

Louisa looked over Mr. Bates' shoulder to see a footman running down the drive in their direction. *Oh, how tiresome*, she thought. A rescue attempt would simply ruin everything.

Apparently, Mr. Bates felt the same way. He stuffed her unceremoniously into the carriage, causing her to lose her crook, and climbed in after her. "Drive, blast it!" he shouted at the coachman, and they took off down the lane with a jarring lurch.

Louisa landed atop Mr. Morland, who set her aright with more wandering hands and leering glances than the act strictly required.

Louisa snatched the bonnet off her head and glared at him from behind her mask. He just smirked back at her. She slid into the corner, as far away from him as she could get. Really, he was even more unpleasant than his cabbage-headed cousin.

"So, now that you have me here, what are you going to do with me?" she asked, smoothing her disarranged skirts.

"We are going to Gretna Green, my dear Miss Richards, where we will be married," Mr. Bates answered.

Admittedly, Louisa's geography was a bit rusty, but . . . "Isn't that rather far away?"

"You will be so hopelessly compromised by the time we reach there, that you will be *glad* to marry me," he said. He was obviously trying for an air of confidence, but Louisa sensed the uncertainty in him.

Really, she thought, it was just too easy. If he had succeeded in making off with the real Cassie, there would have been a thousand opportunities for her to escape between here and Scotland. This was not a very well-thought-out plan on Mr. Bates' part.

If there was anything worse than a villain, in Louisa's estimation, it was a stupid villain. It was just a good thing that soon he would be gone from England forever, and would bother no one with his nuisances again.

Except for the poor people of Jamaica, of course.

Louisa peered out the window, wondering idly when Sir Belvedere and Lady Lettice were going to make their appearances. Suddenly, much to her shock, Mr. Bates grabbed her arm and pulled her onto his lap.

"What are you doing?" she screamed as his wet lips found her bare neck. "Let go of me at once!"

"We might as well start the compromising now," he said, reaching for her skirt while his cousin laughed. "Just in case you have any idea of leaving us soon."

Louisa beat him over the head and shoulders with her bonnet. "Release me, you ridiculous looby!"

"Not just yet," he answered.

Absolutely furious, Louisa squeezed her eyes shut and concentrated very, very hard on her hair, and then on her entire body. Gradually, she felt the faint tingling sensation that meant she was moving from her temporary solid form back to her usual insubstantial state.

When Mr. Bates reached one of his meaty hands to her breast, he found no warm, yielding flesh. Only cold air.

He fell forward, his face turning from scarlet with lust to chalk-white with fear. His mouth opened, but no sound emerged. He just sat there, frozen, staring at her.

Mr. Morland edged back along the seat. "What is happening?"

Louisa took off her mask, sending her now-blond curls tumbling about her shoulders, and turned to look at him.

He gasped for air. "You—you are not Miss Richards!"

"Of course I am not. You stupid men snatched the wrong woman. My name is Louisa, but you may call me Lady Royce. You can find my actual self in the family crypt at St. Anne's Church, but I occasionally come back to pay calls on very special people. Like yourselves."

"As do I," said Lady Lettice, appearing on the seat next to Mr. Morland. "How do you do? I am Lady Lettice Leighton. And that is Angelo down there, beneath the seat. The one who is tying your ankles together."

Mr. Morland looked down, and saw that small hands were indeed busily engaged in tying his ankles. A wizened little face peeked up at him.

"Hello!" Angelo said merrily.

Mr. Morland screamed and fumbled at the door latch. "Stop the carriage right now! This moment!"

"Certainly, sir," Sir Belvedere's voice answered. "Your order is my command."

The carriage ground to a halt, and Mr. Morland finally got the door open and fell out onto the road. He pulled his still-speechless cousin with him, and the two of them ran as fast as they could into the darkness at the side of the road. Mr. Morland was forced to hop rather than strictly run, thanks to Angelo, but he was very fast nonetheless.

It was just as Louisa, Lady Lettice, and Sir Belvedere had planned.

Louisa laughed and laughed as she watched them fade away, the underbrush rustling until finally there was only silence. "Oh, I did enjoy that!" she said happily. "It was over much too quickly, though."

"Are you quite all right?" Lady Lettice asked. "We followed as quickly as we could, but we were not certain which direction you went in."

"I am perfectly well, even though that idiot tried to compromise me." Louisa put her head out to see Sir Belvedere sitting atop the box. "What happened to the coachman, Sir Belvedere?"

"Oh, we set him down about a mile past. He is sure to be at the village by now. He was so foxed I am sure he thought we were a hallucination. I am becoming an excellent driver, don't you think?"

"Superb," said Lady Lettice. "But if we sit about here all night, we shall miss the entire ball. I want to dance at least once."

"And so do I!" Louisa agreed heartily. She looked out the window as Sir Belvedere turned the carriage and set off toward the castle. "You do not think they will try to come back, do you?"

"Of course not. Didn't you see their expressions? They were frightened out of their wits. What little wits they possess, that is." Lady Lettice lifted up the little mirror at her belt and examined her coiffure. "I think, my dear Louisa, that we should resolidify before we reach the castle, if we want to dance without frightening all the guests."

"Forgive me, my lord, but I must speak with you," a footman said in a breathless voice, as if he had just run a great distance.

Phillip and Cassie were talking to Lady Royce, but their conversation ceased at this quiet interruption.

"Of course," said Phillip. "Is there some sort of trouble?"

"Trouble?" Cassie echoed. The only "trouble" she could think of was Mr. Bates. Could he have returned to ruin the ball?

"I think—I fear a lady may have been abducted," the footman gasped. "I saw her being carried away from the ball, down the drive. She dropped this before the man put her in a carriage, and they drove away." He held up a shepherd's crook, trimmed in now-bedraggled blue and yellow ribbons.

"That is my crook!" Cassie cried.

Phillip looked down at her, puzzled. "Your crook, my dear?"

"The one that went with my other costume. The costume I thought I saw someone wearing earlier." She turned to the footman. "Was the lady wearing a blue-and-yellow shepherdess gown?"

He shrugged helplessly. "I fear it was too dark to be sure, Miss Richards. She *was* wearing a light-colored bonnet."

"And the man with her?" Phillip asked.

"He was wearing a sort of hooded cloak, my lord. But I think there may have been two men there."

"*Two* men?" Cassie caught at Phillip's arm. "Mr. Bates and Mr. Morland, it has to be! They have come back."

"Why would you think that?" Phillip asked quietly. "Have you heard something from them?"

Cassie shook her head. "Not at all. But it sounds exactly like something they would do. Mr. Bates was not at all happy to be thwarted in the matter of my land. Oh, poor Louisa!"

"Louisa?" Aunt Chat said, coming up to their small group just in time to hear these last words. "Has something happened to Louisa?"

"I saw someone earlier, walking about dressed in my shepherdess costume," Cassie explained. "I am sure it was her. She left me this gown and took mine. Now Mr. Bates has snatched her, thinking it was me."

"How terrible!" Lady Royce said. "What if he does her harm?"

"Mother, Cassandra," said Phillip. "I do not wish to appear unconcerned about your friend, but how exactly can Mr. Bates hurt her? She is, er, no longer alive."

"I still do not like this," Cassie murmured.

"Let us go find them," said Phillip. "I'm not certain how long they have been gone, but they can't have gone far. I don't imagine Mr. Bates will care to keep traveling when he realizes his mistake! But I do not like the idea of Mr. Bates coming back to the castle to hurt you." His expression darkened. "I do not like it at all."

Cassie couldn't help a small shiver at the thought of being carried off by Mr. Bates. If Louisa had in fact taken her place, she owed her a great debt of gratitude. "Shall we go look for them, then?"

Phillip nodded. "Very well, but we will not go far. Mother, you and Lady Willowby stay here and make certain the ball goes on smoothly."

Lady Royce nodded. "What about your—important announcement?"

"We will make it when we return, with Louisa safely in tow."

So it was that Phillip, Cassie, and Antoinette set off down the drive, still clad in their costumes and armed only with torches and Antoinette's ankh-topped staff. But they did not have to go a great distance. A black, closed carriage, drawn by a coach-man in clattering armor, turned in the gates just as they reached the end of the drive.

"Good eve to you!" Sir Belvedere cried, drawing up on the reins.

Louisa and Lady Lettice appeared at the window. "What are you all doing out here?" Lady Lettice said. "Is the ball over already?"

"Oh, it cannot be!" Louisa complained. "I have not had one dance yet."

"Are you all right, Louisa?" Cassie cried, running up to the carriage, her blue satin skirts held up above the gravel and dust. "Was it Mr. Bates who took you away?"

"Indeed it was," Louisa said. She opened the carriage door and stepped down onto the drive, shaking out her gown. "The cabbage-head. He tried to take some most indecent liberties." Then she laughed merrily. "Oh, but you should have seen his face when I revealed my identity! I do not think we will ever see him or his odious cousin again."

"Liberties?" Cassie said, dismayed. "Louisa! How terrible. I am so sorry."

Louisa gave her a puzzled look. "Why are *you* sorry, Cassie? You did not kidnap me."

"But I was the one he meant to take. If not for me, you would not have been put in such an unpleasant position."

Louisa shrugged. "What could he do to me? I am already dead! We were just happy there was something we could do for you, after all your kindness to us. Besides, it was vastly amusing."

Phillip stepped up to her and gave her a deep bow. "I can never thank you enough, my lady," he said softly, seriously. "I owe you a great debt of gratitude for saving the woman I love."

Louisa looked at him steadily. "I fear I always thought you were rather stuffy. Even as a child, you were so solitary, so intent on your purpose—like my husband. But now I know what a true and gallant heart you have. I am very sorry for all the silly tricks we have played on you over the years, like spilling your ink and disarranging your papers."

"And I, too, apologize, my lord," Sir Belvedere said, climbing down from the carriage box.

"*I* have nothing to apologize for," Lady Lettice said. "Do you, Angelo?"

"Not I!" Angelo's voice piped from the depths of the carriage.

"Then we should go back to the ball, before it is all over and done with," said Lady Lettice.

"I quite agree," answered Phillip. Then he put his arm around Cassie and smiled down at her. "We have a very important announcement to make."

Chapter Twenty-Five

Phillip stood in the center of a group of well-wishers, watching across the room as Cassie was enveloped and carried away by just another such group. Her cheeks were flushed and glowing from the excitement of the evening and the emotion of the announcement of their betrothal, and her eyes were shining like dark stars. She laughed at something Mr. Lewisham said to her, and the sweet sound seemed to hover over the chatter like a silvery cloud.

What a fortunate man he was, he thought, as all the crowd and noise seemed to fade away, leaving only her in his sight and senses. Only weeks before, he had been so solitary, concerned only with his work. Now a whole new life stretched out before him, beckoning him down a new road. A road of love and marriage, a place in a community, and, one day, a family. Children with Cassie's sparkling brown eyes and mischievous ways.

He was not certain he was exactly prepared for it, but he was looking forward to it. Very much.

"Congratulations, Lord Royce," someone beside

him said. "You are so fortunate to have gained the hand of such a fine lady."

Peter looked over to see Sir Belvedere standing there in his armor. "Thank you," he said. "She is indeed a very fine lady."

"She rather reminds me of—of someone I knew once, long ago," Sir Belvedere said.

They both watched for a moment as Cassie moved through the crowd, with Antoinette on one side of her and Lady Lettice on the other. Angelo trailed behind them, holding a bowl of marzipan candies in his hands and smiling down at them blissfully.

"I also wanted to thank you again for your actions tonight," Phillip said. "You and Louisa and Lady Lettice. It was very brave of you."

If Sir Belvedere had had the capability, Phillip was certain he would have blushed. As it was, he shuffled a bit in his armor, causing a great racket. " 'Twas nothing at all, my lord. Why, what could such a knave as Mr. Bates do to us!" He lowered his voice and said confidentially, "We *are* already dead, y'know."

"I know. That does not make it any less brave. When Louisa allowed herself to be carried off in Cassandra's place, she saved her a great deal of fear and pain. I will always be grateful for that."

"I know Louisa did not mind doing it at all. Truth to tell, I think she found it rather exciting."

"I do wish you had let me know what was going to happen. I could have assisted you."

Sir Belvedere shook his head. "We did not want to trouble you, my lord. Especially on such an important night as this, with the announcement of your betrothal."

"Nevertheless . . ." Phillip was interrupted when his mother announced the last dance before supper, the "Sir Roger de Coverley," which Phillip was meant to lead off with his new fiancée. Sir Belvedere melted into the crowd, and Phillip went to claim Cassie for the dance.

She took his hand, and let him lead her into their places in line, giving him the most brilliant smile Phillip had ever seen.

How Louisa had missed dancing! Her feet tingled with joy at moving through the familiar patterns again, and she hummed beneath her breath along with the tune. Oh, it *was* delightful! Truly the finest night she had known since the end of her mortal life.

Her partner, a rather portly Harlequin, twirled her about, and she skipped back to her place in line to await her next partner. When she spun around to meet him, she found herself holding hands with the Cavalier she had glimpsed earlier.

"William!" she whispered, stumbling a bit in her surprise. It had been almost one hundred and thirty years since she had seen her husband, but he had not changed a bit. "It *was* you I saw."

"Hello, Louisa," he answered in his deep, serious voice. Then he spun her back into her place in line and went on to the next lady.

Louisa's feet automatically carried her through the patterns of the dance, but she scarcely even glanced at her new partner. She twisted her neck about, trying to keep William in her sight, but he was always lost in the swirl of dancers.

Perhaps she had not really seen him. Perhaps she had only imagined seeing him again, after all this time.

But then she shook her head. That had not been imagination! She had truly seen William again, touched his hand. And it had been as jolting, as exalting, as it was at the ball where she had first met him.

The dance did not bring them together again. As soon as the music ended, she made her way through the tangle of people pairing off for supper. She searched every face carefully, and found three men costumed as Cavaliers, but none were William.

At last, she felt a soft, feather-light touch on her shoulder and looked up to see him there.

"William!" she cried. She went up on tiptoe to put her arms around his shoulders, burying her face in the familiar curve of his neck. His long hair tickled her cheek, as it always had when they kissed. "It is you. I knew it!"

"Yes," he said, his own arms coming about her waist, pulling her closer into him. "It is me."

"Where have you been all these years? Why did you move on and leave me here? Why did I have to stay so long?"

"So many questions," he said, his voice full of laughter. "You are still the same Louisa."

She pulled back to frown at him. "Do not make fun of me!"

He looked back at her steadily. "I would not do that."

"Would you not?"

"Of course not. We have been apart far too long for that. And as for your questions . . ." He looked about the still-crowded ballroom. "Come with me."

He drew her into the dim, deserted library and shut the door behind them. Louisa went and perched herself on the edge of Lord Royce's desk, and her husband came to stand beside her.

"We are all sent to Earth to learn something," he said. "It just took you a bit longer than some."

Louisa was puzzled. "What sort of lesson do we have to learn?"

"It is different for every person. But yours and mine were very similar."

"What was it?" As usual, William tried her quick-silver patience. But she was so very happy to see him again that it almost did not matter.

Rather than answer her question directly, William smiled and said, "We were in love when we married, were we not, Louisa?"

She thought back to those golden days of their courtship and wedding. "Oh, yes."

"Yet our downfall was that we were selfish people. We cared too much about ourselves and not enough about our marriage. After the king was restored to the throne, I should have come back to you. Instead, I stayed at Court, trying to gain favor. I left you alone here."

Well, not strictly alone, Louisa thought, tears prickling at her eyes. That had been the problem. The memory of those days still had the power to hurt her: the loneliness, the waiting. And the parties she had held here, trying to forget. "That was no excuse for my behavior."

"Perhaps not. But I am as much to blame for that as you were. Just as I was to blame for your death."

Louisa looked up at him, startled. "How so?"

He took her hand in his. "If I had been here, taking care of you as I should have, it would not have happened. We could have had children and a life together. That was the lesson I had to learn, and I learned it well when I heard that you had died. My lesson, and yours, was that only our love, our marriage, our time together, mattered. Not favor at Court, not wealth and land."

"But I always knew that!" Louisa cried, bewildered and touched, and very, very sad.

"No," William answered gently. "You knew that you were hurt, that I could not give you what you wanted. But you did not see that we as individuals were not so important—only the love we found was. And you realized that by helping Phillip and Cassandra to not make the same mistake."

Louisa thought back on so many things, on their own marriage, on the past few weeks with Phillip and Cassie. She had seen how very much they cared about each other and how they tried to deny that at first. Just as she had been denying her love for William ever since the night she drank too much brandy in her despair over him and went tumbling over the cliff.

And she now knew that what William said was the truth, and she had learned her lesson well. It had just taken her decades longer, that was all.

"You see now, do you not?" William whispered. "Cassandra is you, and Phillip is me. And you have helped them to have the chance that we never had, thanks to our own stubbornness."

"I see," Louisa said with a joyful smile. "I see perfectly." She turned her face up to his for a kiss she had been waiting one hundred and thirty years for.

When it was over, William looked at her solemnly and said, "Are you ready to go, then?"

"Oh, yes. I am ready."

Within seconds, the library was utterly deserted, as if no one had ever been there at all.

Except for two shadowy figures in the corner.

"Do you think she is gone forever?" Lady Lettice asked, staring at the spot on the desk where Louisa and William had just been. She would have thought she would be glad to see Louisa gone, to have the East Tower all to herself. But she found that she felt strangely bereft.

"Oh, I am sure she will come back to visit one day," Sir Belvedere said, reaching into his armor to produce a handkerchief, which he presented to her with a flourish. "She will not be able to resist giving us all the gossip from the other side."

"No doubt," Lady Lettice said. "And I am very happy she found her husband again. It is only . . ."

"Only what?"

"Well, I am not sure *I* will ever find my love again. Or if he was ever truly my love in the first place."

Sir Belvedere patted her hand. "You will. We just have to learn our lessons, as William said. And we are intelligent people. We can do that, I am sure."

Lady Lettice smiled at him. "I am sure we can."

"In the meantime, would you care for a card game in the East Tower, fair lady?"

"I would enjoy that. But first, I must snatch Angelo away from the refreshments."

"It was a lovely ball. The finest ever, I am sure," Cassie sighed, leaning on Phillip's arm as he led her up the staircase and down the corridor toward her chamber. She had imbibed just a tiny bit too much champagne at supper, and her heeled slippers wobbled.

The house was quiet now, with all the guests departed or tucked up in their chambers, and the first grayish light of dawn peeped in at the windows. But Cassie still felt like she could dance for hours more.

"It was a splendid ball," Phillip agreed. "Though I hope you will not want to go on having masked balls every year when we are married." He tugged again at the hem of his costume, as he had been doing all evening.

Cassie laughed. "If I do, you will not have to come as an ancient Greek again."

"Will I not?" he said hopefully.

"No. You could be an ancient Roman!"

"Such a great difference."

"Indeed there is." She stopped at the door to her room and leaned back against the sturdy wood, smiling up at him. "But I confess I rather like *this* costume."

"Then I will wear it again, though only for you."

"Hm, that sounds quite acceptable to me." She kissed his cheek. "Thank you for tonight. It was indeed splendid."

"A night worthy to tell our grandchildren about?"

"Undoubtedly."

"Yet also, I fear, a long one. You should be asleep. My mother and your aunt will want to get started with wedding plans later, I am sure."

"I am ready for anything! Even wedding plans." But then she broke into a large, uncontrollable yawn. "I *am* rather sleepy, though. Good night, Phillip dear."

"Good night, my love."

Cassie kissed him once more, then ducked into her chamber, closing the door softly behind her.

Only when she heard his footsteps fading down the corridor did she turn to face the room and see the note that lay on the floor, a white square against the dark blue rug. She knelt down to pick it up, her satin skirts puddling around her, and opened it right there.

She read the short message twice, a smile spreading across her lips. "Oh, Louisa," she whispered. "Good fortune to you, my friend. Good fortune."

Epilogue

Five Years Later

"Penelope! Where are you?" Lady Lettice called, picking her way over the pebbles of the beach to peek into the tunnel entrance. She heard a soft, childish giggle, but pretended to be completely befuddled. "Lady Penelope Leighton. You must come out right this moment, or I shall be forced to fetch your father."

Dark, glossy curls peeped out from behind an upturned, rotting fishing boat. Then the whole child popped up, brown eyes shining with excitement and dust smeared across her dainty pink dress.

"Here I am, Lady Lettice!" she sang. "I was hiding from you."

"Indeed you were. You are becoming far too adept at that." Lady Lettice moved cautiously into the tunnel and took little Penelope by the hand. She had not been in the tunnels since that day more than five years ago, when Antoinette had summoned her there. She was not at all certain that she wanted to be there now, but she had to keep a sharp eye on

Penelope. Cassandra and Phillip had entrusted her
with their daughter's care this afternoon.

"I thought I told you to stay on the shore!" Lady
Lettice said to the grinning child.

"Did you, indeed?" Penelope said ingenuously.

"You know that I did."

"Well, I thought this *was* part of the shore. Does it
not have sand on the floor?" Penelope trailed one
tiny slipper through the grit of the tunnel floor. "Just
like the beach."

The child was too clever for her own good, Lady
Lettice thought wryly. "How did you find this
place?"

Penelope tugged away from her to peek into one
of the old crates stacked along the walls. "The man
told me."

"Man?" Lady Lettice said, puzzled. "Do you
mean Angelo?"

Penelope giggled. "No! Angelo is *Angelo*. The man
is just a man." She picked a stick up off the floor
and used it to poke through the contents of the crate.

Lady Lettice looked warily over her shoulder to
the dark depths of the tunnel. *A man*. Could it possibly be that Mr. Bates, who had disappeared from
England so long ago, and, as they had heard later,
disappeared from Jamaica as well, was here?

No, she reassured herself. Mr. Bates would not
come back; there was nothing for him to gain. Cassie
had long ago sold her land in Jamaica, and she was
long married, with Penelope, Edward, and new
baby Louisa.

But then—who was "the man"?

Lady Lettice did not see anyone, but she had a
creeping feeling about the tunnels. She walked over
to Penelope and pulled the child down from the
crates.

"Come along, now," she said. "We ought to return to the castle."

Penelope's lower lip trembled. "I am not finished exploring yet!"

"It is almost time for tea. Do you not want some of Cook's special lemon cakes, which she has made just for you?" Lady Lettice knew the value of bribery when it came to the Leighton children.

Penelope eyed the crates, obviously measuring their charms against the lure of cakes. "May I come back later, Lady Lettice?"

"If your parents say you may," Lady Lettice relented. "Perhaps Sir Belvedere or your nursemaid will bring you."

Penelope smiled happily and slipped her hand back into Lady Lettice's. As they turned to leave, a man's deep voice stopped them.

"Lettice," it said. "*Ma belle chère* Lettice."

Lady Lettice turned around and felt her breath catch in her throat. She pulled Penelope close to her.

"Jean-Pierre," she whispered.

"So you remember me?" he said, emerging fully from the shadows. After more than two hundred years, he was still handsome, as dark and dashing as a pirate. He grinned at her.

But Lady Lettice would not be lulled by a dashing smile and a French accent. Not again. "Of course I remember you," she snapped. "Unfortunately."

"That is the man I saw!" Penelope piped up, her voice muffled in the silk of Lady Lettice's gown.

Lady Lettice glared at Jean-Pierre. "So now you are using children in your schemes?" she said scathingly.

Jean-Pierre looked crestfallen. He held his elegant hands out to her beseechingly. "I would never have hurt her, *ma belle* Lettice. I merely wanted to bring you here, so I could talk to you."

Lady Lettice felt a tugging at her skirt and looked down to find Penelope watching her with melting dark eyes. "Please, Lady Lettice," she whispered. "He only wants to talk to you. And he is *so* handsome."

Lady Lettice's gaze snapped back to Jean-Pierre to see if he had heard that. He obviously had, as he was covering his laughter with his hand.

Lady Lettice frowned at him, and he instantly sobered. "What could we have to talk about?" she said. "I thought you said everything when you dashed off back to France."

"Please, Lettice," he said, taking a small step toward her. "All of that was not as it appeared. I have been waiting a very long time to explain to you. I may not have very long here. All I ask is that you listen to me, for half an hour, no longer. If you do not believe me, you need never see me again."

Lady Lettice could feel herself wavering, drawn in by the warm, musical cadence of his voice and by the lure of his words. It had been ever thus with him.

She glanced down at Penelope. "I cannot talk to you now," she said, keeping her tone stern and doubting. "I have to take Lady Penelope back to her parents."

"*Certainment*. But you will come back later?" he said hopefully.

"Perhaps." She turned around and walked with Penelope back to the entrance of the tunnel.

As she turned out into the bright sunshine, she heard him call, "Please come back, *ma couer*."

Lady Lettice smiled secretly. *My heart*.

"Are you finished packing yet, Cassie?" Antoinette asked, adding one last book to her own already full valise and snapping it shut.

Cassie knew she should be making the final decision on which gowns to take to Bath. They were meant to leave tomorrow, so that Phillip could discuss his newest book with Aunt Chat's Philosophical Society, and her trunk was not half-full. But she could not resist leaving her task to bend over baby Louisa's basket and tickle her soft little feet.

Louisa laughed and kicked out in infant joy.

"What a brilliant baby you are!" Cassie cooed. "So tiny, but you are already laughing and smiling. You know your mama, don't you? Yes, you do!"

Antoinette came over to peer into the basket, as well, holding out her finger for Louisa to grasp. "She knows her Aunt Antoinette, too! Though you know that her nursemaid says it is only air bubbles that make her laugh."

"That is not true! It is because she has such a merry nature. Penelope is going to be a brilliant scholar, like her father; Edward is going to be a great horseman; and Louisa is going to be my sunshine."

There was a quick knock at the door, and Melinda came in, holding a jewel case in her hand. Behind her was little Edward, galloping on the stick horse Sir Belvedere had made for him.

Edward was a handsome, sturdy little boy, and very swift as he trotted about his mother's chamber. Unlike his older sister, who had long been speaking in full sentences by the time she was his age, he did not have an extensive vocabulary. But he could say "horsie," "saddle," "phaeton," and "Tattersall's" beautifully, as well as doing a perfect imitation of a horse's neighing.

He did this now as he galloped, reining in only to give his mother and aunt kisses.

"Oh, my dears, I need your advice!" Melinda said. "Which jewels should I take to Bath? I asked Eddy, but the little darling is absolutely useless about fashion. He just wanted to put my emerald brooch on his horse's mane."

"Let us see," said Antoinette. She, Cassie, and Melinda sat down on Cassie's bed, and spread the baubles out over the counterpane.

They were debating the merits of amethysts and pearls when Penelope came dashing in, curls and ribbons flying wildly behind her. "Mama!" she cried. "Grandmama, Aunt Antoinette, you will never guess what I found on my walk!"

Edward galloped up to her. "Penny. Horsie."

"Yes, Eddy, your horse is beautiful," she said, pausing to pat her brother's horse on the head before she climbed up onto the bed beside her mother. "I saw a man in the tunnel."

"A man?" Startled, Cassie pulled Penelope into her arms, looking over her dark curls to where Lady Lettice hovered by the door. What sort of a man could her daughter possibly be seeing in the tunnel? "Who was it?"

"A Frenchman," said Penelope, obviously unconcerned. "He was dressed funny, in puffy pants and a short cloak. He wore an earring, like this one." She held up one of her grandmother's pearl drop earrings. "And he knew Lady Lettice. He called her *ma couer*. Mrs. King says that means 'heart,' " she said, quoting her new French teacher.

"Was it Jean-Pierre?" Antoinette asked Lady Lettice.

Lady Lettice gave her a sharp look. "Did you summon him, Antoinette?"

"Certainly not," Antoinette answered. "I have not summoned anyone since you and Angelo. I have been spending my time doing useful things, like studying herbs." And publishing a book of herbology, full of the healing properties of plants and recipes for making soaps and bath oils.

"Well, he is here anyway," said Lady Lettice.

"What does he want?" Melinda asked.

"I do not know. I did not stay to chat with him."

"He wants her to come back later," Penelope said helpfully. "He wants to explain everything to her. He said . . ."

"Yes, thank you, Penelope," Lady Lettice interrupted. "That is enough."

Penelope grinned.

"Will you talk to him?" Cassie asked Lady Lettice.

Lady Lettice shrugged carelessly, but she would not quite meet their eyes. "Perhaps. It would be— interesting to hear what he has to say."

"But even if you talk to him, you will not just— go, as Louisa did, will you?" Cassie asked. She rather liked having Lady Lettice's company. And the children adored her; they would howl with laughter whenever she did her walk-through-walls trick.

"Certainly not," Lady Lettice said. "Jean-Pierre and I are not like Louisa and her husband. William loved Louisa truly in the end. Jean-Pierre—well, I am not certain why he is here, but I do know that he does not love me."

With that, she turned and left the room, so agitated that she did not see Phillip standing there, and floated right over him.

Phillip studied the company gathered there and laughed. "Well! Is this a *soirée* and I am not invited?"

"Papa!" Penelope and Edward shouted. They both ran across the room and leapt on their father.

Phillip knelt down and kissed them both. "You two are behaving as if you have not seen me in a year, when it has only been since breakfast."

"It has been a very long time since breakfast, Papa," Penelope said.

"Indeed it has, my poppet." Holding a child under each arm, Phillip stood and faced the cluster of ladies.

"We were helping your mother decide which jewels to take to Bath," Cassie explained.

"And did you make a decision?" Phillip asked.

"Oh, yes!" Melinda said happily. "All of them. There is simply no predicting what sort of things we will be invited to in Bath. Now, I should go and be sure my maid has finished all my packing." She came and held out her hands for the children. "Why don't you come with your grandmama, Penny and Eddy, and help me."

When they were gone, Antoinette picked up baby Louisa's basket and carried it to the door. "I should finish my packing, as well. Louisa can advise me. One is never too young to learn about fashion," she said.

As soon as the door closed behind them, Phillip drew Cassie into his arms for a lingering kiss.

"Ah, alone at last," he murmured against her neck.

"Yes. I just love the subtle way Antoinette and your mother herded the children out the door." Cassie pulled him closer to her and leaned her head back with a blissful sigh as his teeth found her sensitive earlobe. "Not that I am not delighted, my dear, but why are you here? You usually work straight through to teatime."

He leaned away to gesture toward the papers he had dropped when the children came rushing at him. "I wanted to ask you your opinion on some of today's work. Or perhaps I should have asked Penelope. She can already name the entire pantheon of gods. But all of that can wait." He pulled her close again.

Cassie briefly debated whether she should tell him

about the return of Jean-Pierre, but then decided that that, too, could wait. She lost herself in his ardent kiss.

Children, work, Bath, ghosts—*all* that could wait. This time was just for them.

Read on for an excerpt from
another passionate Regency
romance by Amanda McCabe,

The Spanish Bride

Available March 2010 at
penguin.com or wherever
books are sold.

Spain, 1811

"I pronounce you man and wife. In the name of the Father, of
the Son, and of the Holy Spirit. Amen."

Carmen Montero, known in her Seville home as the Condesa
Carmen Pilar Maria de Santiago y Montero, trembled as the
priest made the sign of the cross over her head. Her fingers
were chill in her bridegroom's grasp.

It was done. She was married.

Again.

And she had always sworn to herself that she would never
again enter the unwelcome bonds of matrimony! She had relished her widowhood, the freedom to live as she pleased, apart
from restrictive Seville society. The freedom to work for the
cause of ridding Spain of the French interloper.

Her husband, Joaquin, Conde de Santiago, had been good
for nothing in life. She shuddered still to think of his cold, cruel
hands, his rages when, every month, she was *not* pregnant with
a son and heir. At least in death his money had proved useful,
working to help free Spain from the French.

Yes, she had sworn never to marry again.

Yet she had not foreseen that there could be anything in the
world like this man.

When she had first seen Major Lord Peter Everdean, the Earl of Clifton, her heart had skipped a beat, just as in the silly novels her friends had slipped into their convent school so long ago. Then it had leaped to life again. He was just as handsome as she had heard whispered by her friends at balls in Seville—the Ice Earl, as the ladies gigglingly called him.

But it had not been only his golden good looks that drew her. There was something in his beautiful ice blue eyes: a loneliness, an isolation that she had understood so deeply. It had been what she had felt all her life, this sense of not belonging.

Now perhaps she had found a place she *could* belong, even in the midst of war. Perhaps they both had.

Carmen peeked up through her lashes at the man beside her, only to find him watching her intently, a faint smile on his lips.

She smiled slowly in return, once she could catch her breath. The only word that could describe Peter was *beautiful*. He was as elegant and golden as an archangel, his fair hair and sun-bronzed skin gleaming in the candlelight of the small church. His broad shoulders gave a muscular contour to his red coat and his impossibly lean hips looked charming in tight-fitting white pantaloons. His rare smiles enticed women the entire length of Andalucia, and everyplace he went.

Now his ring was on *her* finger. Tall, skinny, bookish Carmen. This extraordinary man was her husband, her lover, even her friend.

It was all suddenly overwhelming, the incense in the church, the emotions in her heart. She swayed precariously, only to be caught in her husband's strong arms.

"Carmen!" he said. "What is it?"

"I just need some fresh air," she whispered.

Nicholas Hollingsworth, Peter's fellow officer and their only witness, hurried down the aisle ahead of them to throw open the carved doors. "She is probably exhausted, Peter," he pointed out. "She rode all day to get here!"

"Yes," Carmen agreed. "I am just a bit tired. But the air is a great help."

Indeed it was. Her head was clearer already in the cool, dry night. She leaned her forehead against her husband's shoulder and closed her eyes, breathing deeply of his heady scent of wool, leather, and sandalwood soap.

"I am a brute," he murmured against her hair. "You should have been asleep these many hours, and here I have insisted on dragging you before the priest."

Carmen laughed. "Oh, I do not think I mind so very much."

"It was past time for the two of you to make it respectable," Nicholas said. "You have been making calves' eyes at each other for weeks, every time Carmen comes into camp. It was quite the scandal."

"Untrue!" Carmen cried, laughing. "You are the scandal, Nick, chasing all the *señoritas* in the village."

"I do not have to chase them! I stand still and they come to me." Nicholas saluted them smartly, and turned to make his way back down the hill to the lights of the British encampment. "Good night, Lord and Lady Clifton!"

Carmen and Peter watched him go, silent together in the warm starlit night, and in the sense of the profundity of the step they had just taken.

They had known each other only about two months, from intermittent visits Carmen had made to the various encampments of Peter's regiment. Yet Carmen had somehow *known,* the moment she had seen him, that he was quite special.

"I remember when I first saw you," she said.

"Do you?"

"Yes. The day I rode in from Seville to speak to Colonel Smith-Mason. You were playing cards with Nicholas outside your tent, in just your shirtsleeves. Most improper. The sun was shining in your hair, and you were laughing. You were quite the most handsome thing I had ever seen."

"I also remember that day. You were riding hell-for-leather through the camp, on that demon you call your horse. You were wearing trousers and that ridiculous hat you love so much." He laughed. "I had never seen a woman like you."

"Hmph, thank you *very* much! I will have you know that that hat is the height of fashion right now."

"I stand corrected, Condesa. But I could not believe that anyone so very lovely, so refined, could be a spy."

"I am not a spy," she corrected him. "I simply sometimes overhear useful information that could perhaps aid you in ridding my country of this French infestation."

"So that is not spying?"

"No. It is . . . helping."

Peter laughed, the rumble of it warm against her. "Then, I am very glad indeed that you have decided to help *us*. You, my dear, could be a formidable foe."

"Not as formidable as you." Carmen fell silent, turning her new ring in the moonlight to admire the flash of the single, square-cut emerald. Peter had told her that the ring had been his mother's, who had died when he was a small child. "This war cannot go on forever."

"No." Peter's hand covered hers, tracing the ring with his thumb. "Are you sorry now, Carmen, that we married so hastily? Are you having second thoughts about sharing your life with mine after the war?"

"No! Are you?"

"Of course not. You are the only woman I have ever loved."

Carmen's brow arched doubtfully. "Really?"

His laugh was rueful. "I did not say the only woman I have ever *known*. You would see that for a sham immediately. But you are the only woman I have ever loved."

"Then, you did not ask me to marry you out of some sense of obligation, after—well, after what occurred last week?"

"Are you referring to the fact that we anticipated our wedding vows?" Peter clicked his tongue. "My dear, how indelicate!"

Carmen couldn't help but blush just a bit at the memory of that night, when, tipsy with brandy and kisses and a dance beside a river, they had fallen into his bed and done such incredibly wonderful, wicked things. Peter's hands, his sorcerer's mouth . . .

A giggle escaped.

"No," Peter continued. "I married you because I think it is so charming that, despite the fact that you can ride and shoot like the veriest rifle sergeant, you still blush at the mention of the, ah, small preview of our marital bed."

"Small, *querido*?"

"Well, perhaps not *so* small."

"No." Carmen smiled. "Yet have you thought of after the war, when we must leave here and go to England, and you must present me as your countess?"

"Of course I have thought of it! It is almost all I do when

we are apart. It will be wonderful. I have a sister and an estate that I have neglected these many years, so we must go there as soon as we can."

"You have been doing your duty for your country 'these many years.' Surely your family must understand that?"

"Yes, but it does not make it any easier to be parted from them. Sometimes, when I cannot sleep at night, I think of them, Elizabeth and Clifton Manor. I can almost smell the green English rain . . ." His voice trailed faintly away.

Carmen looked out over the lights of the camp. She had never been to England, or indeed anywhere but Spain. It was all she knew, warm, sunny, tradition-bound Spain. How would she fare in a new, English life?

She leaned her head against his shoulder, her eyes tightly shut. "Will they like me at your home? Will your sister like me?"

Peter tipped her chin up with one long finger, forcing her to meet his gaze. "Elizabeth will love you; you are very much like her. They will all love you at Clifton. As I do. Believe me, darling, it is much easier to be an English countess than a Spanish one, and you have done that wonderfully. You must not be afraid."

Her jaw tightened. "I am not afraid."

Peter laughed "Excellent! I knew that a woman who does the things you do could not possibly be frightened of the English *ton*." He kissed her lightly on her nose. "Are you ready to return to camp?"

"Oh, yes."

The encampment was uncharacteristically quiet as they made their way hand in hand to Peter's tent. A few groups of men played desultory games of cards around the fires. Outside the largest tent, Colonel Smith-Mason stood with some of his officers, talking in low voices over a sheaf of dispatches.

Peter glanced at them with a small frown.

"Do you think there is something amiss?" Carmen whispered. She had lived long enough with the intrigues of war to know that events could change in an instant, but she had hoped, prayed, that her wedding night at least could prove uneventful.

Outside the bedchamber, anyway.

"I do not know," Peter answered, his watchful gaze still on the small group. "Surely not."

"But you do not *know*?"

He shrugged, "We have more important things to think of tonight," he said, bending his head to softly kiss her ear.

Carmen shivered, but waved him away. "No, you must find out. I will wait."

"Are you certain?"

"Yes. Go on. We have many hours before dawn." He kissed her again, and she watched him walk away, his polished buttons gleaming in the firelight. Then she turned to duck into his tent. *Their* tent, for that night.

It was a goodly size, but almost spartan in its tidiness. The cot was made up with linen-cased pillows and a blue woolen blanket; a stack of papers and books was lined up exactly on the table, and the chairs pushed in at precise angles. His shaving kit and monogrammed ivory hairbrush were flush with his small shaving mirror. The only bit of personal expression was in the miniature portrait on a small stand beside the cot: of his younger sister, Elizabeth. Next to it was a portrait of Carmen, painted when she was 16, which she had given him as a wedding gift.

Carmen laid her small bouquet of wild red roses beside the paintings and went to open her own small trunk, which had been brought there while they were at the church. In it were the only things she had brought away on her journey from Seville: two muslin dresses and a satin gown, a pair of boots, rosary beads, men's trousers and shirts, and a cotton nightrail that was far too practical for a wedding night.

She slipped out of her simple white muslin wedding dress, and took the high ivory comb and white lace mantilla from her hair. She brushed out her waist-length black hair. Then she sat down on the cot to wait.

She was quite asleep when she at last felt Peter's kiss on her cheek, his hand on her back, warm through her silk chemise. She blinked up at him and smiled. "What was it?"

"It is nothing." He sat down beside her and gathered her into his arms. He had shed his coat and shirt, and Carmen rubbed her cheek against the golden satin of his skin. "There were rumors of a French regiment nearby, much closer than they should be."

"Only rumors?"

"Yes. For tonight." He wrapped his fingers in her loose hair and tilted her face up to his, trailing small, soft kisses along the line of her throat. "Tonight is only ours, my wife."

"Oh, yes. My husband. *Mi esposo.*" Carmen moaned as his mouth found the crest of her breast through the silk. Her fingernails dug into his bare shoulders. "Only ours."

The bridal couple was torn from blissful sleep near dawn by the horrifying sounds of gunfire, panicked shouts, and braying horses.

Peter was out of bed in an instant, pulling on his uniform as he threw back the tent flaps.

Carmen stumbled after him in bewilderment, drawing the sheet around her naked shoulders. "What is it?" she cried. "A battle?"

"Stay here!" Peter ordered. Then she was alone.

Carmen hastily donned her shirt and trousers, and tied her hair back with a scarf. She was searching for her boots when she heard her husband's voice and that of Lieutenant Robert Means, a young man she had sometimes played cards with of a quiet evening. And fleeced regularly.

"By damn!" Peter cursed. "How could they be so close? How could they have gotten so far without us knowing?"

"Someone must have informed them," Robert answered. "But we are marching out within the quarter hour."

"Of course. I shall be ready. Has captain Hollingsworth been alerted?"

"Yes. What of . . ." Robert's voice lowered. "What of your wife, Major?"

"I will see to her."

Carmen stuck her head outside the tent. "She will see to herself, thank you very much! And what are you doing running about unarmed, *husband*?" She rattled his saber at him.

"Carmen!" Peter pushed her back into the tent. "You must ride into the hills and wait. I will send an escort with you."

"Certainly not! You require every man. I have ridden about the country without an escort for months. Shall I ride to General Morecambe's encampment and tell him you require reinforcements?"

"No! You are to find a safe place, and wait there until I come for you."

"Madre de Dios!" Carmen pulled her leather jacket out of her trunk and thrust her arms into the sleeves, glaring at him all the while. "I will not hide! I cannot play the coward now. I will ride for reinforcements."

"Carmen! Be sensible!"

"You be sensible, Peter! I have been doing this sort of thing for a long time."

"But you were not my wife then!" he shouted.

"Ah. So that is it." Carmen left off loading her pistol to go to him, and framed his handsome, beloved face in her hands. "I cannot give up what I am doing to become a fine, frail, sheltered lady again, simply because I am now your wife. No more than you can stay safely here in camp because you are now my husband."

He turned his head to kiss her palm. "No. Even though I wish it so, you are quite right."

"We shall have many, many years to sit calmly by the fire, *querido.*"

He smiled against her skin. "And will you long for your grand adventures, Carmen, when you are chasing babies about Clifton Manor?"

"Never!"

Peter caught her against him and kissed her mouth, hard, desperate. "I will see you at supper, then, Lady Clifton."

"Yes." Carmen clung to him for an instant, an eternal moment, then stepped away. "Promise me you will fight very, very carefully today, Peter."

"Of course, my love." He grinned at her, the white, crooked grin that had won her heart. "I never fight any other way."

Then he was gone.